About the Authors

Fiona McArthur is an Australian midwife who lives in the country and loves to dream. Writing Medical Romance gives Fiona the scope to write about all the wonderful aspects of romance, adventure, medicine and the midwifery she feels so passionate about. When not writing, Fiona's either at home on the farm with her husband or off to meet new people, see new places and have wonderful adventures. Drop in and say hi at Fiona's website www.fionamcarthurauthor.com

Carol Marinelli recently filled in a form asking for her job title. Thrilled to be able to put down her answer, she put writer. Then it asked what Carol did for relaxation and she put down the truth—writing. The third question asked for her hobbies. Well, not wanting to look obsessed she crossed the fingers on her hand and answered swimming but, given that the chlorine in the pool does terrible things to her highlights—I'm sure you can guess the real answer.

Louisa Heaton is a married mother of four (including a set of twins) and lives on an island in Hampshire. When not wrangling her children, husband or countless animals, she can often be found walking her dogs along the beach muttering to herself, as she works out plot points. In her spare time, Louisa reads a lot, crochets. Usually when she c...

Midwives' Miracles

Midwives' Miracles:
Special
Moments

FIONA McARTHUR

CAROL MARINELLI

LOUISA HEATON

MILLS & BOON

First Published in Great Britain 2021
By Mills & Boon, an imprint of HarperCollins*Publishers,* Ltd
1 London Bridge Street, London, SE1 9GF

www.harpercollins.co.uk

HarperCollins*Publishers*
1st Floor, Watermarque Building,
Ringsend Road, Dublin 4, Ireland

MIDWIVES' MIRACLES: SPECIAL MOMENTS
© 2021 Harlequin Books S.A.

A Month to Marry the Midwife © 2017 Fiona McArthur
The Midwife's One-Night Fling © 2018 Carol Marinelli
Reunited by Their Pregnancy Surprise © 2017 Louisa Heaton

ISBN: 978-0-263-30297-4

MIX
Paper from
responsible sources
FSC™ C007454

This book is produced from independently certified FSC™ paper to ensure responsible forest management.

For more information visit: www.harpercollins.co.uk/green

Printed and Bound in Spain using 100% Renewable electricity at CPI Black Print, Barcelona

A MONTH TO MARRY THE MIDWIFE

FIONA McARTHUR

Dedicated to Rosie, who sprinted with me on this one, Trish, who walked the beach with me, and Flo, who rode the new wave and kept me afloat. What a fab journey with awesome friends.

PROLOGUE

THE WHITE SAND curved away in a crescent as Ellie Swift descended to Lighthouse Bay Beach and turned towards the bluff. When she stepped onto the beach the luscious crush of cool, fine sand under her toes made her suck in her breath with a grin and the ocean breeze tasted salty against her lips. Ellie set off at a brisk pace towards the edge of the waves to walk the bay to the headland and back before she needed to dress for work.

'Ellie!'

She spun, startled, away from the creamy waves now washing her feet, and saw a man limping towards her. He waved again. Jeff, from the surf club. Ellie knew Jeff, the local prawn-trawler captain and chief lifesaver. She'd delivered his second son. Jeff had fainted and Ellie tried not to remind him of that every time she saw him.

She waved back but already suspected the call wasn't social. She turned and sped up to meet him.

'We've got an old guy down on the rocks under the lighthouse, a surfer, says he's your doctor from the hospital. We think he's busted his arm, and maybe a leg.'

Ellie turned her head to look towards the headland Jeff had come from.

Jeff waved his hand towards the huddle of people in the distance. 'He won't let anybody touch him until you come. The ambulance is on the way but I reckon we might have to chopper him out from here.'

Ellie worked all over the hospital so it wasn't unusual that she was who people asked for. An old guy and a surfer. That was Dr Southwell. She sighed.

Ten minutes later Ellie was kneeling beside the good doctor, guarding his wrinkled neck in a brace as she watched the two ambulance women and two burly life-savers carefully shift him onto the rescue frame. Then it was done. Just a small groan escaped his gritted teeth as he closed his eyes and let the pain from the move-ment slowly subside.

Ellie glanced at the ocean, lying aqua and innocent, as if to say, *it wasn't my fault*, and suspected Dr South-well would doggedly heal and return to surfing with renewed vigour as soon as he could. The tide was on the way out and the waves weren't reaching the sloping plateau at the base of the cliffs any more where the life-savers had secured their casualty. The spot was popular with intrepid surfers to climb on and off their boards and paddle into the warm swell and out to the waves.

'Thanks for coming, Ellie.' Dr Southwell was look-ing much more comfortable and a trifle sheepish. 'Sorry to leave you in the lurch on the ward.'

She smiled at him. He'd always been sweet. 'Don't

you worry about us. Look after you. They'll get you sorted once you've landed. Get well soon.'

The older man closed his eyes briefly. Then he winked at Ellie. 'I'll be back. As soon as I can.'

Ellie smiled and shook her head. He'd gone surfing every morning before his clinic, the athletic spring to his step contradicting his white hair and weathered face, a tall, thin gentleman who must have been a real catch fifty years ago. They'd splinted his arm against his body, didn't think the leg was broken, but they were treating it as such and had administered morphine, having cleared it with the helicopter flight nurse on route via mobile phone.

In the distance the *thwump-thwump* of the helicopter rotor could be heard approaching. Ellie knew how efficient the rescue team was. He'd be on his way very shortly.

Ellie glanced at the sweeping bay on the other side from where they crouched—the white sand that curved like a new moon around the bay, the rushing of the tide through the fish-filled creek back into the sea—and could understand why he'd want to return.

This place had stopped her wandering too. She lifted her chin. Lighthouse Bay held her future and she had plans for the hospital.

She looked down at the man, a gentle man in the true sense of the word, who had fitted so beautifully into the calm pace of the bay. 'We'll look forward to you coming back. As soon as you're well.' She glanced at the enormous Malibu surfboard the lifesavers had propped up against the cliff face. 'I'll get one of the guys to drop your board at my house and it will be there waiting for you.'

Ellie tried very hard not to think about the next few days. *Damn*. Now they didn't have an on-call doctor and the labouring women would have to be transferred to the base hospital until another locum arrived. She needed to move quickly on those plans to make her maternity ward a midwifery group practice.

CHAPTER ONE

FOUR DAYS LATER, outside Ellie's office at the maternity ward at Lighthouse Bay Hospital, a frog croaked. It was very close outside her window. She shuddered as she assembled the emergency locum-doctor's welcome pack. Head down, she concentrated on continuing the task and pretended not to see the tremor in her fingers as she gathered the papers. She was a professional in charge of a hospital, for goodness' sake. Her ears strained for a repeat of the dreaded noise and hoped like heck she wouldn't hear it. She strained…but thankfully silence ensued.

'Concentrate on the task,' she muttered. She included a local map, which after the first day they wouldn't need because the town was so small, but it covered everywhere they could eat.

A list of the hours they were required to man the tiny doctor's clinic—just two in total on the other side of the hospital on each day of the week they were here. Then, in a month, hand over to the other local doctor who had threatened to leave if he didn't get holidays.

She couldn't blame him or his wife—they deserved a

life! It was getting busier. Dr Rodgers, an elderly bachelor, had done the call-outs before he'd become ill. She hummed loudly to drown out the sound of the little voice that suggested she should have a life too, and of course to drown out the frogs. Ellie concentrated as she printed out the remuneration package.

The idea that any low-risk woman who went into labour would have to be transferred to the large hospital an hour away from her family just because no locum doctor could come was wrong. Especially when she'd had all her antenatal care with Ellie over the last few months. So the locum doctors were a necessary evil. It wasn't an onerous workload for them, in fact, because the midwives did all the maternity work, and the main hospital was run as a triage station with a nurse practitioner, as they did in the Outback, so actually the locums only covered the hospital for emergencies and recovering inpatient needs.

Ellie dreamed of the day their maternity unit was fully self-sufficient. She quite happily played with the idea that she could devote her whole life to the project, get a nurse manager and finally step away from general nursing.

She could employ more midwives like her friend and neighbour Trina, who lived in one of the cliff houses. The young widowed midwife from the perfect marriage who preferred night duty so she didn't lie awake at night alone in her bed.

She was the complete opposite to Ellie, who'd had the marriage from hell that hadn't turned out to be a marriage at all.

Then there was Faith who did the evening shifts, the young mum who lived with her aunt and her three-year-old son. Faith was their eternal optimist. She hadn't found a man to practise heartbreak on yet. Just had an unfortunate one-night stand with a charismatic drifter. Ellie sighed. Three diverse women with a mutual dream. Lighthouse Bay Mothers and Babies. A gentle place for families to discover birth with midwives.

Back to the real world. For the moment they needed the championship of at least one GP/OB.

Most new mums stayed between one and three nights and, as they always had, women post-caesarean birth transferred back from the base hospital to recover. So a ward round in maternity and the general part of the hospital each morning by the VMO was asked to keep the doors open.

The tense set of her shoulders gradually relaxed as she distracted herself with the chore she'd previously completed six times since old Dr Rodgers had had his stroke.

The first two locums had been young and bored, patently here for the surf, and had both tried to make advances towards Ellie, as if she were part of the locum package. She'd had no problem freezing them both back into line but now the agency took on board her preferences for mature medical practitioners.

Most replacements had been well into retirement age since then, though there had also been some disadvantages with their advanced age. The semi-bald doctor definitely had been grumpy, which had been a bit of a disappointment, because Dr Rodgers had always had a kind word for everyone.

The next had been terrified that a woman would give birth and he'd have to do something about it because he hadn't been near a baby's delivery for twenty years. Ellie hadn't been able to promise one wouldn't happen so he'd declined to come back.

Lighthouse Bay was a service for low-risk pregnant women so Ellie couldn't see what the concern was. Birth was a perfectly normal, natural event and the women weren't sick. But there would always be those occasional precipitous and out-of-the-ordinary labours that seemed to happen more since Ellie had arrived. She'd proven well equal to the task of catching impatient babies but a decent back-up made sense. So, obstetric confidence was a second factor she requested now from the locums.

The next three locums had been either difficult to contact when she'd needed them or had driven her mad by sitting and talking all day so she hadn't been able to get anything done, so she hadn't asked them back. But the last locum had finally proved a golden one.

Dr Southwell, the elderly widower and retired GP with his obstetric diploma and years of gentle experience, had been a real card.

The postnatal women had loved him, as had every other marriageable woman above forty in town.

Especially Myra, Ellie's other neighbour, a retired chef who donated two hours a day to the hospital café between morning tea and lunch, and used to run a patisserie in Double Bay in Sydney. Myra and Old Dr South-well had often been found laughing together.

Ellie had thought the hospital had struck the jackpot when he'd enquired about a more permanent position and had stayed full-time for an extra month when the last local GP had asked for an extended holiday. Ellie had really appreciated the break from trying to understand each new doctor's little pet hates.

Not that Dr Southwell seemed to have any foible Ellie had had to grow accustomed to at all. Except his love of surfing. She sighed.

They'd already sent one woman away in the last two days because she'd come to the hospital having gone into early labour. Ellie had had to say they had no locum coverage and she should drive to the base hospital.

Croak... There it was again. A long-drawn-out, guttural echo promising buckets of slime... She sucked in air through her nose and forced herself to breathe the constricted air out. She had to fight the resistance because her lungs seemed to have shrunk back onto her ribcage.

Croak... And then the *cruk-cruk* of the mate. She glanced at the clock and estimated she had an hour at least before the new doctor arrived so she reached over, turned on the CD player and allowed her favourite country singer to protect her from the noise as he belted out a southern ballad that drowned out the neighbours. Thankfully, today, her only maternity patient had brought her the latest CD from the large town an hour away where she'd gone for her repeat Caesarean birth.

It was only rarely, after prolonged rain, that the frogs

gave her such a hard time. They'd had a week of downpours. Of course frogs were about. They'd stop soon. The rain had probably washed away the solution of salt water she'd sprayed around the outside of the ward window, so she'd do it again this afternoon.

One of the bonuses of her tiny croft cottage on top of the cliff was that, up there, the salt-laden spray from waves crashing against the rocks below drove the amphibians away.

She knew it was ridiculous to have a phobia about frogs, but she had suffered with it since she was little. It was inextricably connected to the time not long after her mother had died. She knew perfectly well it was irrational.

She had listened to the tapes, seen the psychologist, had even been transported by hypnosis to the causative events in an attempt to reprogram her response. That had actually made it worse, because now she had the childhood nightmares back that hadn't plagued her for years.

Basically slimy, web-footed frogs with fat throats that ballooned hideously when they croaked made her palms sweat and her heart beat like a drum in her chest. And the nightmares made her weep with grief in her sleep.

Unfortunately, down in the hollow where the old hospital nestled among well-grown shrubs and an enticing tinge of dampness after rain, the frogs were very happy to congregate. Her only snake in Eden. Actually, she could do with a big, quiet carpet snake that enjoyed green entrées. That could be the answer. She had no phobia of snakes.

But those frogs that slipped insidiously into the hand basin in the ladies' rest room—no way! Or those that croaked outside the door so that when she arrived as she had this morning, running a little late, a little incautiously intent on getting to work, a green tree frog had jumped at her as she'd stepped through the door. Thank goodness he'd missed his aim.

She still hadn't recovered from that traumatic start to her day. Now they were outside her window... Her hero sang on and she determined to stop thinking about it. She did not have time for this.

Samuel Southwell parked his now dusty Lexus outside the cottage hospital. His immaculate silver machine had never been off the bitumen before, and he frowned at the rim of dust that clung to the base of the windscreen.

He noted with a feeling of unreality, the single *Reserved for Doctor* spot in the car park, and his hand hovered as he hesitated to stop the engine. *Doctor*. Not plural. Just one spot for the one doctor. He couldn't remember the last time he'd been without a cloud of registrars, residents and med students trailing behind him.

What if they wanted him to look at a toenail or someone had a heart attack? He was a consultant obstetrician and medical researcher, for heaven's sake.

At that thought his mouth finally quirked. Surely his knowledge of general medicine was buried miraculously in his brain underneath the uteruses? He sincerely hoped so or he'd have to refresh his knowledge of whatever ailment stumped him. Online medical journals could be accessed. According to his father it shouldn't be a problem—he was 'supposed to be smart'!

Maybe the old man was right and it would do him good. Either way, he'd agreed, mainly because his dad never asked him to do anything and he'd been strangely persistent about this favour. This little place had less than sixty low-risk births a year. And he was only here for the next four weeks. He would manage.

It would be vastly different from the peaks of drama skimmed from thousands of women and babies passing through the doors of Brisbane Mothers and Babies Hospital. Different being away from his research work that drove him at nights and weekends. He'd probably get more sleep as well. He admired his father but at the moment he was a little impatient with him for this assignment.

'It'll be a good-will mission,' Dr Reginald Southwell had decreed, with a twinkle in his eye that his son had supposedly inherited but that his father had insisted he'd lost. 'See how the other half live. Step out of your world of work, work, work for a month, for goodness' sake. You can take off a month for the first time in who knows how long. I promised the matron I'd return and don't want to leave them in the lurch.'

He'd grinned at that. *Poor old Dad.* It dated him well in the past, calling her a matron. The senior nurses were all 'managers' now.

Unfortunate Dad, the poor fellow laid back with his broken arm and his twisted knee. It had been an accident waiting to happen for his father, a man of his advanced age taking random locum destinations while he surfed. But Sam understood perfectly well why he did it.

Sam sighed and turned off the ignition. Too late to back out. He was here now. He climbed out and stretched the kinks from his shoulders. The blue expanse of ocean reminded him how far from home he really was.

Above him towered a lonely white lighthouse silhouetted against the sapphire-blue sky on the big hill behind the hospital. He listened for traffic noise but all he could hear was the crash of the waves on the cliff below and faint beats from a song. *Edge of Nowhere.* Not surprising someone was playing country music somewhere. They should be playing the theme song from *Deliverance.*

He'd told his colleagues he had to help his dad out with his arm and knee. Everyone assumed Sam was living with him while he recuperated. That had felt easier than explaining this.

Lighthouse Bay, a small hamlet on the north coast of New South Wales at the end of a bad road. The locum do-everything doctor. Good grief.

Ellie jumped at the rap on her door frame and turned her face to the noise. She reached out and switched her heroic balladeer off mid-song. The silence seemed to hum as she stared at the face of a stranger.

'Sorry, didn't mean to startle you.' A deep, even voice, quite in keeping with the broad shoulders and impeccable suit jacket, but not in keeping with the tiny, casual seaside hospital he'd dropped into.

Drug reps didn't usually get out this far. That deeply masculine resonance in his cultured voice vibrated against her skin in an unfamiliar way. It made her face prickle with a warmth she wasn't used to and unconsciously her hand lifted and she checked the top button of her shirt. Phew. Force field secure.

Then her confidence rushed back. 'Can I help you?' She stood up, thinking there was something faintly familiar... But after she'd examined him thoroughly she thought, no, he wasn't recognisable. She hadn't seen this man before and she was sure she'd have remembered him.

The man took one step through the doorway but couldn't go any further. Her office drew the line at two chairs and two people. It had always been small but somehow the space seemed to have shrunk to ridiculous tininess in the last few seconds. There was a hint of humour about his silver-blue eyes that almost penetrated the barrier she'd erected but stopped at the gate. Ellie was a good gatekeeper. She didn't want any complications.

Ellie, who had always thought herself tall for a woman, unexpectedly felt a little overshadowed and the hairs on the back of her neck rose gently—in a languorous way, not in fright—which was ridiculous. Really, she was very busy for the next hour until the elderly locum consultant arrived.

'Are you the matron?' He rolled his eyes, as if a private thought piqued him, then corrected himself. 'Director of Nursing?' Smooth as silk with a thread of command.

'Acting. Yes. Ellie Swift. I'm afraid you have the advantage of me.'

The tall man raised his eyebrows. 'I'm Samuel Southwell.' She heard the slight mocking note in his voice. 'The locum medical officer here for the next month.' He glanced at his watch as if he couldn't believe she'd forgotten he was coming. 'Am I early?'

'Ah…'

Ellie winced. Not a drug rep. The doctor. *Oops.*

'Sorry. Time zones. No Daylight Saving for you northerners from Brisbane. Of course. You're only early on our side of the border. I was clearing the decks for your arrival.' She muttered more to herself, 'Or *someone*'s arrival…' then looked up. 'The agency had said they'd filled the temporary position with a Queenslander. I should have picked up the time difference.'

Then the name sank in. 'Southwell?' A pleasant surprise. She smiled with real warmth. 'Are you related to Dr Southwell who had the accident?' At the man's quick nod, Ellie asked, 'How is he?' She'd been worried.

'My father,' he said dryly, 'is as well as can be expected for a man too old to be surfing.' He spoke as if his parent were a recalcitrant child and Ellie felt a little spurt of protectiveness for the absent octogenarian. Then she remembered she had to work with this man for the next month. She also remembered Dr Southwell had two children, and his only son was a consultant obstetrician at Brisbane Mothers and Babies. A workaholic, apparently.

Well, she certainly had someone with obstetric experience for a month. It would be just her luck that they wouldn't have a baby the whole time he was here. Ellie took a breath and plastered on a smile.

First the green frog jumping at her from the door, then the ones croaking outside the window and now the Frog Prince, city-slicker locum who wasn't almost retired, like locums were supposed to be.

'Welcome. Perhaps you'd like to sit down.' She gestured at the only other chair jammed between the storage cupboard and the door frame. She wasn't really sure his legs would fit if he tried to fold into the space.

He didn't attempt to sit and it was probably a good choice.

There was still something about his behaviour that was a little...odd. Did he feel they didn't want him? 'Dr Southwell, your presence here is very much appreciated.'

It took him a couple of seconds to answer and she used them to centre herself. This was her world. No need to be nervous. 'We were very relieved when someone accepted the locum position for the month.'

He didn't look flattered—too flash just to be referred to as 'someone', perhaps?

Ellie stepped forward. Bit back the sigh and the grumbles to herself about how much she liked the old ones. 'Anyway, welcome to Lighthouse Bay. Most people call me Swift, because it's my name and I move fast. I'm the DON, the midwife, emergency resource person and mediator between the medical staff and the nursing staff.' She held out her hand. He looked at her blankly.

What? Perhaps a sense of humour was too much to hope for.

His expression slowly changed to one of polite query. 'Do they need mediation?' He didn't take her hand and she lowered it slowly. Strange, strange man. Ellie stifled another sigh. Being on the back foot already like this was not a good sign.

'It was a joke, sorry.' She didn't say, *'J. O. K. E.,'* though she was beginning to think he might need it spelled out for him. She switched to her best professional mode. The experience of fitting in at out-of-the-way little hospitals had dispatched any pretensions she might have had that a matron was anyone but the person who did all the things other people didn't want to do. It had also taught her to be all things to all people.

Ellie usually enjoyed meeting new staff. It wasn't something that happened too often at their small hospital until Dr Rodgers had retired.

Lighthouse Bay was a place more suited to farming on the hills and in the ocean, where the inhabitants retreated from society, though there were some very trendy boutique industries popping up. Little coffee plantations. Lavender farms. Online boutiques run by corporate women retreating from the cities looking for a sea change.

Which was where Ellie's new clientele for Maternity rose from. Women with considered ideas on how and where they wanted to have their babies. But the town's reliable weekend doctor had needed to move indefinitely for medical treatment and Ellie was trying to hold it all together.

The local farming families and small niche businesses were salt-of-the-earth friendly. She was renovating her tiny one-roomed cottage that perched with two other similar crofts like a flock of seabirds on the cliff overlooking the bay. She'd found the perfect place to forget what a fool she'd been and perfect also for avoiding such a disaster again.

Ellie dreamed of dispensing with the need for doctors at all. But at the moment she needed one supporting GP obstetrician at least to call on for emergencies. Maybe she could pick this guy's brains for ways to circumvent that.

She glanced at the man in front of her—experience in a suit. But not big on conversation. Still, she was tenacious when there was something she wanted, and she'd drag it out of him. Eventually.

In the scheme of things Lighthouse Bay Maternity needed a shake up and maybe she could use him. He'd be totally abreast of the latest best-practice trends, a leader in safe maternity care. He should be a golden opportunity to sway the sticklers to listen to the mothers instead of the easy fix of sending women away.

But, if he wasn't going to sit down then she would deal with him outside the confines of her office. She stood and slipped determinedly past him. It was a squeeze and required body contact. She'd just have to deal with it. 'Would you like a tour?'

Lemon verbena. He knew the scent because at the last conference he'd presented at, all the wives had been raving about the free hotel amenities and they'd made him smell it. It hadn't resonated with him then as it did now. Sam Southwell breathed it in and his visceral response set off rampant alarm bells. He was floundering to find his brain. There was something about the way her buttoned-to-the-neck, long-sleeved white shirt had launched a missile straight to the core of him and exploded, and now the scent of her knocked him sideways as she brushed past.

The way her chin lifted and her cool, grey eyes assessed him and found him wanting, giving him the ultimate hands-off warning when he hadn't even thought about hands on—hadn't for a long time until now—impressed him. Obviously a woman who made up her own mind. She wasn't overawed by him in the least and that was a good thing.

He stared at the wall where 'Swift' had stood a second ago and used all of his concentration to ram the feelings of sheer confusion and lust back down into the cave he used for later thought, and tried to sound at least present for the conversation. She must be thinking he was an arrogant sod, but his brain was gasping, struggling, stumped by the reaction he was having to her.

She was right. Being jammed in this shoebox of an office wasn't helping. What an ironic joke that his father had thought this isolated community would help him return to normal when in fact he'd just fallen off a Lighthouse Bay cliff. His stomach lurched.

He turned slowly to face her as she waited, not quite tapping her foot. He began to feel better. Impatience wasn't a turn-on.

'Yes. A tour would be excellent,' he said evenly. She

must think he was the most complete idiot but he was working to find headspace to fit it all in. And he could work fast.

The place he could handle. Heck, he could do it in his sleep. He had no idea why he was so het up about it. But this woman? His reaction to her? A damnably different kettle of fish. Disturbing. As in, deeply and diabolically disturbing.

'How many beds do you have here?' A sudden picture of Ellie Swift on a bed popped into his head and arrested him. She'd have him arrested, more likely, he thought wryly. He was actually having a breakdown. His dad was right. He did need to learn to breathe.

CHAPTER TWO

Sam hadn't slept with a woman for years. Not since his wife had died. He hadn't wanted to and in fact, since he'd used work to bury grief and guilt, with all the extra input, his career had actually taken off. Hence, he hadn't had the time to think about sex, let alone act on it.

Now his brain had dropped to somewhere past his waistline, a nether region that had been asleep for years and had just inconveniently roared into life like an express train, totally inappropriate and unwelcome. Good grief. He closed his eyes tightly to try and clear the pictures filling his head. He was an adolescent schoolboy again.

'Are you okay?' Her voice intruded and he snapped his lids open.

'Sorry.' What could he say? He only knew what he couldn't say. *Please don't look down at my trousers!* Instead he managed, 'I think I need coffee.'

She stopped. Dropped her guard. And as if by magic he felt the midwife morph from her as she switched to nurture mode in an instant. No other profession he knew did it as comprehensively as midwives.

'You poor thing. Of course. Follow me. We'll start in the coffee shop. Though Myra isn't here yet. Didn't you stop on the way? You probably rushed to get here.' She shook her head disapprovingly and didn't wait for an answer but bustled him into a small side room that blossomed out into an empty coffee shop with a huge bay window overlooking the gardens.

She nudged him into a seat. Patted his shoulder. 'Tea or coffee?' It had all happened very fast and now his head really was spinning.

'Coffee—double-shot espresso, hot milk on the side,' he said automatically, and she stopped and looked at him.

Then she laughed. Her face opened like a sunburst, her eyes sparkled and her beautiful mouth curved with huge amusement. She laughed and snorted, and he was smitten. Just like that. A goner.

She pulled herself together, mouth still twitching. 'Sorry. Myra could fix that but not me. But I'll see what I can do.'

Sam stared after her. She was at least twelve feet away now and he gave himself a stern talking-to. *Have coffee, and then be* normal. He would try. No—he would succeed.

Poor man. Ellie glanced at the silent, mysterious coffee machine that Myra worked like a maestro and tried to work out how much instant coffee from the jar under the sink, where it had been pushed in disgrace, would equate to a double shot of coffee. She didn't drink instant coffee. Just the weak, milky ones Myra made for her from the machine under protest. Maybe three teaspoons?

He'd looked so cosmopolitan and handsome as he'd said it—something he said every day. She bit back another snuffle of laughter. Classic. *Welcome to Lighthouse Bay.* Boy, were they gonna have fun.

She glanced back and decided he wasn't too worthy of sympathy because it was unfair for a man to have shoulders like that, not to mention a decidedly sinful mouth. And she hadn't thought about sinful for a while. In fact she couldn't quite believe she was thinking about it now. She'd thought the whole devastation of the cruelty of men had completely cured her of that foolishness.

She was going to have to spend the next month with this man reappearing on the ward. Day and night if they were both called out. The idea was more unsettling than she'd bargained for and was nothing to do with the way the ward was run.

The jug boiled and she mixed the potent brew. Best not to think of that now. She needed him awake. She scooped up two Anzac biscuits from the jar with a napkin.

'Here you go.' Ellie put the black liquid down in front of him and a small glass of hot milk she'd heated in the microwave.

He looked at it. Then at her. She watched fascinated as he poured a little hot milk into the mug with an inch of black coffee at the bottom.

He sipped, threw down the lot and then set it down. No expression. No clues. She was trying really hard not to stare. It must be an acquired taste.

His voice was conversational. 'Probably the most horrible coffee I've ever had.' He looked up at her. 'But I do appreciate the effort. I wasn't thinking.' He pushed the cup away. Grimaced dramatically. Shook his whole upper body like a dog shedding water. 'Thank God I brought my machine.'

She wasn't sure what she could say to that. 'Wow. Guess it's going to be a change for you here, away from the big city.'

'Hmm…' he murmured noncommittally. 'But I do feel better after the shock of that.'

She grinned. Couldn't help herself. 'So you're ready for the walk around now?'

He stood up, picked up the biscuits in the napkin, folded them carefully and slipped them into his pocket. 'Let's do it.'

Ellie decided it was the first time he'd looked normal since he'd arrived. She'd remember that coffee trick for next time.

'So this is the ward. We have five beds. One single room and two doubles, though usually we'd only have one woman in each room, even if it's really busy.'

Really busy with five beds? Sam glanced around. Empty rooms. Now they were in with the one woman in the single room and her two-day-old infant. Why wasn't she going home?

'This is Renee Jones.'

'Hello, Renee.' He smiled at the mother and then at the infant. 'Congratulations. I'm Dr Southwell. Everything okay?'

'Yes, thank you, doctor. I'm hoping to stay until Friday, if that's okay. There's four others at home and I'm in no rush.'

He blinked. Four more days staying in hospital after a caesarean delivery? Why? He glanced at Matron Swift, who apparently was unworried. She smiled and nodded at the woman.

'That's fine, Renee, you deserve the rest.'

'Only rest I get,' Renee agreed. 'Though, if you don't mind, could you do the new-born check today, doc, just in case my husband has a crisis and I have to go at short notice?'

New-born check? Examine a baby…himself? He glanced at the midwife. Who did that? A paediatrician, he would have thought. She met his eyes and didn't dispute it so he smiled and nodded. 'We'll sort that.'

Hopefully. His father would be chortling. He could feel Ellie's presence behind him as they left the room and he walked down to the little nurses' alcove and leaned against the desk. It had been too many years since he'd checked a new-born's hips and heart. Not that he couldn't—he imagined. But even his registrars didn't do that. They left it to Paediatrics while the O&G guys did the pregnancy and labour things.

'Is there someone else to do the new-born checks on babies?'

'Sorry.' She shook her head. 'You're it.'

He might have a quick read before he did it, then. He narrowed his eyes at the suspicious quirk of her lips. 'What about you?'

Her hair swished from side to side. He'd never really

had a thing for pony tails but it sat well on her. Pretty. Made him smile when it swayed. He'd faded out again.

'I said,' she repeated, 'I did the online course for well-baby examination but have never been signed off on it. One of those things I've been meaning to do and never got around to.'

Ha. She thought she was safe. 'Excellent. Then perhaps we'd better do the examinations together, and at least by the time I leave we'll both be good at them. Then I can sign you off.'

She didn't appear concerned. She even laughed. He could get used to the way she laughed. It was really more of a chortle. Smile-inducing.

The sound of a car pulling up outside made them both pause. After a searching appraisal of the couple climbing out, she said, 'The charts are in that filing cabinet if the ladies have booked in. Can you grab Josie Mills, please?'

When he looked back from the filing cabinet to the door he could hear the groans but Swift was already there with her smile.

He hadn't seen her move and glanced to where she'd stood a minute ago to check there weren't two of her. Nope. She was disappearing up the hallway with the pregnant woman and her male support as if they were all on one of those airport travellators and he guessed he'd better find the chart.

Which he did, and followed them up the hall.

Josie hadn't made it onto the bed. She was standing beside it and from her efforts it was plain that, apart from him, there'd be an extra person in the room in seconds.

Swift must have grabbed a towel and a pair of gloves as she came through the door, both of which were still lying on the bed, because she was distracted as she tried to help the frantic young woman remove her shorts.

In Sam's opinion the baby seemed to be trying to escape into his mother's underwear but Swift was equal to the task. She deftly encouraged one of the mother's legs out and whipped the towel off the bed and put it between the mother's legs, where the baby seemed to unfold into it in a swan dive and was pushed between the mother's knees into Swift's waiting hands. The baby spluttered his displeasure on the end of the purple cord after his rapid ejection into a towel.

'Good extrication,' Sam murmured with a little fillip of unexpected excitement as he pulled on a pair of gloves from the dispenser at the door. Could that be the first ghost of emotion he'd felt at a birth for a long while? With a sinking dismay it dawned on him that he hadn't even noticed it had been missing.

He crossed the room to assess the infant, who'd stopped crying and was slowly turning purple, which nobody seemed to notice as they all laughed and crowed at the rapid birth and helped the woman up on the bed to lie down.

'Would you like me to attend to third stage or the baby?' he enquired quietly.

He saw Swift glance at the baby, adjust the towel and rub the infant briskly. 'Need you to cut the cord now, John,' she said to the husband. 'Your little rocket is a bit stunned.'

The parents disentangled their locked gazes and Sam heard their indrawn breaths. The father jerked up the scissors Ellie had put instantly into his hand and she directed him between the two clamps as she went on calmly. 'It happens when they fly out.' A few nervous sawing snips from Dad with the big scissors and the cord was cut. Done.

'Dr Southwell will sort you, Josie, while we sort the baby.' Swift said it prosaically and they swapped places as the baby was bundled and she carried him to the re-suscitation trolley. 'Come on, John.' She gestured for the father to follow her. 'Talk to your daughter.'

The compressed air hissed as she turned it on and Sam could hear her talking to the dad behind him as automatically he smiled at the mother. 'Well done. Con-gratulations.'

The baby cried and they both smiled. 'It all happened very fast,' the mother said as she craned her neck toward the baby and, reassured that Swift and her husband were smiling, she settled back. 'A bit too fast.'

He nodded as a small gush of blood signalled the third stage was about to arrive. Seconds later it was done, the bleeding settled, and he tidied the sheet under her and dropped it in the linen bag behind him. He couldn't help a smile to himself at having done a tidy-ing job he'd watched countless times but couldn't ac-tually remember doing himself. 'Always nice to have your underwear off first, I imagine.'

The mother laughed as she craned her neck again

and by her smile he guessed they were coming back. 'Easier.'

'Here we go.' Swift lifted the mother's T-shirt and crop top and nestled the baby skin-to-skin between her bare breasts. She turned the baby's head sideways so his cheek was against his mother. 'Just watch her colour, especially the lips. Her being against your skin will warm her like toast.'

Sam stood back and watched. He saw the adjustments Ellie made, calmly ensuring mother and baby were comfortable—including the dad, with a word here and there, even asking for the father's mobile phone to take a few pictures of the brand new baby and parents. She glanced at the clock. He hadn't thought of looking at the clock once. She had it all under control.

Sam stepped back further and peeled off his gloves. He went to the basin to wash his hands and his mind kept replaying the scene. He realised why it was different. The lack of people milling around.

Swift pushed the silver trolley with the equipment and scissors towards the door. He stopped her. 'Do you always do this on your own?'

She pointed to a green call button. 'Usually I ring and one of the nurses comes from the main hospital to be on hand if needed until the GP arrives. But it happened fast today and you were here.' She flashed him a smile. 'Back in a minute. Watch her, will you? Physiological third stage.' Then she sailed away.

He hadn't thought about the injection they usually gave to reduce risk of bleeding after the birth. He'd somehow assumed it had already been given, but realised there weren't enough hands to have done it, although he could have done it if someone had mentioned it. Someone.

As far as he knew all women were given the injection at his hospital unless they'd expressly requested not to have it. Research backed that up. It reduced postpartum haemorrhage. He'd mention it.

His eyes fell on Josie's notes, which were lying on the table top where he'd dropped them, and he snicked the little wheeled stool out from under the bench with his foot and sat there to read through the medical records. The last month's antenatal care had been shared between his father and 'E Swift'. He glanced up every minute or so to check that both mother and baby were well but nothing happened before 'E Swift' returned.

An hour later Sam had been escorted around the hospital by a nurse who'd been summoned by phone and found himself deposited back in the little maternity wing. The five-minute cottage hospital tour had taken an hour because the infected great toenail he'd been fearing had found him and he'd had to deal with it, and the pain the poor sufferer was in.

Apparently he still remembered how to treat phalanges and the patient had seemed satisfied. He assumed Ellie would be still with the new maternity patient, but he was wrong.

Ellie sat, staring at the nurses' station window in a strangely rigid hunch, her hand clutching her pen six inches above the medical records, and he paused and turned his head to see what had attracted her attention.

He couldn't see anything. When he listened, all he could hear were frogs and the distant sound of the sea.

'You okay?' He'd thought his voice was quiet when he asked but she jumped as though he'd fired a gun past her ear. The pen dropped as her hand went to her chest, as if to push her heart back in with her lungs. His own pulse rate sped up. Good grief! He'd thought it was too good to be true that this place would be relaxing.

'You're back?' she said, stating the obvious with a blank look on her face.

He picked up the underlying stutter in her voice. Something had really upset her and he glanced around again, expecting to see a masked intruder at least. She glanced at him and then the window. 'Can you do me a favour?'

'Sure.' She looked like she could do with a favour.

'There's a green tree frog behind that plant in front of the window.' He could hear the effort she was putting in to enunciate clearly and began to suspect this was an issue of mammoth proportions.

'Yes?'

'Take it away!'

'Ranidaphobia?'

She looked at him and, as he studied her, a little of the colour crept back into her face. She even laughed shakily. 'How many people know that word?'

He smiled at her, trying to install some normality in the fraught atmosphere. 'I'm guessing everyone who's frightened of frogs.' He glanced up the hallway. 'I imagine Josie is in one of the ward rooms. Why don't you go check on her while I sort out the uninvited guest?'

She stood up so fast it would have been funny if he didn't think she'd kill him for laughing. He maintained a poker face as she walked hurriedly away and then his smile couldn't be restrained. He walked over to the pot plant, shifted it from the wall and saw the small green frog, almost a froglet, clinging by his tiny round pads to the wall.

Sam bent down and scooped the little creature into his palm carefully and felt the coldness of the clammy body flutter as he put his other hand over the top to keep it from jumping. A quick detour to the automatic door and he stepped out, tossing the invader into the garden.

Sam shook his head and walked back inside to the wall sink to wash his hands. A precipitous human baby jammed in a bikini bottom didn't faze her but a tiny green frog did? It was a crazy world.

He heard her come back as he dried his hands.

'Thank you,' she said to his back. He turned. She looked as composed and competent as she had when he'd first met her. As if he'd imagined the wild-eyed woman of three minutes ago.

He probably thought she was mad but there wasn't a lot she could do about that now. Ellie really just wanted him to go so she could put her head in her hands and scream with frustration. And then check every other blasted plant pot that she'd now ask to be removed.

Instead she said, 'So you've seen the hospital and your rooms. Did they explain the doctor's routine?'

He shook his head so she went on. 'I have a welcome pack in my office. I'll get it.'

She turned to get it but as she walked away something made her suspect he was staring after her. He probably wasn't used to dealing with officious nursing staff or mad ones. They probably swarmed all over him in Brisbane—the big consultant. She glanced back. He was watching her and he was smiling. She narrowed her eyes.

Then she was back and diving in where she'd left off. 'The plan is you come to the clinic two hours in the morning during the week, starting at eight after your ward round here at seven forty-five. Then you're on call if we need you for emergencies, but most things we handle ourselves. It's a window of access to a doctor for locals. We only call you out for emergencies.'

'So do you do on-call when you're off duty?' He glanced at her. 'You do have off-duty time?'

Ellie blinked, her train of thought interrupted. 'I share the workload with the two other midwives, Trina and Faith. I do the days, Faith does the afternoons and Trina does the nights. We cover each other for on-call, and two midwives from the base hospital come in and relieve us for forty-eight hours on the weekends. We have a little flexibility between us for special occasions.'

'And what do you do on your days off?' She had the feeling he was trying to help her relax but asking about her private life wasn't the way to do that.

She deliberately kept it brief. Hopefully he'd take the hint. 'I enjoy my solitary life.'

She saw him accept the rebuke and fleetingly felt mean. He was just trying to be friendly. It wasn't his fault she didn't trust any man under sixty, but that was the way it was.

She saw his focus shift and his brows draw together, as if he'd just remembered something. 'Syntocinon after birth—isn't giving that normal practice in all hospitals?'

It was a conversation she had with most locums when they arrived—especially the obstetricians like him. 'It's not routine here. We're low risk. Surprisingly, here we're assuming the mother's body has bleeding under control if we leave her well enough alone. Our haemorrhage rate per birth is less than two percent.'

His brows went up again. 'One in fifty. Ours is one in fifteen with active management. Interesting.' He nodded. 'Before I go we'd better check this baby in case your patient wants to go home. I borrowed the computer in the emergency ward and read over the new-born baby check. Don't worry. It all came back to me as I read it.'

He put his hand in his pocket and she heard keys jingle and wondered if it was a habit or he was keen to leave. Maybe he was one of those locums who tried to do as little as possible. It was disconcerting how disappointed she felt. Why would that be? Abruptly she wanted him to go. 'I can do it if you like.'

'No.' He smiled brilliantly at her and she almost stumbled, certainly feeling like reaching for her sunnies. That was some wattage.

Then he said blithely, 'We will practise together.' He picked up a stethoscope and indicated she should get one too.

Ellie could do nothing but follow his brisk pace down the corridor to Renee's room. So he was going to make her copy him. Served her right for telling him she'd done the course.

In Renee's room when he lifted back the sheet, baby Jones lay like a plump, rosy-cheeked sleeping princess all dressed in pink down to her fluffy bloomers. Ellie suppressed a smile. 'Mum's first girl after four boys.'

'What fun,' he murmured.

He started with the baby's chest, listening to both sides of her chest and then her heart. Ellie remembered the advice from the course to start there, because once your examination woke the baby up she might not lie so quietly.

Dr Southwell stepped back and indicated she do the same. Ellie listened to the *lub-dub, lub-dub* of a normal organ, the in-and-out breaths that were equal in both lungs, nodded and stood back.

He was right. She'd been putting off asking someone to sign her off on this. Before Wayne, she would have been gung-ho about adding neonatal checks to her repertoire. A silly lack of confidence meant she'd been waiting around for someone else to do it when she should really just have done this instead. After all, when she had the independent midwifery service this would be one of her roles.

By the time they'd run their hands over the little girl, checked her hips didn't click or clunk when tested, that her hand creases, toes and ears were all fine, Ellie was quite pleased with herself.

As they walked away she had the feeling that Dr Southwell knew exactly what she was feeling.

'Easy,' he said and grinned at her, and she grinned

back. He wasn't so bad after all. In fact, he was delightful.

Then it hit her. It had been an action-packed two
hours since he'd walked in the door. This physically attractive male had gone from being a stranger standing
in her office, to coffee victim, to birth assistant, to frog
remover, to midwife's best friend in a couple of hours
and she was grinning back at him like a smitten fool. As
if she'd found a friend and was happy that he liked her.

Just as Wayne had bowled her over when they'd first
met. She'd been a goner in less than an evening. He'd
twisted her around his finger and she'd followed him
blindly until he'd begun his campaign of breaking her.
She'd never suspected the lies.

Oh, yes. Next came the friendly sharing of history,
all the warm and fuzzy excitement of mutual attrac-
tion, pleasant sex and then *bam*! She'd be hooked. The
smile fell off her face.

Not this little black duck.

Ellie dragged the stethoscope from around her neck
and fiercely wiped it over with a disposable cleaning
cloth. Without looking at Sam, she held out her hand
for his stethoscope. She felt it land and glanced at him.
'Thank you. I'll see you tomorrow, then, Dr Southwell.'

She watched his smile fade. Hers had completely
disappeared as she'd looked up at him with the same
expression she'd met him with this morning. Polite en-
quiry. He straightened his shoulders and jammed his
hand back in his pocket to jingle his keys again.

'Right,' he said evenly. 'I'll go check into my guesthouse.' Without another word, he strode away to the front door and she sagged with relief.

Lucky she'd noticed what she'd been doing before it had gone too far. But at this precise moment she didn't feel lucky. She felt disheartened that she couldn't just enjoy a smile from a good-looking man without getting all bitter, twisted and suspicious about it. Wayne had a lot to answer for.

She did what she always did when her thoughts turned to her horrific marriage that really hadn't been a marriage—she needed to find work to do and maybe Josie or her baby could give it to her.

CHAPTER THREE

THREE NIGHTS LATER, alone in her big oak bed on top of the cliff, Ellie twisted the sheets under her fingers as the dream dragged her back in time. Dragged her all the way back to primary school.

Her respirations deepened with the beginning of panic. The older Ellie knew what the dream Ellie didn't. Her skin dampened.

Then she was back.

To the last day of compulsory swimming lessons she'd used to love. Now school and swimming lessons made her heart hurt. Mummy had loved helping at swimming lessons, had even taught Ellie's class the first two years, but now all they did was remind young Ellie how much she'd lost, because Mummy wasn't there anymore. Daddy had said Mummy would be sad that Ellie didn't like swimming now, but it made her heart ache.

And some of the big boys in primary school were mean to her. They laughed when she cried.

But today was the last day, the last afternoon she'd see the grey toilet block at the swimming pool for this year, and she pushed off her wet swimming costume with relief and it plopped to the floor. When she reached for her towel she thought for a minute that it moved. Silly. She shook her head and grabbed for it again so she could dry and get dressed quickly, or she'd be last in line again and those boys would tease her.

Something moved out of the corner of her eye and then she felt the cold shock as a big, green frog leaped towards her and landed on her bare chest. She screamed, grabbed the clammy bulk of it off her slimy skin and threw it off her chest in mindless revulsion, then fought with the lock on the change-room door to escape.

The lock jammed halfway. Ellie kept screaming, then somehow her fingers opened the catch and she ran out of the cubicle, through the washroom and outside through the door—into a long line of stunned primary school boys who stared and then laughed at the crying, naked young Ellie until she was swooped on by a scolding teacher and bundled into a towel.

She wanted her mummy. Why couldn't she have her mummy? It should be her mummy holding her tight and soothing her sobs. She cried harder, and her racking sobs seemed to come from her belly, even silencing the laughing boys...

Ellie sat bolt upright in bed, the sob still caught in her throat, and shuddered. She didn't know why frogs were so linked with her mother's death. Maybe it was something she'd heard about her mother's car accident, coupled with her childhood's overwhelming sense of loss and grief—and of course that incident at the swimming baths hadn't helped—but she couldn't hear a frog without having that loneliness well back up in her again. It had become the spectre of grief. All through her childhood, whenever she'd been lonely and missed her mother, she'd had the frog nightmare. She'd eventually grown out of it. But, after Wayne, it had started again.

She hadn't had the dream for a while. Not once since she'd moved here a year ago—and she hoped like heck she wasn't going to start having it repeatedly again.

She glanced at the window. It was almost light. She'd have time for a quick walk on the beach before she'd have to come back and shower for work. Find inner peace before the day.

Then she remembered the new doctor. Sam. Day four. One more day and then she'd have the weekend off and wouldn't have to see him. Was that why she'd had the dream? The problem was she liked him. And every day she liked him more. He was lovely to the women. Great with the staff. Sweet to her. And Myra thought the sun shone out of him.

Ellie didn't want to like Sam. Because she'd liked the look of Wayne too, and look where that had ended up.

Of course when she went down to the beach the first person she saw was Dr Sam. Funny how she knew it was him—even from the spectacular rear. Thankfully he didn't see her because he was doing what his father had done—watching the ocean. Sam's broad back faced her as he watched the swells and decided on where to swim. Then he strode into the water.

She walked swiftly along the beach, her flip flops in her hand, waves washing over her toes while she tried not to look as his strong arms paddled out to catch the long run of waves into the shore that delighted the surfers.

She couldn't even find peace on 'her' beach. She stomped up the curve of sand and back again faster than usual, deliberately staring directly in front of her. If she hadn't been so stubborn she would have seen that he was coming in on a wave and would intercept her before she could escape.

He hopped up from the last wave right in front of her. 'Good morning, Ellie Swift.'

She jumped. She glared at his face, then in fairness accepted it wasn't his fault she was feeling crabby. 'Morning, Sam.' Then despite herself her gaze dropped to the dripping magnificence of his chest, his flat, muscled abdomen, strong thighs and long legs, and her breath caught in her throat. Even his feet were masculine and sexy. *My goodness!* Her face flamed and she didn't know where to look.

Sam said, 'The water's a nice temperature,' and she hoped he hadn't noticed her ears were burning.

'Um…isn't it warmer in Queensland?' Her brain was too slow to produce exciting conversation.

He shrugged and disobediently her eyes followed the movement of his splendid shoulders despite her brain telling her to look away. He said, 'Don't know. I haven't swum in the ocean for years.'

That made her pause. Gave her a chance to settle down a little, even wonder why he hadn't been to the beach back home. She needed to get out of here. Create some space. Finally she said, 'Then it's good that you're doing it here. I have your father's surfboard up at my house. I'll arrange to get it to you. I'm late. See you soon.'

Sam stood there and watched her leave. He couldn't help himself and he gave up the fight to enjoy the sight. She had a determined little walk, as if she were on a mission, and trying hard to disguise the feminine wiggle, but he could see it. A smile stretched across his face. Yep. The receding figure didn't look back. He hadn't expected her to. But still, it was a nice way to start the day. Ellie Swift. She was still doing his head in. He had to admit it felt novel to be excited about seeing a woman again. Could it be that after only these few days here he was finding his way to coming back to life?

He hadn't made any progress as far as breaking through her barriers went. Maybe he was just out of practice. But the tantalising thing was that, despite coming from different directions, he sensed the rapport, their commonalities, the fact that inherently they believed in the same values. And he was so damnably attracted to her. He loved watching her at work and would have liked to have seen the woman outside work hours. He didn't understand her aversion to having a friendly relationship with him, but that was her right and he respected it. Thank goodness for work. He'd see her in an hour. He grinned.

Ellie disappeared from sight and Sam strode up the beach to scoop up his towel from the sand. He rubbed his hair exuberantly and stopped. Breathed in deeply.

Felt the early sun on his skin, the soft sea breeze, and he glanced back at the water. The sun shone off the pristine white sand and the ocean glittered. He'd needed this break badly. He hadn't enjoyed the world so much as he had since he'd come here. Life had been grey and closed off to him since Bree's death.

The only light in his long days had been the progression of his patients' pregnancies to viable gestation—so that, even if the babies were born prematurely, it was later in the pregnancy and, unlike his and Bree's children, they had a fighting chance. Other people's surviving children had helped to fill the gaping hole of not having his own family.

Now this place was reminding him there was a whole world outside Brisbane Mothers and Babies. He really should phone his dad and thank him for pushing him to come here.

Thursday night, the nightmare came back again and Ellie woke, breathless and tear-stained, to the phone ringing.

That was a good thing. She climbed out of bed and wiped the sweat from her brow. She grabbed for the phone, relieved to have something else to drive the remnants of the nightmare away. 'Hello?' Her voice was thick and wavered a little.

'Sorry, Ellie. Need you for a maternity transfer. Prem labour.'

Her brain cleared rapidly. 'Be there in five.' That sounded much more decisive. She was in no fit state to walk in the dark but she'd have to. Hopefully a frog wouldn't do her in. Ellie dragged off her high-necked nightdress and pulled on a bra and trousers. Her shirt was in the bathroom and she stumbled through to get it, glancing at her face in the mirror. Almost composed.

But her hands shook as she buttoned her shirt all the way up. Damn nightmares.

She dragged her thoughts away from the dream. 'Who's in prem labour?' Ellie muttered as she ran the comb through her hair. The fringe was sweaty and she grimaced. It wasn't a fashion show and she'd find out who soon enough.

When she reached the hospital, swinging her big torch, she saw the Lexus. Dr Southwell. Trina had called him in as well.

If she thought of him like that, instead of as Sam, there was more distance between them and she was keeping that distance at a premium. That was what she liked about midwifery—nothing was about her. She could concentrate on others, and some 'other' must be well established in labour for Trina to call the doctor as well as Ellie.

She made a speedy pass of the utility vehicle parked at an angle in front of the doors as if abandoned in a hurry. Her stomach sank.

She recognised that car from last year because it had the decals from the fruit market on it.

Marni and Bob had lost their first little girl when she'd been born in a rush, too early. It had all happened too fast for transfer to the hospital for higher level of care, too tragically, and at almost twenty-three weeks just a week too early for the baby to have a hope to survive. Marni had held the shiny little pink body on her skin, stroking her gently, talking through her tears, saying as many of the things she wanted to say to her daughter as she could before the little spirit in such a tiny angel's body gently slipped away.

There had been nothing Ellie could do to help before it was too late except offer comfort. All she'd been able to do was help create memories and mementoes for the parents to take home because they wouldn't be taking home their baby.

Ellie had seen Marni last week. They'd agreed about the fact that she needed to get through the next two weeks and reach twenty-four weeks, how she had to try not to fear that she was coming up to twenty-three weeks pregnant again. That a tertiary hospital couldn't take her that early if she did go into labour. This was too heartbreaking. When Ellie walked into the little birth room her patient's eyes were filled with understandable fear that it was all happening again.

She glanced at Bob chewing his bottom lip, his long hair tousled, his big, tattooed hand gripping one of Marni's while the other hand dug into the bed as if he could stop the world if only it would listen. Old Dr Rodgers would have rubbed their shoulders and said he was so sorry, there was nothing they could do. So what *could* they do?

Marni moaned as another contraction rolled over her.

Sam looked up and saw Ellie, his face unreadable. He nodded at the papers. 'We're transferring. Marni's had nephedipine to stop the contractions and they've slowed a little. I've given IV antibiotics, and prescribed the new treatment we've just started at our hospital for extreme prematurity with some success, but we need to move her out soon before it hots up again. Are you happy to go with her?' There was something darkly intense about the way he said it. As if daring her to stand in his way.

'Of course.' What did he mean? If he was willing to try to save this baby and fight for admission elsewhere, she'd fly to the moon with Marni. But he knew as well as she did that most of the time other hospitals didn't have the capacity to accept extremely premature labour because they wouldn't be able to do anything differently when the baby was born. Too young to live was too young to live. 'They've accepted Marni?'

His face looked grim for a moment. 'Yes,' was all he said, but the look he gave was almost savage, and she blinked, wondering what had happened to him to make him so fierce.

'Ambulance should be here soon,' Trina said. She'd been quietly moving around Marni, checking her drip was secure, removing the used injection trays. She kept flicking sideways glances at Sam, as if he was going to ask her to do something she didn't know how to do, and Ellie narrowed her eyes. Had he done something to undermine her friend's confidence? She'd ask later.

Her gaze fell on the admission notes and she gathered them up to make sure she had the transfer forms filled out. She heard the ambulance pull up outside and didn't have the heart to ask Bob to move his car. They'd manage to work around it with the stretcher.

She rapidly filled in the forms with Trina's notes,

added the times the medications were given and waved
to the two female paramedics as they entered.

'Hello, ladies. This is Marni. Prem labour at twenty-
three weeks. We need a quick run to the base hospital.
I'm coming as midwife escort.'

One of the paramedics nodded at Marni. 'Hello.
Twenty-three?' Then a glance at Sam that quickly
shifted on. 'Okey-dokey.' She said no more.

Ellie finished the transfer forms and disappeared
quickly to pluck the small emergency delivery pack
from behind the treatment room door just in case Marni's baby decided otherwise. She sincerely hoped not.

Four hours later Sam watched Ellie for a moment as she
filled in paperwork at the desk. He had slipped in the
back door from the main hospital and she hadn't seen
him arrive, which gave him a chance to study her. Her
swanlike neck was bent like the stalk of a tired gerbera.
His matron looked weary already and the day had only
just started. *His* matron? *Whoa, there.*

But he couldn't help himself asking, 'What time did
you get back?' He knew the answer, but it was a conversation opener.

He watched the mask fall across her face. Noted he
was far too curious about the cause of that wall around
her and kept telling himself to stop wondering. Dark
shadows lay beneath her eyes and her skin seemed pale.

She said steadily, 'Five-thirty. It was a lovely sunrise.'

Sam had thought so too—a splash of pink that had
blossomed to a deep rose, and then a bright yellow beam

soaring out of the cluster of clouds on the horizon over the ocean. The bay itself had already captured him, though he preferred to walk down on the pristine sand of the beach rather than along the cliff tops.

He hadn't been able to sleep after the ambulance had left so he'd sat well back from the edge on the small balcony that looked over the road and across to the headland. He'd spent time on the creakingly slow Internet catching up on his email.

By the time the ambulance had returned past his boarding house to drop Ellie back at the hospital, the sky had been pinking at the edges. She still had an hour before she started work and he'd wondered if she'd go in or if someone else would replace her after a call-out.

Now he knew. He was ridiculously pleased to see her and yet vaguely annoyed that she didn't have backup.

'How was Marni after the trip?'

Her face softened and he leant against the desk. Watched the expressions chase across her face whenever she let the wall down. He decided she had one of the most expressive faces he'd seen when she wasn't being officious. No surprises as to what she was thinking about because it was all out there for him to see.

'Of course, she was upset it was happening again. But the contractions slowed right off.' Concern filled her eyes and he wondered who worried about her while she worried about everyone else. He doubted many people were allowed to worry about her.

Her voice brought him back. 'How do you think she'll go?' She looked at him as if he could pull a miracle out of his hat. It was harder doing it long distance but he'd damn well try. Marni would have the benefit of every medical advance in extreme premature labour from his resources he could muster, every advance he'd worked on for the last four years, or he'd die trying. He wouldn't let *her* down.

'My registrar will arrange for the new drug to be forwarded to Marni and they'll start her on that. The OG at the base hospital will put a cervical suture in tomorrow if she's settled. And she'll stay there in the hospital until she gets to twenty-four weeks, and then after a couple of weeks if everything stays settled she can come home and wait. I'll phone today and confirm that plan with the consultant, and will keep checking until she's settled and sorted.'

'What if she comes in again then? After she comes home?'

Then they would act as necessary. 'We transfer again. By then the baby will be at an age where he or she can fight when we get a bed in a NICU.'

'We didn't get to twenty-four weeks last time.' Worry clouded her eyes.

He resisted the urge to put his hand on her shoulder and tell her to stop worrying. He knew she'd push him away. But the really strange thing was that he even wanted to reach out—this need for connection was new in itself.

He had this! He'd never worried about a response from a woman he was trying to reassure before and wasn't sure how to address it. Or even if he wanted to. Instead he jammed his hand into his pocket and jiggled his keys while he kept his conversation on the subject she was interested in. 'With treatment and persistence, we will this time.'

'Then they're lucky you're here.' Now she looked at him in the way he'd wanted her to since he'd met her. But this time he didn't feel worthy.

But he forced a smile. 'Finally—praise. And now I'm going.' The sooner he did the clinic, the sooner he could come back and check on her.

Ellie watched him walk away. Marni was lucky. She didn't feel so lucky, because a nice guy was the last thing she needed. Why was he being so friendly? She couldn't trust him no matter how nice he was. He'd be here in her face for another three weeks, that was all. Then he'd never come back. Why had his father had to break his arm and send the son?

She closed the file with a snap. Life was out to get her.

She heard the plaintive thought even though she didn't say it out loud and screwed her face up. *Stop whining*, she scolded herself and stood up. *We are lucky to have him. Very lucky.*

But she couldn't help the murky thoughts that were left over from the nightmare. The next day was always a struggle when she'd had the dream. And sometimes it meant she'd get some form of contact from Wayne, as if he was cosmically connected to her dream state so that she was off-balance when he did contact her.

'Hello, my lovely.' Myra's cheerful voice broke into her thoughts and thankfully scattered them like little black clouds blown away by a fresh breeze. Then the smell of freshly brewed coffee wafted towards her from the stylish china mug Myra was holding out for her.

'I hear you had a call-out so I've brought you a kick-start. Though it's not much of a kick.' She grimaced with distaste at the sacrilege of good coffee. 'Half-strength latte.'

Ellie stood up and took the mug. The milky decoration on top looked like a rose this morning. Ellie blew a kiss to the silver-haired lady who always looked quietly elegant in her perfectly co-ordinated vintage outfits. She reminded Ellie of the heroine from a nine-teen-twenties detective show, except with silver hair. Myra had said that the only things she'd missed when she'd moved to Lighthouse Bay from Sydney were the vintage clothes shops.

Ellie sipped. 'Oh, yum.' She could hug her friend and not just for the coffee. Myra always made her feel better. 'Just what I need. Thank you. How are you?'

'Fine. Of course.' Myra seated herself gracefully in the nurse's chair beside Ellie. 'I'm going away for the weekend, this afternoon—' she looked away and then back '—and I wondered if you'd feed Millicent.'

'Of course.' Myra's black cat drifted between both crofts anyway and if Myra was away Millicent would miaow at Ellie's front door for attention. 'Easily done. I still have tinned food from last time.'

'Thank you.' Myra changed the subject. 'And how are you going with our new doctor?'

Ellie took another sip. Perfect. 'He seems as popular with the women as old Dr Southwell.'

Myra looked away again and, despite her general

vagueness due to lack of sleep from the night before, Ellie felt the first stirrings of suspicion. 'I know you like him.'

'Sam and I have coffee together every morning. A lovely young man. Very like his father. What do *you* think of him?' There was definitely emphasis on the 'you'.

Myra was not usually so blunt. Ellie's hand stilled as she lifted it to have another sip. 'He seems nice.'

'Nice.' Myra rolled her eyes and repeated, 'Nice,' under her breath. 'He's been here for nearly a week. The man is positively gorgeous and he has a lovely speaking voice.'

Ellie pulled a face. Really! 'So?'

For once Myra appeared almost impatient. 'He's perfect.'

Ellie was genuinely confused. The cup halted halfway to her mouth. 'For what?' Maybe she was just slow today.

Myra's eyes opened wide, staring at her as if she couldn't believe Ellie could be so dense. 'For you to start thinking about young men as other than just partners of the women whose babies you catch.'

'As a male friend, you mean? You seem awfully invested in this doctor.' A horrible thought intruded into her coffee-filled senses. Surely not? 'Did you have anything to do with him coming here?'

Her friend raised one perfectly drawn eyebrow. 'And what influence could I possibly have had?'

It had been a silly thought. Ellie rubbed her brow. She tried to narrow her eyes to show suspicion but suspected she just looked ludicrous. The glint of humour in Myra's eyes made her give up the wordless attempt. So she said instead, 'You seemed pretty cosy with his father last time I saw you.'

Myra ignored that. 'And what have you got against young Dr Sam?' She produced a serviette, and un-wrapped a dainty purple-tinted macaroon and placed it precisely on the desk in front of Ellie. She must have retrieved it from the safety of her apron pocket. The sneaky woman knew Ellie couldn't resist them.

'Ooh, lavender macaroon.' Briefly diverted, Ellie put down her cup and picked up the macaroon.

Myra was watching her. She said again, 'He seems a conscientious young man.'

Ellie dragged her eyes from her prize. 'Think I said he was nice.' She looked at the macaroon again. She'd had no breakfast but was planning on morning tea. 'He's too nice.' She picked it up and took a small but almost vicious bite. Sweetness filled her mouth and re-minded her how she could be seduced by pretty pack-ages. Wayne had been a pretty package… Her appetite deserted her and she put the remainder of the biscuit back on the plate with distaste.

'Poor macaroon.' There was affectionate humour in Myra's voice. 'Not all men are rotten, you know.'

Ellie nodded. Myra always seemed to know what she was thinking. Like her mother used to know when she'd been a child. Ellie didn't want to risk thinking she was a part of Myra's one-person family. Myra would move on, or Ellie would, and there was no sense in be-coming too attached. But she suspected she might be already. It was so precarious. Ellie could manage on her own very well. But back to the real danger—thinking a man could recreate that feeling of belonging. 'I've met many delightful men. Fathers. And grandfathers. The other sort of relationship is just not for me.'

'It's been two years.'

This was persistent, even for Myra. 'Are you match-making? You?' She had another even more horrific thought. 'Did you and old Dr Southwell cook this up between you?'

'I hardly think Reginald—whom I would prefer you didn't call *old* Dr Southwell—would break his arm just to matchmake his son with the midwife at the hospital.'

Ellie narrowed her eyes. 'So neither of you discussed how poor Ellie and poor Sam could be good for each other?'

Myra threw up her hands in a flamboyant gesture that was a little too enthusiastic to be normal. 'For goodness' sake, Ellie. Where do you get this paranoia?'

She hadn't answered the question, Ellie thought warily, but she couldn't see why the pair of them would even think about her that way. She was being silly. Still, she fervently hoped Dr Southwell Senior hadn't mentioned her as a charity case to his son. That would be too embarrassing and might just explain his friendliness. A charity case…please, no.

Myra left soon after and Ellie watched her depart with a frown. Thankfully, she was diverted from her uncomfortable suspicions when a pregnant woman presented for her routine antenatal visit, so the next hour was filled. Ellie liked to add an antenatal education component if the women had time. She was finding it helped the women by reducing their apprehension of labour and the first week with the baby after birth.

Then a woman on a first visit arrived to ask about birthing at Lighthouse Bay instead of the base hospital where she'd had her last baby and Ellie settled down with her to explain their services. Word was getting out, she thought with satisfied enthusiasm.

The next time Ellie turned around it was lunchtime and she rubbed her brow where a vague headache had settled. She decided lack of sleep was why she felt a little nauseated and tried not to worry that it could be one of the twelve-hour migraines that floored her coming on.

Renee's husband arrived, armed with a bunch of flowers, and with their children hopping and wriggling like a box full of field mice, to visit Mum. The way his eyes darted over the children and the worried crease in his forehead hinted that Renee might decide to leave her safe cocoon early and return to running the family.

Ellie suspected the new mum was becoming bored with her room anyway and could quite easily incorporate her new princess into the wild household and still manage some rest.

It proved so when a relieved father came back to the desk to ask what they needed to do before discharge.

'It's all done. Renee has a script for contraception, baby's been checked by the doctor, and she's right to go.'

The relief in his face made Ellie smile at him despite the pain now throbbing in her head. 'Did you have fun with the kids, Ned?'

He grimaced. 'Not so much on my own. They've been good, but…'

Ned carried the smallest, a little carrot-topped boy, and an armful of gift bags out of the ward doorway with a new purpose and possibly less weight on his shoulders. Two more toddlers and a school-aged boy carrying flowers appeared from down the ward, with Renee bringing up the rear with her little princess in her arms, a wide smile on her face.

The foyer in front of the work station clamoured with young voices, so Ellie missed Sam as he returned from clinic and stood at the side of the room.

'Thank you, both,' Renee said. 'It was a lovely holiday.' She was looking past Ellie to the man behind her.

Ellie turned in time to see her new nemesis grin back. She didn't have the fortitude to deal with the 'charity' overtones left from Myra, so she turned quickly back again.

'I think you may be busy for a while,' Sam said to the mother.

Renee nodded calmly and then winked at Ellie. Lowering her voice, she confided, 'It does Ned good to have them for a day or two—lets him see what it's like to be home all day with the darlings in case he's forgotten.'

CHAPTER FOUR

THE AUTOMATIC DOORS closed behind the big family and they both watched them disappear. Sam turned and Ellie saw that flashing smile again. 'Imagine juggling that mob! It wouldn't be dull.'

There was a pause but she didn't say anything. She couldn't think of anything to say, which was peculiar for her, and had a lot to do with the fact that her vision had begun to play up. Small flashes of light were exploding behind her eyes. Migraine.

He filled the silence. 'Do you enjoy watching the women go home with their new babies?'

'Of course. That's a silly question!' He was looking at her with a strange, thoughtful intensity but she was too tired to work it out. She really wasn't in the mood for games. 'Don't you?'

'It isn't about me.' He paused, as if something was not right. 'I'm wondering why a young, caring woman is running a little two-bit operation like this in a town that's mostly populated with retirees and young families.'

Go. Leave me so I can will this headache away. Her

patience stretched nearly to breaking point. 'Me?' She needed to sit and have a cup of tea and maybe a couple of headache tablets. 'Our centre is just as efficient as any other centre of care. What's the difference between here and the city? Are you a "tertiary hospital or nothing" snob?'

'No.' He looked at her. '"Tertiary hospital" snob?'

'Size isn't everything, you know.'

He raised his brows at her. 'I'm very aware of that. Sorry. I was just wondering when you were going to be one of these women coming in to have your perfect little family.'

That stung because she knew it wasn't a part of any future waiting for her on the horizon. Though it should have been. 'There is no perfect little family.'

She looked at him coldly, because abruptly the anger bubbled and flared and her head hurt too much to pretend it wasn't there. 'Where's your perfect little family? Where are your children?'

Lordy, that had sounded terrible. She felt like clapping her hand over her mouth but something about his probing was getting right up her nose.

He winced but his voice was calm. 'Not everyone is lucky enough to have children. I probably won't have any, much to my father's disgust. You're a midwife with empathy pouring out of every inch of you, just watching other women become mothers.'

Easily said. She closed her eyes wearily. 'There's no difference between you and me.'

He didn't say anything and when she opened her eyes he shook his head slowly. 'I saw the way you looked at

Renee's baby. And Josie's. As if each one is a miracle that still amazes you.'

'And you?' She waved a listless hand. 'There's nothing there that spells "misogynist and loner".'

He physically stepped back. 'I really shouldn't have started this conversation, should I?'

'No.' She stood up and advanced on him. She even felt the temptation to poke him in the chest. She didn't. She never poked anyone in the chest. But the pressure in her head combined with the emotion, stresses, and fear from the last few days—fear for Marni's baby, her horrible fear of frogs and this man who was disrupting her little world—and she knew she had a reason to be running scared. Add lack of sleep and it wasn't surprising she had a migraine coming on like a fist behind her eyes.

Stop it, she told herself. She closed her eyes again and then looked down. She said with weary resignation, because she knew she was being unreasonable, 'Sorry. Can you just go?'

She didn't know how she could tell he was looking at her despite the fact she was considering his shoes. His voice floated to her. 'I'm sorry. My fault for being personal.'

That made her look up. He actually did look apologetic when it was she who was pouring abuse like a shrew and had lost it. Her head pounded. She felt like she was going to burst into tears. Actually, she felt sick.

She bolted for the nearest ladies' room and hoped like hell there wasn't a frog in the sink.

Afterwards, when she'd washed her face and didn't

feel much better, she dragged herself to the door, hoping he had gone. Of course, he hadn't; he had waited for her outside in the corridor.

'You okay?'

'Fine.' The lights behind her eyes flickered and then disappeared into a pinpoint of light. She swayed and everything went dim and then black.

Sam saw the colour drain from Ellie's face, the skin tone leeching from pink to white in seconds. His brain noted the drama of the phenomenon while his hands automatically reached out and caught her.

'Whoa there,' he muttered, and scooped her up. She was lighter than he expected, like a child in his arms, though she wasn't a tiny woman with her long arms and neck that looked almost broken, like a swan's, as she lay limp in his embrace.

Unfortunately there was no denying the surge of protective instinct that flooded him as he rested her gently on the immaculate cover of the nearest bed. He'd really have to watch that. He was already thinking about her too much when he wasn't here, when in fact it was unusual for him to feel anything for anybody at all.

Her damn collar was buttoned to the neck again—how on earth did she stand it?—and he undid the first and second buttons and placed his finger gently against her warm skin to feel the beating of her carotid artery.

Her skin was like silk and warmer than he expected. She must be brewing something. Sudden onset, pallor, faint... He didn't know her but she hadn't struck him as the fainting type... Before he could decide what to do she groaned and her eyelids fluttered. Then she was staring up at him. Her blue eyes were almost violet. Quite beautiful.

'Where am I?'

He glanced at the sign on the door. 'Room one.'

She drew her dark brows together impatiently. 'How did I get here?'

'You fainted.'

The brows went up. 'You carried me?' He quite liked her brows. Amusing little blighters. Her words penetrated and he realised he was going mad again. She was the only one who did that to him.

He repeated. 'You fainted. I caught you. Can't have you hitting your head.' She struggled to sit up and he helped her. 'Slowly does it.'

'I never faint.'

He bit back the smile. 'I'm afraid you can't say that any more.'

She actually sagged a little at that and he bit back another smile. Behind her now not-so-tightly buttoned collar, which she hadn't noticed he'd unbuttoned, she wasn't the tough matron she pretended to be. She was cute, though he'd die rather than tell her that. He could just imagine the explosion. 'Stay there. I'll get you some water.' He paused at the door. 'Did you eat breakfast this morning?'

She passed a hand over her face. 'I can't remember.'

'I'll get you water and then I'll get you something to eat.' He could already tell she was going to protest. 'You made me coffee on Monday. I can do this for you. It'd be too embarrassing to fall into my arms again, right?'

She subsided. The fact she stayed put actually gave him a sense of wicked satisfaction that made his lips curve. *Tough luck. My rules this time.*

With a stab of painful guilt that washed away any amusement, he remembered he hadn't looked after Bree enough, hadn't been able to save her, or his own premature children. But maybe he could look after Ellie—at least for the month he was here.

He heard her talking to herself as he left. 'I'll have to get a relief midwife to come in.'

He walked out for the water but didn't know where to get the glass from. He'd have to ask her, so was back a few seconds later.

She was still mumbling. 'I'll be out for at least twelve hours.'

He stopped beside the bed. 'Does your head hurt?'

She glared at him. 'Like the blazes. I thought you were getting water.'

'Cups?'

'Oh. Paper ones on the wall beside the tap.'

Ellie closed her eyes as Sam left the room. How embarrassing! She hadn't fainted in her life and now she'd done it in front of a man she'd particularly wanted to maintain professional barriers with. She'd never fainted with a migraine before. Oh, goody, something new to add to the repertoire.

Where was Myra when she needed her? She wished Sam would just leave. Though when he returned with the water she gulped it thirstily.

'Go easy. I don't have a bowl or know where they live.'

Ellie pulled the paper cup away from her lips. He

was right. She was still feeling sensitive but her throat was dry and raw. She sank back against the pillows. She'd have to strip this bed because she'd crumpled it.

Maybe the weekend midwife could come early. This afternoon. She'd meant to go shopping for food and now she knew she didn't have the energy. She'd just hole up until tomorrow, when she'd be fine. The thoughts rolled around in her head, darting from one half-considered worry to another.

'Stop it.'

She blinked. 'Stop what?'

'Trying to solve all the logistical problems you can see because you do everything around here.'

'How do you know I'm thinking that?' It came out more plaintively than she'd expected. How did he know she did do most things?

He looked disgustingly pleased with himself. 'Because the expressions on your face mirror your every thought. Like reading a book.'

Great. Not! 'Well, stop reading my book.'

'Yes, ma'am.' But his eyes said, *I quite like it*.

She reached down into her fast fading resources. 'If you would like to help, could you please ask Myra to come around from the coffee shop?'

'Myra has left for the weekend. Going away somewhere. There's a young woman holding the fort, if you would like a sandwich.'

Her heart sank. Clarise... Clarise could make toast, which might help, but she'd have to do everything else herself. 'Already? Damn.'

'Can I do something for you?' He spread his hands. 'I've done all my homework.'

Ellie looked at him. Tall, too handsome, and relaxed with one hand in his pocket. Leaning on the door jamb as if he had all the time in the world. She had a sudden picture of him in his usual habitat surrounded by a deferential crowd of students, the man with all the answers, dealing with medical emergencies with swift decision and effectiveness. She had no right to give this man a hard time. Her head throbbed and the light was hurting her eyes. Now she felt like crying again. Stupid weakness.

His voice intruded on her thoughts and there was understanding in his eyes, almost as if he knew how much she hated this. 'You look sad. Is it so bad to have to ask me for help?'

My word, it is. 'Yes.'

Of course he smiled at that. 'Pretend I'm someone you hired.'

'I don't have to pretend. I did hire you.'

He laughed at that. 'Technically the administration officer hired me.'

'That would be me.'

'So what would you like me to do?'

She sat up carefully and swung her legs over the bed. He came in closer as if to catch her if she fell. It was lucky, because her head swam and she didn't want to smack the linoleum with her face.

'Just make sure I make it to the desk and the phone and the rest I can manage. Maybe you could stay in case anyone else comes in while we wait for my replacement.

Even I can see there's no use me being here if I can't be trusted not to fall on my face.'

'Especially when it's far too pretty a face to fall on.'

She looked at him. Narrowed her eyes. 'Don't even go there.'

He held up his hands but she suspected he was laughing at her again. Together they made their way over to the desk and with relief she sank into her usual chair. She reached into her handbag, pulled out her sunglasses and put them on. The pain from the glare eased.

It only took an hour for her replacement to arrive but it felt like six. She just wanted to lie down. In fact her replacement's arrival had been arranged faster than expected, and was only possible because the midwife had decided to spend an extra day at Lighthouse Beach, on the bay, before work.

Ellie had sipped half a cup of tea. She'd taken two strong headache tablets and really wanted to sink into her bed. Standing at the door with her bag over her arm, she wasn't sure how she was going to get up the hill to her croft.

'I'll drive you.'

He was back. And he'd read her mind again. She wished he'd stop doing that. He'd left for an outpatient in the other part of the hospital after Ellie had assured him she'd be fine until the relief midwife arrived and she had been hoping to sneak away.

She'd have loved to say no. 'If you don't mind, I'll have to take you up on that offer.'

'So graciously accepted,' he gently mocked.

He was right. But she didn't care. All she could think about was getting her head down and sinking into a deep sleep.

He ushered her to his car, and made sure she was safely tucked in before he shut the door.

'Do you always walk to work?'

'It's only at the top of the hill.' She rested her head back against the soft leather headrests and breathed in the aroma of money. Not something she'd sniffed a lot of in her time. 'I always walk except in the rain. It's a little slippery on the road when it's wet.'

'Did you come down in the dark, last night?'

She didn't bother opening her eyes. 'I have a torch.'

'You should drive down at night.'

Spare me. 'It's two hundred and fifty metres.'

He put the car into gear, turned up the steep hill and then turned a sharp left away from the lighthouse, onto the road with three cottages spaced privately along the headland. 'Who owns the other ones?'

'I'm in the first, Myra is the end one and the middle one is Trina, so try not to rev your engine because she's probably sleeping.'

'I'll try not to.' Irony lay thick in his voice. He parked outside the first cottage and turned the car off. She'd hoped she could just slip out and he'd drive away.

They sat for a moment with the engine ticking down. Ellie's headache had reached the stage where she didn't want to move and she could feel his glance on her. She didn't check to see if she was imagining it. Then she heard his door open and the car shifted as he got out.

When her door opened the cool salt air and the crash

from the waves on the cliffs below rushed in and she revived a little.

Sam spoke slowly and quietly as if to a frightened child. 'If you give me the key, I could open the door for you?'

'It's not locked.'

'You're kidding me?' The words hung in disbelief above her. Apparently that concept wasn't greeted with approval. He said in a flat voice, 'Tonight it should be.'

She held her head stiffly, trying not to jar it, and turned in the seat. She locked it at night but the daytime was a test for herself. She would not let her life be run by fear. 'Thank you for the lift.'

He put out his hand and Ellie wearily decided it was easier just to take it and use his strength to achieve a vertical position. Her legs wobbled a bit. He hissed out a breath and picked her up.

'Hey.'

'Hey, what?' A tinge of impatience shone through.

'You'll fall down if you try to walk by yourself.'

And then she was cradled tight against his solid warm chest and carried carefully towards her door. He leant her against the solid wood and turned the handle, then they were both inside.

Sam had expected the inside to be made up of smaller compartments but it was a big room that held everything. There was a tiny kitchen at the back with a chimney over the big, old wood-burner stove. A shiny gas stove and refrigerator stood next to it and a scrubbed wooden table and four chairs.

A faded but beautiful Turkish rug drew the sections of the home together in the middle where it held a soft cushioned sofa with a coffee table in front that faced the full-length glass doors out to sea. Bookshelves lined the rear walls and a couple of dark lighthouse paintings were discernible in the corners. There was a fireplace. A big red-and-white Malibu surfboard leant against the wall. His father's. He looked at it for a moment then away.

A patchwork-quilted wooden bed sat half-hidden behind a floral screen, pastel sheets and towels were stacked neatly in open shelves and across the room was a closed door which he presumed was the bathroom. Nothing like the sterile apartment he'd moved into after Bree's death and where he'd never unpacked properly.

The bed, he decided, and carried her across and placed her gently on the high bed's quilt.

'Come in,' she said with an exhausted edge to her voice as he put her down. Talk about ungrateful.

He stepped back and looked at her. She looked limp, with flushed spots in her pale face. Still so pale. Pale and interesting. She was too interesting and she was sick. He told himself she was a big girl. But that didn't mean he liked leaving her. 'Can I make you a cup of tea before I go?'

'No, thank you.'

He sighed and glanced at the room behind him again, as if seeking inspiration. He saw his dad's surfboard again. He'd said the midwife was minding it for him and that Sam should try it out. Maybe he would one day. But not today. It would be a good reason to come back.

He glanced through the double-glazed doors facing the ocean and he could imagine it would be a fabulous sight on wild weather days. But it was also too high up and exposed for him to feel totally comfortable. And she lived here alone.

He thought about the other two crofts and their occupants. It was a shame Myra was away.

'How about I leave a note for Trina and ask her if she'll check on you later?' *Before she goes to work for the night and leaves you up here all alone*, he added silently.

'No, thank you.' Her eyes were shut and he knew she was wishing him gone.

She was so stubborn. Why did he care? But he did. 'It's that or I'll come back.'

She opened her eyes. 'Fine. Leave a note for Trina. Ask if she'll drop in just before dark. I'll probably be fine by then.'

Sounded reasonable. Then she could lock the door.

That was all he could do. He saw her fight to raise her head and tilt it meaningfully at the door and he couldn't think of any other reason to stay.

He walked to the sink. Took a rinsed glass from the dish rack and filled it with water. Carried it back without a word and put it beside her. Then he felt in his pocket, retrieved his wallet and took out a business card. 'That's my mobile number. Ring me if you become seriously ill. Or if you need medication. I'll come. No problem.'

Then he tore himself away and shut the door carefully behind him, grimacing to himself that he couldn't lock it. Anybody could come up here and just waltz in while she was sleeping. Surely she locked it at night?

When he went next door and wrote on another of his business cards, he decided he should at least see if he could hear if Trina was awake. He walked all the way around the little house. Because he could. It was just like Ellie's, though there was a hedge separating them from each other and the cliff path that ran in front of the houses.

Anybody could walk all the way around these houses. The view was impressively dramatic, except he didn't enjoy it. The little crofts clung to the edge of the cliff like fat turtles and the narrow walkway against the cliff made his mouth dry.

At least the dwellings looked like they wouldn't blow off into the sea. They were thick-walled, with shutters tied back until needed for the really wild weather. Daring the ocean winds to try and shift them.

He was back at the front door again. No sounds from Trina's. She could sleep right through until tonight. He'd have to come back himself. Before dark, like Ellie had said.

Sam drove back down the hill to his guesthouse. He let himself in the quaint side entrance with his key and up the stairs to his balcony room. He threw the keys from his pocket onto the dresser, opened the little fridge, took out a bottle of orange juice and sipped it thoughtfully as he walked towards the windows.

She'd sleep for a while. He wished she'd let him stay but of course she'd sleep better without him prowling around. He knew it was selfish because if he'd been there he wouldn't have had to worry about her. Being away from her like this, he couldn't settle.

He felt a sudden tinge of remorse that made him grimace, an admission of unfaithfulness to Bree's memory. It hung like a mist damning him, because he was so fixated on Ellie, but also underneath was a little touch of relief that he was still capable of finally feeling something other than guilt and devastation.

His father would be pleased. He'd say it was time to let go of the millstone of his guilt over Bree, that it was holding him back and not doing the memory of their relationship justice. Was it time finally to allow himself the freedom to feel something for someone else?

His heartbeat accelerated at the thought but he told himself it would all be fine. He was only here for another few weeks, after all, and he'd be heading home after that. Strangely, the time limit helped to make him feel more comfortable with his strange urge to look after Ellie.

The sun shone and turned the blue of the ocean to a brilliant sapphire and he decided he'd go for another swim. No wonder his dad had raved about this place. Then he'd go back and check on Ellie after he'd showered.

CHAPTER FIVE

ELLIE HEARD SAM close the door when he left. She pulled the blanket up higher to calm the shudders that wracked her body. He'd been very good, and she should have said thank you, but the headache had built steadily again. It was easier to breathe in and out deeply, to make it go away and wait for sleep to claim her, and then maybe she'd wake up and all this would just have been a bad dream. Her hair was heavy on her forehead and she brushed it away. She was too disinclined to move to take a sip of the water he'd put there. Mercifully, everything faded.

When she fell asleep she had the nightmare.

She moaned because her head hurt as well.

Slowly the afternoon passed. As evening closed in the nightmares swirled around her, mixed themselves with imagined and remembered events.

But while she slept her troubled sleep there were moments when she felt safe. Moments when she felt a damp, refreshing washcloth on her brow. She dreamt she sipped fluid and it was cool and soothing on her throat. Even swallowed some tablets.

The bad dream returned. Incidents from her time with Wayne mixed in with it. Incidents from their spiral downhill flashed through her mind: cameos of her hurt and bewilderment when he'd barely spoken to her, mocked and ridiculed her…her phobia, her need for nurturing. Screaming he never wanted a family that time she'd thought she was pregnant. *All* she wanted was a family.

The dream flashed to the afternoon at the swimming pool again and she moaned in the bed. Twisted the sheets in her hand.

She fought the change room door. Ran into the boys outside…

She sobbed. She sobbed and sobbed.

'It's okay, sweetheart. Stop. My God. It's okay.'

The words were seeping through the horror and the mists of sweat and anguish. Sam's voice. His arms were around her. Her head was tucked into his chest, her hair was being stroked.

'Ellie. Wake up. It's a dream. Wake up!'

Ellie opened her eyes and a shirt button was pressing into her nose. A man's shirt.

'It's okay.' It was Sam's voice, Sam's big hands rubbing her back. A man's scent. So it must be Sam's shirt. Sam?

She was still foggy but clearing fast. What was he doing here? She pushed him away.

His hands moved back and his body shifted to the edge of the bed from where he'd reached for her. 'That's some nightmare.'

She brushed her damp hair out of her face, muttered, 'Why are you here?'

'Because Trina is at work, Myra's away and I wasn't sure you wouldn't get worse.'

He raised his brows and shook his head. 'You did get worse. It's almost midnight and you've been mumbling and tossing most of the evening. If you didn't get better soon I was going to admit you and put up a drip.'

Dimly she realised her head didn't hurt any more but it felt dense like a bowling ball, and just as heavy. It would clear soon, she knew that, but she couldn't just lie here crumpled and teary. The tendrils of the nightmare retreated and she wiped her face and shifted herself back up the bed away from him, pushing the last disquieting memories back into their dark place in her brain at the same time.

As she wriggled, he reached and flipped the pillows over and rearranged them so she could sit up.

Then he rose. She wasn't sure if that was better because now he towered over her, and it must have shown on her face, because he moved back and then turned away to walk to the kitchen alcove.

He switched on the jug, turned his head towards her and said quietly, 'Would you like a drink? Something hot?'

Her mouth tasted like some dusty desert cavern. She'd kill for a cup of tea. Maybe it wasn't so bad he was here. 'Yes, please. Tea?' She sounded like a scared kitten. She cleared her throat, mumbled, 'Thank you,' in a slightly stronger voice. She glanced down at her crumpled uniform but it was gone and she was in her bra and pants. Her face flushed as she yanked the covers up to her neck.

'You took off my shirt and trousers?'

'You were tangled in them. Sweating. I asked you and you said yes.'

She narrowed her eyes at him. 'I don't remember that.'

He came back with the mug of tea. 'I'm not surprised. You've been barely coherent. If that's a migraine, I hope I don't get one. Nasty.'

'I can't believe you undressed me.'

He waggled his brows. 'I left the essentials on.'

Her face grew even hotter. *Cheeky blighter.*

He put the tea down beside her. 'Do you have a dressing gown or something I can get you?'

'In the bathroom, hanging behind the door.' She took a sip and it tasted wonderful. Black. Not too hot. He must have put cold water in it so she didn't burn her tongue. That was thoughtful. While she sipped he poked his head into the little bathroom and returned with her gown.

Speaking of the bathroom… She needed to go, and imagined taking a shower. Oh, yes…that wouldn't go astray either if she could stay standing long enough to have it. The idea of feeling fresh and clean again grew overpoweringly attractive.

'Um… If you turn around, I'd like to get up.'

He considered her and must have decided she had more stamina than she thought she had because he nodded.

'Sure.' He crossed his arms and turned around, presenting his broad back to her. She shifted herself to the edge of the bed and swung her legs out. For a moment the room tilted and then it righted.

'You okay?' His voice came but he didn't turn. At least he played fair.

'Fine.' She took another breath, reached down and snatched clean underwear and a nightgown from the drawer beside her bed and stood up on wobbly legs. By the time she shut the door behind her in the bathroom, she was feeling better than she expected. *Good tea.*

By the time she showered and donned her night-dress and dressing gown again, she was feeling almost human.

When she opened the door the steam billowed into the room and for a moment she thought the cottage was empty. But he was sitting on the sofa with his head resting back and she remembered he'd been here all evening.

Guilt swamped her and she padded silently towards him to see if he'd fallen asleep. His eyes were definitely open as she tipped her head down to peer at him. There was a black cat at his feet. She'd forgotten Myra's cat.

'Did you feed Millicent?'

He patted the sofa seat beside him. 'Yes. She had sardines. You look better. I'll go soon, but first tell me about your dream.'

Instinctively she shook her head but she saw there were two cups and her teapot on the low table in front of him. She could do another civilised cup of tea after he'd been so good.

She remembered his arms, comforting her, making

her feel safe, as though she were finding refuge from the mental storm she'd created from her past, and her cheeks heated.

She pulled her dressing gown neckline closer and sat gingerly a safe distance along the sofa from him. 'Thank you for looking after me,' she said, and even to her own ears it sounded prim and stilted.

'You. Are. Very. Welcome.' He enunciated slowly as if to a child, and she glanced at him to see if he was making fun of her. There was a twinkle, but mostly there was genuine kindness without any dramatics.

She glanced back at the bed. It was suspiciously tidy. And a different colour. 'Did you change the sheets?'

'I did. The damp ones are on the kitchen chair. Where is your laundry in your little hobbit house?'

She had to smile at that. 'Does that make me a hobbit?'

'If so, you're a pretty little hobbit.'

'That's a bit personal between a doctor and a patient, isn't it?'

He waggled his finger, making the point. 'You are my friend. Definitely not my patient. I'm glad I didn't have to admit you.'

She wasn't quite sure how to take that and then he said very quietly, 'But listening to you suffer through those dreams was pretty personal. You nearly broke my heart.'

She moved to rise but he touched her arm. 'As your non-doctor friend, can I say I think now is a really good time for you to share your nightmares. Stop the power they have over you.'

She shivered but she subsided and glanced around the room. Anywhere but at him. The dish rack was empty. No dirty dishes. Distractions would be good. 'Have you eaten?'

He patted his flat belly. 'I ate early, before I came. In case I needed to stay. But I've helped myself to your tea.'

His arm came out and quite naturally he slid it around her waist. Bizarrely her body remembered that feeling, although her memory didn't, as he pulled her snug up against his firm hip. 'Tell me. Was it frogs?'

She shuddered. 'It's a long story.'

She felt him shrug under her. 'We have many hours until morning.'

She looked at him. 'It's not that long a story.'

He chuckled quietly, and it was an 'everything is normal even though we are sitting like this in the dark' sound, and despite the unconventional situation she felt herself relax against him.

'I'm all ears,' he said.

She turned her head and looked at him. 'They're big but I wouldn't say you are *all* ears.'

'Stop procrastinating.'

So she told him about the frog in the change room at school and the boys and, hearing it out loud for the second time since the therapist, she felt some of the power of it drain away. It was a little girl's story. Dramatic at the time but so long ago it shouldn't affect her now. In the cool quiet of the morning, with waves crashing distantly, she could accept that the frog was long dead and the little boys were all probably daddies with their own children now. That quite possibly Sam's idea of repeating it now could have merit because it seemed to have muted its power.

He said thoughtfully, 'If you could go back in time, to the morning before that, if you could prepare that little girl in some way, how could you help that young Ellie? What would you tell her?'

She thought about that. Wondered about what the misty memory of her mother might have said to her as a little girl if she had known it was going to happen.

'The frog is more frightened than you are?' The words came from some distant place she couldn't recognise but with them came a gentle wave of comfort. Relief, even. She thought of the child that she had been all those years ago. Sad eyes under the pony tail, freckles, scuffed knees from climbing tress to get away from teasing boys.

'If I had the chance. That might help her,' she said, and looked at Sam.

Sam nodded and squeezed her shoulder. 'So it was the same dream. Over and over?'

She looked at the floor. 'The other one's an even longer story and I don't think I'm up to that tonight.'

He looked at her and she shifted under his scrutiny. 'Okay. So, will you invite me back?'

Why on earth would he want to come back after these last exhausting hours? 'For frog stories?'

He shrugged again. 'There doesn't have to be stories. Can't I come back because I'd like to come back?'

She felt the shift in herself. Felt the weight of his arm, suddenly unbearable. Could almost imagine the bricks all slamming together between them, creating a wall like a scene in a fantasy movie.

Her voice was flat. Different from what it had sounded like only minutes ago. There was no way he could miss the change. 'You live in Brisbane. Your world is different to mine. We'll never be friends.' She tried to shrug off his arm and after a moment he let it fall. He shifted his body away to give her space and she appreciated his acceptance.

He looked at her and suddenly she felt the wall go up from him as well. Contrarily, she immediately wanted the openness that had been there before. Served her right.

But his voice was calm. It hadn't changed like hers had. 'I disagree. Friends can be made on short acquaintance. I'd like to come back later today and just check you're okay.'

Was he thick? Or just stubborn? How did she say no after he'd sat up here and minded her? Made her tea? After all, he would be gone in a few weeks. 'Did you give me water and wipe my face?'

He nodded. 'I didn't think you'd remember that. You weren't awake.'

'There were parts of the dream that weren't all bad.' She looked at him. 'It gets cool here in the night. Were you warm enough?'

He gestured to the throw folded at the end of the sofa. 'If somebody had visited, they would have found a very strange man wearing a blanket.'

She digested that and said simply, 'Thank you.' She

shook her head because she couldn't understand the mystery of his actions. 'Why did you stay?'

He shrugged. As if it was nothing special. No mystery for him. Lucky him. 'Because I didn't know if you would actually ring me if you needed help. You might have needed someone and I couldn't see anyone else coming.'

He'd stayed out of pity. The thought sat like dirty oil in the bottom of her stomach. She shouldn't have been surprised, because she was alone. No family. No husband. 'So you felt sorry for me.'

Sam compressed his lips as if being very careful about what came out of his mouth. She could live with the truth as long as it *was* the truth.

'I had sympathy for you, yes. You were unwell. I hope you would have done it for me if the roles had been reversed.'

She thought about that. Narrowed her eyes. 'Maybe. That's a sneaky way of wriggling out of the "pity" accusation.'

He sighed. Stood up. 'I'm tired. And I might yet get called out. I'm going home. I'll drop back before lunch and see how you are.'

'You could just call me on the phone to check on me.'

He studied her. 'I'll drop back after I do a round at the hospital.'

She stood up, careful to keep distance between them. 'You don't have to do rounds on the weekend. Only if they call you.'

He shrugged. 'Patients are still there. I'll do a round every day unless I can't.' He gestured to the corner of the room. 'You should go back to bed. I think you'll sleep better now.' Then he walked to the door, opened it and quietly closed it after himself. She heard the lock click.

Sam walked away but his thoughts remained focussed on the little cabin on top of the hill. There was something about Ellie, and this place, that connected so strongly with his emotions. He didn't know what it was about her that made him feel so anxious to help. Shame he hadn't been able to break through the barriers to Bree the way he seemed to be able to with Ellie, especially as for the last few years he hadn't really connected to anyone. He glanced out over the bay as he walked down the hill to the hospital. The lighthouse seemed to look down on him with benevolence.

CHAPTER SIX

ELLIE WENT BACK to the bed. Climbed into the clean sheets that a man she'd only known for less than a week had changed for her. She saw the hospital corners and wondered who'd taught him to make a bed like that. It certainly wouldn't have been med school. She looked at the half-full glass of water he'd left her in a fresh glass.

Then she thought of the fact she'd been in her underwear when she'd woken properly, and wondered with pink cheeks when he'd undressed her. Had she helped him, or fought him, or been a limp lump he'd had to struggle with? Had she missed the opportunity of a lifetime?

She frowned at the random and totally inappropriate thought. How on earth would she face him? Then stopped herself. *It's done. You're not eight years old now.*

She considered the result of holding in the swimming pool incident for all those years and even now the tragedy was fading. When Sam returned to Brisbane she'd be able to thank him for that, too.

Her eyes closed and it didn't happen immediately but eventually she drifted off and, strangely, she didn't dream at all.

The next morning was Saturday. Ellie woke after the sun was well and truly up and lay with her eyes open for several minutes as she went over the recent events, both hazy and clear, and how a man who was almost a stranger had taken control of her world, if only for a few hours.

Even a few days ago the idea of that happening would have been ludicrous but in the cold light of day she could be grateful if a little wary. He'd been circumspect, really. Except for taking off her uniform but then she would have done the same if she'd been nursing some-one in the throes of sweaty delirium. She tried not to think of stripping off Sam's shirt and trousers if he was sick—but the option to expand her imagination was tantalising her. *No!*

She glanced at the clock. Almost ten. He said he'd drop in after his weekend round.

When she put her feet on the ground her head didn't hurt. The headache had gone. It had disabled her but now her step was steady as she made her way into the bathroom with an armful of clothes.

By the time she came out, hair piled into a towel, teeth cleaned and mouth washed, she was starting to feel the emptiness in her belly and a hankering for fresh air.

As she opened the door to let the world in, Sam was standing outside with his phone in his hand.

That would be Sam who had seen her frogs and all.

Sam who looked ridiculously handsome. Sam who'd carried her into her bed. 'Oh. Hello. Have you been here long?'

'Just a few minutes. I knocked and when you didn't answer I was going to ring you.'

She opened her eyes wide. 'Do you have my number?'

'The relief midwife gave it to me when I said I might check on you again.'

Confidentiality clauses and all that obviously didn't hold much water when it was Sam asking. Nice of her, she thought sourly. But sensible too. 'I'm much better, thank you.'

She examined him in the bright morning light. Tall. Smiling like he was glad to see her. She shied away from that thought. Not too many shadows under his eyes, considering his onerous midnight duties. 'How are you after spending the evening with a raving woman?'

'Starving.' He gestured to the plastic shopping bag that hung from his hand. 'Any chance of a table and chairs where I can lay this out?'

'Food?' Her stomach grumbled and heat ran up her cheeks. She peeked at him from under her eyelashes to see if he'd heard and saw he was biting his lip. She could see the dimple at the side where he was holding it in.

He'd heard her stomach. Not much mystery left about her for this guy. 'Okay. I'm hungry. So in that case you are very welcome.' Although as she said it she remembered she hadn't made her bed yet, then mentally shrugged.

He'd changed the blinking sheets. He'd survive an

unmade bed. 'We'll take it through to the front deck. We can open the doors from the inside.'

Sam followed her and she was very conscious that the collar on her long-sleeved top wasn't as high as normal and there was some cleavage showing. Maybe she should put on a scarf? Again she reminded herself that he'd seen her in her bra and pants so any more than that was not a concern.

She sighed. He had the advantage of more knowledge of her than she had of him and she didn't like it. In fact she wasn't sure how she'd ended up with a guy who knew so much stuff about her and was walking around in her house like he owned it.

Before he followed her out onto the little veranda, he paused. 'Can I put my milk and cold things in your fridge? I came straight here from the supermarket, but have a few supplies for my flat as well.'

'Sure. There's plenty of room in the fridge.' Ellie winced a little at the hollow emptiness of the food supplies in her kitchen. She needed to shop and restock the cupboards herself.

When he'd done that he followed her to the balcony that overlooked the ocean. She noticed he hesitated at the door.

As he stood there he said quietly, 'Who built these cottages? The view is incredible.'

She stopped and looked in the direction he was looking, sweeping her gaze over the little cliff top that held the three tiny homes, the expanse of the sea out in front of them with the wheeling gulls and fluffy white clouds, the majesty of the tall, white lighthouse on the opposite ridge, which drew visitors on Sundays for lighthouse tours, its tiny top deck enclosed by a white handrail for the visitors as they examined the internal workings of the light through the windows.

'The cottages were built for three spinster sisters in the middle of the last century. They were all nurses at the hospital down the hill.'

She laughed. 'Myra said that the three of us who live here now are modern day reincarnations. Their father ran the lighthouse and when they were in their mid-twenties the eldest came into some money and had the cottages built. There's only one of them alive now. I visit her sometimes in the nursing home. She's ninety and sharp as a tack. Just frail and happy to have other people make her meals now.'

'So they lived here, unmarried, until they were too old and then they moved out?'

'Yep. Fabulous, isn't it?' There were privacy hedges between the three dwellings. In the past the sisters had kept the hedge levels down below waist height but since she'd moved in they'd grown and it was their own little private promontory over the ocean. She loved it. She moved to the edge and peered out at a ship that was far away on the horizon.

When she turned back she could see that Sam was looking uncomfortable and she glanced around to see why. 'You okay?'

'Not a fan of being at the edge of heights.'

'Oh.' The last thing she'd do was make someone with a phobia uncomfortable. 'We'll go back inside, then.'

'No. Just sit me on this side of the table and I'll be

fine.' He lifted the bags up and placed them on the little outdoor table. 'It's perfect here.'

She smiled at him. 'As we dwell in Phobia Central.'

For some silly reason she felt closer to him because he'd admitted to having a weakness for heights. It made her feel not so stupid with her phobia of frogs. She had a sudden horrid thought that perhaps he'd made that up, just to get into her good graces, and then pushed the thought away.

Wayne had done that.

But Sam was not like Wayne. She pushed harder on the thought and it bobbed around in her mind like a cork in a bathtub. She couldn't make it stay down. Sam was not like Wayne, she repeated to herself. Sam told the truth. She hoped.

As if he could read her thoughts, Sam said, 'My aversion to heights is not quite a phobia but I might not be particularly keen to fix the aerial on the roof.'

Somehow, that helped. 'And I'll never be a plumber because of the frogs. You're a good doctor. That's enough.'

'I'm a doctor but not your doctor.' He grinned at her. 'That said, I'm pretty impressed with your recovery mechanism.'

She shrugged. 'I don't get many migraines but when I do get one it's bad.' She didn't add that they usually came after she had the nightmare, or had forced contact with Wayne, and that she'd had fewer nightmares and migraines since she'd shaken him off her trail.

'I can see they wipe you out. If it happens again, you could call me.'

Yeah, right. 'All the way from Brisbane?' She raised her brows at him. At least she knew he was joking. 'Good to know.'

She began laying out the fresh rolls and ham as she reminded herself he'd be gone in a few weeks. Maybe she could just enjoy his company while she had it. It was the first time she'd had a man in her house to share lunch since she'd moved in. Not that she could take any credit for him being here. The only reason it had happened was because he'd invited himself.

It was strange but pleasant. Mostly because she knew it was just a window of opportunity that would close soon when he went back to where he'd come from. Back to his busy trendy life with its 'double shot espresso and milk on the side' lifestyle.

Sam paused as if to say something but didn't. Instead he opened a tray of strawberries and blueberries and produced a tub of Greek yoghurt. 'I'll grab the plates and spoons.' He headed back inside and Ellie looked after him.

'I guess you know where they are,' she murmured more to herself. Then she lifted her voice. 'And grab the butter out of the fridge, please.'

This was all very domestic. Apparently there was nothing like being undressed when semi-delirious for breaking down barriers. But what was she supposed to say? *No. That's my kitchen! Stay out!*

Sam was back while she was still staring after him and mulling over the phenomenon of his intrusion into her world.

He looked so at ease. 'You're very domesticated. Why aren't you married?'

His face stilled. 'My wife died four years ago. It's unlikely I'll marry again.' Then he looked down at the food in his hands.

Oh, heck. 'I'm sorry.' Then added almost to herself, 'Don't you hate that?' The last words fell out as if she hadn't already put her foot in her mouth enough.

He looked up. 'Hate what? When wives die?' He was looking at her quizzically, when really she deserved disapproval. But underneath the lightness of tone was another wall. She could see it as plain as the sun on the ocean below. She knew about walls.

She'd done it again. Talk about lacking tact. She'd said what she thought without thinking. She wasn't usually so socially inept but there was something about this fledgling relationship... She paused at that thought and shied away, slightly horrified.

Anyway... 'I'm making it worse. Of course it's terrible your wife died, but I meant when you ask a question and the worst possible scenario comes back at you and you wished you'd never opened your mouth.'

'I know what you mean. Forget it. A *Monty Python* moment.'

His eyes were shadowed and she hesitated. His wife must have been young. She couldn't help herself.

'How did your wife die?'

He looked up, studied her and then glanced away. 'I'll tell you some time.' Then without looking at her, 'Why do people ask that?'

Now she felt even more inept. Crass. He had answered her and deserved an answer himself. 'I don't know. Curiosity. Because they're afraid of their own mortality?'

That made him look up. 'Are you afraid of your own mortality?'

She shrugged. 'That's a heavy question for eleven in the morning.'

'Heavy question any time of the day,' he said quietly.

The silence lay thick between them. He straightened and looked like he'd wait all day until she answered.

So she did. 'No. I'm not afraid to die. I'm not that special that the world will weep when I'm gone.'

A flash of what looked like pain crossed his face. 'Don't say that. Don't ever say that. Everyone is special and the world will always weep when someone leaves it.'

A breeze tickled her neck from the ocean and she shivered. This conversation was the pits. 'Can we just talk about the weather?'

He stopped. He looked at her and then slowly he smiled, mocking them both. 'Sure. There's a very nice ocean breeze sitting out here.'

She smiled at him primly. Relief rolled over her like one of those swells away down below running in towards the cliffs. A hump. They'd managed to get over a hump. One that she'd caused. 'I like the way the clouds make shadow patterns on the ocean.'

He glanced at the blue expanse a long way below, then away. 'Yes, very nice.'

She looked at the food spread out. Okay. Now it was awkward. 'Eat.'

So they ate. Conversation was minimal and that kept them away from such topics as death and dying, which was fine by Ellie, and gradually their rapport returned and desultory conversation became easy again.

Sam said, 'Josie went home.'

She looked up. 'Did you do the new-born check?'

'Of course.' A pained look. 'Very efficiently.'

That made her smile. 'I have no doubt.' She took a bite of her roll and chewed thoughtfully. She swallowed, then said, 'When you return to your real world in your hospital will you make sure all of your registrars are proficient at checking new-born babies prior to discharge?'

He shrugged. 'There's a little less time for leisurely learning than there is here but I will be asking the question.' He pretended to growl, 'And they'd better be able to answer it.'

Which made her remember that he was a very distinguished and learned man, one many people looked up to, and she was eating rolls with him and treating him like a barely tolerated servant. *Oops.*

She put her roll down. 'Speaking of questions I've been meaning to ask... Do you know anything about midwifery-led birthing units? Do you think it would work here?'

He paused eating his own meal. 'I don't know. Work how?'

She shrugged, looking around for inspiration, how to explain her dream. 'It would be wonderful if we could provide a publicly funded service for pregnant women that didn't need locums.'

'Gee, thanks.' He pretended to be offended.

'Nothing personal. But cover isn't consistent.' She grinned at him. 'I'd like to see a proper centre for planned low-risk births here without having to rely on locum doctors to ensure we can have babies here.' She was gabbling. But she half-expected him to mock her and tell her she was dreaming, that big centres were more financially viable—although she already knew that. But he didn't mock her. She should have had more faith.

'There are models like that springing up all over New South Wales and Victoria.' He said it slowly, as if he was searching around in his mind for what he knew. Ellie could feel herself relax. He wasn't going to tell her she was mad.

He went on. 'Not so many in Queensland yet, but I'm hearing that mothers and midwives are keen. But you'd need more staff.' He gestured to the isolation around them. 'You're a bit of a one-man band here.'

She'd get help. She'd already had two nibbles from the weekend midwives to work here permanently. And why not? A fulfilling job right on the ocean and the chance to become a respected part of a smaller community wasn't to be sniffed at. Trina and Faith were also in.

'We may be a small band at the moment. Or possibly five women, anyway—Trina, Faith, and I and the weekend midwives from the base. If we changed our model of care we could attract more midwives. We would certainly attract more women to birth here if we offered caseload. Most women would love to have the option to have their own midwife throughout the whole pregnancy and birth. Then get followed by them for the next six weeks after the baby is born. It's a wonderful service.'

He studied her for a moment as if weighing up what he was going to say. 'It would be a great service.'

She sagged with relief.

Then he went on, 'Though it does sound demanding for the midwives, seeing as babies come when they want and pregnant women have issues on and off for most of the forty weeks. If one person was responsible for all that—and I imagine you'd have a caseload of about twenty women a year—it seems a huge commitment and would almost certainly affect your private life. Are you prepared for that?'

Private life? What private life. She was a Monday-to-Friday, love-my-job romantic. Not the other sort. But she didn't say any of that.

Instead she said, 'We are. And, paperwork wise, I have a friend who has just set up a service like that on the south coast. She said she'd come up and help me in the early stages. And Myra was a legal secretary before she bought her restaurant. She said she'd give me one day a week.'

'So you have gone into it a bit.' He nodded. Paused. 'And how are you going to deal with emergencies?'

'The same way we deal with them now—stabilise and transfer if needed. But the women will be healthy and the care will be excellent.'

'I have no doubt about that,' he said, and the genuine smile that accompanied the statement warmed her with his faith when he barely knew her.

This wasn't about her as a woman. This was about her as a midwife and she could take compliments about that. 'It's women's choice to decide how and where they want to meet their baby, and women here have been asking for that choice.'

It was so satisfying to have this conversation with somebody who at least understood the questions and the reasons behind them. So she didn't expect the turn when it came.

'Very ideological. So you're going to submerge yourself even deeper in these new families—be available for more times when you're needed—because in my experience babies tend to come in waves. Slow and then all at once. You'll be working sixty hours a week. Be the auntie to hundreds of new babies over the next thirty years.'

What was he getting at?'

Her smile faltered. 'I hope so.'

His brows were up. She didn't like the expression on his face.

'And wake up at sixty and say "Where has my life gone?"?'

'No.' She shook her head vehemently. 'I'll wake up at sixty and feel like I'm having a life that enriches others.'

The mood plunged with her disappointment. She'd thought he'd seen the vision but now he was looking at her like she needed psychiatric help. Like Wayne used to look at her. That was sad and it was stupid of her to have thought he would be different.

Ooh… Ellie could feel the rage build. Somewhere inside she knew it was out of proportion to what he'd said. That if she chose that path it didn't mean she'd never have a family of her own. But him saying that seemed to ignite her anger.

She leaned towards him. 'How is that different from your life? You said yourself you're probably not going to marry again or have children. Will you spend the next thirty years working? How is that different to me?'

He shrugged. 'I'm a man. It's my job to work till I'm sixty-five or seventy, so it should be rewarding.'

'You're a chauvinist. My working life deserves reward too. How about you stay barefoot and pregnant and make my dinner while I go to work? Is that okay?'

Sam had no idea how the conversation had become so heated. One minute it had been warm and friendly—she'd been gradually relaxing with him—and then she'd waxed on about giving the rest of her life to strangers like some first world saint and he'd found himself getting angry.

He needed to remind himself that he was a man who respected women's choices, and of course he respected her choice. She was right. He should recognise that what she wanted to do was parallel to his own ambition of single-minded dedication. And look how useless that had been for getting over Bree's death. Maybe it was because he did recognise himself in what she said that he'd reacted so stupidly to seeing it through her eyes.

He took one look at her face and concluded he needed to redeem himself fast or he'd be out on his ear with his blueberries in his lap.

He held up both hands in surrender. 'I'm sorry. I

have no right to judge your life decisions. You should choose your path and do whatever fulfils you. Truce.'

Her open mouth shut with a click and he knew he'd just averted Armageddon. Wow.

She was a feisty little thing when she didn't like what he said. And, come to think of it, what the heck had come over him? If she wanted to grow old in this eyrie of a house, alone every night just living for her work, then that was her choice. A small voice asked if that wasn't his choice too. He might not live on top of a cliff, but it wasn't so different from his trendy city flat overlooking the Brisbane River that he barely saw and the twenty-four-seven availability he gave his own hospital.

He'd known her for less than a week and already he was sticking his nose in. Normally he didn't even see other people and what they were doing with their lives but the idea of Ellie's future life made him go cold. It sounded very like his and he wanted more for her. He shivered.

She sat stonily staring out over the ocean and he could discern the slow breaths she was taking to calm down. Typical midwife—deep breathing experts. His mouth twitched and he struggled to keep it under control. Imagine if she saw him laughing at her.

They were both being silly. Fighting about the next thirty years when they should be enjoying the present moment. He was here with a gorgeously interesting woman. He wasn't sure when she'd changed from pretty to gorgeous, but the word definitely fit her better. The sun was drying her dark hair, bringing out red highlights, and the ocean stretched away behind her. He liked the way her hair fell heavily on her neck when she didn't have it in the pony tail. He could remember the weighty silkiness of it in his hand as he'd held it off her face as he'd soothed her during her nightmare.

He remembered unbuttoning her shirt when she'd lifted her hand to her buttons as if the neckline and collar were choking her. He'd slipped the whole shirt off her shoulders, and she'd pushed at her buttoned work trousers, so he'd helped her with those too. She'd relaxed back into the cool sheets with relief and he'd covered her up, trying to blot out the delectable picture of her golden skin in lacy bra and briefs. Feeling a little apprehensive about what she'd say to him when she woke.

'You.' She turned towards him and his little flight of fantasy crashed and burned. Apparently the deep breathing hadn't worked.

'Tell me how your wife died!' There was nothing warm and fuzzy about the request.

That snapped him out of his rosy fantasies and the guilt he mostly kept at bay from his failure to save Bree swamped him. He didn't know why he answered her.

'She killed herself.'

CHAPTER SEVEN

'IT LOOKED LIKE a parachute accident. Except she left a note.' He kept staring at his clenched fingers. Didn't look at her. He couldn't believe he'd said that to a stranger and opened himself up to the inevitable questions.

Ellie's voice was a whisper. 'Oh, heck.' Closer than before. 'Why would she do that?'

He figured he might as well get the rest out. Be done with it. 'Because we lost our third baby at twenty weeks' gestation and she said she couldn't go on.' His voice was flat because if he let the emotion in it would demolish him. His inability to help his own family had destroyed Bree. 'I was next to useless, and using work to bury my own grief, and she refused to talk about it together. We drifted apart. Each suffering in our own way but unable to connect. Then it was too late.'

Her voice was different now. Compassionate. 'Is that why you were so determined Marni be transferred?'

He jerked back to the present with the question. Her thought processes were way different to his. He took a deep breath of his own. Was that the only satisfaction he'd had in the last four years?

Sam thought about what she'd asked. It had kept him sane, having a mission. 'Probably. Since Bree died I've been working on a regime for women who have repeat extreme premature labours, and the results have been promising with the new treatments.'

When he looked up from his hands he saw she was beside him. Her voice was soft. 'Your way of managing the grief?'

'Or the guilt.' Why was he talking about this? He never spoke about Bree. Her hand touched his shoulder as she bent over him. It was feather-light but he felt the pressure as if it was burning into him like a hot coal through ice. Melting him.

'What was she like? What did she do? Your dad must have been upset as well.'

'Before the babies Bree was happy. A great paediatrician, wonderful with kids. Afterwards…' he paused and shook his head, speaking so quietly it was as if he'd forgotten she was there. 'She hid her depression using work too. We both did. She said she wanted more space. When she died my dad felt almost as bad as I did that we hadn't seen it coming. So it was tough for him as well.'

She leant her head down and put her face against his hair. 'I'm sorry for your loss.' Her lemony freshness surrounded him like angel dust as she reached down and hugged him.

Nobody had hugged him since Bree had died. His dad was more of handshake kind of guy and he didn't have any women friends. Then she slid her hands around his shoulders, pulled his head onto her chest and stroked his hair. Her hands were warm whispers of comfort, infused with empathy. 'I'm so sorry. But it's not your fault.'

He twisted his head and looked at her, saying very slowly and deliberately, his voice harsh and thick, 'You've got as much right to say that as I had to say you can't waste your life the way you're planning to.'

He thought she'd draw away at that. He hoped she would because the scent was fogging his brain and the emotions of the last few minutes were far too volatile for bodily contact. All those fantasies he'd been battling with since he'd arrived in this damn place were rising like mist off the ocean. She was holding him close. Pulling him in like a siren on a rock. Drowning him.

She pressed her face against his. 'I should never have asked. We're both too nosy.' She kissed his cheek as if she couldn't help herself. 'I'm sorry.'

If he'd thought her enticing while he watched her from a distance, up close she was irresistible. The scent of her, the feel of her, the warmth of her, was intoxicating, and when she leaned in to say something else he lifted his mouth and captured hers as it passed. She stilled—she tasted like the first day of spring.

She'd made it happen. The kiss had been an apology. A dangerous one. Kissing Sam was a mistake because when he kissed her back driving him away was the last thing on her mind.

Somehow she was on his lap, both her arms were around his hard shoulders, and he was holding her mouth against him with a firm palm to the back of her head.

Inhaling his scent, his taste, his maleness was glorious. The kiss seemed to go on and on even though it was only a minute. His mouth was a whole subterranean world of wonder. In heated waves he kissed her and she kissed him back in time to the crash of the ocean below—rising and falling, sometimes peaking in a crest and then drawing Ellie down into a swirling world she was lost in...one she hadn't visited before. Until the phone rang.

It took a few moments for the sound to penetrate and then she felt his hand ease back.

He pulled away but his eyes were dark and hot as he watched her blink. She raised her trembling fingers to her lips.

His voice was deep, too damn sexy, and he smiled at her in a way that made her blush. 'Your phone is ringing.'

She blinked. Scrambled off his lap. 'Right.' She blinked again and then bolted for the phone while all the time her mind was screaming, *what the heck made you start that?*

It was the weekend midwife, Roz. 'Can you come, Ellie? One of the holidaymakers from the caravan park is in labour. Just walked in. Thirty-five weeks. Twins. Feeling pushy. I'll ring the doctor next.'

'Twins! Sam's here. I'll bring him. We'll be there in three minutes. Get help from the hospital to make some calls. Get them to ring the ambulance to come ASAP.'

Ellie strode to the door where Sam was collecting dishes away from the edge from his side of the table. 'Let's go, Sam. Thirty-five-week twins. Second stage.'

Ellie was pulling on her sneakers. She could put a surgical gown over her clothes.

Sam matched Ellie's calm professional face. 'My car's outside.'

They were there in less than two minutes. Just before they arrived, Sam said, 'Ellie?'

She looked at him. She was still off-balance but immensely glad her mind could be on a hundred things other than what position she'd been in and where that could have led only five minutes ago.

This was an emergency. She'd had two sets of twins when she'd been working with a midwife in the centre of Australia. She'd need to watch out for so many things in the coming hour. They had very little equipment for prems. They'd either have a birth of two premature babies here or a harrowing trip to the base hospital. Twin births could be tricky.

'Ellie?'

'What?'

Sam's voice was so calm. 'This is what I do. Thirty-five-week twins are fine. Not like pre-viable twins. Everything will be fine.'

Ellie felt the tension ease to a more useful alertness. He was asking for a little faith in the team. She smiled at him. 'Okay. You're right.'

A dusty campervan with flowers and a slogan painted on it sat haphazardly in the car park. There was no sign of anyone as they hurried through the doors to the maternity unit but sounds coming from the birthing rooms indicated action.

'We'll just use the one neo-natal resuscitation trolley. The other's too slow to heat up and warmth will be the issue.' Ellie was thinking of the babies. The twins could stay together if they needed help. They'd been closer than that inside their mum and might even comfort each other if kept together.

The obstetric part, Sam could handle. Thank goodness. The mother might not feel lucky at the moment but she was.

They entered the room one after the other and the relief on Roz's face would have been comical if the situation hadn't been so serious. 'Her waters just broke. Nine centimetres. At least it's clear and not meconium-stained.'

Then Roz collected herself. Glancing apologetically at the mother and father, she explained, 'Dr Southwell's an obstetrician from Brisbane Mothers and Babies, and this is the midwife in charge here, Ellie. This is Annette and Paul Keen.'

Everyone tried hard to smile at each other. Sam succeeded and Ellie gave them a wave on her way to sort out the required equipment in case they needed to resuscitate either baby or, heaven forbid, both.

Roz was reciting, 'Annette's twins were due in five weeks. They were packing up from the park to go home today. Labour started an hour ago but she thought she had a tummy bug because Paul had one a few days ago.'

Annette opened her mouth to say hello and changed it to a groan as the next wave of contraction hit her. She ground out, 'I feel like pushing.'

Sam stepped closer to the bed. He looked into the terrified woman's face as she sat high in the bed with lines of strain creasing her face and touched her arm. 'I'm Sam. It's okay, Annette, we've got this. You just listen to your body and your babies, let go of the fear and we'll do the rest. It's their birthday.'

Ellie's hands paused on the suction as she heard his voice and in that moment realised what she was missing in her life. A safe harbour. It would never be Sam, but just maybe someone somewhere might be out there for her, someone like this man who could invest so much comfort in words and took the time to offer them. Such a man would be worth coming home to. She wondered if he had always been such a calming influence. Whether he'd grown to understand a parent's fears since his own loss.

'It's my fault,' Paul mumbled from the corner of the room as he twisted his hands. 'I should never have pushed for this holiday before the babies were born. It's my fault.' Ellie glanced his way but it looked like nobody else had heard him.

Roz bent down and placed the little Doppler on Annette's stomach. First one and then, after she shifted to the other side of Annette's magnificent belly, another heartbeat echoed around the room.

Sam nodded, patted Annette's arm, turned, walked to the sink and washed his hands.

Ellie checked the oxygen and air cylinders were full and then moved to Paul's side. She spoke very quietly so no one else could hear. 'You heard the doctor, Paul. The time for worrying is gone. Now is the time to be the rock Annette needs you to be. Hold her hand. Share the moment. You're about to be a father.'

Paul's eyes locked on hers and he nodded jerkily. 'Right. Rock.' He looked at his hand and scurried over to his wife. He took up her fingers and kissed them. 'Sorry. Lost it for a minute.'

Annette squeezed his hand and Ellie saw the man's fingers go white. Saw Paul wince as the pressure increased and with a smile her eyes were drawn to Sam as he stood quietly at the side of the bed with his gloved fingers intertwined, waiting. As if they had all the time in the world and this was a normal day. She felt the calm settle in the room and smiled quietly to herself.

Roz folded back the sheets to above Annette's thighs.

The first twin came quickly, a fine scattering of hair on her head, a thick coating of white vernix covering her back, and then she slipped into Sam's waiting hands. Not as small as they'd feared, probably over two thousand, five hundred grams, which was good for a twin.

The little girl feebly protested at the brush of air on her skin until Ellie wiped her quickly with a towel and settled her against her mother with a warmed bunny rug over her back. Annette's hands came down to greet her as she shifted the sticky little body so she could see her. The mother's face was round with wonder.

'Oh, my. Hello, little Rosebud.'

Ellie smiled to herself at the name, actually appropriate for the pink pursed mouth, and positioned the tiny girl strategically to make room for the next baby, making sure her chin was angled to breathe easily.

Ellie slipped a pink knitted beanie on the downy head. The soft cap was too big but would do the job of keeping her little head warm and slow the loss of heat.

When she glanced at Paul, tears were sliding down his cheeks as he gazed in awe at his wife and new daughter.

Annette's brows drew together but this time she was confident. 'I need to push again.'

Paul started, and Ellie grabbed another towel and blanket from the stack Roz had collected under the warmer. They all waited.

'This one's breech,' Sam said quietly.

The contraction passed and they all waited for the next.

Annette breathed out heavily and Ellie looked down and saw the little bottom and scrotum inching out, the cord falling down as the belly and back eased up in a long sweep. First one leg sprang free and then, finally, the other leg. It was happening so fast. The contraction finished and they all waited.

'Going beautifully,' Sam murmured two minutes later as the pale shoulders rotated and birthed one by one, followed by the arms, in a slow dance of angles and rotations that magically happened the way nature intended thanks to the curves of his mother's pelvis.

Ellie stood awed at how quickly the baby was delivering by himself.

Sam hadn't touched the torso. His gloved fingers hovered just above in case baby took a wrong turn as it went through the normal mechanisms and she remembered the mantra 'hands off the breech'. He was certainly doing that.

Then, unexpectedly, the rapid progress stopped. Annette pushed again. Just the head to come, Ellie thought. *Come on.* Annette was still pushing.

'Deflexed head,' Sam muttered and glanced at Ellie. He slipped his arm under the baby's body to support it and gently felt for the face with his lower hand. With the hand she could see he placed his second and fourth fingers on each side of the baby's nape at the back.

'Annette. We need to flex the baby's head for birth. I'm going to get Ellie to push on your tummy just above the pelvic bone.'

Annette hissed an assent as she concentrated.

Sam went on. 'Ellie, palpate just above the pelvic brim. You'll feel the head. Lean on that ball firmly while I tip baby's chin down from here.' He glanced at Annette. 'Don't be surprised if baby needs to go to the resus trolley for a bit to wake up, okay?'

Paul's eyes widened. Annette nodded as she concentrated. Ellie could feel the solid trust in the room and marvelled how Sam had achieved that in so short a time. It was worth its weight in gold when full co-operation was needed.

Sam's firm voice. 'Okay, push, Annette. Lean, Ellie.'

Ellie did as she was asked and suddenly the head released. Baby's chin must have shifted towards his chest, allowing the smaller diameters of the head under the pubic arch and through the pelvis, and in a steady progression the whole head was born. Sam expelled a breath and Ellie began to breathe again too.

The little boy was limp in Sam's hands.

Paul swayed and Roz pushed the chair under him. 'Sit.' The dad collapsed back into the chair with his hand over his mouth.

Sam quickly clamped and cut the cord and Ellie

reached in, wiped the new-born with the warm towel and bundled him up to transfer to the resuscitation trolley. 'Come over when you're up to it, Paul,' she said over her shoulder as she went.

Sam spoke to Roz. 'Can you take over here, Roz? Call out if you need me.' He followed Ellie.

Ellie hit the timer on to measure how long since birth, and dried the new-born with another warm towel to stimulate him, but he remained limp.

Sam positioned the baby's head in a sniffing position and applied the tiny mask over his chin and nose. The little chest rose and fell with Sam's inflation of the lungs through the mask.

Ellie listened to the baby's chest. 'Heart rate eighty.' She applied the little pulse oximeter to the baby's wrist which would allow them to see how much oxygen from their lung inflations was circulating in the baby's body.

'Thirty seconds since birth,' Ellie said, and leant down to listen to his heart rate again, even though the oximeter had picked it up now. 'Seventy.' If the rate fell below sixty they would have to do cardiac massage.

'Okay,' Sam said and continued watching the steady rise and fall of the small chest. They both knew it wasn't great but it also wasn't dire yet. Babies were designed to breathe. Unlike adults, new-born babies needed inflation of their lungs to start, were respiratory driven, and even more important than cardiac massage was the initiation of breathing and the expulsion of the fluid from the untried lungs.

Ellie reminded herself she had great faith in the way

babies had recovered from much more dramatic births than this one.

Sam continued with his inflations for another thirty seconds, Ellie wrote down the observations and finally the baby wriggled a tiny bit. Ellie felt the tension ease. 'Come on, junior.'

'His name is Thorn.' Paul was there and he wasn't swaying. He seemed to have pulled himself together. 'Come on, Thorn,' he said sternly, staring down at his son. 'This is your dad speaking. Wake up.'

Ellie decided it was just coincidence but Thorn's blue eyes opened at the command. The baby blinked and struggled and began to cry. The pulse oximeter rate flew from eighty to a hundred and thirty in the blink of an eye and Sam eased back on the mask.

'Well, that worked,' she said and smiled at Paul. A sudden exuberance was bubbling inside her and she looked across at Sam, who grinned back at her. She guessed he was feeling it too.

'Good work, Thorn,' Roz's relieved voice called across and Ellie heard Annette's shaky relief as she laughed.

Thorn was roaring now and, after a glance at Sam and catching his nod, Ellie scooped the baby up and carried him back to his mother. He was soon nestled in beside his sister on his mother's chest.

There was a knock on the door and one of the young ambulance officers poked her head in. 'Did you guys call us?'

Sam said, 'Thanks for coming. Transfer to the base hospital, thirty-five-week twins, but we'd like to wait half an hour—check the bleeding is settled and babies stable—if you want to come back.'

'We'll have coffee. Haven't had lunch. Ring us when you're ready.' She looked to the bed. 'Congratulations.' Then she disappeared.

Ellie decided that was eminently sensible. The impact of an urgent emergency transfer of all concerned would have ruined the moment when everyone was settled. More brownie points for Sam.

She wouldn't have taken the responsibility for delaying transfer but having an obstetrician on site made all the difference. It was fabulous for Annette and Paul to have a chance to collect themselves before they had to leave.

Roz was standing beside Annette, helping her sort the babies, and Sam and Ellie went over to the sink to strip off their gloves and apply new ones.

'Rosebud and Thorn,' Sam said in an undertone, and his eyes were alight with humour.

The names clicked. 'Cute,' she whispered back, grinning, and realised this was a moment she wasn't used to—savouring the feeling of camaraderie and a sudden urge to throw her arms around Sam and dance a little.

She whispered, 'That was very exciting and dramatic. Thank goodness everything is great.'

'Ditto.' Sam grinned at her.

Normally the nurse from the hospital disappeared as soon as the birth was safely complete, and most of the locums were burnt out and uninterested, so as soon as the excitement was over Ellie didn't usually have a third person to talk over the birth with. 'I'll remember that hint with the after-coming head if I have another un-expected breech delivery,' she said now, thinking back over Thorn's birth. The two breeches she'd been present at before had progressed to birth easily.

Sam nodded sagely. 'He was star-gazing. Silly boy. You have to keep your chin tucked in if you want your head to pop out.'

Ellie bit her lip to stop the laugh. Stargazing... A funny way to say it, but clear as a bell to her. She smiled up at him as the last of the tension inside her released.

She stayed with Roz in birthing until the ambulance officers returned. Thorn and Rosebud were positioned twin style at each breast and did an excellent job with their first breastfeeding lesson in life. Besotted parents marvelled, wept and kept thanking the three staff, so much so that Sam escaped from the room to write up the transfer papers.

Just under an hour after the twins were born, Ellie and Sam stood watching as they were loaded into the back of the ambulance.

'Come back and visit us next year when you come on your holiday. We'd love to see you all.' Ellie said.

She'd offered to go in the ambulance but Roz had laughed and said she should take the easy job and stay with the empty ward. Hopefully nobody would come in. Surely they'd had their quota for the week?

Which left Ellie and Sam standing at the door, waving off the ambulance.

As the vehicle turned out of the driveway Ellie told herself to keep her mind on what needed to be done but she could feel Sam's gaze. She kept her own on the spot where the ambulance disappeared and then suddenly turned away. Over her shoulder she said, 'Thank you. You were great. I'll be fine now.'

Sam didn't move. 'So I should go?' His voice was quiet, neutral, so she had to stop or it would have been rude. But her feet itched to scoot away as fast as she could because this man was the one she had kissed. On whose lap she had squirmed and wanted more. *Oh, my*—where was she supposed to look?

She didn't decide on flight quickly enough.

Still quietly, he said, 'You don't need me any more— that right? And we both pretend this morning didn't happen? Is that what you want, Ellie?' She didn't say anything so he added, 'Just checking.' There was definite sardonic tinge to that last statement.

She forced herself to look at him. Maybe she could tell him the truth about Wayne. Because she wasn't going to pursue any crumbs of attention he wanted to give her for the next three weeks and it was all her fault this morning had got out of hand. Maybe she owed him that—telling him how she'd been made a fool of. Lied to. Ridiculed. Abused. She shuddered at the thought. Or perhaps she owed him an apology. She could do that at least.

'I'm sorry, Sam. I don't know what happened. It's all my fault, and I apologise. Can't we just blame the aftermath of my migraine for the strange behaviour on my part and forget it?'

He was studying her thoughtfully, and for so long that Ellie felt like an insect under a magnifying glass.

Finally he said, 'What if I don't want to forget it? What if I want to hear the rest of your stories?'

Why would he want to do that? She couldn't do that. Should never have started it. 'You'll have to do without. Because there'll be no repeat.' She heard the finality in her voice and hoped he did too. 'I'd like you to go now, please.'

Sam looked at the woman in front of him and felt the frustration of the impenetrable wall between them yet again. The really disturbing thing was an inexplicable certainty that Ellie Swift wasn't supposed to be like this. It made no sense. He could very clearly see that underneath the prickly exterior and gazetted loner lay a warm and passionate woman he wanted to know more about. Wanted to lose himself in kissing again. And more.

That she'd had a disastrous relationship was of course the most likely reason she was like this. Underneath her armour lay something or someone who had scarred her and she wasn't risking that kind of pain again. He got that. Boy, did he get that. But it wasn't all about the frog phobia. There had to be something else.

But whether or not he'd get the opportunity to explore that conundrum and the tantalising glimpses of the woman who had reached down and kissed him with such sweetness was a very moot point.

Maybe he should just cut and run. Do what he always did when he felt things were getting too personal or emotional. But, for the first time since Bree had died, he wanted to explore the way he was feeling. Wanted to find out if this glimpse he'd had of a better life was real, or if he was just suffering from some unexpected aberration he'd forget about when he went back to the real world.

Maybe he'd better research his own reasons for pursuing Ellie first before he caused any more damage to this vulnerable woman in front of him, and it was only that overriding consideration which finally made him agree to leave. Since Bree's death he'd lost his confidence in his own emotional stability.

CHAPTER EIGHT

ELLIE WATCHED HIM go and, after having asked him to leave, now, conversely, wanted him to stay. It was the kiss that stopped her asking him to come back. Ellie had never tried to hurt anyone in her life before—so why had she hurt Sam by asking him so baldly about his wife? He was already punishing himself and didn't need her input. He'd been mortally wounded by his love—she knew how that felt—and she'd broken open his unhealed wound with her harsh request. He'd deserved none of it.

So she'd kissed him better—and to make herself feel better. Although 'better' wasn't really the right word for what she'd felt.

Ellie had an epiphany. She'd wanted to hurt him because that way she'd drive him away for her own safety—she'd had no kind thought for him.

And then they'd kissed and everything had changed. And she was running scared. It had all been pushed back by the birth of the twins but the reality was—things had changed.

Ellie sighed. It would have been good to talk more

about the birth. He could have stayed for that. And that was the only reason, she told herself.

She looked around the empty ward, disorientated for a moment. Then she busied herself pushing books across the desk.

It was Sunday tomorrow and she probably needed the space from this man. He was taking up too much room in her head. Luckily she had a whole day to get her head sorted by Monday.

She slowly turned towards the birthing unit and walked in to strip the bed. What a morning. Premature twins. That was a first for her since she'd arrived last year. Thank goodness everything had progressed smoothly.

She thought about Sam's expertise with Thorn's birth in the breech position. Sam's calmness. She wanted to cry, which was stupid. It was Sam's quiet confidence that had made them all seamless in their care and his rock-solid capability that made it so positive and not fraught as it could have been for Paul and Annette with a less experienced practitioner. How lucky they'd been that it had been Sam. She dragged her mind away from where it wanted to go.

She had to stay away from Sam's hands holding her, his lips on hers, their breaths mingled. No. If she let Sam in and he let her down like Wayne had, she suspected she'd never, ever recover.

She took herself into the small staff change room and opened her locker where she kept a spare clean uniform. She'd been stuck here before out of uniform and didn't like it.

She told herself that was the reason she needed more armour. She took off her loose trousers and blouse and pulled on the fitted blue work trousers and her white-collared shirt and buttoned it to the top. Funny how she felt protected by the uniform. Professional and capable. Not an emotional idiot throwing out accusations and making stupid moves on men who were just being kind.

What an emotional roller coaster the last few days had been. And action packed on the ward.

By rights they should have no babies for a week or more because the ward had been too crazy since Sam had arrived. Maybe he drew the excitement to him like a magnet. She grimaced. He certainly did that in more ways than one and she needed to put that demon to sleep.

By the time Roz returned Ellie had the ward returned to its pristine orderliness, and the paper work sorted and filed. Ellie stood up to leave but Roz put her hand on her arm.

Looking a little worse for wear, Roz said, 'Please stay for a bit. Have a cup of tea with me. I'm bursting to talk about it. Not often you get to see twins born without any intervention. Wasn't Dr Sam awesome?' Roz's eyes were shining and she was obviously still on a high from the birth.

Ellie didn't have the heart to leave. She put the plastic bag with her bundled civilian clothes down.

'Sure. Of course. The jug's just boiled. I'll make a pot while you freshen up if you want?'

Roz nodded and Ellie had to smile at the bouncy excitement that exuded from her.

Roz was right. This was an opportunity to think about how they'd handled the situation, what they'd done well and what they could possibly have done better. All future planning for a unit she wanted to see become one of the best of its kind.

She couldn't believe Sam had driven all her normal thought processes into such confusion. *See?* She needed to stay on track and not be diverted by good-looking doctors who had the capacity to derail all her plans.

As Ellie made a pot of tea and brought two cups to the desk she knew with a pang of discomfort that a week ago Roz wouldn't have been able to drag her away from talking about the birth and the outcomes. Maybe it was just that she'd been sick. Maybe it had nothing to do with the fact that she was running scared because a certain man had disturbed her force field and anything to do with talking about him made her want to run a mile.

'I can't get over the breech birth.' Roz was back. Her hair was brushed, lipstick reapplied and she looked as animated as Ellie had ever seen her. She could feel the energy and excitement and welcomed the uncomplicated joy Roz exuded, because joy was dearly bought.

Yes. They should be celebrating. Every midwife loved the unexpected birth that progressed fast and complication-free with a great outcome. And when it was twins it was twice as exciting.

'I just feel so lucky I was here.' Roz's eyes were glowing and Ellie felt the tension slipping away. She was glad Roz asked her to stay.

Roz went on. 'But I was super-glad when you two

walked in together. Especially since, the last time I saw you, you looked like death warmed up.'

Roz stopped and thought about that. 'Did you say on the phone you were together when I called?'

Ellie fought to keep the colour out of her cheeks. 'Dr Southwell had dropped in to ask if I needed anything. But I'm usually good when the migraine goes. It just takes about twelve hours. I'm feeling normal now.' Or as normal as she could, considering the emotional upheavals of the last few days.

Roz studied her. 'You're still a bit pale. And I shouldn't be keeping you here on your day off. Sorry.'

'No. It's good to talk about it. You're right. You did really well getting us here, and everything was ready. You must have got a shock when they walked in and you realised you were actually going to have the babies.'

Roz nodded enthusiastically, totally diverted from the how Ellie and Sam had walked in together. Thank goodness. Ellie returned her attention to Roz, cross with herself, as her brain kept wandering off topic.

'Paul was almost incoherent, Annette was still in the car and I didn't get that it was twins until she was in here and I saw how big she was. Then he said they were premature and she was booked in to have them at the tertiary hospital and I nearly had a heart attack. All I could think about was ringing you, and I was hoping like heck you'd be able to come.'

'I'm fine. But I guess we need to plan that a bit better for the future too. Maybe make a list to work down if one of the call-ins can't make it, rather than ringing around at the time when you have much better things to do than make phone calls.'

Roz nodded agreement. She said thoughtfully, 'I did get the nurse over from the main hospital, and she could have phoned around if needed.'

How it should be. 'That's great. And the babies came out well, which is always a relief.'

Roz frowned as she remembered. 'The boy was a bit stunned. Annette and Paul weren't the only ones worried.'

Ellie thought about Thorn as he'd lain unmoving under their hands, of Sam's presence beside her as they'd worked in unison, both wordlessly supporting the other as they'd efficiently managed the resuscitation. Her stomach clenched as she remembered. At the time it had been all action with no time to be emotionally involved. It was afterwards they thanked their lucky stars everything had worked out well.

That was why debriefing became important, because clearing stark pictures by talking about them and explaining the reasons let her release mental stresses.

Ellie said, 'He wasn't responding for a bit. We gave him an Apgar of three at one minute but by five minutes he was an eight out of ten. I've only been at a few breech births and they often do seem to take a little longer than cephalic births to get going.'

Roz nodded as she thought about it. 'I guess it could be that the cord is out and it has to be compressed against the body coming through. Or the rapid descent of the head afterwards might stun them too. But he came good by two minutes.'

The door opened and they both looked up. Sam was back. Ellie felt her heart give a little leap but it was followed by a frown as all her indecision and tangled emotions flooded back with full force. Damn. She'd been engrossed in this discussion and should have made her escape.

Her face must have shown her displeasure because he raised his brows. 'Sorry for interrupting.'

'No. Come in. Welcome!' Roz jumped up. 'Have a cup of tea with us. It's great you're here.' She turned to Ellie. 'Isn't it, Ellie? We were just talking about the birth.'

Sam looked at her. 'I'll come back.' Then he turned to Roz. 'I thought Ellie had gone and I wondered if you had any questions, Roz. It was a big morning.'

Ellie heard his words and felt ashamed. She reached down inside and retrieved the normal Ellie from the layers of confusion. Found her equilibrium. There she was—the one who'd greeted him, had it been only six days ago?

She smiled almost naturally. 'Please stay. I was going but you're both right. It's really good to talk over things while they are fresh in our minds. We were talking about breech babies that take a while to respond after birth.'

The conversation that followed was all Ellie hoped it would be. Sam shared his fierce intellect and grasp of the intricacies of breech birth from a consultant's perspective—they even covered a spirited discussion on the pros and cons of breech birth for first-time mums—

and by the time she was ready to leave Ellie was comfortable again in Sam's company.

Or perhaps it would be fairer to say in Dr Southwell's company, because she was every inch the woman behind the uniform in charge of the ward and her feet were very firmly planted in the real world of the hospital that she loved.

'I'll leave you two to talk more. I'm going home.'

Sam stood up. 'I'll come with you. I need to grab the milk I left in your fridge.'

They both stood and as Ellie walked to the door with him she heard Roz murmur after them, 'Better than checking out her collection of stamps.' Ellie winced and pretended she didn't hear.

'The breech was great,' Ellie said to change the subject. They went out into the sunlight and Ellie was thankfully aware of the cool ocean breeze brushing her face—helping calm the blush that heated her cheeks.

'So, was it easy to find the hard baby's head through the abdomen when you leant down on it?' Sam asked her with a smile on his face. They had shared something special.

Ellie thought back to the moment when little Thorn's birth progress had stalled. The sudden increase in tension in the room. The mother pushing and nothing happening. The clock ticking. The baby's body turning pale. Then the calm voice of Sam instructing her to help with downward pressure just above the mother's pubic bone.

'Yes. A solid little ball that just pushed away, and then he was born.' She pictured the baby's position in her mind. 'So his chin must have lifted and changed the diameters of the presenting part which made him jam up. It certainly made a difference to re-tuck his chin in, and then he was born. All great learning experiences that make sense when you think about it.'

'Something simple like that can change the outcome so dramatically. The days of pulling down on a breech baby, which of course made the chin obstruct further, thankfully have gone.'

'I've seen two other normal breech births, the rest have been caesareans, so it was a great learning experience for me.'

'You have good instincts. Listen to them and you'll be fine.'

It was a nice thing to say, but she didn't know what to do with the compliment because it was midwifery-orientated but also personal. So she changed the subject. The crashing of the waves from beyond the headland seemed louder than normal. Instead of turning up the hill to her house Ellie turned her head towards the ocean. 'The sea's rough today! I'm up for a walk out to the lighthouse before I go home. If you'd like to have a look, you could come. I need to lose some excess energy.'

'So, excitement makes you energetic?'

She shrugged. 'I'm energetic most of the time.' Except when she had nightmares, but she was well over that now. Luckily they didn't leave her listless for long. 'So what have you been doing on your time off? Have you looked around the bay? Met anybody interesting?'

Sam nodded mock-solemnly. 'My friend with the

ingrown toenail is my new best bud. He dropped off a dozen prawns yesterday at lunchtime and offered me a trip on his trawler but I said I needed to be on call.'

She'd never been interested in offshore fishing but she was happy to hop on board a small tin dinghy and putt-putt around the creek.

'Would you like to go out on a prawn trawler?'

'It'd be interesting. Different way of spending your life than in a hospital seven days a week.'

She threw a look at him. 'Seven days a week is not healthy.'

He raised his brows. His long stride shortened to match her shorter one. 'I thought we'd agreed to disagree on how the other person spends their life.'

Oops. 'That's true. Let's talk about lighthouses. Lighthouse keepers worked seven days a week and only had one holiday a year.'

There was a pause while he digested that. 'Lighthouses. Yes. Let's talk about lighthouses.' The smile he gave her was so sweet she had a sudden vision of Sam as a very young boy with the innate kindness she could see in him now. She couldn't say why, but she knew without a doubt he would never tease a heartbroken little girl who missed her mummy. He would more likely scold anyone who did. She really liked that little boy.

She blinked away the silly fantasy and brought herself back to the hillside path they were on now. The grassy path wound along the edge of the cliff edge, a pristine white fence separated them from the drop and tufts of grass hid the crumbly edge. It was maintained by the present custodian of the lighthouse who lived off site. Glancing at Sam she manoeuvred herself to the side of the path nearest the cliff.

'The lighthouse was built in the eighteen hundreds and is part of a network that was built right along the eastern seaboard after ships were floundering on the underwater rocks.'

He was smiling at something then paused, turned and looked at her.

'Are you listening to me being your guide?'

He grinned. 'Sorry. I was thinking I could see you as a lighthouse keeper.'

She thought about that. Yes, she could have been a lighthouse keeper. 'Except the position was only open to men—though they did prefer married men with families.'

He smiled at that. 'I imagine they would have big families if stuck in a lighthouse together.'

She grinned at him. 'The first couple who lived here had eleven children. He'd been a widower and he fell in love with a local girl—said the bay and the woman he found here healed him. They ended up with a big family. All natural births and all survived.'

'What an amazing woman. And did they live here happily-ever-after?'

'They moved to a lighthouse with bigger family quarters. Once in the lighthouse business, you tended to stay in the lighthouse business.'

'She should have been a midwife.' He laughed at that. 'The children would have had a wonderful childhood.'

'Some families were very isolated but at least here,

at the bay, the children went to school and played with other children.'

They arrived at the top of the hill. The base of the lighthouse and the tall tower were painted pristine white with concrete walls that were a third of a metre thick, which gave a hint at how solid the lighthouse was. They both looked up to the wrought-iron rail away at the top where the windows and the light were.

'They have a tour tomorrow. You can go up the stairs inside and come out onto the walkway. It's a great view.'

Sam patted the solid walls. 'Is this how thick the walls of your cottage are?'

'Yep. It wasn't usual for lighthouses to be built of concrete but there's a couple on the north coast like that. I think the sisters liked it and that's why they copied it.'

Sam watched her glance across the bay in the direction of the three cliff-top dwellings.

She went on. 'I love knowing my cottage is strong. I know the big bad wolf can't blow my house down.'

He'd suspected that was a reason she was holed away here in her house with thick walls. 'Do you want to tell me about your big bad wolf?'

'Nope.' She glanced his way but her eyes skidded past his without meeting them. 'Why spoil the afternoon?'

She pushed past the lighthouse into the little forecourt that looked over the ocean. The thick walls bounded the scrubby cliff face and they could see right out to where the blue ocean met the horizon. An oil tanker was away in the distance and closer to the shore two small sailboats were ballooning across the waves. The wind blew her hair across her face and he wanted to lean in and move it, maybe trace her cheek.

'I'm glad you're enjoying present company.'

She stared out over the ocean. He could feel the wall between them again. She was very good at erecting it. An absolute expert. Darn it.

She said, 'I enjoy the company of most people.'

That showed him. 'I won't get over myself, then.' He smiled down at his hands as he stroked the round concrete cap on top of the wall. She was good for his ego. He wouldn't have one at all by the time he left here.

The stone was warm from the sun, like Ellie had been warm. Sam remembered big hands cupping her firmly, stroking. Enjoying the feel of her under his fingers too.

He could feel his body stir. She had him on the ropes just by being there. He tried to distract himself with the structure of the building. 'It's been designed well.'

'What?' She looked startled for a minute and he guessed it was too much to hope that she'd been thinking the same thing he'd been thinking. She worried at her lip and he wanted to reach out and tell her not to. He felt his fingers itch to touch that soft skin of her mouth. Gentle it. But he didn't. He kept his hands where they were because of the damn wall. Not the wall under his hands. He patted that one. He guessed he had a few walls himself.

'Yes.' She turned away from him, sent him a distracted smile still without meeting his eyes. 'I've had enough. It's getting cool. Think I'll go home and catch up on my Saturday chores. Maybe even light a fire for tonight.'

Those were his marching orders. Get your milk and go. And he was learning that, when she said enough, it meant enough. He'd love to know what the guy in her past had done to her. And maybe take him out into a dark alley and make him regret it.

Sam didn't see Ellie at all on Sunday. He thought about going up and asking for his dad's surfboard as an excuse but that was lame.

Monday and Tuesday there were no inpatients in Maternity and no births, so apart from a sociable few minutes he didn't see Ellie, who was busy with antenatal women. He was called in to a birth Trina had overnight but the woman went home as soon as the four hours were up.

By Friday he was going stir crazy. Maybe it was the wind. There were storm warnings and the ocean had been too rough to swim in this morning. He thought of her up there, with the wind howling, all by herself. Tomorrow he wouldn't even have the excuse of work to see her.

At the end of Friday's work day, late that afternoon before he left as they stood outside in the warm sunshine, he searched his brain for ideas to meet up with Ellie. She had her bag and he was jingling his keys in his pocket even though he hadn't brought his car.

He needed inspiration for an invite. 'That cyclone far north is staying nearer the coast than they thought it would.'

'So it'll be a windy night up in my cottage.' She looked higher towards her house. Clouds were building. 'I love nights when the wind creaks against the windows and you can hear the ocean smashing against the rocks below.'

'It could turn nasty.'

She looked at him as if he were crazy. Maybe he should have suggested picking up the board. He tried again. Time was running out. 'This one might be more wind than you bargain for.'

She shrugged and began walking out to the road. The intersection loomed where she'd head up to her house and he'd head down to his guesthouse. It had been a forlorn hope she'd invite him up.

Obviously that wasn't on Ellie's mind. 'The warnings come all the time. Cyclones usually veer away at the last minute. Either way, I'll be fine.'

Sam wasn't sure what had gone wrong. He'd thought they were getting along well, not too many pitfalls, but it seemed there always were pitfalls with Ellie Swift. And he kept falling into them. But there was nothing he could do except wave her goodbye. There was something about the set of her chin that warned him this wasn't a good time to ask what she was doing tomorrow. He doubted he'd be lucky enough for another set of twins to call her out.

CHAPTER NINE

OVER THE NEXT few hours the wind blew more forcefully, the trees bent and swayed under it, and branches and twigs were flying down the street in front of the hospital. Sam dropped in to see if there were any medical needs but the wards remained quiet. Maternity sat empty. Empty without Ellie.

As he battled his way back to his guesthouse he glared up towards Ellie's house. Trina had gone away for the weekend and Myra had left as well. Again. Ellie was up there completely alone.

He kept telling himself to stop it. She'd managed perfectly well without him worrying about her before. Her house was built to withstand anything the cliff tops could throw at it, and most likely she'd be offended if he asked if she wanted company. He wasn't silly enough to think she'd want to move anywhere else to take refuge.

He kept checking to see when the cyclone would veer out to the ocean and take the wind with it, but it hadn't died down at all. If anything it blew even stronger.

He drove down to the boat shed to chat to his friend, the prawn-trawler captain, and the seafarer shook his head sagely and said they were in for a 'right good blow'.

On the way back to the guesthouse, the weather warning over the radio finally clinched it.

'Cyclone Athena will hit land just north of Lighthouse Bay in less than an hour.'

That did it.

He turned the car around, drove slowly up the cliff road to Ellie's house and parked outside. He sat for a minute and looked at the other two houses, dark and deserted. He stared at Ellie's. The light behind Ellie's blinds bled into the late-afternoon gloom and the little flowering shrubs outside her door were bending in the wind.

When he opened his car door it was a struggle to climb out. The wind pushed hard and he manhandled his door open and almost lost his grip when the wind slammed into him in a gust that would have broken his arm if he'd been caught between the car and the door.

Now that would be embarrassing—coming up to help and having to be saved by Ellie. The wind pushed him towards Ellie's door like a big hand in the small of his back and he realised that it really was too dangerous to be outside in this.

Ellie only heard the knock at the door because it fell just as there was a pause in the commercial break.

Funny how she knew who it was. When she opened the door, Sam would have loomed over her in his big coat if he wasn't down one decent-sized step from her. As it was their noses were level. 'Didn't you see the weather warning?'

Nice greeting. She had no idea how but she had the

feeling he'd been stewing over something. 'No. I'm watching a movie. It's very peaceful inside!'

'The cyclone is heading this way. You can't sleep up here tonight.'

Was he for real? As he finished speaking, a sudden gust buffeted the little house and the windows creaked.

Ellie glared at Sam and narrowed her eyes. Just then a squall of rain swept sideways into Sam's back and Ellie instinctively stepped aside. 'Quickly. You'll get drenched. Come in.'

Sam bent down to take off his shoes and she dragged his arm impatiently. 'Do that in here.' As soon as he was across the threshold, she closed the door on the splattering raindrops that were making their way around his large body and onto the floor.

Sam stood on one leg and pulled his loafers off. She caught the smell of damp leather, the expensive suede mottled in places, with grass stuck to the edges from where she'd furiously cut the lawn even shorter as she'd tried to exorcise her demons earlier this afternoon.

'You've probably wrecked your shoes coming up here in them.'

His face was strangely impassive. 'Normal people don't live on cliff tops.'

What was his problem? 'Normal people leave other people alone when they've been asked to.' They were both speaking in the polite tones of people with patience tried by another's stupidity.

At that moment a fist of wind slammed solidly against the glass double doors facing the sea. The panes rattled. Then the wind sucked back fiercely before it slammed into the window again.

Ellie stopped and stared. The windows creaked and Sam placed his second loafer onto the little tray of seashells Ellie used for lining up inside shoes off the floor and he wiped the water droplets from his hair with a handkerchief.

'That's strong,' she said lamely in a normal voice.

'Really?' She could hear the exasperation in his voice. 'I couldn't leave you up here by yourself.' Sam was still speaking quietly.

'I wasn't by myself.' She indicated Myra's cat. Millicent appeared absorbed in the television and the antics of a well-dressed woman feeding cat food to a white Persian feline.

'Perfect reasoning,' he said mildly. It was infuriating he had regained equilibrium faster than she had. She'd just have to try harder.

'Would you like a cup of tea?' Politeness was good. The wind slammed against the windows again. No doubt it was slamming against her solid thick walls as well but nobody could tell that. 'My croft won't blow down, you know.'

Sam looked at the walls thoughtfully. 'I can imagine that you are correct. But it has weaknesses.' His voice lowered to an almost undistinguishable mumble. 'And obviously so do I.'

She heard him sigh as he straightened. 'I just want to make sure you...' He glanced at Millicent and corrected himself. 'You're both okay.'

He pointed to the windows. 'I seem to remember

there are shutters that close from the outside—is that right?'

Ellie had forgotten the shutters. Too late. Next time. She didn't fancy the idea of going out in that maelstrom to shut them. 'Yes, but it might be too windy to shut them now.'

Sam looked at her as if she'd grown two heads. What was his problem? 'A woman's logic.'

'Excuse me?'

As if to a child, he said, 'The shutters are there to use during extreme wind.' He spoke as if she was slow to understand. She was getting sick of his 'silly little Ellie' attitude. 'So the glass doesn't blow in?'

'The glass won't blow in.' She said it confidently. At least, the words came out confidently. Ellie had a sudden vision of glass flying all over the room. Of Millicent splattered with dangerous fragments and the wind and rain belting into the little room. Her calmness wavered. Millicent had to be safe. 'You're sure it's going to be that strong?'

Just then Ellie's feline friend disappeared and the serious voice of the weather forecaster broke into the room.

'This is an SES announcement. Severe wind warning for the north coast of New South Wales has been posted. The tail of Cyclone Athena, which had previously been expected to head out to sea, has swung back into the coast with two-hundred-kilometre winds expected right along the eastern seaboard. Residents are recommended to stay in their homes and cancel all unnecessary travel on the roads until further notice.

Flash flooding and wind damage is expected. The State Emergency Service can be reached on this number...'

A six-digit number flashed onto the screen just before the power went out.

The windows rattled menacingly in the sudden silence. Ellie stared at Sam.

He said quietly, 'Now can we close the shutters?'

'Might be a good idea.' The wind slammed again.

Sam was staring at the rain spotting the windows. 'Maybe it is too late for that. I think coming down to the hospital and staying there might be a better idea.'

As if. 'I'm not dragging Millicent through this wind. We'll be fine. But you're right. You should go before the wind gets stronger and you can't make it down the hill.'

He rolled his eyes. 'I'll do the shutters.'

No way! 'I'll do the shutters, because this is my house and I know how they fasten. And you're afraid of heights.'

He sighed, this time with exasperation. 'I'm wary of heights and more afraid that you'll blow off the cliff.'

Her eyes flew to his and the certainty in his face made her stop. He really was worried about her, to the extent he was willing to do something he normally wouldn't consider. Wayne would never have done that. The little voice inside her whispered, *Sam isn't like Wayne.* From the set chin to the determined gaze, he wasn't going to be swayed.

He lowered his voice. 'You need to stay here with Millicent.' He smiled down at the black cat who had crept across and was rubbing against Ellie's leg. He spoke to the animal. 'Can you mind Aunty Ellie while I go out and close the shutters against the wind, please?'

Millicent miaowed and Sam laughed. 'The cat wins.'

Ellie looked around. It was dark without the television.

'Fine. I'll light the lamps that I keep in the cupboard for when the silly old lights and TV go off.' She added breezily, 'It happens all the time when the wind blows strongly.'

'Do you have candles?'

She thought about Sam and her in her house, cut off from the world, with candles. 'I might.'

Ellie's face heated and she hoped he couldn't see. It was pretty dim in here. She couldn't read his eyes but she suspected they'd darkened.

Instead she went to the cupboard beside the door and took out a huge pair of black gumboots and a man's raincoat. 'These came with the house. You might still be able to salvage your loafers if you leave them to dry.'

Sam stood outside the hastily closed door, the wind buffeting him. He was mad. Obviously he still needed to feel as though he was protecting Ellie. Leftover from not protecting Bree, maybe? The wind tore at the belted raincoat and the splatter of needled rain hit his nose, and he turned his face to protect his eyes. This was dumb. Maybe they should have just let the windows blow in.

A picture of Ellie in her rain-damaged room if that did happen made his feet move and he chose to start with the worst of them first—the windows that backed onto the cliff edge. Here the force of the gale was building and he moved into it out of the lee of the building, where the full force struck him and he staggered against the wall of the building on the little porch overlooking the ocean. Ellie was looking at him from the inside with absolute horror on her face. *Great. Thanks. Very reassuring.* He managed to keep his face calm.

'Continue blowing me against the house,' he muttered. 'Happy with that.' And he kept that picture of Ellie watching him through the window in his mind to keep out the one of him being sucked off the porch and over the cliff to his death.

How had he got here? Right on the edge of a cliff in a cyclone, to be exact. Risking his life for a woman who wouldn't let him close to her. Did he hope being the hero might work when everything else hadn't?

Not that she'd wanted him to be there, and it served him right, because now he was clinging for his life, shutting oil-bereft hinges on shutters that should have been closed hours ago.

When he'd said he was more worried she would do it herself, he'd been one hundred percent telling the truth. It was that thought that drove him like a machine, unclipping, manhandling and latching each shutter closed until he was back at the side door.

He couldn't quite believe he'd been all the way around the house. It had been a real struggle, and by the end, when the wind had built to almost twice the strength from when he started, he knew Ellie would not have been able to do it.

When he fell into the room and the door was shut, he

stopped. He was dripping, gasping for breath, his face stinging from the lash of the rain, back on secure footing and out of the wind into the calm of another world. Now he felt as if…he'd come home.

CHAPTER TEN

THE ROOM WAS lit rosily. The fire Ellie kept mostly for decoration was burning merrily and Millicent was lying in front of it washing her paws. The cat barely glanced at him, she was so intent on her ablutions. *It's okay. I saved you, cat.*

But Ellie stared. Her worried face was pale, deathly pale, and he remembered the time she'd fainted, but then she flew across the room and smashed into him. She was pulling at his coat, helping him get out of his boots and then hugging him. And she buried her beautiful head in his chest. Okay. This was nice.

'That was…was dangerous. Don't do that again. I had no idea it would blow up that strong. I should never have let…' She was whispering and gabbling, Sam couldn't help thinking to himself it had all been very worth it, then, and the only way to stop her seemed perfectly reasonable to him.

He kissed her.

Sam kissed her. It was a short, cold, hard kiss, then another slower one, as if he needed to do it again, in case she'd missed the first one. She hadn't missed it. Then he hugged her. 'It's okay. I'm fine.' He spoke quietly into her hair as if she needed comfort. Darn right she needed comfort.

He tasted like the storm. It was different from the kiss they'd shared at lunch that day. Ellie hugged the wet coldness of his skin close to her. He buried her face in his damp chest, inhaling the strong scent of the sea, his aftershave and the briny tang of a man who had struggled against nature and won. For her.

He could have been blown off the cliff and she wouldn't have been able to do anything to help him. She should have gone with him, watched him, held a rope or something... It hadn't sunk into her how dangerous it was until she'd seen Sam battling to stay upright through the balcony's glass doors. She'd been so frightened for him. She'd never experienced wind like that before and even now her heart thumped at the memory.

In fact, she'd never seen someone so close to death before and that it was lovely Sam, who'd only wanted to help her, seemed ironically tragic. And she was so hard on him.

When he'd safely traversed the more dangerous face of the building she'd run around lighting candles and lighting the old fuel stove that always sat with kindling waiting in the corner of the kitchen alcove in case of blackouts. She'd set the old kettle on to heat water.

He put her away from him. 'You'll get wet. Wait until I dry and then you can cuddle me.'

She half laughed, half sobbed. 'Sorry. I got a bit emotional.' She scurried away, grabbed a towel and handed it to him. 'That was terrifying, watching you out there.'

'Tell me about it,' he said and rubbed his hair. 'It was a lot worse from where I was.' He dabbed around his neck and handed back the towel. Smiled at her. 'All good. Done now.' He glanced around and she saw the approval. 'This looks nice. Can I stay till the storm blows out?'

She looked at him. Tall. Tousled. Ridiculously handsome, yet reassuring too. The full package. Obviously he cared about her, and she wasn't stupid…she knew he fancied her. Well, heck, she fancied him too, if she was honest with herself, despite all her kicking and screaming. And he was only here for another two weeks so it wouldn't be a long-term commitment.

The wind howled and continued to build outside. 'I suppose I can't throw you out now,' she agreed a little breathlessly, happy to play down the tension of the last few minutes while he'd been outside. That had been horrible.

She remembered his car. 'Though I'm not sure how happy your lovely car will be out there with all the debris flying round.'

'There are probably less branches up here than down in the town. I'm not worried. Plus, it's there if I get called out.'

Despite the fact every birth helped her numbers and the overall viability of her plans for the hospital, she actually preferred the idea that he would not be called out. *Please.*

Ellie looked across at the stove and saw the kettle

wasn't even steaming yet. 'Are you cold? I've got the kettle on. The good news is I have pasta already cooked, and can just transfer it to an earthen dish and pop it in the fuel stove to reheat.'

He frowned. 'I've landed myself on you for dinner. I should have brought something.'

'You brought lunch the other day.' *And yourself tonight.* Her turn to look around the softly lit room. At the fire crackling. The candles. She'd pretended to herself she'd only set them because Sam had suggested them. But there was no denying the soft light added to the ambience. 'Even if the power comes on, now that I'm sorted, I like the power off.'

She suddenly felt quite calm that Sam was here. Felt strangely peaceful now she'd accepted she was attracted to him, but somehow because of the wind and the fact they were battened down here like a ship at sea in a storm it was bizarrely safe to allow herself the luxury, because it was done. He was here. She even walked across and turned off the television so it didn't blare at them in a surge when they were reconnected. She remembered the light switch and did the same to that.

It was as if some other Ellie had morphed from her body and evicted the prickly one. 'The refrigerator will make a noise when the power comes back on. That's enough to wake the dead.' The other Ellie sat down on the sofa and patted the seat beside her. 'Sit down. Rest after your efforts. Relax.' Then she thought of something. 'I've got a question.' It was a silly question but it had been bugging her.

He sat down next to her, right next to her, his hip

touching hers, and the sofa creaked with his weight. He was warm, so the coat must have worked well or he had a really good reheating system. Her mind took a little wander and she imagined what it would feel like to have a lot more of Sam's skin against hers. She wondered how much heat they could generate together. How his skin would feel? She knew from the solid impact they'd just shared, when she'd thrown herself at him like a maniac when he'd come in, that his body would be rock-solid under her hands. Her face heated and she hurriedly diverted her mad mind. The question. Yes.

After a sideways glance, Ellie decided he looked a little wary and, considering some of the questions she'd asked him, she wasn't surprised.

'I just wanted to know who taught you to make a bed with hospital corners.'

He laughed. His look said, *Is that all?* 'My mother. She was a matron, like you,' he teased. 'Met and married my dad late in life and brought us up to be "useful", as well as doctors. My sister and I were the only ones at med school who made their beds with hospital corners. We had a great childhood.'

Ellie knew his dad was a widower. 'Where is your sister now?'

His answer was easy and affectionate. 'In Italy. Doing a term of obstetrics in Rome.' Ellie could see they were still close. 'She's a workaholic.'

'Imagine. Another person striving for further knowledge.' She thought of his father. 'And your dad doesn't think of retirement? Don't you people have holidays?'

He shrugged. 'Every year when we were kids. My

parents always loved the sea, so we spent summer holidays there. Christmas at whatever beach house they'd rented for the New Year. But we always had to make our own beds.' He smiled at the memories. 'Mum and Dad adored each other until she passed away ten years ago.'

The sadness was tinged with wonderful memories. Ellie wished she had more memories of her mother. 'I'm sorry for your loss. I knew your dad was a widower.'

He smiled gently at her. 'Dad's been surfing ever since. Says it's when he feels happiest.'

Sam's smile wasn't melancholy, so she shouldn't be. 'That makes sense. He always had a smile on his face when he came in after being in the ocean.'

'So, that's my story.' He turned fully to face her. 'You owe me a little about your life, don't you think?'

'Mine's boringly tragic. As you know from my nightmares, Mum died when I was six. My dad brought me up. He never married again, though I had a nice auntie.'

She smiled at him. 'A real auntie—Dad's sister. I'd go for holidays with my Aunty Dell. She was an Outback nurse and I visited her in whatever little hospital she was working at. That was when I was happiest. I admired her so much that nursing and midwifery were the natural way for me to go. We've done a few emergency births together. She can do everything.'

He was watching her and she suddenly felt a little shy at being under such scrutiny. Wayne had asked questions about her early in their relationship, but once he'd established nobody was going to rescue her he'd stopped hearing her answers. It was something she'd missed early on and should have realised it was a danger sign.

Sam's voice brought her back and she wanted to shake off the sudden darkness that had come with thoughts of Wayne. Sam wasn't pretending interest. He *was* interested. 'So, no brothers or sisters?'

She shook her head. 'Nope.'

'And where's Aunty Dell now?'

Aunty Dell. For her, Ellie could smile. 'Kununurra. She's slowly moving around the top of Western Australia in her mobile home.'

His voice had softened. 'So no rowdy family Christmases for you?' Wayne had played on her need for 'jolly family time', and she knew it with a bitterness that stung.

Sam's face was sympathetic but she couldn't help her reaction. It erupted like a little volcano of hurt. 'Don't pity me. I've had lots of lovely Christmases at work. Making it special for people who find themselves away from home.'

Sam's expression didn't change and she took a quick breath to calm herself—remind herself this was Sam, not Wayne—and felt a little ashamed of her outburst.

He said, 'That was empathy, not pity. I can see you have a thing about pity. There's a difference. What I'd really like to know about is the relationship that's made you so bitter and prickly. It obviously didn't work out.'

Wayne hadn't been a relationship. He'd been a debilitating illness that had almost become terminal. The kettle began to sing and she heard it with relief. 'No. My relationship didn't work out.' The old Ellie was back and she stood up. 'I'll make a hot drink. Would you like tea, coffee or hot chocolate?'

He put his hand on her arm. 'Do you know what I'd really like? More than a hot drink?'

The kettle sang louder. 'What?'

Sam seemed oblivious to the noise. 'To hear about that time in your life that still affects you so much now.'

She looked down at him. Nope. She couldn't do that. She knew what would happen. Talking about Wayne and the loss of her innocence, the tearing down of her dreams, the descent into abuse she'd suffered, would spoil what she had here with Sam. Tonight couldn't be the start of a long-term thing but it was special. She wouldn't infect this moment with the past.

This thing with Sam, this fledgling, careful aware-ness that she was only just allowing into her world along with Sam, was too precious. Too easily damaged. 'How about you talk about your marriage first?'

'Touché.' He grimaced. She read it in his face. He knew analysing his past would harm what they had as well. 'Let's have hot chocolate instead.'

Sam sipped his hot chocolate. The fire flickered, the woman who had attracted him crazily for the first time in years sat beside him, while a big black cat purred against his side. A hell of a lot different from work, work, work. It was probably the most peaceful eve-ning he'd spent since well before Bree's death, which was crazy, considering the tempest outside. But since he'd closed the shutters they were locked in an imper-vious cave, immune to the elements. There was just the rattle of rain on the roof and the background thrum of the ocean crashing on the cliffs below joining with it to make a symphony rather than a discordant refrain.

The candles flickered and as far as he was concerned Ellie looked like an angel, her cheeks slightly pink as she laughed about the time when Jeff, the lifesaver and prawn-trawler captain, the meanest, toughest guy in town, had fainted at his wife giving birth.

She turned to look at him. 'You must have had funny things happen in your work?'

'Not often.' Or maybe he'd lost his sense of humour so long ago that he'd missed the occasions. He hadn't smiled as much as he had since he'd arrived here. He wondered if it was the place or the woman beside him. He suspected it was the latter and marvelled that one person could turn his thoughts around so swiftly.

It was almost as if, the first time he'd seen her, she'd magically switched on his party lights.

She nudged him with her shoulder. 'Come on. Something funny must have happened at your work!'

He pretended to sigh. 'Very recently I was called into a birth centre and the husband was stark, staring naked in the shower with his wife and two sons while she pushed the baby out. They were from a nudist colony.'

He could tell she was trying not to laugh but he suspected it was more at his horror than the picture he painted.

She pursed her lips in mock shock. 'What about the midwife?'

He looked sternly at her. 'She was dressed. Thank goodness.'

She let go and laughed. 'You're a prude. I'm guessing

if they'd had a home birth the midwife from their colony would have been naked. Birth is such an important event that, if your belief system celebrates the naked body, I can see why they would want to be naked for it.'

He'd started the story to make her smile but she made him think more about the people, not the events. It was something he'd had trouble doing at the time and now he felt slightly ashamed. 'I'm not really complaining. The mother had had a previous caesarean, which ruled out a home birth, and they were "reclaiming her birthing ability".'

She tilted her head and looked at him. 'It's pretty cool you get that.'

He grimaced. 'I didn't get it.' He shook his head. He couldn't take credit when it wasn't due. 'I'm repeating what the midwife told me when she saw my face.'

Her gaze softened. 'But you get it now. I can see that.'

More than that had shifted since he'd come here. 'I think so.'

He tried to explain. 'I've been living a very narrow existence since Bree died. Concentrating on the end goal, which is my research on extreme premature labour. And, although it's too late to save Bree or our babies, maybe I could save other babies and somehow she'd know I was still trying.' He shook his head. 'I don't know. I've been avoiding where possible the more emotive and connecting aspects of my work. My father saw how distanced from people I was becoming so it's not surprising he saw this place as a change of scene for me.' He glanced at her ruefully. 'A chance to try to jolt me out of it.'

'And have we jolted you out of it?'

You have, he thought, but he didn't say it. He let his gaze drift around the candlelit room. Somehow it was easier to talk about it here, now, in the quiet, with just the two of them. 'I feel different. Even that first fast birth in the first half-hour here, with Josie and John. I felt connected. Involved. Not a separate watcher who only stepped in as needed.' He grimaced. 'I even recall their names.' To his shame he hadn't been able to do that for far too long.

He could see she remembered the moment. He wasn't surprised she smiled at the memory. 'You were needed.'

He shook his head. 'Not really. You had it under control. And you loved it all so much. Lived it. It slapped me in the face that I'd lost that in my work.'

She winced at his choice of words. 'Slapped? I'm definitely not a violent person.'

He smiled. 'It was a gentle, metaphorical slap. But I can change that to "nudged me into realising", if you prefer.'

He bumped her shoulder gently with his own. 'Like you nudged me to remember something funny a minute ago.'

'I'm glad you've seen the light.' She said it simply.

'And since then it's been a roller coaster. Lighthouse Bay doesn't win the birth number-count but every patient has had a story, an emotional tag I'm seeing now. That's a good thing. I think.'

She touched his arm. 'It's definitely a good thing.'

That wasn't all he was seeing. He was seeing a beautiful woman, just out of reach. He really wanted to reach. He just hoped she was also feeling the magic that had snared him.

'Come here.' He lifted his arm and to his immense relief she snuggled in under the weight of it. Then it was easy to tilt her chin with his other hand and brush her lips with his. He could feel the tingle of connection all the way down to his toes. He sighed and suddenly felt ten years younger. Now he was alive.

Ellie had known they were going to kiss. Eventually. And surprisingly she was quite calm about it. It wasn't as if they hadn't before and he was very good at it. That other Ellie was stretching inside her and saying, *Yes, please*, as Sam pulled her close. *Hurry up and kiss me some more*, that other Ellie was saying. She was such a hussy.

His mouth touched hers. Mmm… Kissing Sam tasted crazy good. Strangely their bodies were communing like two old lovers—not new ones—and inexplicably she once again found herself in his lap. She kept her eyes closed dreamily as she slid her arms around his strong neck and savoured the virile hardness and warmth of him. The slowness and languorous progression of his mouth from gentle to intense, hard to soft, and back again. It felt so powerful with him holding her face, her cheeks, cradled between his palms as if he held delicate china in his hands. Tasting her and letting her taste him. As though she was precious and special. Breathing in each other's breath as they shared the most intimate connection with their mouths.

Distantly she heard the rain beat on the roof and the

spiral of delight just went on, deeper and more poignantly, until she wanted to cry with the beauty of his mouth against hers, his tongue curled around hers, until her whole body seemed to glow from the inside out. Kissing and more kissing. She hadn't realised she could love kissing this much. That kissing was actually the be all and end all. That it could be a whole play and not just an act of the play. She'd never been kissed like this—as if he couldn't get enough of her mouth. His hands roamed, as if gathering her even closer, but always they came back to her face, gently holding her mouth to his as if he couldn't get enough. Yes. She couldn't get enough, either.

Sam was staying the night. Tomorrow was Saturday. They had all night—or even all weekend, if they wanted.

He stayed all weekend. Sunday morning, she woke to the warmth of Sam's big naked body snug up against her and her cheek on Sam's skin. The blond hairs on his body tickled her nose and her hand closed over the wedge-shaped muscle of his chest as her face grew steadily pinker. Oh, my. What they had done since Friday night?

As if he'd heard her thoughts, his voice announced he was awake too. 'I'm wondering if perhaps we could do some of that again...'

Sam's voice was a seductive rumble and she could feel the smile curve across her face. No doubt she looked like Millicent after scoring a treat. She knew now what Trina was missing and why the young widow had chosen to work most nights. Waking to someone warm and loving beside her. A man spoiling her until she begged him to stop. Being held until she fell asleep.

Cheeks still red, she tried to not jump on him. 'Aren't you hungry?'

'Oh, yeah, I'm starving.' He pulled her on top of him and kissed her thoroughly.

An hour later Ellie watched the steam follow Sam out of the bathroom and ran her hands slowly over her tingling body. She'd had no idea such a sensuous world existed, though how on earth she was going to face Sam at work and not think lurid thoughts defied her imagination. Sam had told her to stay and enjoy the shower while he made breakfast but what she really wanted to do was drag the gorgeous person back to bed. She'd had no idea she was a nymphomaniac. Must be. Surely other people didn't do it so much as they had in the last thirty-six hours?

She didn't know how it could work between them. If it even could work. He was based in Brisbane. She was here. But they were fabulous together so surely that meant something? Maybe she could learn to trust a relationship with a man. A long-distance relationship. If that man was Sam. No. She wasn't in love with him. Was she? She wasn't going there, but she sure as heck was in lust with him.

And if it didn't work long-distance, that was okay, because he would only be here for another two weeks and she deserved great sex at least once in her life. More than once. She grimaced over the word. They hadn't had sex—Sam had made love to her. Gloriously tender love that healed and nurtured and told her he thought she was the sexiest woman in the world. Who would have known? Her cheeks glowed again.

CHAPTER ELEVEN

MONDAY MORNING DAWNED, blustery, and Ellie tweaked her collar tighter to her throat as she closed her front door. She'd slept deeply after Sam had left on Sunday evening. They'd walked for hours hand in hand along Nine Mile Beach, splashing through the waves, coming back after lunch ravenous again. Ellie was convinced that the sun, the exercise and—she grinned to herself—the loving meant she'd slept the best she'd slept for years.

This morning the air felt damp and exhilarating as she trod lightly down the road to work just before seven a.m. She'd skipped her beach walk this morning—strangely, her hips were tender. Must be all the exercise. She blushed sheepishly.

The sea remained wild, white caps out to the horizon, booming swells smashing against the cliff below, and Ellie breathed in the fresh salt with a sigh of pleasure. She loved the coast. Loved the isolation of her croft, though isolation wasn't something she'd savoured over the weekend. She saw Myra's car was back and smiled to herself. She didn't know. *Tee-hee.*

She laughed out loud and conversely had a sudden desire to share the amusing thought with Sam. There was a little wonky logic in that thought and it was not very loyal to her friend.

On her arrival she saw that Trina had had a slow night. The ward remained empty. Her friend had been bored, hence she had reorganised the whole sterile stockroom—a job Ellie had been putting off until a quiet day—and there was a small pile of out-of-date stock that she needed to reorder from the base hospital. At least she had a chore to start her day with.

Later, if no birthing women came in or needed transfer, Ellie would do the same for the medication cupboard. Spring cleaning suited the feeling of determined efficiency she'd decided she needed to ground herself in. Get her head out of the clouds that her thoughts kept drifting up towards.

The expected arrival of Dr Southwell would not faze her, though seriously she wouldn't be able to look at him without blushing, and she wasn't sure how she was going to manage it.

Maybe, as they had no patients, he could go straight through to the clinic in the main hospital to give her a chance to think of what to say.

Except it wasn't Sam who arrived.

Wayne Donnelly was an undeniable presence. Like everyone's favourite young uncle. You could just imagine him dangling babies on his knees, which was what Ellie had thought when he'd begun to pursue her. Whenever Ellie was around he'd made such a fuss of any child and everyone had smiled at him. He'd made her think of families. Dream families. Christmases, Easter egg hunts. All the things Ellie had ever wanted, and she'd fallen headlong in love with the fantasy.

In truth, he hated kids, and was a narcissist and a sociopath. He had no guilt, no shame, no feeling for other people, and could only see the world through eyes that saw himself first.

But he was like a seasoned politician versed in the art of crowd pleasing. Crinkled laughter lines jumped up at the edges of blue eyes framed by thick, black lashes and high cheekbones. Nothing in his looks gave him away. Except maybe the confident, beaming, too-white smile. He had a small cleft in his strong chin and women instinctively gave him another look.

Later she'd found out there was a pattern. He serenaded his victims, pretended to marry them, created joint bank accounts and then sauntered off after skilfully denigrating the woman so she felt it was all her fault everything had failed. A master of psychological abuse.

When Ellie saw him her stomach lurched with bile. Out of the corner of her eye she saw Trina, about to head home to bed, instinctively pat her hair. Yep. He'd already sucked in Trina.

'What are you doing here?' Ellie watched his smile broaden, the fake smile he used like oil to smooth his way in so he could use someone. She'd been incredibly blind. She wasn't any more.

'Too early in the morning for manners, El? Introduce me to your beautiful friend before we find ourselves bickering.'

'No.' Ellie turned from him to Trina. 'He's a cad and a slime, Trina. I'd leave if I was you.'

Wayne laughed. Trina looked at Ellie and shut her gaping mouth with a click. She blinked a few times as her tired brain tried to work it out. Then she stepped closer to Ellie. 'If you say so, I believe you.'

Ironic choice of words from her friend. One of the people in the room was a huge liar.

Trina frowned. 'But…' She wrinkled her brow. 'If he's a cad shouldn't I stay?'

Ellie shook her head. 'I'd prefer you didn't. He won't be here long. You could ring the security man, though. Ask him to come over and sit at my desk. That would be good in case he won't leave.'

Trina didn't look again at Ellie's acquaintance, just crossed to the desk and picked up the phone. She spoke quietly into it and then picked up her bag. 'If you're sure.'

Ellie nodded again. 'Please. And thanks.'

Trina nodded. 'See you tomorrow morning.'

'Sure.' Ellie Looked back at Wayne. Raised her brows. 'Yes?'

'I need money.'

'Really.' He had taken a great deal of that from her already. Along with her naivety. She looked at the impeccable clothes. 'I've seen people far worse off than you.'

'Thank you.' As if she'd given him a wonderful compliment. 'Nice little caravan park you have here. Think I might stay around for a while. Reacquaint myself with my kin.'

'You have no kin. But I can't stop you. Luckily, it's high season and will cost you an arm and a leg. So you will have to move on eventually.' She wasn't moving on. Not this time.

He spread his hands. 'Gambling debts.'

Nothing new. 'Gamblers tend to get those.'

'This time they threatened to harm my family.'

He'd had three 'wives' that she knew of. 'Which family?'

'All of them. You included. I thought I'd better warn you.'

He didn't give a damn. 'You don't care about anyone but yourself. You'd do better going to the police.'

'I don't think that the police station is a safe place for me to go. Would you look forward to identifying my body?'

'Go away, Wayne. Your disasters have nothing to do with me.' And she could feel the shakes coming on. He'd tried to rape her once. After she'd said she was leaving him. And he'd denied it. Said she'd been playing hard to get.

She'd escaped that night and had begun to plan carefully to get away, because he'd taken all her resources. Her wallet, her licence, her bank accounts… Everything had been unavailable when she'd needed it. She'd stumbled into Myra's coffee shop, distraught, and made a friend for life. Myra had helped her create the wall of protection she needed to be free.

'You've turned all bitter and twisted. Not the sweet Ellie I used to know.'

That wasn't even worth answering. Ellie heard the

door from the main hospital open and was glad the security guard was here. She needed to end this. She pretended she didn't know help had arrived. She couldn't keep running.

'Leave the ward, please, Mr Donnelly.'

'You didn't call me "Mr Donnelly" when we were married.'

'We were never married.' Ellie turned away from him to the security guard and her stomach dropped. It wasn't security, it was Sam. No. No. *No.* Her face flushed and she felt dreadfully, horribly sick. She didn't want Sam to know about this. But then maybe it was best. Then he could see she could never truly give a man power over her ever again.

'Good morning, matron,' Sam said.

Ellie saw him glance at Wayne and give him an inscrutable nod. 'We need to discuss the patients.' Sam's voice was surprisingly crisp. Authoritative. No hint of friendliness.

Ellie raised her brows. He knew there were no patients. 'Certainly, Dr Southwell.'

'Fine. When you're ready, please.'

'She's busy. Talking to me.' Wayne squared his shoulders but he was at a disadvantage in both height and muscle. They all knew it. An adolescent part of Ellie secretly revelled in it.

Still politely, Sam said, 'You're a doctor?'

'No. I'm her…'

Before Wayne could complete his sentence, Sam spoke coldly right over the top of him. There was no doubting his authority. 'This is a hospital. If you are not a medical practitioner, matron's attention is mine. There is a waiting room, though, in the main hospital where you can sit, but this could take some time.'

Ellie added helpfully, 'He's leaving.'

'Excellent. Come with me, matron.' Sam indicated with his hand that he expected Ellie to head down the corridor to the empty rooms in front of him.

She looked at Wayne and made the decision to enforce her freedom from dreaded drop-in visits like this. She didn't know why she hadn't done it before but knew it was a fault she needed to remedy immediately. 'If you don't leave town, I'll lodge a restraining order with the police this afternoon. I've kept evidence of our fake marriage certificate. This won't happen again.'

Then she turned to Sam. 'This way, doctor.'

Sam ignored Wayne and followed Ellie. She could feel his large body blocking Wayne's view of her as they turned into an empty room and stood silently in the centre of it out of sight. Ellie clasped her hands together to stop them shaking, unable to look at Sam. They both heard footsteps retreating, and the automatic doors open and close, and Ellie sagged against a wall. Sam watched her but he didn't come any closer, as if he knew she needed space at this moment.

'Your ex-husband, I assume?'

'He was a bigamist. Or trigamist, if there is such a word. So never legally my husband.'

Sam whistled. 'Ouch.'

She said very quietly, 'There were worse things about him than that.'

Sam studied her. 'Would you like me to follow and punch him out?'

He was deadly serious. She could see that.

She could almost smile at that except her heart was broken. Yes, she was beginning to love Sam. That was so dangerous to her peace of mind. It frightened the stuffing out of her. And she loved him even more for the offer, but Wayne had made her see how impossible it all was. She couldn't do this—start again with Sam. She didn't have the trust in her to build a strong relationship and Sam needed a woman to love him wholeheartedly.

Not one who'd locked him out like Bree had. Bree, who had almost destroyed him while she'd destroyed herself. He deserved that trust. She could give him love. She was more than halfway to falling in love with him already. But she couldn't give him trust. She'd thought she could but she couldn't. Trust had died in her for ever. Killed by the man who had just left.

'Thank you for the thought but I wouldn't like to ask you to sink to his level.' She straightened off the wall.

'Now you can see, Sam, why I'm so wary of men. Why I know I'll never let myself get that close to someone again. I'm sorry if I gave you the wrong idea this weekend. It was lovely, what we shared, but it's finished. You'll leave soon and that's good.' She took a step towards the door and it was the hardest step she'd ever taken. 'Let's go back to the desk.'

His fingers lifted to touch her arm, then dropped. 'Ellie.'

'Yes?' She looked at his caring eyes. His beautiful

mouth. The kindness that shone on his face. It broke her heart.

'I'm sorry you've been wounded by a pathetic man. We're not all like that.'

She heard him. Saw that he meant it. But that didn't help. She wished she could believe it as deeply as she needed to be fair to Sam. 'I know. I really don't think you are that sort of man, but I don't have the capacity in me to risk a relationship again. A relationship needs to be good for both of us and I wouldn't be good for you.'

'But—'

She cut him off. 'Thank you. I don't want to talk about it any more.'

Sam sighed impatiently. 'I can understand that here. But later, I think we should.'

'No, Sam. We won't.' Then she turned and walked away.

Sam left Ellie soon after. He went out the front door to make sure her ex-bigamist had departed but there was no sign of him. He actually would have liked to slam the sleazy little mongrel up against a wall and warn him never to approach Ellie again, but he might find a place in himself that would do more than that, and he'd taken an oath to not harm.

His fingers clenched by his sides. No wonder she had trust issues and didn't want to ask any man for help. Even himself. He wasn't a violent man but after what they'd shared the last two days the idea of some-one abusing Ellie's trust to that extent devastated him. And made him furious. But in the end it wasn't any of his business unless he was looking for something long-term—which wasn't his intention. Or was it? Hell, he didn't know. Did he even have a choice?

Ellie spent the next five days rearranging antenatal schedules and managed to book a different pregnant woman for antenatal appointments for every morning during the time Sam would be around.

They had two normal births, one on Faith's shift and one on Trina's, so Ellie was spared having to call Sam in. She could only be glad the babies were being kind to her. But every afternoon when she went home the house was empty, where before it had been welcoming.

Sam came on Wednesday afternoon for his father's surfboard and she gave it to him, refused to talk and didn't invite him in.

On Thursday Myra cornered her and told her Sam had asked her to see if Ellie would change her mind. Spend some time with him. They had their first ever disagreement when both women were so determined to change the other's mind about what was right.

By Friday Ellie knew she needed to get away or she would make herself sick, so as soon as she finished work she took herself off availability for call-backs and loaded her car.

Ellie felt the need to abandon her cottage and head to a different world. It had everything to do with avoiding a certain visitor who just might drop in again.

She didn't know where to go, so she drove north to the Gold Coast, where she could find a cheap hotel and just hibernate for two nights in a place that no-body knew her.

She stayed in her room all day Saturday and drove back Sunday via the base hospital where two of her patients were still inpatients.

She did her own visiting, with a quiet chat in the big antenatal ward with Marni, who was going home tomorrow. Bob arrived not long after she did, and she was pleased to hear that the young mum's contractions had settled down, and Bob had painted inside their house while Marni was in hospital so she didn't have to be exposed to the smell of new paint.

She showed Ellie the quilt she was making the baby, and there was something about Marni's determined optimism that made her feel ashamed. Marni had explained that when she was bored she sewed another little animal onto the patchwork cot-blanket, pouring love and calmness into it, determined to do everything asked of her to keep her pregnancy on track.

After Marni, Ellie visited the postnatal ward area, where Annette sat happily with her twins, who were being star patients and were almost ready to go home.

'Still perfect?' Ellie grinned at the two sleeping bundles and the relaxed mum sitting with a magazine in her lap.

'They have their moments. Rosebud is the impatient one, so has to be fed first, while Thorn needs a bit of encouragement to keep at it.'

'So they are still how they started out, then.'

'Exactly.' Both women laughed.

'How is that gorgeous Dr Sam?'

'Fine.' Ellie felt her face freeze, as if all the muscles had suddenly stopped working. 'He's here for another week and then he's gone.' Her voice was bright. 'Then I guess we'll have another new locum. Did you know his father was here first? He was a surfer, though I'm not sure how good his surfing will be for a while, because he broke his arm. That's why his son came.'

'So Dr Sam's not coming back?'

'No.' It would be better if Sam never came back. She suspected every time he came it would hurt more to keep saying goodbye to him. 'He has a high-flying job in Brisbane. He was only doing everyone a favour.' Including her.

On the drive home she thought about her dilemma. She'd had sex with a man she'd known for only two weeks by that point, and who was just passing through. Maybe she even understood her friend Faith, who had never said she regretted the man who'd come, disappeared and left her with a baby. She'd never been close to understanding before.

Sex. She grimaced and reminded herself that that was all it was. Then her sensible voice returned. That was okay. She was a grown-up. Afterwards she could go back to how it had been before and concentrate on work.

On Monday morning when Sam walked in to the maternity ward the Ellie he found was the woman from three weeks ago. White shirt buttoned to the neck, grey eyes serene and cool, her manner very businesslike.

'Good morning, doctor.'

His temper was less than sunny after being frustrated all weekend. He'd thought if he just waited until Saturday morning they could sort it all out. He'd taken croissants and blueberry yoghurt, as she'd liked that last time, and then had stood there like an idiot until he'd realised she'd left. He'd rung Myra each morning and afternoon all weekend to check in case she'd returned.

Now he stared with narrowed eyes as she stood officiously in front of him. 'Good morning, Ellie.' He stressed her first name, disappointed but not surprised this ice maiden didn't resemble the woman he had held in his arms all weekend just over a week ago. He was back to square one, and despite his best efforts there was no breaking through her barriers. Maybe he should just give up.

They had five days to go. Then he'd be gone. He could lose himself in his work again. Treat it as an interlude that had shown him he could finally care for another woman. But he wasn't so sure he could care for one as much as he'd grown to care for Ellie.

On Friday morning, Sam's last day there, Ellie went back to the beach. She'd been avoiding it all week in case Sam was there in the mornings surfing but she missed the peace she gained from her daily walk. Peace was at a premium at the moment and she needed it before facing today.

It had rained last night, and the ocean was too rough for surfers out there. As she trod down the path even the frogs weren't penetrating the gloom she was wrapped in. At least she had Sam to thank for losing the majority of her phobia. She wasn't going to touch one but the croaking barely bothered her now—there were worse things that could happen than frogs. Such as Sam going and never seeing him again.

She reached the sand, slipped off her footwear and stood for a moment. Gazing out. A new weather pattern was coming in. More high winds and rough seas. She breathed in deeply and let the crash of the waves on the cliffs across the bay penetrate, feeling the cool white sand between her toes, the turbulent, curving waves tumbling onto themselves and running up the sand to kiss her better. The biggest waves made a cracking noise as they slid all the way up to her to foam around her toes then crackle into the sand as it drank in the water and the cries of the gulls overhead. This was why she lived here. Because it made her strong.

Yes, it was sad that Sam was going, more than sad, but it was good as well. It would never have worked and what he'd given her in the two days they'd been together was something she could hold to her heart in the years to come. She wished him happiness with a woman who deserved him. She just wished she could have been that woman.

Ellie lifted her head and breathed in another gulp of sea air past the stinging in her throat and then she set off along the beach. She would get through today, kiss Sam's cheek and say goodbye.

Sam knew she was going to kiss his cheek. He didn't want her platonic guilt. If she wasn't going to kiss him properly then he didn't want her to kiss him at all. He stepped back as she moved forward to say goodbye and saw her blink in confusion as he avoided her.

That's right, Ellie. Feels bad, doesn't it, to be knocked back? He didn't say it but he knew it was there in his eyes. He was still pretty darn angry with her for not fighting for what they might have had.

'Goodbye, Ellie Swift. I wish you a great life with your midwifery centre.' He turned away quickly because if he didn't he'd grab her and kiss her until she begged him to stay. But that wouldn't happen.

He'd driven an hour towards Brisbane when the radio alert of another storm warning jerked him back to sense. Ellie was on the seaboard. Right on the edge of a cliff, to be exact. Her little house would bear the brunt of the storm and he wouldn't be there to make sure she was all right.

Not that she'd want him to be there, but suddenly he asked himself why would he drive away from a woman who'd finally made him want to look at the future again? One he wanted to wake up next to for the rest of his life? He loved Ellie. How many times did real love actually come to a man?

After he'd stepped back from her he'd seen the look of hurt on her face and it came back to haunt him now. What if she was feeling the same pain he was? Wasn't he as bad as she was for not fighting for what they could have?

He'd loved Bree, and it had destroyed him when she'd died. But Ellie was right. It hadn't been his fault. He didn't know she'd been so unstable that she would take her own life. And he'd lost himself in work.

If it wasn't for Lighthouse Bay and Ellie he might be still lost. He could have woken up in thirty years and realised he'd been a shell for decades. He didn't want to be a shell. He wanted to be the man who held Ellie every night. The man who held the babies she was destined to have with him, and might never have if he kept driving away. He loved her. He wanted her. And he would fight for her.

He pulled over and turned around. The storm up ahead was flashing lightning across the hills. Great sheets of white light. Ellie was over there somewhere. Alone.

The thunder crashed outside. The scent of ozone filled the air, lighting up the sky all the way out to sea. This storm was more electrical than the other one. She shied away from those memories of the night Sam came, like Millicent had skidded away from the window.

Myra was gone again and Ellie suspected she had a male friend she was visiting. She even suspected it might be the 'elder' Dr Southwell. Good for her.

But Ellie knew the man she should have fought for was gone. Sam was gone. In her head he was gone. In her heart he was buried under protection so thick she felt like she was walking around inside a big, white cotton-wool ball, adding more layers all week, so that by the time Sam had left this afternoon she could barely hear, she was so distanced from everyone. He'd turned away from her coldly in the end and she deserved that. She'd been a coward and deserved his scorn.

She wished she'd never ever started this painful process of letting someone else in. Because for the first time in a long time she wondered if, if she'd tried a little bit harder to let go of the past, she just might have had a future. With Sam. Was it too late? Could she contact him through his father? Myra would be all over her like a rash if she asked for Sam's phone number. Or his flat address. Maybe she could turn up at his flat. Her heart began to pound and she looked down at Millicent. 'Am I mad to think of it or mad not to do it, cat?'

She had a sudden memory of Marni, determined to fight for her baby. Shoring herself up with positive actions. Stitching her quilt of love so that she would be ready when the good things happened. Ellie had done the opposite, undermined her own confidence with the past every time Sam broke through her barriers.

Stop it. Too late, it's over. She stroked the soft fur between Millicent's pointy ears.

She sat up straight. 'You know what, Milly? It's not over till the fat lady sings. I'll find him tomorrow and see if we can at least spend some time together.' She would try and, if it didn't work out, then she might just have to get a cat of her own. Maybe a kitten so she could have the full experience of being a mother. Yeah, right. Full experience.

The knock came in between two claps of thunder and she frowned at the improbability of visitors.

Then, there was Sam. Standing on the bottom step, his nose level with hers, his dark eyes staring into hers.

'Can I come in?' A flash of lighting illuminated them both and a nearby tree exploded into sparks. The explosion made her ears ring and she put out her hand to drag him in.

'Damn it, Sam. You could get killed standing out in that. You're mad.' Her heart was thumping at the closeness of the strike and the concept that again she could have got Sam killed by keeping him outside her house.

Then he was inside, the door was shut and they both stood there, panting, a few inches of air and a huge chasm between them.

He didn't seem perturbed about what had almost happened. He just said softly, 'You haven't closed the shutters again.'

She couldn't believe he was here. As if she'd conjured him. 'I know. It's not that windy. And you can't do it because it's too dangerous to go out in case the lightning gets you.' She licked her dry lips. 'Why are you here, Sam?'

He was staring down at her. She couldn't read the expression in his eyes but it was nothing like the one he'd left with today. It was warm, gentle and determined. 'Can I share the storm with you?'

Her cheeks were heating. He looked so good. Smelt so good. She knew he would feel so good. 'That would be nice,' she said carefully.

His brows rode up. 'Nice?' He put down his coat. 'It could be more than nice. Because I've decided to fight for you.'

This was all happening way too fast for her to erect the barriers she needed. Hang on—she didn't need barriers. Her brain was fogging. Softening. Revelling in the fact that Sam was here.

Sam said, 'I'm going to wear you down until you say yes.'

He wasn't gone. She hadn't ruined everything. Yet! Then his words sank in. 'Yes to what?'

'Will you marry me, Ellie? Be my wife. We'll work out the logistics—our work, your fears, my baggage. But driving away from you today and knowing I wasn't coming back was the loneliest thing I've ever done in my life, and I don't want to do it again. I love you.'

He loved her. 'Oh, Sam.' She loved him. Lord, she loved him so much. She lifted her head. She loved him too much to push him away for a second time. She would just have to break free from the past and be everything Sam needed. For the sake of both their futures. 'I love you too.'

He closed his eyes. 'It was too close, Ellie. We were too close to losing this.' Then he stepped in and picked her up. Hugged her to him and swung her around. And she laughed out loud. Sam's arms had her. They both were laughing and then he kissed her, and Ellie knew, at last, that she had found her 'for ever' family.

CHAPTER TWELVE

SAM STOOD WAITING, his heart pounding as he watched for the first signs of the bridal car to descend the gravel road to the beach, and he appreciated the grounding effect of the cool sand under his bare feet as he waited for the warmth of the sun. But, more impatiently, he waited for the glowing warmth of the woman he would spend the rest of his life with. Where was Ellie?

The light touch of a hand on his arm broke into his thoughts and he turned with a smile to his father. He saw the old man's eyes were damp and shadowed with that memory of past sadness, yet glowing with pride too. Happy and sad at the same moment. Sam knew all about that. They both glanced at Sam's sister as she stood with her Italian friends, back on sabbatical to her old hospital while she attended her only brother's wedding.

His dad cleared his throat and said quietly, 'Your mother would have been so proud of you, son. So happy for you.'

Sam patted his shoulder. Felt the sinewy strength under his hand and was glad his dad was healed again.

'She'd be happy for you too. We've both been blessed twice with wonderful women.'

'I can see you love your Ellie, Sam.'

Sam felt his face relax, felt his mind expand with just thinking about her. Felt the joy surge up into his chest. Such elation. 'She's turned the world on for me, Dad. Ellie, this place, the future.' He shook his head, still unable to believe his grey life had been hit by a sunburst called Ellie Swift. Soon to be Mrs Southwell. 'I just wish she'd hurry up and arrive.'

The first rays of the sunrise struck the cliff in front of them at the exact moment an old-fashioned black saloon descended the steep slope and finally drew up at the place reserved for the bride in the crowded car park.

The whole town had come out in the dark to wait for the sunrise and for Ellie. The dapper chauffer, not resembling a prawn-trawler captain at all, opened the door onto a long blue roll of carpet that reached all the way across the sand to Sam.

He helped the two golden bridesmaids in their beautiful sheath dresses, Trina and Faith, and the stately Matron of Honour in a vintage gold dress, his dad's fiancée, Myra, and then Sam heard the hushed gasp from a town full of supporters as Ellie stepped out in a vision of white with her father's hand in hers.

Ellie had been shy about a veil, a white dress, the fact that she'd thought she was a bride before and had been mistaken, but Sam had taken her in his arms and told her his dream…of Ellie on the beach dressed as a bride. Sam had spoken quietly of the pureness of their love, the freshness of their commitment and his desire for her to feel the bride of her dreams—because their life together would be that dream.

And there she was, drifting towards him, the veil dancing at the sides of her face in the morning breeze, walking a little too quickly in her bare feet as she always did, her eyes on his, her smile wide and excited as she closed the gap between them. She came first, not after the bridesmaids, almost dragging her dad, and Sam was glad, because he could watch her close the gap between them all the way, and he barely saw the three smiling women behind her. He'd told them he wasn't talking to them anyway—they'd kept his Ellie at Myra's house last night sequestered away from him. They and her Aunty Dell, back from Western Australia for her only niece's wedding.

When Ellie stopped in front of him her eyes were glowing behind the fine material of the veil and he took her hand in his and felt the tension drain from his shoulders like an eddy rushing from a freshly filled rock pool. Ellie's dad released his daughter's hand, smiled wistfully and waved them on.

The sun chose that moment to break free of the ocean and bathed the whole wedding party in golden-pink rays as they rearranged themselves in front of the minister. The crowd drew closer, the waves pounded on the rocks by the cliff, Sam's hand tightened on Ellie's and the ceremony began, accompanied by the sound of the gulls overhead.

Afterwards the wedding breakfast was set out on white-cloth-covered tables on the long veranda of the surf club restaurant that looked out over the bay. The local Country Women's Association ladies had whipped up a magnificent repast and Ellie's new husband kept catching her eye with such love, such devotion and pride, she constantly fought back happy tears which she refused to let free. Not now. Not today. She had never thought she could be this happy.

She touched the sleeve of his white tuxedo coat. 'Sam, let's take a minute to ourselves. Walk with me on the beach.' She watched his face soften, saw it glow with love and pride, and those blinking tears that had stung her eyes threatened again. She willed them away.

So they turned down the steps of the surf club, away from the revelries, and people parted smilingly and nudged each other. 'Let them go. Young lovers.'

Finally it was just Ellie and Sam walking along the beach, barefoot in the morning sunlight, Ellie's dress hitched over her arm, toes making fresh footprints in virgin sand, and every now and then the froth of the chuckling waves tickled their ankles.

'I love you, Sam.'

'I love you too, my wife.'

She hugged the words to herself and used them to make her brave. She had news and she wanted to share it but they hadn't had a moment together alone all morning.

'This morning…' she began, and felt the nerves well. Hoped desperately he would be glad. 'This morning, I did a test.'

His big, dark brows, those brows she loved and traced

at night with her fingers, drew together. He didn't get it. 'And did you pass your test?'

'It was positive.'

She let the words hang suspended with the sound of the sea between them. Squeezed his hand in hers and waited. Felt his fingers still beneath hers.

'Pregnant?' His voice was almost a whisper.

Her heart squeezed and she nodded. 'Our baby. Just weeks in time, but it feels good. The feeling is right. Everything will be fine, Sam.' She stopped and turned to him, took his face in hers instead of the other way around. Felt the skin of his cheeks tense as he realised what she'd been trying to tell him 'My darling, everything will be perfect.'

His face stilled and then slowly, ever so slowly, he smiled. It rose from somewhere so deep inside him that she was blinded by the joy she had been so afraid would be missing, consumed instead by fear that what had happened to Bree would happen to her too.

He smiled, then he grinned, picked her up and swung her around as if she were a feather, and then he hugged her. Fiercely. Put her down. Glanced around and then picked her up again. Laughed out loud. Ellie was giddy with relief, giddy with swinging, giddy with Sam.

The only minor glitch would be the time she spent on maternity leave.

But Lighthouse Bay Mothers and Babies would be fine. Sam had taken the post of Director of Obstetrics at the base hospital an hour away and his father had become the permanent GP for Lighthouse Bay. Soon Ellie would have the midwifery service she dreamed of, because now she had a straight pathway of referral to a higher level of service if needed. She knew the obstetrician in charge—her new husband—very well, and he was extremely supportive. And in the wings was Trina, ready to come off night duty and take over when Ellie stepped down. And after her there was Faith, and then Roz, and other midwives waiting to be a part of the journey travelled by the midwives of Lighthouse Bay.

* * * * *

THE MIDWIFE'S
ONE-NIGHT FLING

CAROL MARINELLI

Dear Lucinda

Love you more xxxx

PROLOGUE

'YOU MUST BE getting excited about the big move to London?'

It was a question Freya Ross had heard many times in recent weeks, and although the knot in her stomach tightened at the thought of what lay ahead she smiled.

'I'm very much looking forward to it.'

As a midwife at the birthing centre attached to Cromayr Bay Hospital, Freya was examining Mrs Roberts while her three little boys ran amok in the rather small cubicle. Most patients preferred to be called by their first name, but not Mrs Roberts.

'Jamie!' Mrs Roberts scolded as her boisterous three-year-old climbed on a chair.

Freya was more than used to working with toddlers underfoot, and she was also very used to holding in her thoughts.

She had told no one of her misgivings about moving to London. Not her parents, nor her best friend, nor her colleagues. Certainly she would not burden a patient with her worries.

No one could possibly guess that now her leaving date was almost here Freya was dreading making the move from the small Scottish town of Cromayr Bay to London.

The news of her leaving had come as a complete surprise to everyone. No one had known she'd gone to London for an interview. This was no mean feat in Cromayr Bay! Even swapping her off-duty days had been complicated—Freya hadn't been able to lie and say that she was visiting the dentist, given that the dentist was the husband of Betty, her senior midwife. And, had she called in sick—well someone would either have mentioned that her car had been seen at Cromayr Bay station, or they'd have dropped in to check that she was okay.

In the end Freya had said that she was catching up with a friend with whom she had trained.

'Oh? Who?' Betty had asked...

Feeling as if her nose must surely be an inch longer after such a complex lie, Freya had taken the train to Edinburgh's Waverley Station and from there had travelled down to London to the Primary, a large, modern hospital.

Freya's general nursing training had taken place in Cowdenbeath, and she had done some placements in Edinburgh during her midwifery training, so she wasn't unfamiliar with busy hospitals. The Primary was incredibly large, though, and the interview had been very thorough.

Her training had been excellent, and Freya had kept her skills up to date with regular shifts in the main Cromayr Bay hospital, which the birthing centre was attached to.

She had been offered a six-month contract by the London hospital, commencing in the middle of July, and Freya was starting to get nervous.

Not that she showed it.

Instead of revealing her feelings now, she made small talk with Mrs Roberts as she palpated the baby. 'We've got my leaving do tonight, over at the Tavern,' Freya said. 'You're actually the last patient that I'll see before I go.'

'I'm sorry that you shan't be here for the birth.'

'I am too, Mrs Roberts,' Freya agreed. 'Although I know you are going to do just fine.'

'I expect Alison is feeling the same as I do about your leaving?'

Freya's hands paused mid-examination. Alison had made it clear that she didn't want the news about her pregnancy getting out just yet.

'We're best friends.' Freya decided to give a non-committal answer, just in case she had misinterpreted the question. 'So, yes, she was a bit upset when I told her that I was moving—but I'll be coming home regularly.'

'I meant about the baby,' Mrs Roberts said. 'It's okay, I'm not asking you to break any confidences. I just heard the other day that she's expecting again. It's lovely news.'

'It is,' Freya agreed, though inwardly she sighed for her friend at the fact that the news had got out. Very few people knew. And, even though Alison was past her first trimester, she had wanted to keep it to herself for a while yet.

But nothing stayed a secret for very long here.

'I just hope…' Mrs Roberts voice trailed off. 'Well,' she said. 'I hope that things go better for her this time.'

Freya gave a small nod, but refused to be drawn into a discussion about the loss of Andrew.

Last year had been a hard one.

Following an uneventful pregnancy, Alison had arrived at the birthing centre in active labour. But while checking the foetal heart-rate Freya had realised something was terribly wrong.

Alison had been transferred to the attached hospital and a crash Caesarean had been performed. The little boy had been resuscitated and then transferred to Edinburgh, where there had been a NICU cot available.

He'd been beautiful and utterly perfect. A chunky baby, with long, dark lashes, big cheeks and pudgy hands. But the lack of oxygen from cord compression and subsequent meconium aspiration had left him severely brain damaged.

Despite best efforts Andrew had died two days later, leaving Alison, her husband Callum and their families shattered.

Freya had been his godmother and proxy aunt, and she still woke regularly from nightmares, with the ominous sound of the CTG bleeping seeming to fill her bedroom. It felt as if her chest was being crushed whenever she recalled the devastation on Alison's face when it had become clear that things were going terribly wrong.

'*Freya?*' Alison had pleaded.

The fear in Alison's voice was something that Freya would never be able to erase from her memory.

Alison had never blamed Freya. In fact she had drawn on her friend, and Freya had stayed strong for Alison even through a serious relationship break-up.

And now, not by a flicker did she reveal her own heartache as she focussed on her patient and the little life beneath her hands.

'Everything's looking grand,' Freya said as she felt the baby's position. 'The head is down and baby is a good size.'

'Aye.'

For Freya, the real beauty of working at Cromayr Bay was the chance to really get to know her patients and their families, and now, after being more than willing to chat about Alison's pregnancy, Mrs Roberts's short response when discussing her own, concerned Freya.

It wasn't just that, though. Over the months Freya had been trying to gauge Mrs Roberts's feelings.

This pregnancy had come close after the birth of twins, but Mrs Roberts insisted it was all part of the plan as she wanted her children to be near each other in age.

Freya was quite certain that Mrs Roberts was struggling, but she was a very proud and private woman. Earlier, though, she'd seemed more talkative, and Freya wondered if she actually wanted to speak to her.

Jamie, the eldest, was getting restless, and the twins were going through their mother's handbag. Freya was in no doubt that Mrs Roberts would want to dash off as soon as her appointment was done.

As she went to the desk to write up her findings Mrs Roberts dressed and then came over and took a seat.

'Jamie!' She scolded her son, who had pulled over a jar of cotton balls. 'I'm so sorry, Freya.'

'It's not a problem. I shouldn't have left them at a three-year-old's level.' As Mrs Roberts went to retrieve them Freya stopped her. 'He might as well play with them,' she said—not just because the cotton balls would now have to be discarded, but also because it might keep Jamie amused for a few minutes.

'He's into everything,' Mrs Roberts explained. 'I need eyes in the back of my head.'

'You're certainly going to be busy when the new baby comes,' Freya agreed. 'Is there anyone who might be able to help once the baby is here?'

'Och, I'll not be bothering others. I just have to get on with things.' Mrs Roberts straightened herself in the chair.

Freya felt for her. She too was very private.

With two younger brothers, Freya had always been 'the sensible one'. Her mother, Jean, had relied on her to look out for the boys and soothe their hurts rather than her own.

As Freya wrote up her notes she thought how she came across to her patient. Her long dark curls were pulled back into a ponytail and she knew that her green eyes could sometimes come across as guarded rather than shy. She was a quiet person, and that generally suited her patients just fine.

However, like Mrs Roberts, Freya could appear a touch

aloof at times—abrupt, even—although not, she hoped, with her patients. And, while she tended not to chat too much about herself, that wasn't an issue in Cromayr Bay, where everyone knew everyone else's business anyway.

But Freya wanted to reach her patient and to be sure that she was coping, so she decided to open up a little to Mrs Roberts in the hope that the woman would reciprocate.

'Actually,' Freya said, 'although I'm telling everyone that I'm excited about moving to London, I'm really quite nervous. It's a big hospital and I shan't know anyone.'

'You'll be fine...' Mrs Roberts started, and then paused as Freya gently spoke on.

'I expect everyone is asking if you're excited now that the baby will soon be here?'

Mrs Roberts nodded. *"Not long now!"* She mimicked the regular phrases being thrown daily her way. *"You'll be hoping for a girl after three boys."*

'Are you?' Freya asked. She knew the sex of the baby.

'Of course not. I didn't get pregnant to try for a girl. In fact, I didn't...' It was the closest Mrs Roberts had come to admitting the pregnancy had been an accident, but she quickly rallied. 'Healthy will suit me just fine.'

'Of course,' Freya agreed, and Mrs Roberts changed the subject.

'So you're nervous about leaving?'

'Terrified,' Freya now admitted. 'And I'm wondering how I'm going to fit in.'

'You'll fit in just fine.'

'I hope so,' Freya replied. 'But I'm starting to think I've made a mistake.'

'Well, I know *that* feeling.'

Freya watched as Mrs Roberts closed her eyes and finally admitted the truth. 'It's not that I don't want it—well, I'm sure I will once the baby's here. I just honestly don't know how I'm going to cope. The twins are into everything and Jamie runs wild. Davey's no help. Och, he tries—but he's out the door for work at seven, then not back until six and wanting his supper. I'm trying to freeze a few meals for when the baby comes...'

'That's good.'

'It'll take more than a few frozen dinners to see us through, though.'

Freya saw the flash of tears in Mrs Roberts's eyes and then watched as she buried her face in her hands and started to weep.

'Mam!' Jamie toddled over and pulled at her skirt. 'Mam!'

'Mummy's just a little tired,' Freya said as she gave Mrs Roberts some tissues.

When his inquisitive eyes fell on her stethoscope, Freya took it from her neck and played with it on him, to give Mrs Roberts time to cry by herself.

'Do you want to have a play with it now?'

Delighted with his new toy, Jamie wandered off.

'I'm sorry, Freya.' Mrs Roberts sniffed into the tissue that Freya had pressed into her hand. 'How on earth am I going to manage with another one? I don't get a moment to myself as it is.'

'Have you thought about asking your sister to come and stay with you for a wee while once the baby arrives?' Freya knew that the two women were close.

'I have,' Mrs Roberts nodded, 'but it's a huge imposition.'

'Did she say that?'

'No, no—she offered to come. But I think it's asking too much from her.'

'You'll need help at the start, Mrs Roberts. It's better to take it than to do too much and find yourself overwhelmed and exhausted. If you talk about it with her now she can start to make plans.'

And making plans was what Freya and Mrs Roberts did next.

Her sister Norma would come, and also there was a small crèche that Mrs Roberts occasionally used.

'I might see if they can go there—just one afternoon a week, maybe two—so I can have some time with the new baby.'

'I think that's a wonderful idea,' Freya said. 'Did you know, once I've moved, I've got Mrs Hunt coming in to service my cottage between tenants?'

'I dinnae need a cleaner.'

'Well, I'm only mentioning it in case you might. She's very thorough and her prices are reasonable.'

The appointment went well over time, but it was worth every minute because Mrs Roberts was actually smiling as she retrieved the contents of her bag from the floor.

'You wee monkeys,' she said to the twins. 'Jamie, give Freya back her stethoscope.'

Before the cubicle door was opened Freya had a final word. 'If you're ever feeling overwhelmed when the baby is here—'

Mrs Roberts broke in. 'Then I'll speak to Betty. I honestly will. I feel so much better for talking with you.'

Mrs Roberts rounded up her three sons and Freya saw them to the desk. There she pulled up the appointments on the computer screen and made one for the next Thursday.

'Thanks so much, Freya.'

'You're welcome, Mrs Roberts.'

'Leah, please.'

Freya smiled, for it was high praise indeed to be invited to call Mrs Roberts by her first name.

'I wish you all the very best in London.'

'Thank you.'

Once Mrs Roberts had left Betty came over, and Freya explained a little of what had happened.

'It would have taken a lot for her to admit she's struggling,' Betty agreed. 'Well done, Freya. And don't worry—I'll be keeping a very close eye on her.'

Freya took in Betty's knowing eyes and kind face and knew Mrs Roberts was in the very best of hands. Betty had been a midwife here for nearly forty years. She had, in fact, delivered Freya herself. Right now, though, she was just trying to get the clinic closed somewhat on time.

'I'll shut down the computers and you go and tidy up the cubicles,' Betty said. 'You're going to be late for your own leaving party.'

Goodness, Freya thought when she saw the chaos of the cubicle. It looked as if it had been snowing!

Yet not for a second did she regret that the check-up had spilled more than an hour over time.

Freya tidied up and as she came out saw the waiting room was in semi-darkness.

'Everything's done,' Betty said. 'I'll lock up.'

And then it was finally here—the end of her time at the Cromayr Bay birthing centre.

Freya looked around the waiting room and beyond the desk, thinking of the two birthing suites behind. Then she walked out through the familiar room and into the office to collect her coat before a dash home to get changed for her leaving do.

She hoped her ex wouldn't show up.

Alison would be there. She had cried when Freya had told her that she was moving to London,

'I'll be back all the time,' Freya had reassured her.

'It won't be the same.'

No, it wouldn't be. But then, things hadn't been the same between them since Andrew had died.

Freya had always been private. The only person she really opened up to was Alison—but of course the loss was Alison's, so Freya had tried to remain stoic and strong for her friend, not burdening her with her own grief.

She said goodbye to Betty, who promised she would join them all at the Tavern shortly, and then drove the short distance home in her little purple car.

It was July. The holidaymakers were back and the town was busy.

She parked outside her tiny fisherman's cottage which, although a bit of a renovator's nightmare, was certainly a home.

Each of the houses along the foreshore was a different colour, and Freya's little cottage was a duck-egg-blue with a dark wooden door. Opening it, she stepped into the surprisingly large lounge with its open fireplace, seeing on the mantelpiece her favourite pictures and little mementoes.

Freya headed into the tiny alcove kitchen. It needed a complete overhaul, but everything worked—and anyway, Freya wasn't much of a cook. In pride of place was a coffee machine that Freya was having to leave behind in the move, as there really wasn't that much room in her father's car.

It would be nice for the tenants, Freya thought as she made a very quick coffee.

Freya had the house rented out over the summer, but in October it was going on the market to be sold.

In the cellar she had boxed up some of her belongings. The tiny spare bedroom looked a little bare, but it was ready for its new occupant with a pretty wrought-iron bed and a small chest of drawers.

Freya headed into the main bedroom to change out of

her uniform and get ready for her leaving do, but for a moment she paused.

The unobstructed view of The Firth had sold the place to her on sight. Often at night she simply lay there in bed, looking out, and she had watched the new Queensferry crossing being built. It was a spectacular cable-stayed bridge, and Freya had watched the huge structure unfold from either side until finally the two sides had met.

It was her favourite view on earth, and as she gazed out to it Freya asked herself again what the hell she was doing leaving. Here, she had a job she loved and friends she had grown up with as well as her family, to whom she was very close.

Yet, the very things she loved about Cromayr Bay, were the very reasons she felt she had to leave.

The loss of Alison's baby had hit everyone.

After it had happened Freya had often walked into a shop or a café, and on too many occasions the conversation would suddenly stop.

Everyone knew everyone's business—which wasn't always a good thing. Take tonight—there was a fair chance that her ex, Malcolm, would be at the Tavern. Not that she really thought of him much, but it was always awkward to run into him and see the hurt, angry expression in his eyes before he turned his back on her.

It wasn't just about Malcolm, though. Freya wanted more experience and a fresh start.

She would be thirty soon, she reasoned. If she didn't make the move now then she never would.

Deep down, though, she knew she was running away.

It was going to be hard to leave, but for Freya it was simply too hard to stay.

CHAPTER ONE

'Is anyone...?'

Freya looked up and quickly realised that the woman in theatre scrubs wasn't asking if she might join Freya at her table in the hospital canteen. Instead all she wanted was one of the spare chairs at Freya's table.

People, Freya thought, didn't even bother to speak in full sentences down here.

'Help yourself.' Freya nodded.

And so the lady did.

It was orientation day at the Primary Hospital, and apart from being asked her name and shown where to go Freya really hadn't spoken to anyone. She had tried during the coffee break, but Rita, the woman she had sat next to during the lectures, had gone off to call her husband.

The schedule had been a full one. First there had been an introduction to the Primary—a large general hospital with a major trauma centre. The volume of patients seen in Casualty per annum was, to Freya, staggering, as was the number of deliveries in Maternity, which had reached seven thousand last year.

There was no such thing as orientation day at Cromayr Bay—a new staff member would be shown around and introduced and made welcome. Here, though, Freya sat with approximately fifty fellow nurses, admin staff and

ancillary workers who were commencing, or had just commenced work at the Primary this month alone.

Freya felt like a very small fish in a very large and
rather cold sea.

On Friday she had been in to collect her uniforms and
her lanyard and had got rather lost on her way out of the
huge building. Today, though, sitting in the lecture theatre,
she had found out that the red strip painted on the corridor
wall led to Casualty and the main exit. So that was good
to know. The yellow strip, she had then been told, led to
Maternity and the blue to Outpatients.

'It helps not just the staff and the patients,' the admin
manager had said, 'but it is also far easier to give directions to visitors. We shall soon be adding a green strip for
the Imaging Department. Any more than that and the walls
will start to look like rainbows!'

After a morning of lectures and films they had been
told to head off for lunch and to be back at one.

There was no coloured strip that led to the canteen,
but by following the overhead signs Freya had found it
quite easily.

The place had been packed, and Freya had rather wished
she had thought to bring her own lunch, as most of her fellow orientation candidates seemed to have done. Perhaps
that was why she sat alone.

She hadn't brought any change for the vending ma-
chines, so she'd queued up and selected a salad wrap,
a packet of cheese and biscuits and a coffee, and then
scanned the busy canteen for a table.

They'd all been rather full, but there had been a couple
of seats that had seemed free on a table for four.

'Do you mind if I join you?' Freya had asked.

'We're just leaving,' the man there had said.

They had also left their plates, glasses and cups.

She had to stop comparing things to Cromayr Bay, but all this was just so unlike anything she was used to.

Since her father had left her at her one-bedroom flat, four days ago, Freya hadn't really spoken to anyone. Well, apart from a couple of shop assistants and a worker on the Underground who had helped Freya to buy a travel pass.

She had rung her mother and assured her that everything was fantastic.

'Your dad said the flat's a bit grim.'

It *was* rather grim, but Freya had reassured her mum that it was nothing a few rugs and pictures wouldn't pretty up, and reminded her that it was a brilliant location—just a ten-minute walk to the Underground.

'Is anyone...?'

Freya looked up as another unfinished question was asked by an elderly man in a porter's uniform.

'No,' Freya said, and gestured to an empty seat. 'Help yourself.'

He said nothing in response, just took a seat at the table and opened up some sandwiches, then pulled out a newspaper and started to read.

There was no conversation.

Having finished her wrap, Freya peeled open the foil on her cheese and crackers. But she really wasn't hungry so she put them down and pushed away her plate.

Glancing at her phone, she saw that there were still another fifteen minutes left until she was due back.

'Is this seat...?' asked a snooty, deep, but far from unpleasant male voice.

Freya was suddenly sick to the back teeth of unfinished questions.

'Is this seat *what*?' she asked, but as she looked up her indignation took a rapid back seat as she was momentarily sideswiped by six feet plus of good looks dressed in blue theatre scrubs.

He had straight brown hair that was messy, and was so crumpled-looking that, despite the hour, he appeared to have just got out of bed. A stethoscope hung around his neck, and in his hands was a very laden tray.

Freya regretted her brusque response, but consoled herself that he probably hadn't understood a word she had said.

Oh, but he had!

'Is this seat *taken*?' he enquired, more politely, though the smile he wore had a tart edge.

'Please,' Freya said. 'Help yourself.'

He put down the tray, and Freya assumed when he looked around and then wandered off that he must be locating a spare chair for his companion. On his tray there were two mugs of tea, a carton of milk and six little boxes of cereal—the type that her mother had used to get when the family had gone camping, or in the holidays as a treat, when she and her brothers would fight over who got what.

But instead of a chair and a companion he returned with a spoon.

'Len,' he said to the porter by way of greeting. He got a 'humph' in return, but the good-looking stranger didn't seem in the least bothered by the less than friendly response.

As Freya drank her coffee she tried not to look at him, and pretended not to notice when he opened each box of cereal in turn and poured them into the one bowl with all the flavours combined. It was a heap of cornflakes and chocolate puffs and coloured circles, and then he added to his concoction the small carton of milk.

No, there was no companion about to arrive, for next

he added sugar to both cups of tea and made light work of the first.

And still Freya tried not to notice.

A domestic came round with a trolley and started to pick up the collection of cereal boxes, as well as the mess that the previous occupants had left in their wake.

'Done?' she asked Freya as she reached for her plate.

'Yes, thank you,' she said, and then blinked as the porter—Len—actually spoke.

'Do you mind?'

'Sorry?' Freya asked as he pointed to her plate.

'You're not going to eat those?' he asked, pointing to the open cheese and crackers that Freya hadn't touched.

'No.'

'Do you mind if I have them?'

'Go ahead,' Freya agreed—because, really, what else could she do?

'Ta very much,' Len said, and took out a piece of kitchen paper from his pocket and wrapped the cheese and biscuits in them.

The domestic didn't seem in the least perturbed by this odd exchange, and cleared up the boxes and plates. Then as she wheeled her trolley off, The Man Who Liked His Breakfast Cereal, spoke.

'Here you go, Len.' He pushed a granola bar across the table to him.

'Cheers!' Len pocketed his bounty as he stood up and then walked out of the canteen.

Goodness, Freya thought, people here were *so* odd. She simply couldn't imagine asking a complete stranger for the leftover food on their plate.

But then that deep, snooty voice spoke again and attempted to clarify things a little.

'He only talks to the animals.'

'I'm not with you.'

'Len,' he explained. 'He's miserable around people, but he visits an animal shelter in his free time and he's always after treats for them.'

'Oh!' Freya let out a little laugh.

'You're new,' he said, glancing at her lanyard.

He had realised she was staff, but was quite certain he would have noticed her before if she wasn't new.

She wore a dark shift dress that accentuated her pale bare arms, and her black curly hair was loose and down to her shoulders. From the little he had heard, he guessed she was far from home.

'I'm here for my orientation day,' Freya said.

He grimaced. 'I've done a few of those in my time. The fire lecture, the union rep...'

'We haven't had a fire lecture yet,' Freya said. 'That's this afternoon. I think it's a film, followed by a demonstration.'

'Fun,' he drawled as he rolled his eyes. 'Mind you, I did have a patient who tried to set fire to the ward once...'

She waited for more, but he'd gone back to his cereal.

'Breakfast?' Freya asked.

'And lunch.' He moved on to his second mug of tea. 'Are you new to London as well as the hospital?'

Freya nodded. 'I got here last week.'

'I worked in Glasgow for a while.'

'For how long?'

'A year. I couldn't understand a word anybody said. "Pardon" became my most-used word.'

'I'm having the same problem—although in reverse,' Freya admitted. 'I have to keep repeating myself.'

'I can understand you.'

'Then you're the first.'

'You're not from Glasgow, though?'

She was far too soft spoken for that, he thought. But not soft. He had liked the edge to her tone when he'd asked if the seat was taken. Richard *loved* the challenge of a sullen woman.

'No, I'm from Cromayr Bay.'

'Never heard of it.'

'Fife,' Freya said. 'Overlooking the Firth.'

'Never heard of it,' he said again.

But this time he smiled just a smidge and she couldn't tell if he was teasing.

'How are you finding London?'

'It's early days.' Freya gave a small shrug.

'Ah, after a few late nights you'll come to love it.'

It was then that she noticed his eyes—or rather, it was then that she *properly* noticed them.

In his good-looking face there were several standouts. If she'd been describing him to Alison, his sculpted cheekbones and attractive full mouth were two features she might easily have named, and that his hazel eyes were just so much *more* than hazel. They were the colour of burnt amber, with a smatter of golden flecks, and they made Freya feel as if she were gazing upon an open fire.

Or was that more from the way he absolutely held her gaze as she replayed his words in her mind?

'Ah, but after a few late nights you'll come to love it.'

Those words had sounded like an invitation.

As Freya held their eye contact steady, she wasn't quite sure how, but he made her his sole focus.

And he was hers.

Gone was the canteen, and gone too was the noise.

But then he spoke, and Freya found herself blinking at the intrusion of words.

'So, where will you be working?'

'Maternity. I'm a midwife. The name's Freya,' she

added, and she was not just being polite. His stethoscope was hanging over his lanyard and she wanted to know his name and just who this delectable stranger was.

She would have to wait to find out, though. His pager was trilling. As he looked at it he scooped the last of his cereal into his mouth and then gulped down the remaining tea as he stood.

'I expect you to be fully versed in the operating of a fire extinguisher the next time we meet.'

'I'll do my best,' Freya said, but he had already gone, his large frame moving swiftly through the tables as people made way to let him past.

She watched.

And not idly.

The overhead chimes started then, and Freya heard that the Cardiac Arrest Team was needed in Casualty.

Through the glass windows of the canteen Freya watched as he ran down the corridor, and then she turned her head and surveyed his empty cereal bowl and the two empty cups of tea.

Freya didn't know his name, just that he was gorgeous. Effortlessly so. And way more gorgeous than *she* could handle.

She hadn't been born yesterday. In fact, Freya's thirtieth birthday was fast approaching. And there was something about him that told her he had learnt to flirt from the cradle. There had certainly been a tease and a flirt in his eyes when they spoke—especially with that little quip about late nights.

Well, there would be no late nights spent with *him*! She was far too guarded and sensible for that.

With her lunch break over, Freya headed back to the lecture theatre for the afternoon session of her orientation day. Sure enough it was the fire lecture. She watched the film and tried not to smile when they were given a demonstration on how to use the various fire extinguishers.

And even as she watched and listened Freya wanted to know more about the time her lunch companion's patient had tried to set fire to the ward.

And she wanted to know his name.

Fully versed in the fire policy at the Primary, as well as in the various codes used for emergencies of different natures, and how to report safety hazards, Freya found that it was time for coffee—and, she guessed, another fifteen minutes of standing alone.

'There's a lot to take in, isn't there?' said Rita, the woman who had earlier been sitting next to her.

'There is,' Freya agreed. 'Where will you be working?'

'I used to be a domestic on Maternity. I'm hoping they'll send me back there, but I haven't been told where I'm going yet. You?'

'I'm a midwife, so I'm *certainly* hoping that they'll be sending me there!' Freya joked.

'Pardon?'

'Maternity,' Freya said instead.

'Well, I hope to see you there.'

They headed back for their final lectures about the pay office and superannuation. Rita took furtive notes and Freya did her level best not to tune out completely.

Finally orientation day was concluded, and the fifty or so new Primary Hospital workers all headed for home.

Freya followed the red line, and sure enough was soon approaching Casualty.

And there he was.

The man who had understood her when she spoke.

He must be hungry again, Freya thought, watching him feed coins into a vending machine.

Gosh, he really was good-looking—and just so tall and

broad. Even side-on there was a presence to him. She wondered if she could come up with a witty line about fire extinguishers in the few seconds she'd have before their paths crossed again.

Except she didn't come up with any witty lines, and neither was one needed—because he collected a bottle of water and a bar of chocolate and headed back into Casualty without noticing her at all.

Freya headed towards the Underground, as did seemingly fifty million other people, and stood squashed between them for the four stops to her flat. And surely those same fifty million people were getting off at the same stop, for they all seemed to be herding towards the escalator with her.

She thought of her little purple car at home. The one that would never have survived the motorway—which was the reason her father had driven her here. And she thought of the short drive from the hospital to her home and the gorgeous view that awaited her there.

'Cheer up love!' called out a man working at a flower stall. 'It might never happen.'

Freya jolted as she realised he was calling out to her.

She walked into her dingy flat and let out a sigh.

The place looked no better for her efforts over the past four days. She had washed down the walls, but really they needed several coats of paint. The curtains she had washed had shrunk, Freya had realised when she'd put them back, and now they didn't properly close, falling a foot short of the floor. And there was an awful picture of a horse and cart that had to come down!

Tomorrow, Freya decided. When she would also get a rug to cover the mustard-coloured carpet, she thought as she headed into the kitchen.

It was even worse than her kitchen at Cromayr Bay.

But it wasn't just the flat that was upsetting her. Apart from that gorgeous guy at lunchtime she had barely spoken to a soul since she'd arrived here.

It would be better soon, Freya told herself. Once she got to the maternity unit she would start to make friends.

Wouldn't she?

She was starting to think the flower seller had picked up on her mood correctly. 'It' had indeed happened.

Moving here, Freya was sure, had been a mistake.

CHAPTER TWO

'FIONA, CAN YOU go to Labour and Delivery? I mean Freya.'

Freya nodded. She was getting rather used to being called the wrong name by Stella, the associate unit manager.

'Sure.'

'And can you buddy with Kelly?'

Freya had been working there for a fortnight now, and today she was to go to the labour and delivery unit. 'Buddying' meant that she and Kelly would check each other's CTG readings to ensure that two sets of skilled eyes overlooked the tracings. Even after two weeks it was no less daunting than it had been on her first day.

She had spent the first week in the antenatal clinic and the past few days on the maternity ward, and now she was on her second day in L&D.

There were *so* many staff, and each day there seemed to be new faces. Freya had really clicked with one midwife yesterday, but as it had turned out she'd just been doing an agency shift, so Freya had no idea if she would see her again.

Everyone was so busy, and though they were all professional and nice, there just wasn't the same vibe from her colleagues that Freya was used to.

As she walked to L&D Freya rolled over the top of her

trousers as they were way too loose. Her uniform consisted of dark blue trousers and a pale blue top and it was less than flattering. She couldn't care less, but the sizing must be off because it hung off her. Although she *had* lost a bit of weight since she'd arrived, due to the constant busy pace and the lack of time to do a proper shop.

As she pressed the green button and the doors to L&D parted she saw a woman pushing an IV, walking the corridor with her support person. Freya gave them a smile.

She checked the board and saw that Dr Mina was the obstetrician in charge today. In the short while she had been at the Primary, Freya had worked with her several times, and found her incredibly efficient as well as a calming presence to the patients.

The hand-over was in depth, so that everyone was well-versed on all the patients—both those present now and those expected to arrive over the course of the shift.

'Freya, can you take over from Angela in D5?' asked Pat, the midwife in charge of L&D today. 'She's awaiting an epidural, but finding an anaesthetist this morning is proving a rather hard ask.'

'Has the second-on been paged?' Freya asked, and that earnt her a wry smile from her colleague.

'*Everyone's* been paged, but there's been a five-car pile-up on the M25 and there was already a dissecting triple A being rushed to Theatre, along with a collapse on the paediatric ward. Then we had to call the Crash Caesarean Team out half an hour ago. Right now Anaesthetics are snowed under, and it's a case of if a patient's screaming then at least they're breathing.'

Freya took a breath of her own. That patient-load sounded like a full week's work in Cromayr Bay at the height of summer, but it was just another morning at the Primary.

Or not. Because then Pat explained that it had been an exceptionally busy night in Casualty too.

'Just remind Kathy in D5 that she hasn't been forgotten. Her husband, Ben, is getting upset.'

Freya checked her patient's details and then went into the delivery suite. The lights were low and the suite was dim, and Kathy was kneeling up and holding on to the head of the delivery bed as Angela pressed a hot pack into her back.

'Hi, there,' Freya said as she approached. 'I'm Freya. I'm—'

'Are you an anaesthetist?' Kathy's husband snapped.

'No, I'm a midwife,'

'Not good enough! My wife has been waiting for two hours for an epidural.'

'Please, Ben,' Kathy implored, but then her face screwed up and she leant on her forearm as a contraction came.

Angela helped her through it as Freya checked all the equipment. Angela brought her up to speed with Kathy's progress, but then gestured with her head to the door. Freya followed her out.

'The husband is getting really tense and it's upsetting Kathy,' Angela said.

'I can see that.' Freya nodded.

'He's a great guy—he's just terrified. But Kathy has still got a good way to go. I've called down to Casualty but two of their patients are currently being transferred to ICU, so they're very tied up. The anaesthetist in our theatre is aware, though he's probably half an hour or so away.'

'Okay…'

'You could try calling Switch and asking—'

'No need.'

A voice she recognised, though she hadn't heard it since her orientation day, caused Freya to turn around.

'Oh, Richard!' Angela sighed in relief. 'Am I pleased to see you.'

'Not as pleased as your patients will be. What room?'

'D5 is first,' Angela said. 'It's all set up for you.'

'Thanks, Angela,' he said. 'Freya.'

She gave him a smile. 'Richard.'

Finally she knew his name.

And, more than that, he was still *stunning*.

He had been wearing scrubs when they'd met, but this morning he wore a dark suit and a crisp white shirt with a silver-grey tie. His straight hair was damp, and rather more in need of a cut than the last time she'd seen him, and he was unshaven.

In seconds she took in every delicious detail, and the last few didn't quite fit. He was so well turned out that the unshaven jaw stood out for Freya.

Instead of heading to the suite, he took the patient's notes and walked over to the desk. The sharp, fresh scent of his cologne lingered. Freya saw him removing his jacket as she followed Angela back into D5.

'Good news,' Angela said. 'The anaesthetist is here.'

'Well, where is he, then?' Ben demanded.

'Dr Lewis is just reading up on the notes.' Angela gave Kathy a lovely smile. 'I shall leave you in Freya's hands. You've been amazing, Kathy.'

Kathy nodded and tried to say goodbye, but was overwhelmed by another contraction. Freya took over, rubbing Kathy's back and trying to establish a rapid bond with the woman, and also with her husband.

'Would you like to come and rub her back?' Freya suggested, but Ben stood against the wall and gave a tense shake of his head.

Yes, it was all terribly different from anything she was

used to. Usually Freya would have seen her patients at antenatal clinic, and often their partners too.

'Well done, Kathy,' Freya said as the contraction faded. Knowing that the anaesthetist was here, Freya suggested that Kathy empty her bladder and walked with her, pushing the IV pole, to the en suite bathroom attached to the delivery room.

'He's nervous,' Kathy said, explaining Ben's behaviour.

'Of course he is,' Freya said. 'It's hard work for the women but it's hell on the men.'

That made Kathy laugh a little.

Freya waited outside, and when Kathy came out after washing her hands, she asked Freya a question. 'Do you have children?'

'No.' Freya said. 'I've got nieces and nephews, and my best friend's expecting, but I'd definitely like my own someday.'

She was actually enjoying getting to know the women here, and opening up to people who didn't know her at all, Freya realised. At home, had she said that, it would have been all around town that she and Malcolm were trying for a baby.

'We tried for ages...' Kathy sighed. 'I thought it would never happen.'

'Well, it clearly is.'

'Thanks, Freya,' Kathy said as Freya pushed the IV pole. But as they got to the door she paused. 'Please...' she said. 'Don't mind Ben. His bark is far worse than his bite.'

'I know that. You'll be feeling a lot more comfortable soon, and I'm sure he will too.'

She was just helping Kathy back onto the delivery bed when the door opened and she saw the beautiful man she now knew was called Richard come in.

'Where the *hell* have you been?' Ben said by way of greeting.

'I'm Dr Lewis,' he responded. 'Consultant anaesthetist.' Then he smiled at his patient. 'Hello, Mrs Hudson.'

But Ben wasn't finished yet. 'She was booked to have an epidural hours ago, but she's been left screaming in pain.'

'I'm aware of that, Mr Hudson, and I agree that it's unfortunate, but I'm here now.'

'It's more than unfortunate, it's not good enough,' he retorted.

'Ben, please...' Kathy pleaded, but her husband still wasn't done.

'Where were you?'

'Actually,' Richard said as he rolled up his sleeves, 'I was in bed when I was called to see if I could come in. I'm not supposed to be here until eight.'

It was only just after seven. And Freya understood now why he hadn't shaved.

'Now...' He looked over to his patient as he tied on a plastic apron. 'Would you prefer me to call you Mrs Hudson or Kathy?'

'Kathy.'

'Well, Kathy, we'll have you feeling a lot more comfortable soon.'

He was very meticulous. As Freya helped Kathy to sit on the edge of the bed for the procedure Richard Lewis went through all that had been set up. He made no small talk as he checked and rechecked everything.

'Right,' he said, as if to himself, and then he addressed Kathy. 'You're going to feel a sting from the local anaesthetic and then a bit of pressure. I'll need you to stay as still as you can—do you understand that?'

'I do—but what if I get a contraction.'

'It's fine. I'm used to them. I'll work around it.'

He went through everything that she could expect to feel, and as the next contraction came he put on gloves, waiting for the pain to diminish before the procedure commenced.

'I'm sorry,' Ben said suddenly.

'It's fine,' Richard responded. 'It's awful to see someone you love in pain. However, by all accounts your partner has been doing marvellously. Let's try and make this last bit a whole lot easier for her, shall we?'

Whoa! Freya thought as she held on to Kathy. He had somehow accepted the apology while reminding the husband just who this day was about.

'Why don't you come this side?' Freya suggested to Ben. She knew he was really just terribly anxious. 'You can hold Kathy's hand.'

This time he didn't shake his head and came and took his wife's hand.

Richard worked quietly and soon the epidural was in. Kathy lay back on the delivery bed.

'You'll need to stay in bed now,' Richard reminded her as he disposed of his sharps and then removed his gloves. 'Thank you, Freya. Can I leave my mess to you? I believe I'm wanted in D3.'

'Sure.'

Freya checked Kathy's obs, and those of the baby, and by the time she had tidied up Kathy was indeed starting to feel the benefits of the epidural.

'You should try and get a little rest now,' Freya suggested. 'I'll be in and out, and there's the call bell if you have any concerns at all.'

'Freya!'

Her name was called the second she stepped out of the room. 'Can you go and take the baby in D7?'

Freya nodded and headed to delivery suite number

seven. 'Taking' a baby was wonderful indeed. It combined all the joy with barely a hint of the pain.

Stepping in to the delivery suite, she found the atmosphere was lovely and peaceful. Kelly, one of the other midwives was there, along with the soon-to-be father, who had his arms wrapped around his wife's shoulders.

In fact Kelly was so calm that even when she told Freya that Dr Mina and the anaesthetist had been paged she did it in such an open way that there was no jolt of alarm from the mother.

'The baby is small for the dates and the head is smaller than expected,' she said, and Freya checked all the equipment was ready.

Despite the unexpectedly small head, everything seemed to be under control.

'Try not to push, Sita,' Kelly said. 'Just pant.'

'Okay,' Sita said, and fought against the urge.

'Good girl,' said Kelly. Her focus was totally on the delivery, and she didn't look over when the door opened.

'Hello, there,' Richard said quietly, and Kelly calmly told him the reason for him being paged.

'Thirty-seven weeks and small for dates,' Kelly explained.

The room was getting crowded. Stella had come in after Richard, followed by Dr Mina just as the head was delivered. And now there was Guy Masters, the paediatrician on call, whom Freya had already met.

'Well done, Sita,' Dr Mina said. 'Just breathe and do as Kelly says. Dr Masters is a paediatrician and he's here to check your baby.'

The head really was tiny, and Freya found she was holding her breath as the body slithered out. But even as she accepted him he started to cry. His huge eyes were blinking at the light and his little face was wrinkled.

He was utterly gorgeous, Freya thought as she held this tiny piece of the future in her hands. Tiny, but perfect. And as she rubbed him down Guy was already examining him.

'One that is better out than in,' Guy said.

The baby had clearly not been getting sufficient nutrition in-utero, but he was angry and defiant and utterly perfect.

'I don't think we need you, Richard,' he said as loud cries pierced the room and the baby pinked up beautifully.

'Not with those lungs,' Richard agreed. And it was just as well he wasn't needed because his pager was going off.

He left unnoticed by all, Freya thought. All except her.

'I think he's ready to meet his mum,' Guy said, and Freya popped a little hat on the baby to keep him warm, wrapped him, then carried him over to his waiting parents.

She smiled as she watched a family being born. Freya loved delivering babies, but *taking* them was special too. They always tried to deliver them straight to the mother, but sometimes, as with this unexpected small size, the baby needed a proper examination. Apart from his size this one was doing just fine. Another perfect new life.

The day seemed to be running away from her. Busy, a bit crazy, and after her hectic morning she could only take a coffee break on the run at the desk.

There, Dr Mina was speaking with Richard and Kelly was chatting with Stella about a film they were going to see at the weekend.

'It's supposed to be really good,' Freya commented, subtly fishing to be asked to go with them, but Kelly just nodded her head.

Freya took her lunch in the staff room, and just as she returned she was told that Kathy was ready to push.

When she got to the delivery room Ben was white with fear and Freya gave him a smile.

'I thought you'd gone home,' Ben said.

'And miss out on this?' Freya asked.

Ben proved to be a champion when it came to coaxing Kathy to push. It was clearly an excellent epidural, because she could feel the sensation and some pressure but had no pain.

'Another big push,' Freya encouraged. 'Come on—a really big one, right down into your bottom.'

This time it was Kelly who arrived to take the baby and soon Freya delivered a chunky baby boy. He was gorgeous, and there were tears from both Ben and Kathy as he lay on her stomach, blinking at the world.

'Are you going to cut the cord, Dad?' Kelly asked, and Ben came over with tears in his eyes to have that special moment with his son.

Baby Hudson didn't have a name yet, but by the time Freya was ready for home he'd had his first feed and Kathy had had a well-earned cup of tea.

It hadn't been a particularly busy day, or so Freya had been told, and yet she was exhausted.

The high of Baby Hudson's birth lasted right through the Tube journey, but faded as she began the walk for home.

Freya had never been surrounded by more people, and yet she had never felt more alone.

There was a social club at the hospital, but she was hardly going to walk in on her own, and making friends was proving a lot more difficult than she had anticipated.

However, later, rather than sit alone with her noodles, Freya reminded herself that she did indeed have friends and called Alison.

'How are things?' Alison asked.

'Busy,' Freya said. 'Well, work is—the social life, not so much.'

'But you're in *London*!' Alison said.

'I know…' Freya sighed, because Alison's observation just made it worse. 'I *am* trying,' she admitted. 'I sort of hinted to a couple of girls at work that there was a film I'd like to see, but I felt like a bent coin in a vending machine.'

'Rejected?' Alison laughed.

'Exactly.'

'Keep at it. Just say yes to anything you're invited to.'

'I'll have to be invited somewhere first.'

'You *will* be.'

'How are *you*?' Freya asked. She felt her throat clamp tight, but she swallowed and pushed through, trying to keep her voice casual and light. 'How's the baby.'

'All good. I'm fifteen weeks now, and I swear I've got a bump, although Callum says it's too early.'

Freya hesitated, because women sometimes showed more quickly with a second pregnancy, but she couldn't gauge whether or not that was the right thing to say to Alison now.

Freya dealt with pregnant woman every working day, and she dealt with loss too. And, what was more, she prided herself on dealing with it well. Yet when it came to her friend she felt like an absolute novice, and simply didn't know how to be around the subject of Alison's pregnancy.

Freya was terrified she might break down, and Alison didn't need that. Of course they had both cried together in the days following Andrew's birth, and then his death, but right now Freya was sure it was time to be strong.

'When's your ultrasound?' Freya asked.

'In two weeks' time. I'll believe it's really happening once I've heard its little heart.'

Alison's voice broke then, and Freya closed her eyes when she heard it. 'It will be okay,' she offered.

'You don't *know* that, Freya,' Alison snapped.

'I know, but...' Her voice trailed off.

'Sorry,' Alison said.

'Don't be.'

And then Freya turned on her midwife voice and said all the right things, just as she would to a patient.

But Alison was her best friend. It was awkward and it was difficult and things were different between them.

There was no escaping that.

CHAPTER THREE

RICHARD LEWIS REALLY was stunning.

Even asleep he managed to bring a little skip to Freya's heart when she walked in and saw him, lying across several chairs in the staff room.

Pat and Kelly were deep in conversation there, and didn't seem bothered in the least by the sight of Richard sprawled out.

It bothered Freya—or rather it bothered her senses. She tried not to peek as she stirred her soup, but she didn't try very hard because her eyes kept wandering over.

He hadn't shaved again, and Freya knew he must have been working all night. It was now late morning.

She had been at the Primary for a month now, and he was no less intriguing and no less gorgeous.

During the course of her working week Freya saw him regularly. He had a new registrar, who wasn't yet able to do epidurals unsupervised, so Richard was in L&D quite often to oversee his work. And he was always called if there was a difficulty with a delivery or a Caesarean.

There was rarely time for conversation, though.

Freya considered the Maternity Unit here extremely busy, but *his* workload was incredible. He rushed to emergencies all over the hospital—and that was aside from Theatre and patients in the ICU.

Of course there were many anaesthetists in such a busy hospital, but Freya, despite her warnings to herself, was only interested in one!

Her instincts had been right. He was a heartbreaker, indeed. She had found that out from the other midwives. Not that they'd actually confided in her! No—she was still struggling to fit in. But she had overheard a couple of conversations, and apparently he'd just ended a brief fling with a nurse in Casualty. And Von, one of the other midwives, was *still* hoping that she and Richard might get back together.

She looked over at him. He needed a shave and a haircut. Or rather *he* might think that if he looked in the mirror, but to Freya he looked just fine.

Better than fine!

He was like a bear, Freya thought. Not a fat bear, more like a bear just out of hibernation, all slender and restless and hungry.

And then she smiled at her mad thoughts.

Pat was chatting to Kelly about the film that Freya *still* hadn't seen. 'I was thinking I might go this weekend,' Pat said.

'You *have* to,' said Kelly. 'It's amazing.'

Freya again tried to be brave. 'I'm dying to see it,' she admitted.

'You should.' Kelly looked over and nodded, and then she stood. 'Come on, Pat. We'd better get back.'

Once they'd gone Freya let out a sigh. Over and over she'd been mentioning that she'd love to go and see the film, but there had been no takers. How much more of a hint was she supposed to give?

She sat staring at the television and took a sip of her revolting packet soup. And then a voice—one she had really come to like—chimed deep and low.

'I'll take you to the bloody film.'

She looked over.

'I can take a hint.'

'Sorry?'

'You keep suggesting it every time I'm near. All you have to do ask.'

'I wasn't hinting for *you* to take me!' Freya said, and actually found herself going red. 'I was waiting for one of *them* to ask me along.'

'You're too subtle,' he said, and lay there smiling at her. 'Poor Freya-no-Friends.'

'Don't!' she said, but she was smiling.

'You have to invite yourself—or just go along with them.'

'What? Just turn up? Like a stalker?'

'Well, maybe not.'

'I've *always* had friends,' Freya said, for she had been giving it some considerable thought. 'But I've realised that's because we all grew up together. I've never actually had to *make* any.'

'Rubbish,' he scoffed. 'You're saying that because you grew up in a village you all get along?'

'It's not a village.'

'Well, town or whatever,' he said. 'But I'm sure there are people you don't like there. You're not automatically friends with everyone you grew up with. God, I loathed Derek next door, and we had to play together all the time.'

'Why?'

'That's for another time.'

He stretched and yawned and sat up, more bear-like than ever as he gave himself a sort of shake.

'I'm starving,' he said.

'I've got some soup.'

'No, thanks.' Richard pulled a face. 'I'm going to head down to the canteen. What time do you finish?'

She'd thought he must have been joking about going out. 'Not until nine.'

'Well, I'm covering for Simon until eight, so I doubt I'll get away much before then. I'll meet you at the entrance to Casualty.'

'I don't even know if the film's on,' Freya said. 'Or the session time.'

'Times,' he corrected. 'It's on everywhere. You're not in Cromayr Bay now, where they have to come and change the reels…'

He was teasing, yet it made her laugh. 'It's not *that* bad.'

'Give me your number and if I can I'll text you if I'm not going to make it. But if I'm not there by a quarter past, just head for home. It'll mean I'm stuck somewhere—nothing else. I won't be avoiding you!'

He even turned the subject of her being a little lonely into a smile.

'I'll look forward to it,' Freya said, and recited her number. 'And, no, I won't be upset if…' she started, but her voice trailed off as Stella came in.

'Freya, I know you're not due back yet, but we've got a bit of a rush on.'

'Of course,' Freya said, and she stood and finished the last of her soup, a little surprised when Richard spoke again.

'I'll see you around nine, then?'

Freya felt her cheeks were a little warm as she walked back round to the unit—because he had made it clear in front of Stella that they were meeting up tonight.

It meant nothing, she told herself. It was just two colleagues going out. If it had been Kelly or Pat or anyone else she wouldn't be giving it too much thought and Stella was surely the same.

'See Rose?' Stella said, and pointed over to Rita, the domestic who had done her orientation with Freya on her first day.

'Rita,' Freya corrected as they walked.

'Rita, then.' Stella nodded. 'See how it looks like she's emptying the rubbish…?'

'Er…yes,' Freya answered.

'Well, she's not—she's actually collecting all the discarded hearts…'

Freya pressed her lips together as she realised what Stella meant, and even managed a wry smile as Stella spoke on.

'Oh, look, she's going under the bed. Must have found another one. You know how he dashes from one emergency to another?' She didn't await Freya's response. 'Well, he's the same with women.'

'Stella.' Freya stopped walking and gave her senior a wide smile—because she knew his reputation and because Stella had made her smile. 'We're going to the cinema. No more, no less.'

'Don't say I didn't warn you.'

It was a slow evening by Primary Hospital standards, which would have meant a chaotic one back home! But by nine Freya was in the changing room. She took her phone from her locker, as she chose not to have it on her at work, and found herself letting out a breath of relief that there was no text from Richard to say he couldn't make it.

And then she swallowed, because relief possibly wasn't the right word.

Freya was nervous about tonight.

She so wanted to make friends.

Only this didn't feel like any friendship Freya had ever known!

She pulled off her horrible uniform, changed into the grey linen dress and ballet pumps she had worn into work and let her hair down, pulling her curls out with her fingers.

In the end it was actually Freya who was a little late, and when she arrived at the entrance to Casualty he was checking his phone.

He was out of scrubs and in a suit, although minus a tie, and beside him Freya felt rather drab.

She looked far from drab, though. In fact, Richard thought as she walked towards him, she was wearing the same dress she had been on the day they had met.

And that was concerning, because usually he couldn't recall what any woman had worn the previous night, let alone in previous weeks. He'd even joked to a friend that he'd be hell at reporting a missing person because he'd be unable to tell the police what the missing person was wearing.

He didn't really notice such things, other than thinking, *Oh, she looks nice.*

With Freya though he'd be able to describe in detail to any police officer that the dress was grey linen, and it was a touch looser than it had been on the day they had met.

Yes, Officer, she had on black pumps and no stockings, just pale slender legs. And her hair was worn down. It didn't actually sit on her shoulders since it's too curly for that, it just holds its wild shape there. And she has green eyes, Officer, and soft full lips.

Anything else? the officer would ask.

Well, she's been a bit lonely since she arrived here, he would say. *I didn't give it too much thought at the time...*

But he was giving it some serious thought now.

Not that he showed his concern. Richard, thanks to his job, was incredibly good at that.

'Right,' he said as they headed out onto the street. 'The film is on at ten, so if we skip all the trailers we'll have time to go and get something decent to eat. I am sick of eating on the run.'

'That sounds brilliant.'

'Are you on in the morning?' he asked.

Freya nodded.

'And me.'

And then Freya was delivered another thinly veiled warning as Stella dashed past them to a car in which presumably her husband had come to meet her. 'Enjoy *the film*, Freya!'

'I will,' Freya called back.

'Has she been telling tales about me?' Richard asked as they walked out onto the street.

'No!'

The street was busy enough that it could have been a Saturday during the day back home, and she was glad it was dark enough that he'd hopefully missed her blush as she lied.

'Of course she has,' Richard said. 'And they're all true.'

'Then it's a good job we're just heading out to see a film,' Freya said.

'Indeed.'

But first they would eat...

'Is Italian okay?' he checked, and she nodded as he led them to a very lovely casual-looking restaurant, tucked away from the main street.

Freya only realised just how hungry she was as the gorgeous scents inside hit her, and they were guided to a table looking out onto the street.

'Can I get you some drinks to start?' the waiter offered.

'Freya?' Richard asked.

'Just water.'

'And me,' Richard said. 'Sparkling?'

'Lovely,' Freya agreed.

The menu was delectable, and she decided on a creamy carbonara, while Richard settled for *osso bucco*.

'So,' he said when their order was in, 'how are you finding it at the Primary?'

'It's fine,' Freya said, and she saw his eyes narrow. 'Well, it's a bit overwhelming. I expected it to be busy, of course, but I didn't realise it would be quite so full-on.'

'What was it like where you worked before?'

'I was in a birthing centre attached to a hospital. We saw the mothers for all their antenatal care, then right up to the postnatal check.'

'How many deliveries at the centre?' Richard asked.

'About a hundred a year. So it's been a big change for me to come somewhere that averages more than that in a week. Still, I wanted the experience.'

'You could have got that more locally,' Richard said, tearing open a bread roll. 'The Women's Hospital in Edinburgh surely delivers a similar amount?'

'Yes,' Freya agreed. 'I did a stint there during my training. But I wanted something completely different, and it was sort of now or never.'

'Are your parents back home?'

'And my brothers.' Freya nodded.

'Do you all get on?' he asked, because despite himself he wanted to know more. Surely there must be more of a reason she had left—not just in her work, but her home, friends and family too?

'Oh, yes. I've got my own place, but I see plenty of them. The older brother, though they're both younger than me, has got two children. I delivered the younger one.'

'I can't imagine having a sister-in-law, let alone being that close to her.'

'Don't you have siblings?' Freya asked.

'No, there's just me.'

'And are you from London?'

'Kent.'

'Do you get back there much?'

'Now and then,' Richard said, and then he hesitated.

He rarely spoke about his family, but he felt no sense of her probing beyond what he was comfortable with, and actually he found it was nice to sit and chat.

'I see my father sometimes, and my mother's here in London. She's just got engaged.' He rolled his eyes, just as their meals were delivered. *'Again.'*

Then came the pepper grinder, and the parmesan cheese, and he thought certainly they would speak about the food now, or the film they were about to see—or even, as Richard usually would, get on with flirting. And yet he was still curious to hear more about her.

'Do you miss your old job?'

'Yes and no,' Freya said. 'I was often delivering the babies of people I'd been to school with, or their wives. And I know a lot of people around town. And while it's nice knowing your patients…'

He nodded. 'My father's a GP. I know only too well the downside. He was never off duty—even going out for a meal like this he'd be interrupted. The only time I remember him getting away from work was if we went on holiday, and even then patients would call him for advice.'

'I don't mind that so much,' Freya admitted.

Her dismissal of the intrusion aspect of things surprised him.

'It's more the fact of everyone knowing everyone else's

business,' she explained. 'And of course when a pregnancy goes wrong it's much harder.'

'It's just part of the job,' Richard said.

'Yes, but it's more difficult when you know the patient.'

'Perhaps…'

To Freya, he didn't sound as if he necessarily agreed. 'There's no *perhaps* about it.'

He opened his mouth to say something, but then changed his mind. It had been a very long day, and they were here to relax after all.

Still, there was something he really would like to know. 'Was there a break-up involved?' he asked.

'Sorry?'

'Is that the reason you left—is there an ex-Mr Freya back home…'

'No!' She laughed. 'I've never been married, but I did break up with someone earlier in the year. It really didn't have anything to do with my decision to leave, though.'

'Are you sure?' Richard frowned through disbelieving eyes.

She was very guarded and, although they were chatting easily, he sensed she was being prudent in her responses.

For once he wanted to dig for the truth from a woman.

'Well, it might have had *some* influence on it,' she admitted reluctantly. 'There's nothing much worse than going into a pub or a restaurant and knowing there's a pretty good chance that your ex will be there. It was a bit messy, I guess.'

'Who ended it?'

'Me,' Freya said. 'We'd been together for ages and I just…' She didn't want to talk about Alison's baby and the pregnancy that had gone wrong. But it had been that which had heralded the end for her and Malcolm. 'I was going through a bit of a tough time and he didn't help matters…'

She gave a thin smile. 'And so, before even the very curl of his hair started to irk me, I ended it. I guess he wasn't the love of my life.'

'There's no such thing,' Richard declared. 'Work is the only love of my life and I intend to remain faithful to that.'

'How do you do it?' Freya asked. 'I know how wrung out *I* feel after an emergency, and yet you deal with them each day.'

'It's my oxygen,' Richard said. 'There's nothing I'd rather be doing. Although,' he admitted, 'I don't want to end up like my father. There has to be a balance. I go away a lot on my days off—try to get well away from the hospital.' He gave a tight smile. 'I have some choices that need to be made.'

'Such as…?'

He gave a small shake of his head that told her not to go there. And when she didn't push for more information Richard could have reached over and kissed her there and then.

He didn't, of course, but the thought was there as their eyes locked.

Freya felt the heat spread over her cheeks as their eyes held, and yet she did not tear her gaze away.

God, he was good, Freya thought, for he turned her on without so much as a touch.

And despite her insistence that tonight was about nothing more than seeing a film, she was now heeding Stella's warnings.

It had been lust at first sight, she knew.

And she would not be acting on it.

Freya wasn't like that. One boyfriend at the end of school and throughout her nursing training. A gap of two years and then Malcolm.

A fling with a sexy anaesthetist was so *not* something

Freya would do. And it *would* be a fling, for he'd warned her—was warning her right now—that everything she'd heard about him was true.

So she reached for her water and tried to think of something to say as she peeled her mind away from sex.

Because that was all it would be.

Sex.

Ah, but it would be sex with *him*.

'So your mother's engaged?' Freya asked. 'Again?'

He knew she was changing the subject.

Although they were speaking about his family, their minds had just been on sex. He wanted to feel her hair... he wanted to delve into those mixed message eyes.

She almost scalded him with a look, and behind the walls she'd put up there lurked desire.

And he liked her odd sullen moments, interspersed by the brightness of her smile.

But, no, this was not what she needed.

He might have a well-deserved reputation, but he wasn't an utter bastard.

Freya was by her own admission a little lonely, a touch overwhelmed, and he would not be meddling with that pretty head.

So, back to her question. He had to think for a moment what it was. Ah, yes, the many loves of his mother's life.

'My mother is about to enter into her fourth marriage. My father isn't quite so bad. He's only been married and divorced twice. I doubt he'll be taking that step again.' He gave a tight smile. 'Thank God! It really is hard coming up with a new speech each time.'

'Her *fourth*!'

He nodded. 'She left us when I was fifteen, and I'm now thirty-three, so it's not quite as bad as it sounds.' He saw her wide eyes. 'Well, maybe it is. My mother is high-end drama and she just wasn't cut out to be the wife of a country GP. She loathed it. And since she broke up with my father—'

He went quiet, for the first time since they had met. And then...

'Freya?' he said.

'Yes?'

'We've missed the film.'

'Oh!'

She looked around the restaurant and noticed the other diners were thinning out, and then she glanced at her phone. It was coming up for eleven.

'Do you want dessert or coffee?' he offered.

'No, no...' She shook her head.

He walked her to the Underground station and there, she assumed, they would go their separate ways.

'I'll see you home,' he said, when she told him where it was.

'It's only four stops,' Freya protested—but not too much. She still wasn't quite used to the Tube, and she did feel a bit nervous at night. It would be nice to have company.

Or rather it would be nice to have *his* company.

'We're here,' Freya said as they arrived at her flat.

'Well, I'm sorry you didn't get to see your film.'

Freya wasn't sorry.

'It's fine,' she said, toying with whether or not to ask him in and deciding that it would be foolish at best. There was a kiss in the air—she could feel it—and as she looked up at him she wondered how that gorgeous unshaven jaw would feel pressed hard against hers.

'Well, another time, then,' Richard said, resisting the urge to kiss her against the wall.

She wanted a friend, he reminded himself. No more than that.

'Thanks for a nice night. It was good to...' She gave a shrug. 'Well, it was nice not to be talking about babies.'

'All work and no play?' Richard said.

'Something like that.'

She took out her key and he watched as she put it into the lock. That was the difference with Freya—she didn't stand there awaiting his kiss. She didn't seem to want the complication of *them* either.

And yet there was want.

It was a sultry summer night that deserved to end in bed, but Richard was behaving himself.

'Night, Freya.'

'Night, Richard.'

She walked inside, closed the door behind her and leant against it, taking a long breath in.

Had there been a double-lock she would have turned it. Instead she made do with the security chain.

But only to keep herself in.

There was a kiss waiting on the other side of that door— she was sure of it.

And not just a kiss.

Who was she kidding?

It hadn't been a kiss in the air out there—it had been *sex*.

But a fling with Richard Lewis would be foolish at best. Freya didn't do that type of thing. And it *would* be a fling—she knew that. He'd as good as told her so himself.

She told herself that she could never regret a sensible decision. That in the morning she would wake up and be delighted that she'd avoided the awkwardness that would have surely followed.

Except in the morning Freya didn't feel delighted.

She only felt regret.

CHAPTER FOUR

'How was the film?' Stella asked as Freya walked with her from the changing room.

'Great,' Freya answered. 'It's well worth seeing.'

She was saved from further questioning as the overhead chimes went off, summoning the Trauma Team to Casualty.

She certainly wasn't about to tell Stella that they'd never actually made it to the cinema, as she knew Stella would just read more into it than there had been.

It was unusually quiet, so Freya took the lull in proceedings as a chance to check stock. She had just pulled out the suction catheters and was ticking the order form when the overhead chimes went off again.

They were a common occurrence in a busy hospital such as this, but the summons that came was one that Freya hadn't yet heard.

'Obstetrics Squad to Casualty.'

Freya wasn't a part of the Obstetrics Squad. She had been told about it during her interview, though. Each Maternity shift, a senior midwife carried a pager and would attend to any obstetric emergency elsewhere in the hospital, along with an obstetrician and anaesthetist.

New staff had to attend at least three off-unit emergencies as an observer, and then Dr Mina had to approve them before they were made a part of that team. But just because she wasn't part of the team it didn't mean that there was nothing for Freya to do.

She ran down to the equipment room and opened up the door, and was pulling out the emergency trolley as Stella and Kelly came running from opposite directions.

'Dr Mina's already down there,' Stella informed Kelly, who held the pager for the Obstetrics Squad today. 'Freya, go and observe.'

Freya nodded. She was nervous about this role, yet keen for the experience.

The chimes were pinging again.

'Here…'

It was Len the porter, who had caught up and took over the other side of the trolley, allowing Kelly to run on ahead.

There was everything that might be required, including a neonatal cot, even though there would be one in Emergency. The trolley was set up for any eventuality.

As she swept into Casualty, Freya acknowledged that she was nervous but consoled herself that she was just there to observe. Even if she never made the team it would be good experience for when she went back to Cromayr Bay.

When.

There was no time to dwell on that word, though it jolted her.

Richard was at the head of one of the resuscitation beds and only briefly glanced up when she came in.

'Next bed,' he said, clearly knowing that she wouldn't have been down there before. He gestured with his head to a curtained area beside him, from behind which came the sound of equipment and people, and above all that the screams of a woman.

They were terrified screams and the woman sounded in pain.

'Thanks.' Freya stepped in and saw there was organised chaos taking place.

Dominic, his registrar, was at the head of the bed and the trauma team were around the woman. So too was Dr Mina, tiny in green scrubs and yet authoritative all the same.

She had a Doppler on the woman's stomach and there was the sound of a rapid heartbeat.

'Stay back and observe,' Kelly said. 'You'll be doing this yourself soon.'

There wasn't actually room for her to do anything *but* observe.

An older woman dressed in scrubs was talking to the patient. 'You're okay, Louise,' she said in an Irish brogue. 'We're taking care of you now…'

Louise had on a hard collar, and from what Freya could make out she had been involved in a high-impact motor vehicle accident. There was blunt trauma to her chest and abdomen as well as a head injury.

And she was twenty-six weeks pregnant.

'Louise.' Kelly moved near the head of the bed. 'Your baby has a strong heartbeat…'

But nothing would calm the woman. Louise Eames was absolutely terrified and perhaps, after her head injury, confused too.

There were also concerns that she had abdominal bleeding.

'I'm May, the Unit Manager in this madhouse.' The Irish woman stepped back and spoke to Freya as Kelly took over reassuring the patient. 'I'm a midwife myself. All looks well but, as you know, pregnant women can mask symptoms. I'm worried that she's worse than her observations are showing.'

It was nice to be talked through it all. Most of it Freya

knew, but she hadn't actually seen the Obstetrics Squad in action.

'I've told NICU to hold a cot, in case she has to be delivered.' May said. 'Here's Richard now.'

Richard spoke for a moment with Dominic, and then Dominic stepped out—Freya guessed to take over the patient in the next bed.

'Hello, Louise.'

He spoke as if they had already met, Freya thought. There was just something so reassuring about his voice.

'I'm Dr Lewis, Consultant Anaesthetist.'

Louise screamed again.

'No,' he said. 'No screaming. Save that oxygen for your baby. Now, I want to have another listen to your chest.'

'That's a good girl,' Kelly said to Louise, who was quietening down—though that wasn't necessarily a good sign.

'We're going to get her round for a CT,' Dr Mina said. She and Richard discussed sedation, but Louise seemed a lot calmer now.

The CT was swift, and showed a small tear on Louise's spleen, but everything looked fine with the baby.

'Louise.' Dr Mina spoke to her. 'The hard collar can come off now and you'll be more comfortable. The baby is doing well, but we're going to move you now to the Intensive Care Unit, so that we can keep a close eye on both of you.'

'Will my baby be okay?' It was all Louise wanted to know.

'Everything is looking fine for now,' Dr Mina said. 'But, Louise, if we need to deliver you, then we will.'

ICU was all ready and waiting, and absolutely the right place for Louise to be.

Freya listened as May gave a detailed hand-over to the Critical Care Nurse. It was scary for Louise to be there, no doubt, but after the noise of Emergency it was certainly a lot calmer here.

'Thank you,' Dr Mina said to the midwifery staff as they gathered up their equipment to leave.

Richard didn't look up as he was already with another patient and completely focussed.

God, what a job he had, Freya thought as they headed out.

'Poor thing,' Kelly said, as they made their way back, but then she moved straight on to business. 'We'll have to check the trolley as soon as we get back,' she told Freya. 'Just in case we're called again.'

'I hope we're not,' Freya said.

But hope didn't work.

Just after three the chimes went off again. Freya was taking a baby for Pat when she heard them, and they didn't even share a glance—instead they focussed on the little life coming into the world.

Working at The Primary was, Freya thought as she came out of the delivery suite, just all so *intense*.

'Were the chimes for Louise?' Freya asked Stella, who was writing up the board against a background of screams from a woman in the bathroom.

'Yes.' Stella nodded. 'Maternal compromise.'

And then there was paperwork—so much paperwork—only today Freya used it as an excuse and a reason for lingering at the nursing station until well after four, when Kelly came back.

She was wearing a pink theatre cap and still somehow brimming with energy as she and Stella commenced restocking the emergency trolley.

'Mum dropped her blood pressure. Thankfully they were straight onto her. The baby's out.'

He was doing well for dates, but it was Louise that was

the main concern. The small tear on her spleen had extended and, as Dr Mina had explained, the signs of hypovolemia were more subtle in pregnancy.

Freya was utterly exhausted as she made her way home.

'Cheer up, love, it might never happen,' said the flower seller, and Freya managed not to shoot him a look.

She stepped into her flat and just flopped onto the couch—lay there staring at the peeling paint on the ceiling, feeling utterly wrung out. Every second at work she felt as if she were on a roller coaster that didn't allow time for catching her breath, or time to reflect.

Poor Louise… She'd been incredibly well taken care of—Freya knew that—but it was all so different from everything she was used to.

Which was what she had wanted, of course. And she was certainly getting experience. But it was draining her.

Stella had told her there would be a case follow-up for Louise, in which Dr Mina would go into greater detail, and Freya was truly grateful that she'd been sent down to Casualty to observe. She really was gaining experience, and if ever a mother came into Cromayr Bay with blunt force trauma…

Freya halted herself there, but it was too late. She knew in that moment that she was imagining herself back at home, just as she had this morning.

But she wasn't *just* here to gain experience. If she'd wanted that, as Richard had pointed out, she could have gained it rather more locally.

No, she had *moved* to London.

Freya hauled herself to the shower and then, having pulled on a robe, surveyed the contents of her fridge.

There wasn't much. She had meant to stop and pick up a few things on her way home. Now she had neither the energy nor the enthusiasm to go out again.

A knock on the door had her padding down the hall— she guessed it would be her neighbour, as their post got muddled on occasion.

Instead it was an unexpected sight for sore eyes.

Richard.

He'd had a haircut and was clean-shaven. And he was wearing a suit, but no tie, and he looked incredibly tired but still breathtakingly handsome.

'What are you doing here?' Freya asked.

He tried not to notice that she wore only a robe and that her hair was wet as he answered. 'We have a film to see.'

CHAPTER FIVE

'STELLA ASKED ME earlier if I'd enjoyed it…' said Richard.

'She asked me too.' Freya smiled. 'What did you say?'

'I said it was very good, and then I had the awful feeling I was going to be questioned further, but thankfully she had to rush off…'

'Yes, it's been one helluva day,' Freya said. 'How's Louise?'

'Critical.'

'I'm not a reporter, Richard. You can tell me how she really is.'

'She's very unstable. She's had a splenectomy and a Caesarean and has been given a lot of blood. It's going to be a very long night for her.'

'Poor thing.' She was about to let him in, but then she shook her head. 'To be honest, I'm not really in the mood to go out.'

'Fair enough.' Few women refused him, but he found it was rather refreshing. Richard liked her ways.

'We'll do the film another time, maybe?'

'Sure.'

Freya looked at him. He was a man she could never keep, but that didn't matter now. For in her heart Freya knew she would be leaving London soon.

'You can come in,' Freya said. 'If you want to.'

And Richard did want to.

He came through the door and Freya could feel his eyes on her bottom as she led him down the hallway.

His eyes *were* on her bottom—for a moment—but then he looked at the trail of moisture her hair had left on her robe, and then he looked down to her long, bare legs.

He didn't notice the mustard carpet, nor the curtains hanging too short, he simply noticed *her*. As he had from the very first day they had met.

They faced each other, and the want that had been there for a long time, certainly on the doorstep last night, seemed to have followed them into her flat.

'I'll go and get dressed.'

Please don't, Richard thought, but didn't say.

As if she could hear him Freya looked up into his eyes.

'If you disappear on me, at least I'll know what to tell the police,' he said.

'Sorry?'

'She was wearing a pale robe...'

'Oh.'

Freya didn't really understand, but there was a smoky edge to his voice, and as he further explained their eyes locked.

'I don't usually notice what women wear—well, not to the extent that I do with you.'

This morning Freya had regretted her sensible decision last night not to invite him in. Now she wanted to be reckless.

Richard felt as if he could see the barriers between them tumbling down before his eyes. And, yes, desire *did* reside behind her green gaze.

'What else was this woman in a pale robe wearing?' Freya asked. 'Slippers?'

'No,' Richard said, his eyes never leaving hers. For he

had already seen her painted toes. 'Her feet were bare and her hair was damp…' His hand came up and he picked up a heavy coil of black hair, as he had ached to do from day one. 'And,' he added, 'I'm quite sure she didn't have any underwear on…'

He watched her mouth part in a smile and lust punched like a fist as they teased and flirted and turned each other on.

'I wish you hadn't shaved,' she whispered as his mouth came to hers.

And then she changed her mind, because instead of rough kisses she got the tang of cologne and Richard's clean-shaven cheek against hers.

'Smooth can be good,' he told her as his hand slid behind her neck.

Her skin flared beneath his fingers and the feel of his cheek had her mouth searching for his.

But then he spoke. 'Freya…'

She frowned at the slight hesitation in his voice, for it was unfamiliar. He was always, *always* so confident and direct.

Freya pulled back her head and those gorgeous eyes of his awaited her.

Richard was not one to spoil the moment, but his conscience niggled and he wanted to make things absolutely clear to Freya. People could trust him with their lives, but not with their hearts, and he wanted to be sure she understood that before things went further.

'Don't rely on me.'

It was the oddest thing to say, perhaps, and yet the kindest.

'I get it, Richard.'

He wasn't going to be the cure for her loneliness. Richard Lewis wasn't going to be the love of her life.

Yesterday it might have mattered. But now she knew it didn't have to last for ever, or even for more than this night, because her time in London was finite. And she *wanted* this night with him.

It was Freya who moved to close the gap between their mouths. But it was definitely Richard who kissed her, softly at first, but warmly and thoroughly. Freya's mouth felt so exquisitely tender that even the gentlest of his kisses felt bruising.

The moan as his tongue slipped inside came from her. And then, for the first time since she'd arrived, London fell silent. Save for the sound of *them*.

His breathing was ragged and their mouths were frenzied. And surely he'd kissed the oxygen from her because he made her dizzy, and his tongue was so expert and thorough that it made her crave more of him.

His hands undid the belt of her robe. He freed one arm, then the other, and as it slid to the floor she felt cool air on the back of her body—a contrast to the warm rough fabric of his suit and the press of metal and buttons on her naked front.

Freya had never known such raw passion. Their tongues jostled and then she was pressing herself into him, her hands clutching his hair as his hands spanned her waist.

He guided them so that they moved to the wall as if as one. His kisses were certainly not smooth now—they were indecent and delicious and Freya was lost in them. Their chins bumped, their teeth clashed. She wanted to climb him and wrap her body around him.

Freya was tackling his belt, to free him, and then she felt his hard warmth leap towards her hand.

Richard reached into his jacket pocket for a condom, and it was an impatient pause for them both as he sheathed himself. She ached to have him inside her, and he ached to be there too.

And so he rectified things, thrusting in and taking her against the wall.

Freya had never been so thoroughly taken, and it felt sublime. He lifted her so that her legs could wrap around him and she knew she had never moved so seductively. He exposed a side to her that she did not recognise, because she had always been a touch reticent in bed.

Not now.

His fingers dug into her buttocks as she ground against him, and instead of feeling herself holding back, she was *more* herself with him.

She was so light that he could put one hand against the wall and hold her round her waist with the other. And then he changed the pace...

There was a scream building in her throat, which was clamped closed, so it waited there, trying to burst free. And then there came a breathless shout from him, followed by a rush of energy along her spine as he came deep within her. Finally her scream found its release, but it came out in staccato sobs as she throbbed to his beat.

His hands soothed now, rather than inflamed, and he seemed to know that this wasn't a Freya she knew.

And it wasn't.

Her head came to his shoulder and she felt the fabric of his jacket. He was completely dressed, and she was utterly naked. And now there was a smidgen of shame creeping in for Freya—just a curl of guilt as he lowered her down to the floor, yet still held her tightly.

He buried his head in her damp hair and then she felt his lips near her ear. 'I only wanted a cup of tea.'

Richard made her laugh. He just did.

Having sorted out his clothes, he picked up her robe

and helped her into it, then did up the very same belt she had so readily allowed him to open.

They were both still a touch breathless, still trying to find their balance again,—but, *God*, they felt better.

She went and sat on the sofa, where she'd been lying earlier. Richard looked utterly normal—not even particularly dishevelled. His hair fell into perfect shape, whereas Freya was quite sure hers was in knots.

But she didn't care.

He came and joined her on the sofa, and though they didn't speak it wasn't awkward. It was nice to lie down with her head on his lap, looking up at him as he played with her hair. It was relaxing *not* to speak.

He looked around at her flat and saw for the first time the mustard carpet and odd curtains. Even odder, though, was the fact that there was nothing that spoke of *her*.

Well, there were some books and magazines on a shelf, but there was a large picture on the wall of a horse and carriage, and he was certain it hadn't been wrapped in a blanket and lovingly moved down from Scotland.

'Do you like horses, Freya?' he asked.

'Not particularly. Why?'

'There's a picture of one on your wall.'

She looked over to where his gaze fell. 'I know. I can't get it down.'

Well, that wasn't quite true. Freya had a little step ladder, which she'd used when she'd re-hung the curtains, but she simply hadn't got around to taking the horse and cart picture down. It wasn't as if she had anything to replace it with. It would do for now.

And, anyway, there were far better things to look at. Gosh, it was nice to lie there, Freya thought, looking up at Richard.

And for Richard it was nice too—nice to feel her hair, because it had entranced him.

He looked down, but not into her eyes. Her robe was hanging open a little, and he could see the curve of her breast and the edge of a pink areola beckoning. He wanted to slip his hand in…

But sustenance first.

'I'm starving.'

He wasn't asking her to cook for him—a bowl of cereal was his usual choice when in a rush, and he *was* in a rush. To resume proceedings!

He hauled her off his lap and walked through to her tiny kitchen, where he opened up the cupboards while Freya lay there, liking it that he hadn't asked if he could do so.

Usually that would have made her tense. She recalled well how she had sucked in a breath when she had bought her little cottage and Malcolm had opened her fridge. But now she lay smiling as Richard opened and closed her cupboards.

'You have absolutely nothing to eat,' Richard said when he came back. 'Not even cereal.'

'I meant to stop at the shops on the way home from work. I think there's some soup…'

'That's not going to cut it. Come on,' he said. 'Get dressed.'

'We could always ring for pizza,' Freya suggested.

He was tempted. There was a huge appeal in the thought of having pizza delivered and then moving straight to bed. And he had seen from his search of the fridge that there was a bottle of wine there.

A perfect evening.

Except—rarely for him—the pleasure was laced with guilt.

Did she fully get that he didn't *do* the dating thing?

He wasn't that bad—it wasn't *all* bed. Just…mostly.

He had come here tonight fully intending to take Freya to that damned film—which was actually quite a concession for him. Richard couldn't remember the last time he had been to the cinema.

But now he had to be clear. Richard wanted to make sure that she didn't think this might lead to anything more than a few casual dates and a whole lot of bed.

While he hoped he had spelled things out yesterday— and although getting pizza and going straight to bed would be easier and far more pleasant—Richard knew that he needed to tell her that this night wouldn't change anything.

Yet clearly it was going to.

For they were soon back at the Italian restaurant—but as lovers this time.

CHAPTER SIX

TONIGHT IT WAS Richard who had the carbonara.

Freya chose spaghetti, and it came with a rich, meaty tomato sauce.

'You did it again,' Richard said.

'What?'

'When I saw your carbonara last night I regretted my choice...' And then he stopped, because he'd been about to say that next time they came here the spaghetti with the rich, meaty tomato sauce was what he'd want.

But he didn't.

Instead he remembered he was off work tomorrow and ordered a bottle of red.

'I don't like drinking if I'm working the next day,' he explained. 'But I've got a few days off now.'

'And me.' Freya smiled.

He wondered if she was waiting for him to suggest they do something together.

Ah yes, *The Talk*, Richard reminded himself.

Except Freya got there first.

'I'm going home for a couple of days before a stint on nights,' she said. 'I've got a new lot of tenants arriving at my cottage next week.'

'Holidaymakers?' Richard said.

'Yes, they're there for two weeks and then I've another

lot coming in. I've arranged for someone to come in and clean, and change the sheets and things, but I just need to sort a few things out.'

'Don't you hate having people staying at your house?'

'I've put a lot of stuff in the cellar,' Freya said. 'And that's locked. It doesn't bother me.'

'But isn't it a hassle?'

'Not really.' Freya shrugged. 'And even if it is at times, then it's worth it. It helps a lot with the mortgage, though in a couple of months it's going on the market...' Freya halted.

Or was it?

She recalled that just before Richard had arrived her plans had started to change. She needed to be alone to think about that, to decide what she was going to do, and so she asked about him instead.

'What about you? Do you have plans?'

'I have an interview.'

'Ah, that explains the haircut,' Freya said as she twirled spaghetti around her fork.

'Not really. I was well overdue for that. It's not an interview as such—more an informal lunch to suss things out...'

He let out a sigh and promptly forgot the reason he had brought her here. Instead he told her what tomorrow was about. No-one else knew.

'There's a role coming up.'

'I thought you loved what you do?'

'And I do, but it *is* consuming. I'm actually heading to the airport after the lunch. I'm going to Moscow tomorrow for a few nights, to get away completely.'

'Moscow?'

'It's a bit drastic, I know, but I love getting away. I don't put my phone on, so the hospital can't call me to come in—or if they do I don't hear it.'

'Well, you don't need to go all the way to Moscow for that. There are more than a few places in Scotland where you can't get a signal.'

'Please...' He grinned. 'I was teasing about changing the movie reels.'

'I know you were,' Freya agreed. 'But, trust me, there really are plenty of places you can't get a signal. I went away for Christmas with my family last year and we all had to keep going for walks just so we could make a call, or check emails and things. And in summer, depending on what provider they have, the tourists often can't get a good signal. We have a wee laugh, watching them walking around with their phones in the air.'

'Well, I'll bear that in mind,' Richard said.

'So, are you keen for this job?'

'I'm curious, certainly.'

He told her the name of a very exclusive private hospital which made her look up from her pasta.

'I've a friend, Marcus, who's director of anaesthetics there, and there's a position coming up—a very attractive one...' He didn't get to finish, for Freya had a question.

'But won't you miss the adrenaline?'

'Yes,' he said. 'But there are days when I think no, I won't miss it at all. It's a big decision—but you'd know all about that, given you've just made a big move yourself.'

Freya gave a shrug. 'I just knew that I wanted to get away.'

He looked at her through slightly narrowed, assessing eyes. 'Why?'

'Lots of reasons,' Freya said. 'I had a bit of a rough year. Well, not myself, exactly...' She didn't know why it was so hard simply to say it. 'My best friend lost a baby last year... Andrew.'

'Were you present at the birth?' Richard asked.

'Not at the actual birth, but I was there on admission.' Freya said. 'Alison ended up having a crash Caesarean. She came in a week before her due date, everything about the pregnancy had been fine, and then I went to check the foetal heart-rate...' She paused a moment as she recalled it. 'At first I thought I had picked up Alison's...'

She didn't, of course, need to explain to him that the mother's heart-rate was usually a lot slower than the baby's.

'But then I knew the heart-rate was the baby's...'

'Not good.'

'No.' She shook her head. 'My senior, Betty, was there, and a doctor was there within a minute, and everything was set in motion. We got her straight upstairs to Theatre. I didn't go in. Betty knew I was too involved. He was born flat and was resuscitated but died two days later. Cord compression and meconium aspiration...' Freya screwed her eyes closed for just a second but then opened them and gave an uncomfortable shrug. 'Anyway, it was a difficult time.'

'Did she blame you?'

'Oh, no—nothing like that. It was more...' Freya didn't know how to describe how she'd felt when she didn't really know herself.

'You blamed yourself?'

'A bit,' Freya said. 'Well, I questioned myself. It made me realise that being so involved with my patients isn't always ideal.'

'So you came to nice, anonymous London?'

'It wasn't just because of that,' Freya said, 'but it is nice to be not so involved with the patients.'

'I'm sorry—you don't get to do a job like yours and *not* get involved.'

'It's not that easy...'

'I never said anything about *easy*.'

That annoyed her. Richard was too brusque, too direct, and he had hit a nerve.

'You don't know me.'

'I'm trying to.'

It was a rare admission for him, because while he might be talking about getting involved professionally, he certainly did his best not to on the personal front.

'You cannot do this job, Freya, and not care. Or rather, you cannot do this job in the way you want to do it and not care.'

He signalled for the bill and then remembered that they still hadn't had *The Talk*.

It didn't seem so important now. Freya was off to Scotland tomorrow and he to Moscow. And she certainly wasn't jumping up and down demanding to know when they would see each other again as they headed to the Underground.

'You really don't have to see me home,' Freya said.

'I'm not,' Richard said. 'I believe in equality—it's your turn to see me to my door.'

CHAPTER SEVEN

UH-OH!

Freya woke to a very un-lumpy mattress—in fact, she felt as if she was wrapped in cotton wool. And then she heard Richard speaking into the phone.

Her one and only one-night stand was over.

And, instead of regretting it, she smiled as she lay there, recalling last night.

They had arrived back at his gorgeous apartment and he'd poured them a drink and headed off for a shower.

She'd ended up in there with him.

And then they'd taken their drinks to bed.

Oh, it had been bliss.

She lay there listening to his lovely deep voice.

'No, I'm away until Tuesday, so I can't,' he said. 'How is Mrs Eames?'

As soon as the call ended, his phone went again.

'No,' he said, very brusquely. 'You cannot come and stay.'

Freya wondered if it was an ex, trying to get her toes back past the bedroom door, but she blinked when he spoke again.

'Mother, I have a friend staying at the flat while I'm away.' Pause. 'I *do*. Currently she's living in a terrible rental and I've loaned her the place for a few days. So, no, you can't come and stay. If you need a break from your fiancé then I suggest that perhaps you actually speak to him about that fact, rather than go away.'

Another pause and Freya rolled over and looked at him, not even politely attempting to pretend she was asleep.

'What do you mean, you don't believe me?' he said. 'Freya, would you tell my mother that my place is yours for a few days?'

Gosh, what a way to meet the parents, Freya thought as he handed her his phone.

'Hello, Mrs…' Freya didn't know what to call her, given she had divorced Mr Lewis three husbands ago.

'Amanda,' the woman said for her. 'So you're staying at Richard's?'

'Just for a wee while,' Freya said. 'While my landlord's sorting…'

'Pardon?' his mother said.

Richard took back the phone.

'So you see there is no spare room at the inn. I'll talk to you when I'm back from Moscow.'

He ended the call and his phone rang yet again.

'Work,' he muttered, and Freya didn't blame him a bit when he turned it off.

'Thanks for that!' Freya said with an edge, more than a little annoyed to have been put in that position and at his jab about her home.

'I never said you were my lover,' he pointed out, 'just that my apartment wasn't free. Anyway, she can afford a hotel.'

'Fair enough.' Freya said, but she was still sulking a little.

'I am *so* tired of her dramas.'

Freya said nothing.

'Can you see why I've been put off relationships for life?'

'I think so.' Freya nodded. He was *almost* forgiven. 'How's Louise?' she asked.

'Mrs Eames?' he checked. 'She's made it through the night and is holding her own. She's a lot better than yesterday at least.' He looked over. 'Do you want some breakfast or are you still cross?'

'Still cross,' Freya said and told him why. 'My flat isn't terrible.'

'I just said that as an excuse to my mother. She's hardly going to drop in and see it.'

'I guess…'

She let it go, and she decided he was completely forgiven when he got out of bed and returned with coffee, and toast topped with grapefruit marmalade.

Or was it the fact that she simply had to know more about this man?

'Were she and your father ever happy?' Freya asked as they ate their breakfast and got crumbs in his gorgeous bed.

'I think so. But she wanted a livelier social life and he is rather wedded to his job. She gave him an ultimatum and it backfired, I fear, because he chose work.'

'Your father married again?'

'Yes—his housekeeper. Or rather the woman who had been *their* housekeeper, so you can imagine how well that went down. My mother was convinced there had been something going on all along…' He rolled his eyes and then, putting his plate down, moved to take her mug. 'Can we talk about *our* sex-life instead, please?'

'But your parents' sex-life is so much more interesting!'

'Then I must be losing my touch.'

They made each other laugh and then, to Freya's surprise, and seemingly to Richard's, instead of taking her mug he lay back on the pillows and told her some more.

'She walked out when I was fifteen—a couple of days after their twentieth wedding anniversary. My father wasn't giving her the attention she felt she deserved. He had a terminally ill patient and had had to cancel their anniversary trip. I felt terrible for my father after the break-up—he just moped around. Then, just when I was starting my "A" Levels, he announced he was marrying Vera.'

'The housekeeper?'

'Yes. And the following summer my mother married an old friend of my father's. A more glamorous version of him, really.'

'What happened to him?'

'She left him after five years, and after that I kind of tuned out. Now all I know is that she's engaged to Roger.'

'Have you met him?'

'Yes—a couple of dinners. He's a cosmetic dentist.' He pulled a face.

'What's wrong with being a cosmetic dentist?'

'Nothing. I just feel his eyes on my mouth every time we speak. I think he's trying to work out if I've got crowns. In *my* line of work we just ask!'

He looked over to Freya and gave her a very nice smile that showed stunningly even teeth.

'And *do* you have crowns?'

'Two—thanks to rugby.'

She looked right back at him, and as she did so she thought about him asking his patients about their dental work before he put them under. She looked into his eyes and Freya understood why patients so clearly trusted him.

Because *she* trusted him.

Of course she didn't know him very well yet, but that much she knew. And, Freya thought as they stared at each other, if she were terrified and scared for her life, or her baby's, his would be the eyes she would want to see.

No, she would never regret this. In the twelve hours since their lips had first met she had come alive to her body in a way she never had before.

She wanted to put down her mug and reach for his kiss. Or at the very least to ask him what day he'd get back from his trip, in the hope that she could see him. But then she recalled their rules, and peeled back the sheet rather than leaning in to his embrace.

'I'd better go. I have a train to catch.'

'What time?'

'Ten.'

'Then there's plenty of time.'

'No, I need to get back to mine to pack.'

'Fair enough,' Richard said.

He lay there with his hands behind his head as she dressed. He kept his mouth firmly closed.

It was deliberate, because a long weekend in Scotland with Freya sounded tempting—rather than flying to Moscow by himself and cramming in some sightseeing.

'Have a great trip,' Freya said.

'I will.' He put out his hand and she came and sat down on the bed.

'And good luck with your lunch,' she added.

'Thanks.'

It wasn't awkward when she left. More, it felt...*unfinished*.

Freya thought about him more than she ought as her train slid its way northwards.

It was packed, and there were no seats in the quiet carriage, so Freya put in her earbuds and tried to listen to music—but every song sounded as if it had been written

about *them*. So she gave up with the music and chatted to
the woman in the seat beside her.

She was a fellow Scot, so neither had to say *sorry,* or *I
beg your pardon* once, and Freya found out from her that
on weekends and public holidays you could sometimes get
a cheap upgrade to First Class.

'I'll remember that,' Freya said, and then gazed out
of the window and watched the rolling countryside. The
clouds gathered and right on cue, as they crossed the border at Berwick-upon-Tweed, she saw grey skies and rain,

It made her smile.

The train travelled the rugged Scottish coastline, eating
up the miles until they reached Edinburgh Castle. It was
dark and powerful and towering over them, and her first
glimpse of it in what felt like a long time caused Freya's
heart to swell.

The train pulled into Waverley Station and it felt very
good to be home. The station was busy as she checked the
board for the next train to Cromayr Bay and saw that she
had half an hour to kill.

Freya decided to buy some flowers for her little cottage, to brighten things up. As she was paying she could
hear her phone beeping, and assumed it was Alison, or
her mother, checking on what time her train would get in.

She nearly dropped the phone when she saw that it was
Richard.

Lunch went well. I'll have my phone off for a few days now,
but just wanted to say that I hope you have a nice break.

No kisses or fun little emojis. No clues to anything,
really—but even getting a text was more than she had expected.

Freya hadn't expected anything. She'd hoped that she

might see him again—of course she had—but this simple text… Well, it confused her. This didn't fit with how he had said it would be.

She honestly didn't know how to respond.

A part of her wanted to fire back smiley faces and pictures of tartan berets and Russian hats—just to keep it all light and breezy. Yet light and breezy wasn't how she felt when it came to Richard.

And so, when most women would be firing off a rapid response to a text from Richard Lewis, Freya—because she didn't know how to respond—instead sent the promised text to Alison, and then stuffed her phone back in her bag.

Freya had no intention of telling people about Richard. Certainly she wouldn't be telling her parents. While Freya adored them, her mother Jean loved 'a wee natter', and—as Freya well knew—nothing stayed a secret in Cromayr Bay for very long.

Alison was a different matter. And she was there waiting when Freya got out at Cromayr Bay.

The clouds had parted and the sky was high and blue, and Alison was smiling widely as she waved to her.

'Look at you!' Freya smiled, because in the weeks that Freya had been away Alison had changed and was now sporting a lovely little bump.

'I know!' Her friend smiled back. 'Betty said that you can sometimes show a lot more quickly the second time around.'

Betty had clearly said easily what Freya hadn't been able to. And still Freya did not know why.

She had been dwelling on it for months now, and had even discussed it with Richard, but still she had a huge block when it came to speaking about the loss with her friend.

'I booked us a table at the Tavern for tonight,' Alison said as she drove her home.

'In the *restaurant*?' Freya checked, because usually they went for a curry, or just to the Tavern's bar. The restaurant was pricey, and rather grand, but she had heard right.

'Yes, it's closing for renovations next week. They're going to put a function room in at the top, and they're refurbishing the restaurant.'

Freya didn't like the sound of that—she loved it as it was.

'The bar's staying open, as well as the hotel, but I thought you might want to see the restaurant as it is one more time.'

Oh, she really did.

They took the hilly street approach and, rarely for summer, there was a parking spot close to Freya's cottage. They pulled in behind her little purple car.

'Do you want to come in?' Freya offered, but Alison shook her head.

'I've got to go and do a shop—I'll meet you in the Tavern bar at seven.'

'I'll see you there, then.'

'It's good to have you home, Freya.'

It was good to be here, Freya thought as she pushed open the door.

The drapes had been closed by Mrs Hunt after the last tenants, and Freya went around opening them up and letting in the late-afternoon sun. Then she turned on the hot water and caught up on her mail while she waited for it to warm.

And she did all she could not to think too much of Richard and what had happened last night.

She wouldn't be telling Alison. At least she didn't know whether or not to tell her.

Alison and Callum had been childhood sweethearts. And Freya wasn't sure her friend would understand.

Freya herself didn't understand.

She liked it that there was no risk of getting overly involved with Richard.

The break-up with Malcolm had been tricky. He'd kept messaging and coming round, turning up wherever she went, wanting to talk, to see if they could give it another go.

Well, she wouldn't be having that problem with Richard!

It was rather freeing.

It was nice to dress up and go out. She hadn't brought much with her, but she had a nice copper-coloured dress, and with heels it was dressy enough. Her hair was still rather wild from going to bed with it damp last night, so Freya wore it up and then added a dash of lipstick.

She glanced at her phone as she put the lipstick back in her bag, and then decided she'd do well to leave the phone at home, to prevent herself from replying to Richard.

She had no idea what she would say anyway.

Freya headed to the Tavern bar, and she felt herself tense a little as she walked inside. It was Friday night in Cromayr Bay, and that meant there was a fair chance Malcolm would be there. But thankfully there was no sign of him, and a moment or two later Alison arrived.

The Tavern really was gorgeous—a boutique hotel just off the main street, it was set high on a hill and offered a stunning version of Freya's favourite view of the Firth.

They climbed the steps to the restaurant and were shown to their seats by a waitress. Then Gordon, the owner, came over.

'Are you two here for a last trip down memory lane?'

'Something like that.' Freya smiled.

'I remember you coming here when you passed your midwifery exams—och, and for your eighteenth too...'

'I'm going to miss the old place.' Alison sighed.

'Well, hopefully you'll love the new one just as much,' Gordon said, and then he talked them through the menu.

They made their choices—which was tough, because there was lobster brought in from the pots just that afternoon, and there was Dornoch lamb, as well as Freya's favourite, game pie. But she'd had that the last time she was here...

'I'm going to have the lamb, please,' Freya said.

'And I'll have the spelt and mushroom risotto,' Alison said.

Freya had wine, and Alison a mocktail, and they chatted about Freya's move to London.

'So, have you made any friends there yet?' Alison asked.

'Not really,' Freya admitted. 'They're very cliquey...' she started. Only that wasn't quite right. They were all very nice. 'I don't know what it is. I try, I just don't seem to fit in. Richard says I'm too subtle.'

'Richard?'

'A friend,' Freya said.

'So you *have* made one.'

'A temporary one.' Freya said. 'He's being interviewed for a plum new job in a private hospital.'

'In London?' Alison checked.

Freya nodded. 'And he'll get it—he's brilliant.'

'Well, if it's in London that doesn't have to stop you from being friends. So you *do* have one.'

'I guess...'

Alison smirked, because she knew Freya well, and from

the little flush on her cheeks it was clear to her he was more than just a friend.

'It's just a temporary thing,' said Freya.

'Why?'

'Because temporary is all he does.'

'But that's not like you.' Alison frowned.

'Well, maybe it is. Look, we've been out a couple of times, and both of us know that it won't be going any further, and that actually suits me just fine.'

'Why?' Alison asked again.

'It just does,' Freya said, and gave an uncomfortable shrug.

She wasn't ready to tell Alison she was thinking of coming home for good once her contract was up, but thankfully then their meals arrived.

The lamb was delectable and the conversation became easier. Alison chatted about her and Callum's tenth wedding anniversary, which was soon coming up.

'Can you believe it?'

'Not really.' Freya laughed. 'It feels like just a couple of years ago that I was your bridesmaid.'

'Are you coming home for your thirtieth?' Alison asked.

'I think so,' Freya said. 'Though I'm doing all I can not to think about that.'

They had a wonderful night catching up. Although not about the things that hurt.

As Freya walked down the hill for home the air was salty, and despite the late hour the sky was still dusky. It was so much lighter here than in London. But autumn would soon close in.

It was one of the reasons she'd come home.

Tomorrow she had to speak to the estate agent about house prices and things, as soon the families renting for summer breaks would fade away and her little slice of potential heaven would be going on the market.

It would be a relief, Freya told herself. The rentals covered the mortgage, but there was a lot of work to be done on her home.

A lot.

She let herself in and smiled at the pretty flowers she'd set by the window. Then she made herself a hot chocolate, frothing the milk in her coffee machine, and took herself to bed.

Freya rarely closed the curtains. There was nothing between her little cottage and the water, and the sight of the bridges always had her in awe. They were miles away, of course, but it looked as if fairy lights had been expertly strung in the sky, and the new Queensferry Crossing was magnificent.

Tomorrow she was catching up with a few friends, and then there was a huge Sunday dinner at her parents' house to look forward to.

And then she thought about Alison and what she'd said about 'temporary' not usually suiting her. Perhaps now it did.

She took out her phone and read again the text he had sent.

Freya liked Richard.

A lot.

From the moment she had first seen him he had captivated her.

Yet she wanted to keep things breezy and light.

Or rather, she *had* to.

And not just because Richard Lewis had told her that it was the only way they could be. It was also because this place was home. Not London.

Freya had made up her mind now—she would not be selling her home.

* * *

He'd noticed her lack of response to his text.

Of course he had.

Richard had been moving through Security at Heathrow when he'd fired it off, and had regretted the simple message the second after he'd hit 'send'.

He did not report in to *anyone*—certainly not about things like interviews—and, furthermore, he loathed the cascade of texts that all too often came when he was seeing someone.

When he'd collected his phone on the other side of Security he'd seen that she hadn't responded.

Good, he'd told himself. A mistake had been made, but a lesson had been learnt, he'd decided as he had boarded the plane.

'Phones to be turned off now, please,' the steward said, but Richard had checked his again before he did so.

Four hours later, as he stood at Moscow airport, even though the very reason for his trip was to get away from the constant buzz of pagers and phones, he found himself turning it on.

No, she had not replied.

Freya could not have known the effect on him.

It made him want her more.

And that did not sit well with Richard.

CHAPTER EIGHT

'HOW WAS MOSCOW?'

This time it was Freya who put her tray down at his table in the canteen. It was morning—just after seven—and he was eating cereal.

Unlike her, though, he was starting his day rather than at the tail-end of a shift.

They hadn't really spoken since she had got back. Freya was just finishing a two-week stint on nights and their rosters hadn't crossed.

'Beautiful,' Richard said. 'But far from relaxing. All the signs are in Russian.'

'I wonder why!'

'Still, it was nice to get away. How was Scotland?'

'I had a great time. It flew by, though.'

'Have you finished on nights?' He frowned, because it was odd to see her down here at this time of the morning.

'Officially I have.' Freya nodded. 'But there's a twin pregnancy to deliver soon.'

Freya was lacking in experience there, as the birthing centre at home didn't accept multiple pregnancies. So she was more than happy to stay back—especially as through the night she had got to know Jeanette and her partner.

'Stella just came on, and she suggested I go and get

something to eat. Then she and Dr Mina are going to hold my hand, so to speak.'

Neither mentioned catching up with each other again. Some things were best left, Richard had decided.

He liked her a lot—perhaps because he couldn't quite read her. She was private, and he liked that. And her eyes could be sullen at times, but then she punched out a smile...

All Richard knew was that he liked her a whole lot more than he was comfortable with.

'Your interview went well?' Freya checked, alluding to the text she hadn't responded to.

'It was just lunch.'

He offered no more, for he had already told her more than he should. Yet deep down he knew she wouldn't have told anyone his potential news. He'd never have shared it with her otherwise.

Richard hadn't expected to be as impressed as he was by the private hospital set-up. The hours were far fewer, though he could take on more if he chose, and he would have considerably more annual leave.

'It would be a step up—a big one.'

'A step back too,' Freya said. 'From the pace here.'

It wasn't a criticism. She looked at him and could see his exhaustion, and then she looked down at the pile of cereal with which he fuelled his day.

She looked up again, at the closed look on his face, and knew she should not have come over. It wasn't just their rosters that had kept them apart. He was politely avoiding her.

Thankfully, this time around it was her pager that interrupted them. 'Woohoo!' Freya said as she glanced down and read the message it was time for her to go back up to Maternity. 'Wish me luck.'

She didn't wait around to hear him do so. Instead, she

made her speedy way along the yellow line to Maternity and pushed the gorgeous Richard Lewis out of her mind.

Having washed her hands, she headed into D4.

'You've been busy,' Freya said to Jeanette as she tied on a plastic gown. 'Well done, you.'

The next hour was sheer hard work for Jeanette and she did it brilliantly. Freya made sure there was no trace of tiredness in her own reactions.

The room started to fill up. Guy Masters and his registrar came—one for each baby—as well as Stella and Kelly.

'Listen to Freya,' Dr Mina said as Jeanette started to panic.

'You're almost there,' Freya encouraged. 'A big one now...'

She had never delivered twins before, but with so much experience in the room she didn't feel at all scared. And as Twin One was delivered onto Jeanette's stomach there was a sense of elation.

Yet there was more work still to do.

'Is she okay?' Jeanette kept asking over her baby's cries.

'She's wonderful,' Kelly said. 'Dad, do you want to cut the cord?'

With Twin One in Kelly's extremely capable hands Freya prepared to deliver Twin Two. The baby was in a good position, and Freya looked up and saw that Jeanette was starting to push.

'Well done,' Freya said. 'Jeanette, you are doing *so* well...' Being a midwife was such a privilege, she thought. 'Okay, I need another big push.'

And then Twin Two was there, a little stunned and straight off to Stella, and soon there was the delicious sound of two babies crying.

'Well done,' Dr Mina said quietly to Freya.

'Thank you.'

There was still the single placenta to come, and when it did both Freya and Dr Mina carefully examined it and checked the membranes.

Soon the room was clear. The paediatric team were happy, and Stella and Kelly had dashed off. Everything was under control here.

They were utterly adorable, Freya thought as she helped Jeanette feed her twins one by one. Once Jeanette was on the ward and wasn't feeling so shaky she would be helped to feed them both at the same time, but for now they lay in their mother's arms one at a time.

'You were completely wonderful.' Freya smiled.

'So were you,' said Jeanette.

Freya was feeling a little shaky herself after her first twin birth. She wrote up her notes and filled in all the paperwork, but the words blurred a little on the page.

Because of tears.

She was tired, that was all, Freya told herself as she pressed her fingers into her eyes. She was tired and over-emotional. And now that the birth was over she could take her thoughts back to the canteen, and to the ending of her and Richard.

Oh, but she'd been warned. Not just by Stella but by the man himself.

'Home?' Stella gently asked.

'Yes.'

Freya stood and made her way to the changing rooms. And suddenly, coming down from the L&D theatre, there he was.

'How did it go?'

'It was brilliant.' She smiled deliberately.

'Have a well-earned sleep, now.'

'Thanks.'

And that was it, Freya thought as she closed the door.

They were back to niceties on passing in the corridor and no more.

She peeled off her baggy top as she started to change so she could finally go home. But then came a knock on the door.

'Freya...?'

She lifted her top to cover herself, and then didn't know why she needed to bother, given it was him.

He wanted to apologise—to tell her the problem was him, not her—but they didn't get there.

Richard never brought any personal awkwardness to work. He had his pickings, but he never allowed things to get awkward *here*.

Yet suddenly they were kissing.

Deep, frantic kisses.

She found out that his rough unshaven jaw was possibly her preference over the clean-shaven version. And then he was thumbing her nipples through her bra.

'Not here...' he said, even as he pressed into her.

He had moved from her mouth and was kissing her neck, and his hand was creeping into the back of her navy trousers.

The scent of him was potent and she found his mouth again and...

Oh, God, she was nearly coming.

'Not here,' he said again, and sort of shoved her off him.

It was probably just as well, or they'd have been on the floor of the changing room, where anybody could walk in.

They both breathed through it and waited for it pass, but it was a couple of minutes before Richard was ready to head back out there.

'I'll text you about tonight,' Richard said.

Freya noted that he didn't sound happy or flirty or teasing. He sounded frustrated. As if it was *her* fault for the situation they were in, when it had been Richard who had followed her in here.

'And answer my text this time, Freya.'

CHAPTER NINE

BOTH OF THEM kept waiting for the bubble to burst.

Yet it didn't.

They tended to end up at his place, but one morning
two months into *them*, and three months after Freya had
moved to London, Freya stirred on her lumpy bed with
Richard spooned in behind her.

It should be over with by now, she knew. Freya was
waiting for Richard to discard her with the practised ease
he was known for.

And, oh, it would hurt.

It would hurt like hell.

London would be lonely without him. Friends had
proved very hard to come by, and the pace of the work
still completely floored her. She missed being more involved with the mothers, and found she craved the community that had felt too small.

Freya was homesick.

For home, for family and friends.

Apart from during her time with Richard—which was
wonderful, of course—Freya ached for home.

She was starting to do what he'd told her not to.

She was starting to rely on him.

And while Freya waited to be summarily dumped, Richard waited, as Freya had once said, for the very curl of her hair to irk him.

For the gloss to fade.

For the joy to wear off.

But it hadn't. It didn't.

If anything, it had intensified.

He lifted her hair and in the darkness could see her pale skin. He pushed down the sheet.

It was a cold mid-October morning and she shivered, both from the chill of the air and also the heat as he ran a finger down her spine.

And then he brought his tongue to her neck.

He slipped a hand under her so he could play with her breast, and she groaned as he toyed with her nipple.

'Wake up,' he whispered.

'I don't want to,' Freya whispered back. 'I'm having a lovely dream.'

She could feel him hard against her thighs, so she parted them a little and he slipped between their warmth.

He really should reach for a condom. But this was so nice...

He probed between her thighs, teasing, rubbing, caressing the edges of her intimate space without pushing in.

Freya knew she should halt things. Yes, she was on the Pill, but that wasn't the point. They had made no promises to each other—just sex for as long as they both wanted it.

But then there were the dinners and the breakfasts. and the talking into the small hours at times.

Though there was little talking now...

But, ever the sensible playboy, he did not slip into her inviting warmth. He pulled away from between her thighs and Freya lay with her eyes screwed closed in frustration as he sheathed himself.

She was losing her head—Freya knew that. And she dared not check her heart.

He came back to his previous position and groaned, '*God*, Freya,' as he slipped in.

She was so ready and tight, and pre-dawn sex had never felt better. He filled her and stretched her, and his body wrapped around hers felt like a blissful vice. He toyed with her breast in the way she had come to adore.

They moved in delicious unison, their bodies tuned to each other, pressing together until they found their climax.

They lay on their backs on her lumpy mattress, both sated and breathless, but when the near-miss with the condom came to her mind Freya gave him a scolding.

'We have to be more careful.'

But he hadn't *wanted* to be careful, and, Richard knew, neither had she.

'We'll talk about it.'

'No,' Freya said, 'we already have.'

She was not sleeping with someone who had told her never to rely on him without a condom.

And yet Richard was starting to rely on her in a way he had never considered he might.

Life felt a whole lot better with Freya in it.

Yes, work was crazy, but there was a counter-balance to it now, and he needed far fewer trips overseas to get away from the pressure.

Instead, he looked forward to the end of a work-day and to nights spent with her.

He didn't like coming *here* so much, mind… He didn't like her poky flat. But last night he hadn't finished until midnight, and he had hardly been able to ask her to hop on the Tube and come to his place. Or give her a key and tell her to come to his at the end of her shift and let herself in.

Surely it was way too soon for that? And, anyway, he'd sworn never to get so involved.

Yet more and more he found he was.

It was Richard who broke the silence. 'Marcus is pushing me for an answer on the new job.'

'And have you decided what you want to do?'

'Not yet. It would mean starting in the New Year.'

'That's ages away.'

'It will be November in a couple of weeks,' he pointed out. 'And I'd have to give a month's notice—more if possible. So if I want some time off between jobs then I need to give him an answer soon.'

'Which way are you leaning?'

'I'm still not sure,' Richard admitted. 'The private work would be at a slower pace, and seriously more money...'

'But you *love* what you do.'

'I know that, but...' He ground down on his jaw.

He wanted her take on things, but whenever he broached it with Freya she asked only what *he* wanted to do. And, while he liked it that Freya never put any kind of pressure on him, he kind of needed her view on this.

Because it might affect her.

God, he thought. He was staring up at the ceiling and wanting someone else's input into his future because he was starting to think, to *hope*, that the 'someone else' might be involved in it.

He thought it better not to say anything just yet, though. He really needed to think this through, and he needed to get the hell out of here before he went and said something stupid.

He had always been incredibly focused where work was concerned, and independent in his choices too. This way of thinking was a huge shift for him, and lying in the warmth of her bed it would be all too easy to offer her his keys, to move her in, because he did not want her here in this horrible flat.

He wanted her at his home.

'I'm going to go,' Richard said.

'There's still an hour before you have to leave.'

'Yes, but I want to have a shower...'

'Have one here.' Freya frowned.

'I don't like your shower, Freya,' Richard said, and climbed from the bed.

Ooh, what was that all about? Freya pondered as Richard dressed. He was in an odd mood, and as he went to leave he gave her only a brief kiss on the cheek—more like a family member might at a gathering, rather than a lover who had just left her bed.

Freya could not let it go. 'Thanks, Uncle Richard.'

'What?' He frowned.

'That's the sort of kiss my uncle gives me,' she said, and looked at him with accusing eyes.

He smiled, because he couldn't help but smile when she was around, and because she was such a snarky thing that he was tempted to dress her, pack a case and haul her back to his place.

For good.

'We'll talk tonight,' Richard said. 'You're on a late?'

'Yes.'

'Well, I finish at six, but I'll stay back and then we can go to mine.'

He walked out of her flat and Freya heard the slam of the door. She lay there, not quite so brave now.

Richard wanted to talk.

To Freya that could only spell one thing.

They were done.

She had known the winds would change eventually, and that one day he'd tire and Rita the domestic would be reaching under a bed with a broom for her soon to be discarded heart.

She had been duly warned.

Freya had sworn to herself that when the time came she would be ready for it and fully prepared to deal with it. Except she hadn't factored in how deeply feelings could be etched. Never had she felt such kinship with someone. And as she got up and pulled back the curtains a world without Richard in it suddenly looked a lot less friendly than even a cold grey day in London.

She showered and told herself she was overreacting. Of *course* Richard wanted to go home to shower—because hers was horrible, with dark green tiles, and the water ran cold for ages before you could get in. And the shower curtain needed to be replaced.

She had meant to get another one, but she was always running out of time in between work and Richard. Still, after her shift today she had two days off. She would get on with sorting out the flat then.

God, imagine being here without him, Freya thought as she sat on the Underground and looked at the endless faces that refused to acknowledge her and the eyes that flicked away the second the mistake of eye contact was made.

It was another busy late shift, and close to the end of it she turned at the sound of her name.

'Freya. There's a phone call for you. Private.'

'Oh.'

Very deliberately, Freya had left her mobile in her locker. The only people she could think of who might call her at work were her parents.

Tentatively she picked up the phone. 'Freya Ross speaking…'

'Freya?'

If ever the sound of your own name could drench you in ice, it did then to Freya. There was a begging tone in the voice that sounded like a final grab for a rescue rope.

It wasn't her mother, it was Alison, and Freya knew only too well the inflection of her friend's voice when it was laced with fear.

'I didn't want you to find out from anyone else,' Alison said, 'but Aunt Shona's already put something on social media and I'd rather you heard it from me...'

'What's happening?'

'I've had a bleed,' Alison said. 'I'm having tests, and Dr Campbell says that I might I have an abrupt—' She stumbled over the word.

'An abruption.'

This might well be serious and Freya felt sick.

And angry.

And scared.

But she held in her fears as Alison spoke again.

'They're not sure where the bleeding is coming from, but apparently I have an irritable uterus and they're monitoring how the baby is faring.'

'Are they looking to deliver?' Freya asked, and knew her voice had that odd, distant note she saved for Alison these days.

'Not at this stage,' Alison said, 'but they're monitoring me, and might transfer me from Cromayr to Edinburgh, if needed. Freya, I'm so scared.'

'I know you are, but sometimes bleeds happen. It doesn't necessarily mean—'

'Freya!' Alison interrupted. 'Can you come?'

Her request was unexpected. Welcome, yet unexpected. They were best friends, and yet somehow Freya had felt Alison might want her to stay away this time.

'Of course I'll come,' Freya said. 'I've a couple of hours

to go on this shift and then I'm off for a couple of days. I'll turn my phone on now and you can call me if anything changes. If you're transferred, tell Callum to let me know and I'll come straight in to see you at Edinburgh. I'll be there in the morning.'

'Is everything okay, Freya?' Stella asked as she hung up the phone.

'No,' she admitted. 'My best friend's pregnant and she's had a bleed and has been admitted. She lost a baby last year, so I'm going to head home at the end of my shift. I'll take the train.'

'Do you need me to take a look at the off-duty?'

'I should be fine. I've got a couple of days off.'

'Well, the night staff will be arriving soon, and there's enough of us on if you want to go.'

As their conversation was ending Richard arrived at the desk. He dealt with some questions that Stella had for him, and then the first chance he could Richard spoke to Freya. 'I shouldn't be too much longer,' he said. 'If I run a little over can you wait in the staff room?'

Oh, right, Freya thought. Their talk. He wanted to speak to her, and Freya was quite sure that it was about the end of them.

'I can't come over tonight,' she told him. 'Alison's had a bleed and she's asked me to go and see her. Stella's letting me go early, so I'm just about to go home and pack and then I'm heading to Euston.'

'How bad is it?' Richard asked.

'It sounds as if it's under control,' Freya said. 'And if there are any further issues then she'll be transferred to Edinburgh. I think she's just terrified…'

'And needs a friend?'

'I guess… Or maybe she doesn't understand what's happening and wants me to translate what's been said.'

'I'm quite sure they've told her exactly what's happening,' Richard said. 'If you can give me half an hour to sort out some cover, I'll drive you.'

Freya shook a head. 'It's fine. I'll just go home and pack a few bits—the Tube's just as quick.'

'I meant that I'll drive you up to Scotland.'

She'd thought he'd meant he would drive her to Euston.

'Sorry?' She frowned, unsure if she was hearing things right. 'Don't be daft. You're back on in the morning, and you're first on call.' Freya knew his roster as well as her own. 'We wouldn't even get there until then.'

'It's not daft at all,' Richard said. 'I'll sort it out. Just give me some time to arrange cover.'

'You don't have to do that.'

'Freya, in the same way I'd do it for them, my colleagues will cover for me when it's urgent.'

He could not know how much those words meant to her.

'You're sure?' Freya checked.

'Of course I am.'

This was unlike anything Freya was used to. *She* was the fixer. The one who sorted things. Even as she had hung up the phone on Alison she had already been mentally working out the off-duty roster and the train times to Edinburgh.

And yet here was Richard, calling on colleagues and rearranging his schedule.

Stella was marvellous too and, unasked, swapped around her next set of days off, so that she had four days off in a row.

'Though if Kelly is swapping her weekend with you, then I'll need you back for an early on Monday.'

Freya nodded. 'That would be great,' she said. 'Thank you so much.'

She had a quick shower in the staff changing rooms, and by the time she came out Richard was ready.

'All done.'

Richard made it sound like a simple feat had been achieved. He didn't burden her with the drama of it, he simply sorted it, and within the half-hour they were driving towards her flat.

There wasn't a hope of him getting a parking spot, but he said he'd drive around while she packed.

'Wait on the pavement for me.' Richard said.

He drove around and in the end he did find a spot, beside a small café. He ordered two coffees and four pastries and then headed back to her street. She was waiting for him, dressed in jeans and a long baggy jumper with an overnight bag beside her.

Richard negotiated the car through the traffic and filled her in with what he'd achieved while she'd been in her flat.

'I booked myself a room at the Tavern.'

'Why?' Freya frowned.

'Well, given your cottage is being rented out, I didn't want you to have to go to the bother of explaining me to your parents.'

'No,' Freya said, 'the last tenants are gone.'

'Oh, that's right—it's on the market.'

Except it wasn't on the market. Because Freya had decided against it, given that she knew she was coming back once her London contract was finished.

But she couldn't deal with telling him that tonight, Freya thought. She would save it for when she was summarily dumped.

Yet it didn't *feel* like the end of them, Freya thought, still more than a touch stunned that Richard had changed his busy schedule just to make things easier on her.

'The satnav estimates that we'll be there at seven,' Richard told her. 'Maybe call when we get closer and check that she hasn't been transferred?'

'I will.' Freya nodded. 'I'll pop in and see her when I get there, if she's still in Cromayr Bay, though I might have to wait until visiting hours if she's been transferred to Edinburgh.'

'We'll know soon enough,' Richard said.

They chatted idly for the first couple of hours, but then she decided to be brave and address what he had said this morning. 'You said that you wanted to talk to me?'

'It's nothing that can't keep.'

'We have five hours to go,' Freya pointed out.

But Richard shook his head. 'It's nothing that can't keep,' he said again.

Perhaps he didn't want a hysterical crying female in the car as he drove, Freya pondered, although she was determined to at least *pretend* to take it well.

She looked over to him and her heart skipped, as it always did. Yes, she'd sworn to take it well—it was what they had agreed on after all. But she would miss him so.

Richard turned the conversation to his work, and she could not know, just how rare that was—because usually he didn't discuss such things in depth with someone he was seeing.

Generally it was just a case of replying, 'Busy day,' to any enquiries about work.

Not tonight, though.

'I just signed off on Dominic performing epidurals,' Richard said. 'That's going to make things a lot easier.'

'That's good.'

'He's brilliant,' Richard mused.

'Have you told *him* that?' Freya both smiled and yawned as she asked the question.

'Not yet.' He glanced over. 'Why don't you try and get

some sleep?' he suggested. 'I'll wake you when we stop for petrol.'

'Okay, then I can drive when you get tired.'

'I'll be fine.'

Freya rested her head against the window and very soon was drifting off.

Occasionally she stirred, but there was just the radio playing and the lulling sound of a car eating up the miles.

When she finally woke she glanced at her phone.

'Anything?'

'No.'

'Well, no news is good news,' Richard said. 'We're coming up for the border—we'll stop after that.'

And there it was, the blue and white flag of Scotland as they crossed the border, and it felt both odd and nice to be doing it with Richard. It was good to be home.

The motorway stop was efficient.

She went and bought them something to eat while he filled up the car. 'Why don't you get flowers here for your friend?' he suggested.

Freya bought a gorgeous orchid, and a bunch of flowers for herself, and soon they were back in the car for the last leg. They were just merging onto the motorway when he let out a curse.

'What?' Freya said, looking around, assuming a car had cut them up or was driving too closely behind them.

'I forgot to get condoms.'

Freya was shocked, because she'd been expecting to be dumped but then she smiled. 'We do have shops in Cromayr Bay.'

'I know. But I've never run out of supplies or not had any to hand...'

'Never?'

'God, no. I wouldn't leave it to someone else. There

would be little Richards everywhere...' He gave a shudder at the very thought.

'I'm the same,' Freya said.

She didn't leave that type of thing to anyone else either, and kept right on taking her Pill regardless.

The hills were dotted with wind turbines, but rather than soothe her as they drew closer to their destination Freya found she was nervous.

'I don't know what to say to her,' Freya admitted as they neared the stunning Queensferry Crossing. 'I was so hoping that what happened last time was just a one-off.'

He glanced over. 'She's had a bleed—it could just be a scare,' he pointed out. 'Did the same thing happen last time?'

'No...' Freya shook her head and then sighed. 'It's not just the baby I'm worried about. Things have been a bit strained between us. I don't know how to *be* with her.'

'Just be yourself.'

Freya let out a laugh that was so close to tears it was almost a sob. 'I don't think she needs my anxiety right now. I'll just keep things calm and point out that this type of thing...' She halted, because when she had tried to say that to Alison on the phone, Alison had suddenly cut in and asked her to come.

'Can you stop being a midwife?' Richard asked.

'I'm trying to. We're really close, but I just don't know how to be around her lately. I keep saying the wrong thing, or not saying what I know I should. It's ironic, really, when I've been taught, and I'm well-versed on how to deal with grieving mothers.'

'Well, you can be trained to the back teeth, but it's very different when it's a private grief. No one *always* knows what to say,' Richard said. 'You try, of course, and then you find out that it wasn't the right thing at the right time, or it was the right thing but at the wrong time.'

He was speaking about himself, Freya realised. 'Did you lose someone?'

Richard nodded. 'Marcus—the guy I'm considering working with—his son died a few years ago. He came in at nine in the evening with meningococcal and was dead by sunrise the next day.'

'Were you working at the time?'

'No.'

He looked over again and saw the slight dismissal in her eyes that told him he couldn't understand what she'd been through. Richard had stayed quiet on the subject before, because that was when he had still been determined to keep things light between them. When Freya had still just been his way of getting away from things for a while.

He wasn't trying to get away from things now, and so he spoke on. 'For a long time I wished to God that I *had* been working.'

She looked at him. 'You don't mean that.'

'But I do,' Richard said. 'For close to a year, nearly every day I wished that I'd been on call that night and been the one dealing with him.'

He thought back to that time, and to the hopelessness and anger he had felt.

'I convinced myself that had I been on then I'd have picked things up sooner. In my God-like moments—' he gave a black smile '—the moments when I'm able to control the world, I decided that had I been there I could have changed the outcome. But in the end I worked out that no matter how much I wanted things to have been different, there are some outcomes that can't be changed.'

'No...' She had never really thought of it like that.

'Just stop for a moment and imagine that you hadn't been on that night.'

'I can't,' Freya said. 'I still have nightmares about it.'

'I know you do,' Richard admitted.

He'd never mentioned it, but he had felt her panic sometimes as he'd held her through the night. She would sit up for a moment, and then eventually settle back to sleep. It had felt like a private thing—something she perhaps didn't want him to have seen—and so he had left it. Because they weren't supposed to have the kind of relationship where you noticed things like that.

But he wasn't leaving things unsaid now.

'Suppose you were a teacher, or you worked in a shop, or even on one of the other wards and you hadn't been there that night…'

'But I *was* there.'

'Just stop,' he said again. 'Just take yourself out of the picture. Suppose you hadn't been on duty that night—how would you have felt?'

'I can't take myself out of the picture, Richard. I was *there*.'

They stopped talking about it then, because some sights were just too beautiful not to pause and take them in.

The dark sky had turned to grey, with soft blushes of pink starting to emerge, but now, as they approached the crossing, they were bathed in gold and pink and it felt as if they were driving through fire.

'That's stunning,' Richard commented.

'I know,' Freya said. 'I never tire of it. I can see the bridges from my bedroom. It's a sight to behold.'

She rang and found out that Alison hadn't been transferred and they arrived in Cromayr Bay along with the morning. Freya directed him along an easier route than the satnav recommended, and soon they were pulling into the parking area near the ambulance bay.

'I'll try not to be too long,' she said.

'Take your time,' Richard said. 'I'll be asleep.'

It was nice not to be running up the corridor harried after two train journeys and weighed down with an overnight bag. Instead Freya had on lipstick and was carrying a huge orchid as she made her way up the corridor. And, no, she did not need a red arrow to find her way.

Laura, the Matron, greeted her warmly. 'Things are looking better,' she said as Freya approached, putting her at ease straight away. 'We were going to transfer her last night, in case the baby needed to be delivered. It's still an option, of course, but everything has settled down and Dr Campbell thinks for now she can stay here. Any further bleeding, though, and she'll be off to somewhere with a NICU.'

Freya let out a breath of relief as Laura took her through.

'She's going to be so pleased to see you.'

And Alison was.

Sitting up in bed, strapped to a CTG monitor, she was having a cup of tea. She put it straight down and then promptly burst into tears when she saw her friend.

'It's fine,' Freya said, and gave her a cuddle.

She could hear the rapid bleep of the baby's heart and it was just the sweetest sound in the world. Especially now, today, here with her friend.

'I am so sorry to drag you up here. Especially now that things seem fine. But when they mentioned delivering me I just panicked.'

'Of course you did.' Freya said. 'But it sounds like things have settled down?'

Alison nodded.

'These things happen,' Freya said. 'It doesn't mean it's related to what happened with Andrew and that it's going to happen again.'

'So everyone keeps telling me—and the sensible part of me knows that,'

'But you're not thinking with your head?'

'No.'

They spoke for a good hour, but still Freya felt more midwife than friend—though by the time she was heading off Alison seemed a lot calmer.

'How long are you staying?'

'For a few days,' Freya said. 'They let me swap my off-duty, but I need to leave on Sunday. I'll come back at visiting time.'

'Did you come by train?'

'No.' Freya shook her head. 'A friend drove me.'

'Which friend?' Alison asked, with a look in her eye that Freya couldn't ignore.

'A good one.' Freya answered. 'And that's all I'm saying on the subject. I'll be back this afternoon.'

And that 'good friend' hadn't slept the hour away.

Richard had tried to, but he had found himself watching the distinct lack of emergencies at the casualty department at Cromayr Bay Hospital.

Oh, there was *some* activity—there were staff arriving for their shifts and some leaving—but not a single ambulance had pulled up.

One patient had arrived—a car had come into the forecourt and an elderly gentleman had spoken to a porter, who seemed also to man the doors. The porter had gone off and returned a few moments later with a wheelchair.

Richard had watched as they'd both helped a woman out of the front seat of the car. She'd been holding her wrist in a familiar way.

'Colles' fracture,' Richard had diagnosed from a distance.

God, he'd go out of his mind with boredom here.

And it was cold. So much colder than mid-October in London that he'd sat with the heating on in the car.

And now he saw Freya, smiling and walking. She stopped and chatted to the same porter, who must also be on duty for wheelchairs and things.

She was happy here. Richard could see that.

'Hey.' He gave her a smile as she climbed into the warmth of the car. 'How is she?'

'Better than it sounded last night. If she has another bleed they'll transfer her, though things are calm for now. I'll go in and see her again later today.'

'Sounds good.'

'It does.' Freya nodded. 'I can't thank you enough for this. It all seems like a bit of a false alarm now.'

'Well, thank God it was.'

'Did you cancel the room at the Tavern?'

'No,' Richard said. 'I thought that so long as your friend's okay we might both go there for dinner tonight. It sounds amazing.'

'The restaurant's new,' Freya said as she directed him the short distance to her home. 'I really want to see it. I hope they still do their game pie. It's the best you'll ever have tasted.'

'It will be the *first* I've ever tasted,' Richard admitted, and then he gave her thigh a squeeze. 'And maybe we can slip upstairs to my room after.'

'I think I like the sound of that.' Freya smiled—and then brought them down to earth with a bump. 'I need milk.'

'I need sleep.'

They pulled in at a small store, but after a moment, rather than wait in the car, Richard, knowing the emptiness of her shelves in London, got out to make sure that she got things like bread and eggs too.

Yes, he was hungry.

And, no, he would not be buying condoms, Richard decided.

Another thing to add to the discussion list tonight.

Romantic dinners in Scotland, discussing his work and then sex minus a condom—he'd be asking her to move in next.

The oddest thing of all was that the thought didn't terrify him...

He held open the door for a woman who was wheeling a pram and saw that Freya was standing behind a large gentleman, waiting to pay for her milk.

'Did you get bread?' he asked patiently.

'No.'

'Do you have butter?'

'No.'

'Is there anything else you need?' Richard checked.

'I don't believe so.'

'Anything else *at all*?'

He meant for tonight, and they both knew it.

And when he looked at her like that, when he smiled, she forgot her fears. She forgot the temporary nature of *them*.

'Nothing I can think of.' Freya smiled.

As he headed off to get bread and butter, and nothing else, he heard someone call her name.

'Freya!'

She turned and gave a huge smile. 'Mrs Roberts!'

'It's Leah,' she reminded her, and Richard watched as Freya peered into the pram.

'Oh, she's beautiful!'

The baby really was. A gorgeous smiling baby, who was wide awake and looking up at her. There were certain babies that just had to be held.

'Do you mind?' Freya checked.

Leah laughed 'Go ahead.'

Richard was back, so she handed him the milk to hold as she unstrapped the baby.

'Oh, my…' Freya said. 'She is absolutely *gorgeous*.'

'She really is,' said Mrs Roberts, and then she glanced to Richard.

Freya remembered her manners. 'This is Richard Lewis—he's a friend of mine from London.'

'It's lovely to meet you, Richard. I'm Leah Roberts. I went through a bit of a time and…well, Freya really helped.'

'I'm glad to hear it,' Richard said. 'What have you called your daughter?'

'Freya,' Mrs Roberts said, and then looked to Freya. 'And, no, it wasn't just because I like the name—though of course I do. You really helped me. You were so kind through my pregnancy. I kept wanting to talk to you, though I didn't know how to.'

'You did it in the end,' Freya pointed out.

'Yes—Norma came down to help, and I had Mrs Hunt come in for the first few weeks…' She looked at her daughter. 'I got to actually *enjoy* her. And though of course I didn't care if it was a boy or a girl, she was a wonderful surprise.' As Freya handed her back, Leah gazed fondly upon her daughter. 'She's a true blessing.'

'Everything went well with the labour?' Freya checked.

'It did. Betty was wonderful, of course, but I did miss you so.'

He drove the last few minutes to her home, with Freya directing him.

'Mine's the blue one—though we'll have to park a bit further up. It can be hard when there are lots of visitors.'

Richard parked, and as he climbed out the scent of the sea reached him. The sun was glistening on the water and there was an angry seagull squawking above as they walked down to her cottage.

Richard had to stoop to get in.

Her home was cold from being empty, and Mrs Hunt had closed the curtains. And yet it was gorgeous, Richard thought as they stepped in and she pulled back the lounge curtains and let in some light.

'I'll put the heating on,' Freya said. 'It's a bit early to light a fire.'

Freya ran a vase under the tap and put the flowers on the table, in the hope of brightening it up.

'Do you want a coffee?' she called out.

'No, all I want right now is bed.'

He was beat. A long day at work and a very long drive up to Scotland meant all he wanted to do was stretch out.

'I'll just have a shower first.'

'You'll have to wait for the water to warm—it will take half an hour or so.'

After turning on the tank in the airing cupboard she showed him the tiny bathroom, and then took him through to her bedroom. The curtains were already drawn closed, and as he stepped into the soft darkness of her room and saw the large bed, the thought of waiting half an hour for hot water held no appeal. So Richard started to undress.

'Are you coming to bed?' he asked.

'Not yet,' Freya said, because unlike Richard she had slept in the car. 'I should maybe let my family know I'm here, and then I might go and...' Her voice trailed off.

Because that was what looking at him did to her at times. Freya needed no reminders as to his beauty. All she ever had to do was turn her head. But here in the dark bedroom, with the lights off, it was not that which swayed her—more the thought of Richard in *her* bed, and the waste of a morning spent on the phone, taking care of a hundred little jobs, when she could be with him.

'I might just join you.'

He was already in. 'God, your bed's comfortable.'

'I know,' Freya agreed. 'I found this mattress topper...'

She was speaking to a less than captivated audience. The bear was asleep. In her bed.

Bears could be many things. Intimidating, irresistible... She stood there, mulling it over, but couldn't think of another adjective. She just knew that she wanted to lie with him, her bear, in her bed.

Freya set the alarm on her phone, so that she'd be up for visiting time, and undressed. She had forgotten how cold her house could get. Or maybe the goosebumps could be labelled as a sign of tiredness.

Either way, she was cold as she slipped into bed, and then she was colder still from the chill of neglected sheets against her skin.

But then Richard rolled over and wrapped her in his arms and she no longer felt cold.

She slept warm in his embrace, and struggled to wake to the sound of an alarm that was pinging somewhere, reminding Freya of where she needed to be.

She rolled onto her back and her brain scrambled to orientate.

She was home...

Alison. Visiting hours. Get up. Get dressed. Be there.

Except she was here.

Feeling his hot mouth on her breast and the sensual slow suck that had made a place low in her stomach draw tight.

It was as if he knew, for his fingers traced slow circles there, and then crept down, down, all the way down...

And then he left her breast, and as his mouth found hers his fingers worked magic.

She moaned, and he liked it. She should really reach for him, but she was feeling too selfish to move.

The alarm went off again, but neither of them cared. She was locked in the bliss of a kiss that delivered ten thousand volts and a hand that did the same.

Her hand went to the back of his head and he swallowed her throaty gasps. Freya could hear the sound of her sex, slick and wet, as he brought her to the boil. He kissed her while she came, and when he rolled atop her it didn't feel disorientating, more like the right place to be on this earth.

As he slid, unsheathed, inside her, her whole body shivered with desire.

It had never been better for either of them. The tight and yet slippery grip of her...the absolute union of them.

He moved, but it was slowly, and he savoured the feel of each thrust and the slow draw-out followed by the faster pushing in.

She was digging her fingers into his back in an effort to hold on to her thoughts and reel them in. Because they were making love, Freya knew. They were *making love*.

They had done many things, but never this.

They were kissing and then pausing to look at each other. And she was in a heated frenzy of passion and emotion as he took her deeply, because a part of her wanted him to pause, while the other part wanted him never to stop.

He took her harder now, and she forgot to hold on. Her thoughts simply unravelled until there was nothing left in her mind but the shattering of *them*. As he shuddered he spilled himself deep inside her and she throbbed against him. The bliss of her clenching made Richard moan, and those last precious drops came to the fading twitches of her climax.

And as he lay there, spent and still inside her, Freya opened her eyes and stared at the ceiling as she found the word she had been missing before.

Irreplaceable.

There would never be another who came close to him.

Richard Lewis was irreplaceable in her heart.

And that shook her to her core.

This wasn't some fling. It might have started as such, but now it couldn't end without regrets.

Not any more.

Freya knew that when it ended he would be leaving with her heart, and she must not let that show.

And so she wriggled out from under him and then climbed from the bed. 'I have to go and visit Alison.'

She really did have to go, or she'd be late for visiting time. But she knew her voice was distant, cold, detached.

'I'll just have a quick shower,' Richard said, pulling back the sheet.

But Freya stopped him. 'You don't need to get up—my car's outside.'

That surprised him. Richard didn't really know why. He'd just assumed that the little purple car blocking his way belonged to a tourist—a visitor or a neighbour. It had never entered his head that it was hers.

'My dad drives it to work once a week,' Freya explained as she headed for the shower. 'To keep the battery from dying.'

Richard dozed as Freya showered, and then she came back in, wearing the same grey dress she'd had on the day they had met. Now, though, underneath it, she had on a long-sleeved black top, as well as thick black tights. Her hair was up, and he saw she'd added a little lipstick as she came and sat on the bed.

'I'll be a couple of hours.'

'Take your time.'

'There's everything you need in the kitchen. Well, there's coffee, and your bread and things, but I'll bring us back a fish supper. They do the best here.'

'And there was me thinking you were finally going to cook.'

They parted with a smile and he heard her footsteps leave and then the sound of the door closing behind her.

Her father needed to drive her car rather more frequently than he currently was, Richard thought as he lay there, because it was taking her a few goes to get the engine ticking over.

Richard was fully awake.

Automatically he checked his phone, and then checked and checked again. But, as Freya had once predicted, he had no signal.

The seagull which had been calling for the last half-hour had found a friend or two, and they were all being rather vocal, yet it wasn't that keeping him from going back to sleep.

'To keep the battery from dying.'

Louder than the seagulls, Richard replayed Freya's words, frowning as he mulled over them. They felt important, and yet he told himself it had just been a throw-away phrase.

He gave up on sleep and headed through the lounge and into her tiny kitchen, taking a moment to work out her rather fancy coffee machine.

As he got the milk out Richard read a note on the fridge, presumably for holidaymakers, reminding them to turn the water off at night and explaining a few nuances of the place.

He walked through to the lounge, and while, yes, it needed a helluva lot of work, it really was gorgeous.

There were books on the shelves, and little ornaments and shells dotted around. As well as that there were paintings on the wall that *she* had put there—not prints of some ugly old horse and cart. And there were throw rugs on the sofa.

'To keep the battery from dying.'

Now he understood why he had stalled on those words. *This* was Freya's home.

And she was keeping it going as it awaited her return.

Richard walked through to the bedroom and opened the drapes and let in the view.

It was stunning.

Afternoon had given way to dusk and the lights from the bridge had come on. Richard found himself wondering what it must look like deep in winter.

He made another coffee and lay there, looking out but not enjoying it as he had on first sight. For he really knew her some more now.

'Two fish suppers, please.' Freya smiled as she placed her order. 'And a large tub of the homemade tartar sauce.'

'It's good to see you back, Freya. Are you here to see Alison?'

Of course the world already knew.

'Aye, I've just been in to see her—she's looking well.'

It was just the kind of normal idle chatter that happened in this place all the time, Freya thought, and she realised she had missed it.

'Will you be wanting pickled onions?'

She was about to say no, even though she loved them,

but perhaps they would both be eating them, Freya thought with a smile. 'Two, please.'

As she drove up the hill to the cottage Freya felt her spirits buoyed. Their lovemaking had been blissful, and Alison had been looking brighter. And now she was simply enjoying the familiar rhythm of home.

Made all the better because Richard was here.

Yes, her mood was good.

It was a lot darker here than in London, and the clocks changing in a couple of weeks would make it darker still. But, unlike many, Freya loved winter and embraced its grey approach.

She'd said before that it was a bit early to be lighting a fire, Freya thought as she parked on her street, but there was a cold chill in the air as she got out. A fire would make the cottage so very cosy.

And, Freya thought as she turned the key in the door, it would be nice to sit by the fire with him.

The house was in darkness. She guessed that Richard must still be sleeping, so she put the supper down and got out plates, then found glasses for wine.

And to hell with it.

She lit a fire.

'Richard?' Freya pushed open her bedroom door. 'Supper's...'

Her voice trailed off as she saw that he was awake and sitting up in bed.

'Enjoying the view?' Freya asked as she looked out fondly to where his gaze fell.

'Not particularly.'

She frowned at the unexpected response and looked out to the bridges. Such had been his tone that she had almost expected them somehow to have changed. For a fire to have broken out on one of them. Or some drama to be unfolding with flashing lights.

But the change was in him, in the room.

'You never really moved to London, did you?'

She frowned at his question, and at the slightly hoarse note in his usually smooth voice.

'I don't know what you mean.'

'I mean,' he snapped, 'that you've never really left here.'

'Of course I have.'

'Is the house up for sale?'

'Not yet.'

'Freya, why didn't you bring your coffee machine down to London?'

It was the oddest question, and she frowned as she gave a simple answer. 'Because I couldn't fit it in my dad's car.'

'And you bought flowers without thinking about it for this place, to pretty it up, yet your flat in London barely gets a look.'

'Richard, I've been busy, and most of my time off is spent at yours.'

'Oh, come off it, Freya,' he snapped again.

Since the moment she'd left to visit Alison he'd been giving it some considerable thought. And all his thoughts pointed to the same conclusion.

'Is this why you've no real interest in whether I take the private job or carry on at the Primary?'

Freya swallowed.

And Richard saw her swallow and knew he was right.

God! He had been going to ask her to move in with him—to take things further! He had even gone to Freya for her take on his career in case it affected *them*.

Well, he decided, she never needed to know that.

'It's been your intention to come back here all along.'

'No,' Freya argued. '*No.* Richard, when I left I thought

it was for good. I truly did. I was so tired of this place, and everywhere I went there were…' She didn't know how to explain it. 'Reminders.'

'Of Malcolm?'

He hoped not. God, he seriously hoped not. But he *had* to rule that one out.

He saw her eyes screw up and the tiny, impatient, shake of her head as she completely discounted that. He believed that it had had nothing to do with the other man.

'The baby?' Richard checked, and her silence was his answer. 'You left because you were upset about your friend's baby?'

He didn't say it scornfully. She saved the scorn for herself.

'Not just the baby. Alison too. I know it shouldn't get to me the way it does. Even Alison seems so much better, and I guess I appear so too. I should have got over it—I know that…'

'Freya, you're grieving.'

'No.' That sounded too dramatic a word. 'Maybe at first, but it was Alison who lost—'

He spoke over her. 'There aren't numbered tickets given out for grieving. You don't get sent to the back of the queue just because the baby wasn't yours. You went through a bad time at work and the loss was a very personal one. Then you ended a long-term relationship.'

'I was right to.'

'Yes, but it might have been more than you could deal with at the time so you ran away.'

'No.'

But Richard wouldn't let her off that lightly. 'Did you know Alison was trying for another baby?'

'Yes.'

'You couldn't face it if anything went wrong and so you left, but you were always going to come home.'

Had she been?

Freya thought of her last days in Cromayr Bay and the ache in her heart as she had walked out of the delivery centre for the last time.

Not the last time *ever*.

A part of her had known that even then.

Even if she had brushed it from her mind.

'Yes.' She admitted it now. 'But I didn't know that when I applied to work at the Primary. I didn't even know it for certain when I started seeing you.'

'But you do now?'

Freya nodded.

And, for the first time in his life knew that the biter had been bitten.

'Richard, you and I…'

'We were a fling.' He let out a mirthless laugh.

She had meant them to be just that, Freya knew. It had never been going anywhere, or so she had thought, and so she had been able to close her heart and have fun for once. But it had been a grown-up game she'd been playing, which meant when it went wrong there was a greater risk of hurt.

He climbed out of bed—and it was odd the things you noticed, she thought, but he turned away from her to get dressed, when he had never come close to doing so before. A glimpse of that beautiful body was denied to her.

'Do you know what *really* annoys me?' Richard's voice was as brusque as the hands that tucked in his shirt.

'That I wasn't honest with you? I accept that, but I truly didn't know how I felt—'

'No,' Richard interrupted. 'The part that *really* annoys me is that you never gave London a chance.'

'I did.'

'No, you had it pegged from the start as cold and unfriendly.'

Given the circumstances, Richard figured he deserved a chance to be mean, and he used it well.

'I'll tell you why you've got no friends, Freya. It's because—unlike me—people probably sensed that you were never really serious about being there.'

'I take my job very seriously.'

'I'm not questioning your midwifery skills. I'm saying that you never gave London a chance.' He shook his head. 'I'm going.'

'Where?'

'To the Tavern. I hear they do a nice game pie.'

'Don't go,' Freya implored. 'We can talk. Surely?'

'And say what? Is it your intention to come back and live here?'

There was no point dressing it up, so Freya told him the decision she had made. 'I'm going to see my contract out and then I'm moving back here. It doesn't mean we have to stop seeing each other. Lots of long-distance relationships work out…'

His laugh was almost a shout. Every word sounded foreign to him.

Long. Distance. Relationship.

A few months ago it might have been ideal. He had been growing tired of casual relationships. With Freya in Scotland he could still focus on work…

God, they were so bloody good together that if he stayed—if they ended this row in bed—he could actually see himself saying that he might consider moving here.

But his decision as to what to do was already complicated enough. He did not need another iron in the fire. He was not, *not*, going to consider living here.

Never.

'Enjoy the view, Freya.'

He didn't need to slam the door, for the bitter tone to his voice reverberated through her far more than the sound of wood on wood could.

Her one-night stand had proved to be more.

And yet he had gone without working through it.

Gone without hearing her side.

Gone.

CHAPTER TEN

First class.

It felt incongruent to Freya that she should lug her broken heart back to London in style, but she'd learnt a few tricks, having made the journey so often, and, given it was Sunday and there was a spare seat, she'd got a cheap upgrade.

Freya wasn't just lugging her heart home, though.

She had thought hard about what Richard had said about her never having given London a chance, and she had spoken about it to Alison too, when she'd visited.

'I'm torn,' Freya had admitted. 'If I stay it will only be because of him. And what happens when he decides it's not working out? He won't even talk to me about it. No.' She'd shaken her head. '*This* is home.'

'Well, why don't you try and make *London* home for a while?' Alison had suggested.

'That's where I'm headed tomorrow.' Freya had given her friend's stomach a tender caress. 'If this wee one behaves.'

Between visits to her friend Freya had braved the cellar of her home and filled up some cases.

The coffee machine would have to wait. It was simply too heavy. But she had packed some rugs and photos and ornaments, and now she sat on the train with her luggage stowed as a tall woman pushed the buffet cart to the side of her table.

An elderly lady stirred nearby and gave Freya a smile as she selected a Ploughman's sandwich and a bag of crisps and then promptly fell back to sleep.

Freya was grateful for the silent carriage, for there was only the lulling movement of the train and the stunning countryside to take the edge off the frequent barbs of her thoughts.

Richard's words had stung so much because they were true. Freya hadn't set out to hurt him, yet inadvertently she had.

And so she looked at her phone, which was on silent, and this time there was no thought of Russian emojis or tartan berets.

This time her text was from the heart.

I never thought I would feel the way I do about you.

While he sat in his gorgeous apartment, surrounded by tiny pieces of Freya—a silk scarf over his sofa, a pair of earrings on his table—knowing that there was some of her washing in the tumble dryer, he read her second text.

Does it have to be all or nothing?

Her question was both sensible and ridiculous.

Sensible because they'd been seeing each other for just a couple of months, and it was too early in the piece to be speaking of career and country moves. Ridiculous because they both knew how they felt.

Richard texted back.

Can you see yourself staying in London?

Freya answered.

I don't know.

Freya had answered, but sensed that now wasn't the time to lie.

She looked out of the window as the train slowed down and they arrived at Berwick-upon-Tweed. She recalled being in his car as they crossed the border. The feeling of being home.

And then, as they left Berwick-upon-Tweed behind, she felt torn from the land of her heart. No, she could not see herself permanently in London.

Not really.

And so she sent another text.

No.

Silence was his first response. But as the train pulled into Newcastle her phone pinged.

There's no point, then.

He was as brusque as ever.

Richard, we can't do this by text. I'm on the train now. Can I come over?

He read the message and gave a wry smile, for all too often a lover had pleaded with him via this very vehicle not to end things, and asked could they please just come over and talk.

This felt like a very different message from the familiar.

It would end in bed, rather than tears, Richard knew, and they would be no further along than they were now.

No, you can't come over. I'll meet you at Euston.

Richard wasn't on the platform, but as she came through the barrier and stepped out into brighter skies her heart sank. He looked amazing, in black jeans and a thin black jumper, but when she saw her own bag over his shoulder Freya knew that the things she'd left at his flat were inside.

'I'm sorry I wasn't honest with you,' Freya said. 'That first night we went out I'd only just started to figure out that I wasn't planning on staying after the end of my contract.'

'Pardon?'

She looked into his gorgeous eyes and managed a pale smile, because she knew he was teasing, as well as trying to ease the pain and make their parting of ways as good as it could be.

'I kept waiting for you to dump me,' Freya said, and poked at his lovely big chest. '*That's* what it said on the box. I went into this with eyes wide open, knowing we had a fast-approaching use-by date...'

'I know you did.' His sigh was a weary one, and it came from lack of sleep—though for once that had nothing to do with work, for he had been on days off.

'Nothing has to change...' Freya attempted, but even she could hear the futility behind her words, because so much already had.

He handed her the bag. 'I don't want us to see each other any more.'

'Richard, please,' Freya said, even when she had sworn she would never beg him not to leave. 'Don't rush off.'

He had to.

Lest he stayed.

'You don't have to make a decision now,' Freya reasoned as she ran after him.

'I've already made it,' Richard said.

'I can't believe you won't let us talk.'

Infuriatingly, he shrugged.

She spoke on. 'I've still got a couple of months to go here, and *some* long-distance relationships work…'

He didn't want to hear it. Richard did not want this dragged out. He did not want his precious days off spent on the motorway, and he did not want her the best part of a day away. So, rather than admit to the hurt he felt, instead he was blunt.

'I like sex a bit more regularly than once a fortnight.'

Her mouth clamped closed. She really didn't have an answer to that.

But Richard hadn't finished yet.

'You wanted a bastard you could readily leave behind, Freya,' he reminded her. 'Don't complain when I deliver.'

And, as she had been promised by all and sundry, as she had known would happen on the day she had accepted a night out in his company, Richard Lewis broke her heart.

'Don't!' Freya warned the flower seller at the Underground station, before he could tell her again to cheer up because it might never happen.

But then she relented.

It had already happened.

She had lost Richard.

And the worst thing about that was that in everything he'd said he'd been right.

So she bought a huge bunch flowers, even though she didn't really feel like it, and lugged her cases up to her flat.

As she opened the door Freya winced.

Really! Imagine her bringing Richard back *here*.

The carpet was vile, but she had ordered a huge rug online that would soon be here, and she had brought loads of things from home.

Loads.

Okay, she only had three more months left here, but she was *not* going to just sit it out.

So she threw some gorgeous quilts over the sofa and scattered cushions on top, and then she set to work putting out ornaments and pictures.

It was better that than focussing on a seriously broken heart.

At work, he ignored her.

Not in front of the patients, of course. And Richard was far too smooth to do something silly like call her 'Nurse'. He still called her Freya if he had to—just not quite in the same way he had said it before.

A couple of weeks into her heartache he came to the nurses' station, where Freya and Stella were sitting. He was wearing scrubs, and still had on a paper theatre hat.

Stella was sorting out the off-duty rota and Freya was feeding a very fussy Baby Glover, whose mother had been taken to Theatre post-delivery when complications had set in.

'How's Mrs Glover?' Stella asked.

'She's fine.' Richard nodded. 'And she should be back on the ward soon.'

He didn't look over or say hi to Freya. He just sat and caught up with the notes he'd been writing before he'd had to dash off. Mid-stroke of his pen, though, he peeled off his cap and tossed it into the bin.

The cap had left his hair messy, just as it had been on the day they had met.

Now Freya knew why.

'Felicity,' Stella said. 'I mean Freya—can you swap from an early to a late on Tuesday?'

'That's fine.'

Freya no longer took it personally when Stella got her staff's names muddled up, because when it came to babies and mother's names she never did.

Never. Not once.

And with twenty-eight mothers and babies on the maternity unit this morning alone, Stella had a lot on her mind.

'You don't have plans?' Stella checked.

'No,' Freya said. 'Well, actually I'm trying to make some curtains, but I'm sure they won't care if I don't get to them that night.'

'You should speak to Pat,' Stella said, but didn't elaborate, and then, having finished sorting out the off duty, she got up and walked off.

There wasn't silence.

That would be too much to ask mid-morning on a maternity ward.

But there was silence between *them.*

How she missed him.

'Richard?' Freya said, and looked up from the little infant she was feeding, 'Do you think—?'

'Is this about a patient?'

'No.'

'Work?'

'No.'

'Then you don't get to know my thoughts.' He stood. 'Dominic and my SHO are stuck in ICU, so I'm going down to Surgical to do the Pain Round. Tell Stella I'll be back to finish these notes when I get a chance.'

'Sure.'

He walked off.

Richard didn't *stalk* off—he didn't do anything other than put her neatly in her place.

He did the Pain Round and asked the patients over and over, 'On a scale of one to ten—ten being the highest—how would you rate your pain?'

'Ten,' some would say, while reaching for their cup of tea.

'Three,' some would say, just a few hours post-op, while wincing from the pull of stitches on their wound or the weight of a sheet.

And that night, when he went home to an apartment minus any little pieces of Freya, Richard dared not rate his own pain.

He had returned to London after their row to the sanity of a single life. It was now two weeks post-Freya and the pain should have improved considerably. In fact the old Richard would have been well onto the next woman by now. At the very least he should be out with a friend and mocking the fact that he had almost considered giving up all this for a career in Cromayr Bay.

Mocking it.

Laughing at the fact that in the days after they had ended things he had placed a call to the head of anaesthetics at Cromayr Bay and made tentative enquiries.

He had been invited for an informal visit in a couple of weeks, to be shown around. There were currently no vacancies, but he'd set the ball rolling. Richard knew he should halt it now.

He wasn't hungry enough to order take-away, so he ate cereal and then took off his suit and stepped into his pristine glass shower. But the trouble with that was he missed those awful green tiles at Freya's place, and the inevitable search for a towel.

Here he had his choice from eight white fluffy ones, all folded and waiting. Yet for all its luxurious bliss, his apartment felt as sterile as an operating theatre now that Freya wasn't there.

He lay in his non-lumpy bed and, though he might appear comfortable to some, he decided to rate his pain.

One to ten…with ten being the highest.

Seven? he attempted, because although it had hurt seeing her today he had been effective in cutting her off.

And yet he'd badly wanted to hear what she'd had to say.

Eight? Because he still hadn't cancelled his visit to Cromayr Bay, simply because he missed her so much.

Nine? Because he was a stubborn bastard and where his career was concerned he never backed down.

This damn thing called love hurt more than he'd considered it might.

Yes, love. And he missed her.

Ten.

Yes. Losing Freya was definitely a ten.

CHAPTER ELEVEN

As STELLA HAD SUGGESTED Freya had spoken to Pat—who, it turned out, was a fantastic seamstress.

'I'll do them for you,' Pat offered.

'I can't just bring you in a pile of fabric!'

'Don't be daft. I'll bring my sewing machine to you.'

It had been arranged for Sunday afternoon, and Kelly had come along, Stella too. As nervous as for a first date—in fact far more nervous than she had ever been on a date—Freya had bought cheese and nuts and crisps and worried.

But then they'd arrived, and it had been so much fun. Pat on the sewing machine, Stella on the ladder. And by the time they had left there had been deep crimson curtains.

They changed the entire room.

And he would never see them, Freya thought.

'Do you see him at all?' Alison asked one night when she called.

'A bit,' Freya said. 'Well, quite a lot. But it's not like before. His registrar, Dominic, can do most of the epidurals now, so I only really see him if there's an emergency.'

'Have you tried talking to him?'

'There's no point,' Freya said. 'He's made things completely clear. I don't see why I should have to give up coming home when he won't consider moving.'

There was silence. From both of them.

'I want you here,' Alison said finally. 'You know I do. But if Callum had to move for work—well, that's where I'd go.'

'Yes, but the fact is *you're* not working. You've finished work to have a baby,' Freya snapped, and then realised what she'd said. 'Sorry...'

'No!' Alison laughed. 'I'm delighted to hear the return of the real Freya. You've been...'

'What?'

'Too *nice*,' Alison said. 'Too *midwifey.*'

'I shall have to snap at you some more, then. Anyway, enough about me—how are *you* doing?'

Alison was doing well. The baby was due early in the New Year and Freya's contract was up in mid-January— which meant that Freya wouldn't be around for the birth.

Alison was having the baby in the main hospital, and if there were any further bleeds she would be transferred elsewhere, so there would have been no chance of Freya delivering her friend anyway.

Yet still she would have *been* there.

She thought back to the time when she had first put in her application to London. She and Malcolm had long since broken up, and Alison had just told her that she and Callum were expecting again.

They'd sat in the bar at the Tavern and Alison had said she wanted Freya to be with her in the delivery room.

'Callum's going to be so tense,' she'd explained.

'That might not be possible,' Freya had said, and had told her best friend that she was considering moving to London.

It had just tumbled from her lips, even before it had been a cohesive thought, and it had grown from there. Freya had applied for a job at the Primary the next week.

Richard had been right. She'd been running away.

There was no avoiding heartbreak, though. It just morphed into something else and found you wherever you were hiding.

Until you faced it.

CHAPTER TWELVE

RICHARD NO LONGER crashed out in the staff room, and they merely nodded if they met in the canteen.

Freya ached to know whether he had decided to stay with the NHS or go and work at the private hospital. Each week when the hospital newsletter came out Freya scanned it for information, but there was no mention of his leaving, nor of his replacement.

She'd find out on the intranet, perhaps. Or one day she would realise he was no longer here, Freya thought as she sat on the labour and delivery unit, where she'd been allocated today.

'It's so quiet,' Freya commented to Stella, for there was only the sound of a woman loudly humming her way through her contractions.

Pat was in there with her. And Kelly was in D5.

'Why don't you go and have your coffee break while it is?' said Stella.

'Freya,' Kelly called, because they were 'buddies' today. 'Can you check this CTG with me before you go?'

Freya did so. They both checked it carefully. There were a couple of anomalies—enough that they called over Stella, who then buzzed for Dr Mina to come and asses mother and baby.

'Go and have your coffee now,' Stella said.

Freya made a coffee and thought how odd it was that it would be a normal day in Cromayr Bay while she was here in London. They'd have the antenatal and postnatal clinics running through the day. And then there were care-in-the-home visits.

Freya loved those. Going into a home and seeing the new baby and its family. If there was a part of her job in Cromayr Bay that she missed the most, then it was that—following the entire journey.

Of course she followed up on certain cases here.

Louise Eames was doing incredibly well and had been discharged home. She was recovering from her trauma and visiting her tiny son.

But it didn't feel the same. Freya missed her old work, the longer preparation and anticipation of birth and the follow up too.

She was about to open a magazine when the overhead chimes went off.

Freya didn't rinse her mug. Instead she put it down on the coffee table and headed straight back to a department that was no longer quiet.

The light was flashing over D5, and Stella was running for the phone. Then she saw Freya.

'Let Theatre know we've got a crash Caesarean coming,' she told Freya, and then got back into D5.

Freya made the call and saw Richard running down the corridor and into the same suite.

'Freya?' Stella put her head out through the door. 'Can you check this?'

As Freya went over to check on the drugs she could hear a tense conversation taking place between the father of the baby and Richard.

'But I'm her husband—absolutely I'm going into Theatre with her.'

'He won't get in the way,' the patient pleaded.

She was lying on her side, with oxygen, and Freya could hear the sound of the baby's heart-rate. It was ominously low. Her waters were thick with meconium, which was usually the baby's first bowel movement after birth.

It felt like a replay of what had happened to Alison.

Andrew had died from meconium aspiration.

Of course it happened—Freya knew that—but she could hear the fear in this mother's voice and it sounded just like Alison's had...

'What's happening?' she asked.

Her calls did not go unanswered as Stella, Dr Mina and Kelly all took time to explain as they prepared her for urgent transfer.

'Baby doesn't like the contractions,' said Dr Mina. 'The slow heart-rate tells us that.'

Then Stella spoke. 'And the meconium shows us that baby's distressed...'

Guy Masters arrived then, and got the hand-over from Dr Mina.

'I want Abigail in theatre,' Dr Mina said, and looked over to Stella. 'Now, or we go ahead here.'

'They're preparing.' Richard said, a touch breathless.

No one would move from this room until a theatre was ready, even if it meant that the baby was delivered here.

'I want my husband with me,' Abigail said.

And then Freya found out what Richard Lewis could accomplish in seconds.

'I understand that you want your husband to be there for the birth, Abigail,' he said in his deep voice. 'But you're having general anaesthetic so it just isn't possible. We need to get your baby out quickly.'

'I *insist* on being there!' the husband cut in.

'Mr Dunstan,' Richard said. 'We don't have time to

debate. You *cannot* be there. From this point, I won't be leaving your wife's side.' He crouched down to be at eye level with Abigail. 'I will be with you the whole time until you are brought round.'

He didn't make false promises and say he'd be there after that, because he knew she would be handed over to the post-anaesthetic care unit, and at that point he might well be called to something else. He had just told the terrified parents how it would be, and had obviously reassured them at the same time, because Abigail nodded.

'Now,' he said as he stood, 'I've got another IV line in and I've gone through your history. I just need to ask if you have any dental crowns.'

'None.'

'Or any loose teeth that I should know about?'

'No.' Abigail shivered.

Everything was ready to go, and the emergency packs were ready for the short dash to Theatre, but until they were told it was ready they would not be leaving.

'Theatre's ready!' someone called.

And then they were off. Running down the corridor in a race to save the baby.

'Can you clear up?' Stella asked, when she saw Freya simply standing there in the middle of D5.

'Of course.'

She cleared all the discarded wrappings and equipment, and as she replaced the oxygen masks and tubing could see that her hands were shaking.

And then she stopped.

Just for a moment.

It felt as if she was shrouded in black lace.

Freya simply stood there and felt the fear and the absolute horror of that night with Alison. And then she did what Richard had suggested on the day that had ended them.

Her mind was in a time that had never been. Imagining a phone call and hearing that Alison had had the baby and it hadn't gone well. Or coming into work and hearing the news. Or Callum, Alison's husband, calling her.

'How would you have felt?' Richard had asked her.

Now Freya felt that moment without herself in the picture.

Devastated.

Only Richard wasn't there to know her answer.

Richard knew this patient would have upset Freya. It had been an incredibly close call.

Their aim was thirty minutes from alert to delivery, and in this instance it had been twenty-eight.

There could not be a more valuable two minutes saved, Richard thought now as he heard the cries of his patient's new baby and Abigail Dunstan was wheeled through to the post-anaesthetic unit. She had been extubated in Theatre and would soon come round.

Richard went over and spoke to Kelly. 'How is he?'

'Lucky,' Kelly said. 'He's well enough for a quick cuddle with Mum when she comes round, and then we're taking him up to NICU—but really just to be observed.'

'Good.' Richard said. 'Well done.'

'And you.'

It had been a good day. Or rather, a good hour. But at any given second that could all change.

Richard looked around at the efficient unit that he'd frequented so often and knew he was going to miss this place.

He was going to go private.

His decision was made.

Rather than hover, he headed straight from Theatre back to the Maternity Unit.

Yes, he should stay away from Freya, Richard knew that, but he was certain this case would have upset her.

He would check up on *any* staff member, Richard told himself. But he knew that he was lying, for every day involved drama after drama. If he checked in on everyone he'd never get anything done.

'Hey,' he said to Stella. 'Well done back there.'

'I heard he's doing well. What can I do for you, Richard?'

'I was actually looking for Freya.'

He didn't dress it up, or pretend he was here for another reason.

'She's gone home.'

'Oh.'

'A migraine, apparently.'

'I see…'

'She's back on tomorrow—on a late,' Stella said. 'And that reminds me… It's her birthday tomorrow. Can you sign the card?'

'I haven't got time for that. I need to get down to Surgical.'

'It will take two seconds!'

They did it for everyone. Just a cake and a card. It was nice that a staff birthday didn't escape unnoticed.

And so he took out his pen and scribbled a message.

Best wishes
Richard Lewis

Richard wrote what he always wrote—but he didn't feel like he always felt.

He needed time to think—but when did an anaesthetist in a busy hospital get that?

By the end of the day the good outcome with Baby Dunstan had been countered by the loss of a twenty-year-old, and as he drove home Richard changed his mind—no, he would *not* miss the place.

And the drama didn't end at work.

As the garage door beneath his apartment opened he was just pondering calling Freya, to check how she was faring, when he caught a flash of blonde hair. And as he got out of his car she rushed over to him and promptly burst into noisy tears.

Oh, God, Richard thought. *Not now. Please!*

CHAPTER THIRTEEN

THIRTY!

How the hell had *that* happened?

Freya awoke in a far less lumpy bed, thanks to the amazing mattress topper she had bought, and commenced her fourth decade on earth.

Whether she looked older or not, Freya thought as she came out of the bathroom and looked in the mirror, she didn't *feel* older—and she didn't feel wiser.

Freya just missed him so.

She was working a late shift, so she took her coffee back to bed and lay checking her messages. There were plenty, but Alison must have been waiting for her to switch on because her phone rang straight away.

'You're catching up to me,' Alison said.

'Ha-ha.'

'Thirty! It's awful, isn't it?'

'Not really. I feel the same as I did when I went to bed. It's just the numbers that have changed.'

'There's a parcel here for you,' Alison said. 'I'm not going to lie and pretend I've posted it. You're not coming home for your birthday?'

'No,' Freya said. 'I messed up my days off.'

'Any word on the man?'

'No. He's being very polite at work.'

'Well, that's good.'

'Not really.' Freya sighed. 'And I'd be mad to base staying on here just for a chance with him.' She was thinking out loud, really. 'He told me never to rely on him...'

Only that had been right at the start.

'And we were only together two months...'

'Freya,' Alison broke in. 'You're arguing with yourself.'

She had a lovely morning, spent mainly on the phone and opening the door to flower deliveries. There were some from her parents, from the staff at the Cromayr Bay birthing suite, and even a posy from Leah Roberts.

There was also a message in her inbox from Malcolm, saying that if she was coming home for her birthday perhaps it would be good to catch up and see where it might lead...

Hell, no!

Freya slammed her computer shut.

And then later she felt the utter joy that came with the job of delivering a little one who'd share the same birthday as her.

Sophie Reece started to arrive in the world one foot first, causing her midwife more than a moment of internal panic. But there was Stella, coming in through the door and being amazing, followed by Dr Mina, who was the most calming presence. And soon there was the body out, with just the head to come.

'Patience...' Dr Mina said.

Guy Masters came in, and Richard did too, just in case this little one needed some more help. But, no, she was fine. Better than fine.

'Happy Birthday!' Freya said to the tiny new girl, once she was settled with her very delighted mum.

She was ready for her coffee break—seriously so—as well as a sit-down, but that wasn't going to happen just yet.

'Happy Birthday!'

And there they all were. Stella, Kelly and Angela, and there was Rita, and Guy Masters, and even Richard, no doubt hauled back to come in while passing.

And there was a cake, with '30' written in glitter balls. Apparently Rita had made it.

But no candles.

'They set off the smoke detectors,' Stella explained.

Freya briefly met Richard's eye and tried, as she had that first day, to think of a quip about fire extinguishers.

But she didn't say anything—couldn't think of what to say that would fit the moment.

She read her card.

Best wishes
Richard Lewis

She looked up, about to ask him what the hell that was supposed to mean, but he was suddenly gone.

So she ate cake, and laughed with her friends, and when Len came sniffing round for leftover cake for his animals Freya had it ready and wrapped for him.

It really was a lovely birthday.

Almost brilliant, in fact.

Just minus him.

But deep into her shift, coming up for nine o'clock, Freya was holding little Sophie while her mother got some very much deserved sleep and he came to the desk.

'Hello, *Richard Lewis*,' Freya snarked.

'Hello, Freya Ross,' he said, and took a seat at the computer.

'Why are you still here, Richard?' Stella checked. 'I thought you finished at six?'

'Yes, well, I'm covering for Simon, but I'm just about done.'

By the time little Sophie was asleep and about to be put in her crib he'd turned off the screen.

'I'm out of here.' But he spoke too soon, for immediately there came the ring of his phone.

'Excuse me,' he said to Stella as he answered the call.

But then he stopped being polite.

'What?'

He was *very* curt.

'I don't know—and I told you not to call me at work. I'm heading to a long case in Theatre, so I can't speak.'

He clicked off his phone.

'You are *such* a bastard.' Stella smiled. 'You just told me you were going home!'

'God, no,' Richard said. 'I'm checking into a hotel tonight. That was my mother. She's broken off her latest engagement and is currently staying with me and she's driving me crazy.'

Stella laughed and headed off.

Freya didn't know where to look, so she turned her eyes down to gaze at Sophie.

'Freya?' he said.

'What?'

She was still smarting about him writing *Best wishes* in her card and the use of his surname.

'You know how you used me?'

'I didn't *use* you, Richard, any more than you used me.'

'Yes, you did—but it doesn't matter right now. I don't want to go to a hotel. Can you please use me again tonight?'

She laughed but did not answer him. And he watched

as she walked away and put down the baby, taking time to wrap her carefully.

'This is the best birthday ever,' Freya whispered to little Sophie, and then she took a key from her pocket and headed back over to Richard.

'No strings,' he warned. 'And no talk of long-distance relationships and other such unmentionables.'

'Just sex, then?' Freya checked.

'Just that,' Richard agreed. 'But with my *very* best wishes.'

She slid over her key and he took it.

Richard hadn't really given much thought to his reaction when he entered her home. But it *was* a home now.

The scent of flowers hit Richard even before he had turned on the light, and when he did click it on the room felt different. There were deep red curtains that fell to the floor, and as he walked around he felt a soft rug underfoot. There were photos of family and friends on the shelves, and he knew he would love to be among them.

But they weren't friends.

They were lovers.

Only it felt a whole lot more than that.

And then he did something silly—which struck him as odd, because he never did things like that. He went to his car, where there was a mobile printer which he occasionally used for looking at cardiac tracings.

Today, though, he printed a photo of himself and tucked it behind one of the pictures on her shelf.

And then he headed to the kitchen. He saw there was still no coffee machine. But there were bananas on the bench and lots of lovely food in the fridge.

He went into the bathroom and saw there were new shelves there, and a shower curtain covered in pictures of shells that he recognised from her home in Cromayr Bay. When he turned on the taps the water ran hot within a minute, so Richard had a shower.

Then he put the door on the latch, so Freya could let herself in, and got into bed.

'Happy Birthday,' said Richard.

Freya sat on the bed. 'Everyone keeps asking me how it feels to be thirty.'

'How *does* it feel?'

'I delivered a baby for an eighteen-year-old today,' she said, and he smiled. 'I don't think I like it,' she admitted.

'You got a lot of flowers.'

'I did—and there are presents waiting for me at home.' Then she remembered the message from her ex and gave a little shake of her head.

'What?'

'Nothing,' Freya said, but then decided that if there was anyone she could tell it was Richard. 'My ex wanted to see if we might catch up.'

'And will you?' Richard asked. He found that he had to concentrate on keeping his voice even as a little snake of jealousy slithered up his chest.

'Of course not!' Freya laughed at the very thought.

And the little snake slithered away as she put her hands around his neck.

He was curious. 'Why did you break up?'

She gave a shrug. 'Just... Why does anyone break up? Why do *you* break things off with women?'

'Because I get bored.'

She looked into those hazel eyes that never seemed restless when they looked into hers.

'So why?' he persisted.

'We wanted different things,' Freya attempted. Only

that wasn't right, because she did want a family one day. 'When I moved into my cottage he seemed to think it was his. And then, when I had the worst day at work ever—possibly the worst day of my life—I came home and told him.'

'And...?'

'He told me he was sorry, and he told me that he believed me when I said I'd done nothing wrong...'

'And...?'

'And then he went to work.'

There was silence as they stared at each other.

He would never have left her that day. Richard knew that.

And so too did Freya, because on the day when a woman he had never met had happened to be bleeding, he had dropped everything, swapped shifts, got in the car and driven her to Scotland.

'Freya,' Richard said, trying to give the other guy a chance. 'You sometimes have to ask for help. You can shut the world out with one glare, and...'

He could see behind the guarded look in her eyes though. Freya didn't need to stand semaphoring her needs—he read them and he felt them. Pity the fool who left her on a dark, dark day.

And more fool *him* if he didn't follow his heart, Richard thought as Freya stood up, peeled off her top and then unclipped her bra.

She slid down her jeans, and then her knickers too, and then climbed onto the bed, sat on his thighs and began to play with him.

'Shouldn't I be taking care of *you* on your birthday?' he asked as he reached up to trace the curve of her breast.

'I'm using you—remember?'

'So you are...'

And she was—but in the nicest of ways, imprinting his beauty on her mind. His flat nipples and the swirl of his chest hair. His dark hair and the soft skin of his balls as she held them. The way he grew to her touch, and the way he put his hand over hers and showed her just how rough he wanted her to be.

'Get on,' he said.

And as she did so she closed her eyes—not just because of the bliss, but because of the threat of tears, for she had thought they would never be together again.

Then she opened them and they stared at each other as he moved her hips, and then they melded into a kiss. He cupped her buttocks, feeling the softness of them, and feeling the way her hair was so silky as it spilled onto his cheeks.

He loved it that she held on to her cries. That this private woman, even as she squeezed her thighs and gripped him tight, even as she groaned and he felt her tension, did not reveal her hurt.

He held her by the shoulders and pushed her up, so he could see the concentration in her face and the parting of her lips as she came. He lifted and drove into her, and shot deep and she took every precious drop.

He loved it that they did not speak of love.

Not yet.

And that there was no need for either of them to ask if there had been anyone else since the last time.

Freya collapsed onto him.

'Happy Birthday,' he breathed again.

'It is.'

Truly it was.

But then, every day was made better, even the sad ones, when it was shared with him.

CHAPTER FOURTEEN

HE LOOKED TIRED, Freya thought when she woke the next morning. Even asleep he looked tired.

And it wasn't down to last night—she knew that.

He'd looked tired on the day she had met him and every day in between.

And if ever there was a man who deserved breakfast in bed it was him...

Richard woke to the sight of Freya holding a tray.

There was toast and *loads* of mushrooms, and a poached egg too, as well as a glass of orange juice. There was even a flower on the tray from one of her many birthday bouquets.

'What's this for?'

'I don't know.' Freya smiled. 'It's a rarity.'

'Well, thank you,' he said as she climbed into bed. 'What are you up to today?'

'Not much,' Freya said. 'On Friday I'm doing the London Eye at sunset with Stella, Kelly and Pat. I told them I wanted to cram in more of London before I went home and so we're going for my birthday.'

She looked over to him and they stared at each other. It was such a relief to be honest now about her leaving London.

'You're making friends, then?'

She nodded, but nothing had really changed—home was still home. So she addressed it. 'Richard, you warned me never to rely on you...'

'I know I did,' he said.

'So I'm making the best decision for *me*. I don't know yet if I'll go back to the birthing unit, I'm actually considering the main hospital. I've got a lot more experience now. I can go up a level—maybe two.'

The lack of rental income from her cottage was starting to bite, plus there was her rent in London...

'I'm not moving to Siberia.'

'I know.'

'Have you made up your mind about the private job?'

But they were teetering on the edge of long-distance relationship speak now, and he could not stand the thought of that. So instead of answering he gave her a kiss.

'I'm going to go.'

'Why?'

'Because I don't want to say something I might regret.'

He sounded as if he was cross with her, but it went a whole lot deeper than that. He didn't want to tell Freya that he too was considering moving.

To Cromayr Bay.

He would only say it when he was sure.

Until he'd properly thought it through, Richard wouldn't be sharing it with a soul.

It didn't stop his mother from finding out about it, though...

'What the *hell*, Richard?' Amanda said by way of welcome as he stepped through the door.

She was holding a letter.

'Did you open my mail?' Richard snarled.

'I was looking for an envelope and it just fell on the

floor. Where the hell is Cromayr Bay and why on earth is the hospital there inviting you to come and have a look around?'

'It's none of your business.'

'Well, I'm making it my business. You would die of boredom. I know you, Richard. You're like me.'

'Don't terrify me, I beg you.'

'I mean it. You would seriously keel over from a lack of adrenaline. I should know. Have you *any* idea what it was like being married to your father and playing second bloody fiddle to his patients while looking at sheep all the time?'

Richard rolled his eyes.

'You've got an opportunity to go into the private sector.'

'I don't want to.'

'Oh, for God's sake stop lying to yourself.' Amanda was so appalled that she forgot to lie about her snooping. 'You've already signed the contract for the private hospital. You can't back out now.'

'You've seen that too?' Richard said, and he was so furious at this invasion of his privacy that he lashed out. 'I believe *you* signed a contract too…"till death us do part"… and then you went and did it another two times.'

'Don't!' Amanda roared. 'I only married in church once and I meant every word.'

'Please…'

'Richard, for our twentieth wedding anniversary I told your father to get a locum, and he did, but then some patient needed him…'

'Mrs Lockley was terminally ill,' Richard reminded her wearily, because he knew the story well.

'And so was our marriage! Yet she survived longer than *we* did! Two more months, in fact. Your *hero* father didn't want to leave her, and in staying with her he neglected me.

On the night of our wedding anniversary. When a locum could surely have dealt with things for once. But instead *he* had to be the one to go out to her.'

Richard just stood there, stunned, as his mother spun the mirror and for the first time ever he could see her side.

'Do you know,' Amanda raged, 'when he got back that night he asked me to make him some Horlicks and then complained that there were lumps in it? I told him he wanted a live-in nurse or a housekeeper—not a wife. I gave him an ultimatum…'

And then she started to cry.

Really cry.

Not the dramatic tears he had grown up with.

'I thought he'd change when I threatened to leave him, that he'd beg me to stay, but instead he let me go…'

She really hadn't meant to end it. Richard knew that now.

'And then what did he go and do?' Amanda sobbed. 'He married our *housekeeper*. I'm sure there was something going on before…'

'No,' Richard said. Of that he was sure. 'He was gutted after you'd gone. He just moped around. He's a stubborn old mule, he would never have begged you to come back, and I guess Vera felt like routine.'

'You're positive there was nothing going on between them while we were still married?'

'I'm as certain as I can be,' Richard countered, for though he'd always felt sure, he wasn't in the game of giving absolute guarantees. 'Anyway, they're divorced now, and I don't think it was a love match—though I bet she got all the lumps out of his Horlicks,' he said, and through her tears his mother laughed.

'I loved your father, Richard, very, *very* much. But he completely refused to compromise.'

'I can see that now.'

And now Richard wasn't only terrified of being like his mother, but like his father too. While he knew he'd shut Freya out, he wasn't merely being stubborn.

For this decision had to be his.

He had to be certain before he made it.

He would not offer her a life spent with even a shade of resentment. He'd grown up on that. So many ruined dinners because his father had been working.

He thought of Freya coming in with the breakfast tray, all smiling and being nice. Of course she'd understood that he'd had to dash off.

But what if it happened every morning?

Most nights?

'I don't think I was cut out to be a doctor's wife,' said his mother.

'I don't know about that,' Richard said. 'I don't think he knew what he had.'

Until it was gone.

Freya would soon be gone too.

But Richard would only make the move if he was absolutely sure he'd never begrudge the fact that he had.

He made his mother a cup of tea, and by the time he had done so Amanda had calmed down.

'Think again about going private, Richard. You wouldn't have signed the contract if it wasn't something you wanted.'

'I was just trying the idea on for size. It's signed—but it's not sealed, nor is it delivered.'

'What on earth are you doing, looking at Cromayr Bay?'

'I've met someone.'

'Freya,' his mother said.

'How do you know?'

'I spoke to her,' Amanda reminded him.

Richard remembered the first morning he had awoken with Freya in his bed, when he had handed her the phone.

'She's Scottish,' Amanda added. 'So I'm guessing it's no coincidence.'

'Freya was born there—she's got family and friends there. She's tied to the place in a way that I'm not tied anywhere. I don't get your argument,' he went on. 'You're saying my father put too much into his work and never gave you enough attention. This move might be my way to negate all that.'

'It was never about the hours he worked, Richard. It was about the way he spent the hours he had at home. He gave all he had to his patients and left nothing for me.'

Richard had, up to this point, been quietly on the side of his father. He'd tried to stay loyal to both parents—of course he had—but in truth he had thought his mother a little shallow.

He didn't feel that now.

'I'm sorry,' Richard said.

'For what?'

'All the eye-rolls over the years.'

She smiled.

'But you are *never* going through my mail again.'

'I won't—but don't rush into this, Richard,' she warned. 'Don't end up like me...resenting the person you love.'

CHAPTER FIFTEEN

'RICHARD'S LEAVING.'

It was said just like that—and not even specifically to Freya.

They were lining up to board the London Eye, Stella, Kelly and Pat, all present, and Freya's heart felt as if it had fallen through a trap door.

'How's Von taking it?' Kelly asked.

'She's hoping to get off with him again at his leaving do!' Stella laughed, and then grimaced. 'Sorry, Freya. You had a bit of a thing going on with him for a while, didn't you?'

Freya nodded, and then pushed out a smile. 'I can't say I wasn't warned.'

The view from the London Eye was incredible.

It was the beginning of December and the sky was white, the trees bare and silver in the evening sun. Freya's heart twisted at the sight of the majestic city. Buckingham Palace, the Houses of Parliament, and the grey of the River Thames.

It was beautiful, and in that moment, high above London, Freya wished they might never have to come down.

Afterwards they went for a curry.

Freya's diary was filling up now, because it was nearing Christmas and she'd been invited to a couple of parties.

He would be gone by then.

She let herself into her flat and it was a relief to close the door and be home.

Home.

Freya looked at the curtains. Though they didn't block out the noise from the street she found the sound of cars and buses quite soothing now. And then she looked at the cushions, and the flowers sitting on the coffee table, and thought, yes, this was starting to feel like home.

Yet soon there would be no Richard.

No chance of seeing him at work…no hope of him asking to be 'used'.

And no scold in his voice when he told her off for her empty cupboards.

Oh, why did he have to leave *now*? Just when her world was coming right?

She went over to the shelf and looked at a photo of her little house in Cromayr Bay. Then she picked up the picture of her and her friends taken when they'd passed their midwifery exams.

And then she saw it.

Freya wasn't really one for efficient dusting, and she'd never taken the photos down until now.

But there it was.

A black and white picture of *him*, cut out on paper. And she wished, how she wished it was colour—because one day soon she might not remember the details of his eyes. Or the way he said her name—the change in his voice—so subtle at times that no one else would notice—that made her his lover and was audible only to her.

This is what you've lost, Freya.

And then her phone rang and the world suddenly felt better.

'Hello, Aunty Freya.'

Freya could hear the rise of elation in her friend's voice. 'Alison?'

'It's a girl—a little girl—four weeks early, but everything's fine. She's not even an hour old yet…'

There was a waver in her voice and Freya closed her eyes as elation dimmed and Alison dipped into the valley of pain.

'She looks like her brother.'

And then, for the first time since that awful day, Freya knew what to say. If his sister looked like Andrew then it was certainly true. 'She must be perfect, then.'

For Andrew *had* been. Utterly, utterly perfect. From his soft brown hair down to his tiny toes.

And Freya had been so busy taking care of her friend, helping her through, that she'd somehow stuffed down her own grief.

It had been such a gut-wrenching loss. For Alison and Callum and their families, and for their friends and all who loved them too.

It was sometimes said that it took a village to raise a child.

Well, Cromayr Bay had mourned when Alison and Callum had lost theirs. He had been one of their own.

'When can you come and see her?'

'I'll see what I can do,' Freya said. 'I have to go in tomorrow, but I'll see if I can swap over the next couple of days. I'll call you in the morning. Go and enjoy…?'

'Eleanor,' Alison said.

It was hard to cry herself to sleep after such wonderful news, and Callum had been sending over pictures and, yes, Eleanor was utterly, utterly perfect.

But just after midnight Freya lay back on her pillow and sobbed.

* * *

Morning arrived and she woke with Richard's picture in the bed beside her. Before she headed for work she took a photo of it with her phone.

At work, she made a beeline for Stella.

'I hate to do this,' Freya said, 'but my friend just had her baby and Kelly has said that she'll swap with me. I'll work the weekend.'

'You haven't carried the Obstetric Squad pager yet, though,' Stella said, and then looked through the roster. 'It's okay—Pat's on, so she can do it. You need two more times observing and then Dr Mina needs to supervise you heading one.'

Freya nodded.

'What did she have?'

'A little girl—Eleanor.'

'Gorgeous,' Stella said.

Richard was coming out of ICU when Freya saw him. He was with Dominic.

'Hi.' Freya smiled.

'Freya,' he said as he passed. But a few steps on he excused himself and caught up with her. 'Are you free tomorrow?'

'I haven't got the energy to be used,' Freya admitted—because really she was terrible at flings.

When he was present she could forget for a while the hurt that awaited when he left. But when they were apart it was hell.

'I just wondered if you'd like to go to dinner.'

So you can tell me you're leaving?

She guessed it was for that.

A bastard he might be, to some, but she *liked* him—very much indeed—and perhaps he considered a hospital corridor with his registrar waiting not the ideal place for a goodbye.

'I can't,' Freya said. 'I'm away home after my shift. I'm getting the overnight train. Alison had her baby late last night.'

'You'll be wrecked. What time does your train get in?'

'Seven—though I'll hang around at Waverley for the shops to open and then I am buying up pink.'

'So a little girl?'

'Eleanor.' Freya nodded. 'Then later we'll all be over to the Tavern to wet the baby's head.'

'Well…enjoy.'

Of course there were no offers from Richard to drive her this time, and she had an awful feeling this might be the last time she would see him.

He gave her a nice smile and then, because he was Richard, no conversation lasted very long without the interruption of his phone or pager.

This time it was the phone. 'My mother,' he said and pocketed it. 'I'll call her back in a moment.'

'How is she?'

'Well, she's found an apartment that isn't mine, so that's good. I don't know,' he said. 'I think that I misjudged her…'

And he left it at that.

Yet she desperately wanted to know more.

There was just so much to talk about—so much of each other to explore and to know.

And she had blown it, Freya knew.

CHAPTER SIXTEEN

WHEN SHE GOT to Waverley Freya drank coffee and ate almond croissants until the shops opened, and then went on a little frenzy of buying pink.

Then she took the train to Cromayr Bay. And as she crossed the bridge she gazed out over her home.

Home?

Yet London was also home.

Freya had never felt more confused in her life.

Visiting Alison was brilliant—to see her holding the tiny bundle and to know that they were both healthy and thriving, even though she might be struggling more than most new mothers today, was wonderful.

Callum went for a walk, and to meet some aunties who were arriving, and Freya had her first hold.

Oh, the baby was so soft and pink, and she had beautiful little eyes and a pretty snub nose. And when Freya put her finger to Eleanor's hand little fingers closed around it.

'She's gorgeous—and she really does look like…' Freya hesitated and then made herself say his name. 'Andrew.'

Oh, grief was so hard when it was personal. At work she could do it, but here, sitting on the bed, it wasn't just Alison she was scared of hurting.

It was herself.

Richard, damn him, had been right again. *She* was grieving too. Because right about now she should be taking Andrew down to the café to give Alison and Callum a break.

And as she gazed down at Eleanor a tear splashed down Freya's cheek for a little toddler who wasn't there.

'Freya?' Alison asked. 'Talk to me.'

'I don't want to say anything that might upset you,' Freya admitted, and as she looked up she could see that Alison was crying too.

'You might,' Alison said, 'because I'm easily upset. Right now I'm both the happiest and the saddest I've ever been. Andrew should be here.'

'Yes,' Freya said, and her tears fell freely now. 'He should be.' And then she said something else too. 'I'm sorry if I haven't been here for you, Alison.'

'You have been.'

Alison was honest. She had no reason not to be.

'You were there every step when he was born, and at the funeral too. And you were here when I had the bleed and you're here now. Freya, losing Andrew changed things. Not for better or worse, but his death changed things. The world felt out of order. In many ways it still does. But even if you'd still lived down the street it was still something that I had to get through alone.'

'You've got Callum.'

'Of course I do. And we've got through this together. But there are parts of this that you can only do on your own. Look…'

She gestured to the window and Freya looked out, and sure enough there was Callum, walking on the green. And as Freya watched he ran the back of his hand over his eyes before heading back in.

He was crying alone and trying to be strong.

'Is there anything I can do?' Freya asked, not really expecting there to be. After all, if there was she'd have done it already.

If love could have fixed this, then there would have been a big brother in the room.

'Could you take this to him for me?' Alison asked, and untied a little pink balloon from Eleanor's crib. 'Can you tell him he has a sister? And can you buy a blue one for him?'

'Of course.'

And they were friends again—well, they always had been, but they had both needed to find their own way to grieve.

The door opened and in came Callum, all smiles but with glassy eyes, and several aunts and uncles who had just arrived.

'Freya!' His voice was bright. 'We've waited for you to get here but we can wait no more. We're wetting the bairn's head over at the Tavern tonight.'

'I can't wait.' Freya smiled.

She headed down to the gift shop with the pink balloon in hand, and bought a blue one as Alison had asked. She bought flowers and a little windmill too.

Freya hadn't been to the cemetery since Andrew's funeral, yet she found his grave easily, for that sombre walk was etched in her heart.

She had been looking out for Alison then, worried that after surgery and all the exhausting emotion her friend might faint.

Alison almost had.

Freya walked down the path and there it was, his tiny grave. She looked at his name and the dates on the little cross. Two days he had lived, but he would never be forgotten.

'You have a wee sister,' Freya said, though the wind took her words, and it was so cold the heat of her tears stung her cheeks as she tied the balloons and then put the little windmill into one of the pots and watched it whirling for a while.

The wind was biting as she walked the short distance to her home, and once there Freya lay on the bed, a jumble of emotions pounding through her heart.

Was she considering staying in London for a chance with a man who had told her never to rely on him?

Only it wasn't just for Richard—she was coming to love the place too. The noise and the people and the flower seller who had, for no reason, given her a rose the other day. And grumpy old Len. Oh, and not forgetting cynical Stella.

Yet she loved it here too.

At six, Freya dressed for the celebrations.

She did her hair and her make-up, and put on a dark red wool dress, black stockings and boots.

She made every effort—because she was thrilled and happy and she wanted to celebrate Eleanor's arrival. And she was so pleased that they'd waited until she was there.

And then she put on a warm overcoat and headed for the Tavern.

The party was in full swing when she arrived, and Freya knew she had been wrong before. The hardest thing wasn't walking into a pub knowing your ex might be there.

It was knowing he couldn't possibly be.

She hung her coat up and then headed over to the bar, where a large whisky was thrust into her hand. It was as if the entire town was out, celebrating the marvellous news.

Betty and Dr Campbell were in good spirits and even Leah Roberts had found a babysitter and was there with her husband, Davey.

It was absolutely the best night.

Even with a piece of her heart missing.

A big piece.

Actually, now she thought about it, just a tiny part of her heart remained.

And then she saw him.

He was standing in the doorway, wearing a suit and looking around...

Not Malcolm.

Richard.

She thought she must be seeing things, surely, but then she met his eyes and gave him an uncertain smile as he walked over.

'What are you doing here?' Freya asked.

'I've got a booking in the restaurant,' Richard said. 'If you'd care to join me?'

The newly refurbished Tavern Restaurant was both stunning and familiar. The gorgeous traditional Scottish stone walls had been retained, but a deep moss-green carpet gave the momentary feeling that they were outside a rugged castle. The tables were dressed simply in white, and in the candlelight the silverware gleamed, while on each tablecloth stood a small vase holding thistles.

And she was here with Richard.

Over and over Freya had to keep telling herself that—not that she could forget it—in order to hold on to the dream, else he might disappear.

They ordered drinks and made small talk with Gordon and between themselves as they waited for them to arrive. But when Gordon started to go through the menu, she blinked at the slightly impatient note to Richard's voice.

'Could we have a moment, please?'

'Certainly...' Gordon nodded.

Freya looked over to Richard and could see his discomfort. And then she knew why he was here. They had been more than a fling—they both knew that—and now, Freya guessed, knowing she was in Scotland, Richard had decided that she deserved a little more than a hospital corridor goodbye.

'I'm not sure if you've heard,' Richard said, 'but I've given in my notice.'

'I heard.' Freya nodded and thought her voice was a little high, as if braced for pain.

'I've been doing a lot of thinking,' Richard said. 'I didn't want to rush into things. I don't like snap decisions.'

'But they're what you do best,' Freya pointed out. 'You think on the run.'

'At work, perhaps,' Richard agreed, 'but I've had fifteen years of training and supervision and amazing mentors. When it comes to matters of the heart I have no clue. I didn't exactly have exemplary role models in that department…' Then he paused, because that wasn't quite right. 'I never thought I'd be asking my mother for relationship advice, but I have been.'

'And what advice did she give?'

'To take the private hospital position and to hell with you—and, frankly, I agreed with her.'

And then he saw Freya's pain, and knew that his job, when at all possible, was to take away pain.

He took her hand. 'I agreed with her for about two weeks,' he said. 'I accepted the role with Marcus and gave notice at the Primary. But then I spoke to my father too.'

'And…?'

'I didn't ask him for advice,' Richard said. 'Instead I gave it. I told him that he could quit telling me he was lonely, because it was his own bloody fault. He lost the love of his life. I don't intend to do that.'

Freya looked up.

'My ties to London are through work and friends. I didn't go to school there. I don't have family there. I understand that this is your home—the place you love. Now, I'm not sure if Cromayr Bay Hospital is big enough for me, but I'll try it for size if it means being with you. I love you.'

She had it all in that moment.

The gift of his love was like a shiny parcel, momentarily blinding her, and this gift came with a velvet box. He opened it and there was a ring. She could see it, but not really see it, for it was blurred by the tears in her eyes.

They were not all happy tears.

She had everything she wanted, Freya thought. Yet all she truly wanted was him. Richard.

'That won't be necessary.' She looked up and saw his face bleach pale, realised he thought she was rejecting the ring. 'I mean the move—not the ring.'

'Freya…?'

'I went on the London Eye and it was an amazing view,' Freya said. 'Not better, nor more beautiful than here, just different. Richard…'

She tried to explain the jumble of her feelings with a heart that was pounding and a head that was slightly giddy.

'After we broke up I was scared that I was thinking of extending my contract in London just in the hope of getting back with you…'

There—she had said it.

'I'd been warned by several people—including yourself—not to count on a future with you. And so I made my decision based on what I knew. I'm falling in love with London and, as exhausting as it is, I love the work. And…' She could be honest now. 'I love *you*. I had to give us a chance.'

'You're staying in London?'

Freya nodded. 'Can you retrieve your notice?'

'God, yes,' Richard said.

He slipped the ring on her slender finger and they toasted their news with a single malt whisky that tasted amazing on his lips when they kissed.

'And now,' Richard said, 'I'm having that game pie.'

He'd been waiting for it for a very long time.

CHAPTER SEVENTEEN

A WEDDING IN Cromayr Bay would never pass unnoticed. That was the beauty of home, Freya thought as she dozed on the train on her way up to Waverley.

In the end it was the bride who had struggled to get time off from work. She'd had one more Obstetrics Squad Emergency to attend before she could be signed off, and Stella had wanted it done before she renewed her contract. As well as that, her trips to Scotland had meant she had very limited days off to indulge in planning a wedding.

A winter wedding.

Richard, though, didn't start his new contract until the end of February, so he had been up to Cromayr Bay a few times without Freya, and had finally sorted out his phone so that Freya could call him.

It was a silent coach, so instead of calling she texted him to say she'd arrived at Waverley and was taking the train to Cromayr Bay. She was secretly hoping that he would meet her.

I'll see you in the morning, then.

Freya was dying to see him, but there was just so much to fit in.

Has your mother arrived?

Not yet.

They were both worried about that, and pretending not to be. Richard's parents hadn't been in the same room without a judge present for seventeen years. But he refused to think of that now.

Richard loved Cromayr Bay. It had the bracing, salty, sharp air that his body required. It was a place he could retreat to and a place he could learn to relax in, for that was necessary indeed.

And then his parents arrived.

The day before the wedding.

The concierge at the Tavern, who doubled as the duty manager, called Richard down to meet Amanda, who stood in Reception bristling.

'My room's not ready.'

'It will be soon,' Richard said.

'You don't understand,' she hissed. 'Your *father's* here. He's over there at the bar.'

Great.

A fight between his parents on the eve of his wedding was the last thing he needed, and so after a few nips of whisky with Freya's brothers, along with many other new friends who had joined them, the bear retired to his cave.

And then a horrible thing happened.

From the room above his own he heard his mother laugh.

Not a bad thing on its own.

But then he heard the unmistakable rumbling sound of his father's laugh too...

By morning Richard had decided that, while the res-

taurant might have been refurbished, the squeaking beds
at the Tavern still needed an overhaul.

He *had* to tell Freya—except it wasn't Freya who answered her phone. Instead it was Alison.

'No, you *can't* speak to her!'

Freya frowned when she heard Alison's firm tone.

She had seen that it was Richard calling, but, given
that she was getting her make-up done, Alison had taken
the call.

'Let me speak to him,' Freya said, holding out her hand
for the phone.

'No!'

It would seem that Alison was taking her Matron of
Honour duties very seriously.

'Is it a medical emergency?' she asked Richard.

It would seem not.

'Are you going to jilt the bride?'

Freya rolled her eyes and snapped her fingers, indicat-
ing that she wanted to be given the phone, but Alison had
other ideas.

'Then there's nothing that can't wait. Anything urgent,
have the best man call *me*—not the bride!'

The flowers in Freya's bouquet were the very same as
the ones she had bought on the day she had decided to give
London a go. The bunch of pale lilacs perhaps didn't appear a very opulent display, but they were now the flowers that made her 'cheer up, love'.

And Freya was both cheered up and nervous as she felt
her father's arm beneath her hand and she walked towards
the love of her life.

Richard did not stare ahead, instead he turned and
watched her every step.

*Yes, Officer, I will remember what she was wearing
for ever.*

Her dress was the colour of a pearl moon as it hung over the local bridges, and on her feet were silk ballet pumps. The flowers he couldn't name, but he knew that she bought them often.

As for her hair... Freya wore it down, and yet it sprang up in curls about her face. Wild and dark, it moved with her.

Make-up? That he would never recall. For as her father let go of her arm and Richard took her hands nothing else mattered.

'You made it,' he said.

'Just.'

They shared a smile and a couple of words in that moment before proceedings commenced.

The vicar spoke of the seriousness of the vows before them as he addressed the packed congregation. And Richard's voice was lovely and clear as he repeated the words which became his promise to her.

'To love and to cherish, till death do us part.'

Those words had always made her a little sad, talking of death at a wedding. And yet they were actually rather gorgeous to hear, she thought, when she was being held by Richard's eyes.

He was taking this as seriously as she, Freya knew. He had avoided and hidden from love, but—like heartache—love found you and chased you until you either denied it or faced it.

And they faced each other now, and smiled as they were pronounced man and wife.

Richard kissed his bride. Their smiling lips met, but he felt the tremble of hers beneath his as emotion caught up with her.

'It's okay,' he said, and briefly held her, 'we've got each other for life.'

They turned and walked down the aisle to see many smiling, friendly faces. Some were familiar to Freya but new to Richard, and some were the other way around.

Freya knew there were friends from the Primary, who had made the trip, but first she smiled to her parents and her brothers, and then to Richard's parents, who stood side by side.

Freya seriously hoped there would be no arguing between them tonight—though Richard had told her it was his parents' problem if they did.

And then there was Kelly, Stella, Pat, Rita and Angela and, it seemed, half the anaesthetics department, including Dominic, who was looking forward to having his old boss back.

They stood and smiled for the camera, and it actually wasn't too painful because Freya had insisted on only a few formal shots.

'It's too cold to stand outside,' she had said, and so, surprisingly quickly, they were back at the Tavern, in the gorgeous new function room at the very top of the hotel.

Freya hadn't seen it before. Only Richard, who had organised things, had been inside.

It was stunning.

Huge long tables were dressed with tall white candles, and there were large bunches of wild Scottish flowers.

It felt as if they were in a castle, Freya thought. And the arched windows looked out on the view she loved—though she really didn't notice the view as Richard made his speech.

He kept it short and sincerely thanked everyone, especially those who had travelled from afar—'Including me,' he quipped.

He got through the formalities, then admitted a truth.

'I never thought I'd be doing this,' Richard said, 'but

I am so honoured to be here. As some of you will know, Freya and I have two places we call home—one in London, another here in Cromayr Bay. I love them both. And, as I've found out, so too does my *wife*.'

He paused, not for effect, but more because it didn't even sound odd to be saying that. It felt right.

And it sounded just right to Freya, too, and she gave him a smile before he spoke on.

'It's not the house, or the location, or even the view. It's the *people* who make a place feel like home. But at the end of the day you close the door. Freya,' he said, 'I will always be happy to come home to you.'

It was the loveliest day of her life.

Freya found out via the best man about a few of Richard's more colourful escapades, and she shared a smile with Stella. She couldn't say that she hadn't been warned.

And then there was a toast to the bridesmaids and the formalities were done.

Almost.

'This is our first dance,' Richard said.

'As man and wife?'

'No,' Richard said. 'This is our very first dance.'

Indeed it was, Freya realised.

She and Richard hadn't yet made it to the cinema, let alone the dance floor. And so it was utter bliss to rest in his arms for a moment and savour their first dance. One she would remember for ever.

Perhaps they should be gazing into each other's eyes, Freya thought, but it was nice just to be held and to breathe in the scent of him and enjoy a quiet moment.

That was how he made her feel. Safe in his arms, whatever the adventure. And he made her feel something else too...

She looked up to him. 'I want to break out of my skin

and dance,' Freya admitted, and they both knew how rare
this was, since she was not a dancing type of person.

'When we're alone,' Richard said in his most deadpan,
sexiest voice, 'you can certainly break out of your skin
and dance. I might even join you!'

He made her toes curl.

And he made her smile in a way no one else did.

But then she saw something.

His parents were dancing and it didn't look strained.

In fact, they were gazing into each other's eyes.

'Richard…' She raised her head, but he knew what she
had seen.

'I know.' He spoke low into the shell of her ear. 'That's
why I tried to call you. I think they might be getting back
together.'

'No!'

'Yes,' he said, and then he lifted her chin, so that she
looked deep into his eyes. 'We'll never be like them. I'm
going to take care of the love we've found.'

'And me,' Freya told him.

They would both take the best of care of this very precious love.

EPILOGUE

'BUT WHY WOULDN'T you have him *here*?' Amanda asked.

They were discussing Richard and Freya's baby, which was due in three weeks.

'Firstly, it might be a she,' Richard pointed out to his mother. 'Secondly, it should be Freya's choice. We're going up at the weekend for a few days and we'll decide then.'

Except that they wouldn't.

Richard didn't know it yet, but Freya was already in labour.

She did *not* want a false alarm, nor to get to the hospital and find out that she wasn't very far along and so she had been keeping quiet.

But she was certain now.

The contractions were fifteen minutes apart and they were getting stronger. The decision as to where to have their baby had now, as of this afternoon, become a moot point.

They went home to Cromayr Bay a lot.

Richard's job remained as constant and as high pressure as ever, but now, instead of him flying away, they drove to there. And if they didn't feel like driving they took the train, because it really was the most wonderful train journey and so relaxing.

Apart from at Newcastle. Each time the train pulled

into there Freya and Richard would exchange a glance as they recalled that text exchange that had nearly put an end to them for ever.

Her cottage was slowly coming on, and Richard loved their time there so much that a role at Cromayr Bay Hospital still wasn't completely off the cards.

After a couple of days spent catching up with friends and loved ones, or simply unwinding alone together, they'd get back in the car, or board another train, and come home.

Freya had fallen in love with London.

Properly.

She had started to fall in love with it when she and Richard had broken up. It had been her friends there who had helped her through, even if they hadn't known just how broken-hearted she'd really been.

They had both been a bit undecided as to where they wanted the baby to born.

Amanda, though, had clearly made up her mind. 'I hope you have it here.'

'Why?' Richard asked. 'I thought you enjoyed your stay at the Tavern.'

'I did.'

'Good.'

There had been no reference to that night—no mention, no comment. If Richard hadn't been unlucky enough to land the room beneath them he might never have known.

'Richard,' Amanda said now, 'can I have a word?'

'Go ahead.' He would not be following her into the kitchen so they could speak quietly. 'I'll be telling Freya what you say anyway, so you might just as well say it here.'

'Very well. Now, I know after I called things off with Roger, that I said I was through with men but... Richard, please don't roll your eyes. Your father and I have been seeing each other since your wedding.'

Richard said nothing.

'We haven't rushed into anything. We've both done that before, and we didn't want to put you through another wedding, but we…we got married last week.'

Richard just stood there.

'It was a quiet wedding,' Amanda said. 'We didn't want a fuss—or rather I didn't want a fuss—and so we went to Gretna Green, and had a little honeymoon at the Tavern.'

'Why aren't you both here to tell me?' Richard asked. 'Is he too busy working?'

'No, we were both going to come, but then we decided that it might be a bit much for the two of us to turn up at your door saying everything's all right now. While it is for us—well, we know that it can't have been easy on you. That's why I came alone.'

He smiled and kissed his mother the perpetual bride. 'Congratulations. And I really do mean that.'

Freya kissed her too, and then Richard got out some champagne. As he did so, Freya excused herself and went into the bedroom.

The pains were getting strong now, that was for certain, but also there was a need to be alone as she thought of Richard and all he had been through with his parents.

For what?

Nearly two decades apart and a whole lot of heartache in between—because neither would back down or consider the other person's side.

Freya knew she had a lot to be grateful for.

Of course, when she came out Amanda showed them the wedding pictures, and Freya made herself scarce now and then, because she wanted to tell Richard that she was in labour alone.

At last Amanda looked at the time. 'I really do have to go or I'll miss my train…'

'Does my father want his dinner?' Richard asked, and his voice was wry.

'No, he's taking me out.'

'Good for you.'

They saw her out, and although Richard hadn't jumped up and down at the news, Freya could tell he was pleased.

'At least it will make things easier on the baby.' Richard commented once she had gone. 'Just plain old Grandma and Grandpa Lewis. We'll have to wait until he's old enough to fill him in on the last twenty years.'

He recalled what they had been discussing before his mother had shared her news. They *did* need to make their minds up.

'Freya, if you want to have the baby in Scotland then…'

'We're having it here, Richard.'

'You don't have to make your mind up now.'

'The baby already has. The contractions are ten minutes apart.'

'Is that why you kept ducking out of the room?'

'Yes.'

But she didn't duck out for the next one, and he felt her stomach turn to rock.

'They're getting worse,' Freya said.

'They're getting *stronger*,' Richard teased, because he heard a lot of midwife-speak every day at work.

But then he saw the chink of anxiety in those guarded green eyes that only he could read.

'Do you want to go to the hospital now?'

'Yes.'

It was a wise choice, Freya had decided. The Underground wasn't an option, and she knew the traffic was terrible on a Friday night, even though the Primary wasn't a particularly long drive from where they lived.

'Oh, God!' she shouted as they didn't even move an inch through one traffic-light-change.

'You're doing really well.'

'No, seriously, Richard! I can't have it in a car.'

'You're not going to. We'll be there soon.'

'How soon?'

'Soon-*ish*,' he said.

'I'm stuck in traffic with an anaesthetist and I'm going to be too far along for an epidural!'

Richard said nothing.

And then there was the hospital, and the ugly grey building had never looked more beautiful to Freya.

He held her hand as they walked the terribly long walk along the yellow line, and when they pushed open the doors to the maternity unit Freya had never been more relieved to be anywhere in her life.

'Freya—welcome!'

Stella had got her name right for once. But she was a patient now, Freya realised as she was helped into a gown and examined.

'You are doing an amazing job,' Stella told her. 'You're four…nearly five centimetres dilated.'

'Only four centimetres!'

'Nearly five—and that's a great time to call for an anaesthetist,' Stella said, because that was on Freya's birthing plan.

Richard said nothing, even though he'd guessed that Freya wasn't really about to have the baby. After all, he had given many, many epidurals.

He said nice things as he felt her disappointment that she wasn't further along. 'You're well into active labour. Sometimes having an epidural too early can slow down the contractions.'

And again he said nothing when Stella informed them

that Dominic would be getting to them very soon—well, just as soon as he could…

Richard knew that if Dominic was delayed when his boss's wife was here then it would be with good reason.

Yet after some more waiting Richard better understood just how awful it was to see someone you loved in pain and be unable to help them. Worse, to be able to help them but to have to step back.

But then the door to D5 was opened and a very nice sight for any labouring mother was there.

'Hi!'

Dominic was a bit breathless, but his smile was so nice he put Freya at ease immediately. And both Freya and Richard knew and trusted everyone in this room.

'I think I'm in love with Dominic,' Freya said when the pain had eased.

'I bet you say that to all the anaesthetists,' Stella teased.

It was a gentle evening.

Dr Mina came in and checked that all was well, and as always she made Freya feel calm, and then Freya dozed on and off and later was thrilled when the night staff came on and she saw that her midwife was Kelly.

Things really had moved along because now, just after ten, when Kelly examined her she told her it was time to start to push.

The lights stayed dimmed and with Kelly's encouragement she was soon pushing effectively. It was a good epidural that had been administered, because she could feel the pressure of the contractions but not the pain—though it was still exhausting first-baby work.

And then the room started to fill up.

Pat came in to take the baby.

And Dr Mina came back in too.

Freya assumed it was just because she was a member of staff.

Not so.

The room was still calm, but Richard could see that forceps were fast becoming an option.

He pulled back Freya's leg as Pat did the same on the other side, while Dr Mina tied on a plastic gown.

'Freya,' Kelly urged, 'I want you to give me a big push *now*.'

The last moments were here, and Freya went inside herself.

'Freya,' Kelly said again, and it felt as if her voice came from afar. 'I need you to *push*.'

'Good girl,' Dr Mina encouraged her.

Except Freya was both scared and spent. She was slight and slender, and Richard wasn't, and this baby was large.

'Freya?'

She opened her eyes to him and Richard stared deep into the darkest of greens. He loved this sullen woman and the fight it had taken to gain her trust. He loved how she did not jump to anyone's command nor readily hand over her guarded heart.

Yet with time she had handed it to *him*.

And now he watched as she rallied again, and then, deep in the early hours of morning, a promise for the future arrived.

A boy.

He lay on Freya's stomach, curled up and stunned for half a moment, but then he let out a husky cry.

'Richard?' Pat said, and held out scissors for him to cut the cord.

Unexpectedly, he declined.

For once neither Richard's head, hands nor heart were steady.

The boy was perfect.

Freya pulled him up into her arms and held him, taking in every finger and toe and tasting his breath as he cried.

'Do we know his name?' Kelly smiled as she wrote on the little birth tags.

'William,' Freya said, and looked down at little William, unable to believe he was really here.

And then everyone melted away and they were left alone to have time to get to know their baby.

Richard had a hold of his son. He held him to his chest in those lovely strong arms.

Freya had never felt so happy and so balanced with the world.

'There are going to be a lot of people thrilled to know you're here,' he said to his son, in that lovely low voice.

And there were.

Yes, soon the phone calls would start, and visitors would be welcomed in, but for now it was phones off and time alone.

For both knew the importance of time.

Time together, spent as a family.

* * * * *

REUNITED BY THEIR PREGNANCY SURPRISE

LOUISA HEATON

For my mum and dad, who had their
own amnesia story.

CHAPTER ONE

HER HEELS CLICK-CLACKED down the hospital corridor, a hurried, tense staccato, as Emily headed for the familiar room that Sam had been moved to after his short stay in the ICU.

She cut a striking figure in her stylish clothes, her long honey-blonde locks held back by sunglasses on her head and her large expensive bag swinging from the crook of her elbow. Her face, beautiful without the aid of make-up, was today showing strain. Lines and dark circles framed her eyes. And those who saw her noted the way her fingers twisted and fidgeted at her wedding band.

The Beverly West Hospital was the biggest and most prestigious hospital in Beverly Hills, Los Angeles, California. Sam's care here had been amazing. From the second he'd been scooped from their crumpled, steaming vehicle and blue-lighted to its doors, Emily had not doubted for one second the level of care they had both received. Apart from that split second when she'd first received her pregnancy test results…

Outside Sam's room she could see Dr Waters and her team, standing discussing something in low voices, with the occasional glance at Sam's notes on a clipboard. They looked serious. Concerned. But why? Hadn't they just

rung her with the news that he was starting to wake up?
That was *good*, right?

Dr Waters looked up as she became aware of Emily's
approach and, meeting her by the door to the room,
pasted a polite smile onto her face. 'Mrs Saint—'

'Is he awake?' She bit her lip and again twisted the
wedding ring on her finger.

This was it. *Now or never.* She would go inside her
husband's room and either find a man who was happy
to be alive and willing to work on any problem, or the
bear of a husband she'd been used to over the last few
difficult months.

'He is. He's tired, and occasionally lapses back into
sleep—which is normal considering the trauma his brain
has been through. Coma patients usually take a day or
two to wake properly.'

'I can go in and see him? Talk to him?'

The call from Dr Waters had come in the early hours
of the morning. The phone ringing had not woken her.
She'd already been awake. Lying in her very empty bed,
staring at the ceiling and trying—still—to decide what
was best to do.

Leave Sam? Or stay and fight for their marriage?

She'd even pulled a suitcase out and laid it on the bed
one day, stood staring at it in numb indecision. Her heart
wavering. It had all seemed so very clear-cut before the
car crash. But now…? Knowing that he was sick…know-
ing that she was pregnant?

She had returned the suitcase to its storage spot and
closed the doors on it. Her mind ran back to the times
when Sam had refused to talk to her about having children, clamming up the second she raised it. Why had he
done that? Over and over again? What hadn't he been telling her? There had to be something, but his refusal even

to talk to her about it had been hurtful. They'd got to a point when they had barely been speaking to one another.

Her brain had almost torn itself in two, trying to figure out his secret. Thinking of one scenario and then another. None had seemed likely, and she'd begun to believe that maybe he just didn't want to have a child with *her*.

Emily had stared at the closed closet doors, knowing that she would do what was *right*. And the right thing here was to give Sam time to recover and then let him know about the baby. Because then there was a small chance—a tiny, infinitesimal chance—that now the baby was no longer hypothetical but real and *here* he might change his mind.

She couldn't leave him without him knowing the truth. And if he heard the news about the pregnancy and *still* didn't want to be there for her and their child *then* she would go. Step out into the world on her own, even though doing so would break her heart. She didn't want to leave Sam, but he'd made life unbearable—had backed her into a corner.

Dr Waters shifted, looking at her colleagues, who all understood the implicit suggestion that perhaps they should leave, allow her to talk to Mrs Saint alone. They gave her sympathetic smiles and scurried away.

'Of course, but before you go in there's something you need to know.'

Her blood ran cold. Was there a problem? Brain injury? Dr Waters had mentioned that there might be the possibility of something like that once before. But Sam had recovered so quickly! His coma had been short, the ICP had dropped to normal levels incredibly quickly...

'What is it?'

Sam could have anything wrong. Be blind. Deaf. Find it difficult to talk or maybe swallow.

'We spoke once before about the damage that might have occurred to Sam's brain because of the injury to his head, and after a quick examination of your husband we believe that there seems to be some sort of memory deficit—mainly amnesia. It could be temporary, of course. He might remember everything after he's had another good sleep. But right now Sam seems...*confused* about his own timeline.'

Emily let out a long, slow, measured breath. Amnesia? She'd been fearing the worst! Temporary amnesia they could deal with.

'Is that all?'

Dr Waters frowned. 'Amnesia is a significant condition. I'm not sure you understand the full—'

'I'm going in to see him.' She cut off the doctor and stepped into Sam's room. She'd been waiting long enough for this moment. Ten long days. Nothing more could keep them apart.

Ten days. It had seemed like a lifetime.

Sometimes in those ten days she'd held his hand in hers, taking advantage of the fact that he was unconscious, remembering the happier times when they'd been close, pretending it was still that way. Sometimes she'd read to him from that day's newspaper, hoping that the sound of her voice would bring him back. And sometimes she'd just sat and stared at him, mulling everything over in her head, thinking of where they'd gone wrong and how she could fix it. Imagining the day he would wake— the day his eyelids would flutter open and he would see her, sitting by his bedside like a sentinel. How he would smile and say her name, reach out slowly for her hand and kiss her fingertips...

Okay, so maybe she lived in a fantasy land at times, but surely a touch of escapism had never hurt anyone.

'Sam?' So much hope, so much need was in the pitch of her voice.

Her husband lay in bed, his face pale and relaxed against pure white starched hospital pillows, his blue eyes slowly opening, wincing at the light in the room before fixing his gaze upon her.

And *smiling*!

It's been too long since you smiled at me like that...

It was like when they'd first been going out. The way he would look at her as if he was already in love with her. As if she was pure joy for him. Had no faults. Had not driven him crazy yet with endless requests to start a family. Okay, maybe not *crazy*, but she had tried to start that conversation lots of times. In the end even *she* had refused to talk. It had been too hard. Their conversations would always somehow end in arguments, and it had been easier just not to talk at all. She'd feared what would happen if they did.

Perhaps that had been a bad thing to do. Shutting down their communication. But she'd been trying to protect their relationship. She hadn't wanted it to end.

Sucking in a breath, she rushed to his side, dropping her bag on the floor, not caring as she reached for his outstretched hand, stooping down to kiss him, feeling his bristles scrape her face as his lips met hers. Nothing mattered at that moment apart from the fact that he was alive. Awake. Back with her. She never wanted to go through those ten days ever again.

It didn't matter that they'd been arguing. She was just happy that he was awake. Reacting. That he was looking at her and he was smiling and—

'How are you feeling?' She stroked his face, looking for clues, looking for any sign of discomfort that he might be trying to hide. Making sure that he wasn't in any pain. Her professional skills as a nurse-midwife were coming to the fore.

'Better for seeing you, Em,' he croaked, squeezing her fingers, and she looked down at their entwined hands and smiled.

All those days she had sat holding his hands and he had *never* squeezed back. Never shown any sign of life in his fingers. They'd just lain there, limp. Breaking her heart. It felt so good to be touching him again. Gaining strength from him.

'I've been so worried!' She sat on the bed facing him and ran her thumb over the backs of his hands.

He closed his eyes briefly, as if he couldn't stand the knowledge that she'd been so concerned for him. 'The doc says we've been in a car accident?'

The confusion in his face was heart-rending, but Emily guessed that this was the amnesia that Dr Waters had mentioned. Sam couldn't remember the crash. Sometimes people's brains would exclude certain bad experiences or memories, to help prevent itself from feeling hurt. Like a safety mechanism. If that was all that had happened to him then they'd both got away from this lightly.

'Yes.'

'Were *you* hurt?'

The concern in his voice and the way his blue eyes darkened at the thought relieved her. He *did* care for her! He *wasn't* angry at what had happened between them prior to this.

That was good, right? It took something like this to wake people up. To make them notice what was important in life. *Each other.* They were stronger together than they were apart. Even if they *had* been disagreeing. Giving each other the cold shoulder.

'Not really. Just whiplash.'

He frowned. 'Whiplash can be serious, Em. Have you been checked out by the doctors?'

He reached up to stroke her face, then his hand fell to her shoulders and neck to rub at her muscles, but he must be feeling tired because his hand dropped back to the bed, his eyes closing as he drifted in and out of sleep, before opening them again.

'Look at me. Weak as a kitten.'

'You need to rest. You've been out of it for ten days.'

'Ten days?' He looked upset.

'They had to put you in an induced coma, Sam. Your brain got shook around in that hard skull of yours.'

He sighed and closed his eyes again and she realised with a sudden pang that he had drifted back to sleep. And she hadn't had a chance to tell him their news, yet.

It can wait. It's waited this long. What's a few more hours?

Right now he was happy to see her. Relieved. All signs of their previous turmoil was gone. They were speaking to each other. Something they hadn't done properly for weeks, and she'd missed that.

But it was odd, wasn't it? That he should be so happy to see her? After the last few days of stony silences, the weeks of arguing and disagreement...

She liked it that he was being nice. Concerned about her whiplash, concerned about *her* health, but she wasn't used to it. It was throwing her slightly.

Having to wait a little longer to deliver the news that she was pregnant was just fine. Because she had no idea how he would react to that. Probably not very well, and then they would be back to being at war with each other. She didn't mind holding off on that for a while.

She liked what they had right now, thank you very

much. The talking. The concern for each other's wellbeing. The holding hands.

Emily stared at his hand in hers, lifted it to her mouth and kissed it, inhaling the scent of him, breathing it in like vital oxygen. Then she got up off the bed and settled into her usual chair, staring long and hard at her husband.

She was getting him back. He'd smiled at her!

She felt sure there was a chance…all this just might be okay.

Sam slowly came to. He had a wicked headache, but he appeared to be still in hospital, attached to God only knew how many wires and monitors and, beside him, her head slumped to her shoulder, asleep, was his beautiful fiancée Emily.

She looked tired. Exhausted, even. Her face was a little pale beneath wave upon wave of that gorgeous hair of hers. But then he assumed she would be. Hadn't she, or someone, told him that he'd been out of it for ten days? After some accident he couldn't even recall?

Ten days. What had he missed? Probably nothing too much. That serial he'd been watching on television had been scheduled to show its last episode the other week, so probably that. There was still another month or so before Emily's birthday, so thankfully not that. He had a big surprise planned. He was hoping to take her to Las Vegas.

It was strange, though. Only ten days and he could swear that her hair seemed longer. A little more sunbleached. Those honey tones were brighter than normal. And were those new clothes? He hadn't seen them before. But then again, Em did enjoy shopping. Perhaps she'd gone out and treated herself whilst she'd been waiting for him to recover? A little pick-me-up?

He lifted his head off the pillow to check himself out.

There didn't appear to be any limbs wrapped in bandages, no plaster casts or anything like that. Had he just got a head injury? That would explain the headache, and the fact that he'd been out of it for a while. He hated it that he was laid up in hospital, because they still had so much to do. Not only did they need to tell everyone that Emily had accepted his proposal of marriage, but there was so much to do at work, too!

His idea, of building an exclusive five-star birth centre—the Monterey Birth Centre—was close to fruition. They'd toured the halls just last week and everything had looked perfect. Almost ready for their Grand Opening.

It was going to be massive. He wanted the Monterey to be the premier birthing centre in the whole of the US. He wanted people to aspire to have their babies there, to be treated as if they were royalty and enjoy the ultimate birthing experience, which he and his team would provide whilst their patients were being fed with delectable dishes provided by a team of Michelin-starred chefs in the kitchen.

It had taken a lot of planning. And sourcing funding. But he'd found people—mainly people whose babies he had already delivered safely—to sponsor and endorse the Monterey. He'd secured a great board of directors—along with himself and Emily, of course—and his excitement for this project had driven him onward like nothing he had ever experienced before. There'd been so much to think about! But he enjoyed that.

Asking Emily to marry him had been the icing on the cake. And she'd said yes. So he guessed now he'd be busy planning a wedding, too!

They hadn't been going out long. Six months? But there was something about her—something that had reached out and grabbed him. She'd seemed so...*vul-*

nerable when they'd first met, and he'd been cautious not to scare her with his desire to be by her side. He'd not been able to pinpoint the source of that vulnerability and, to be honest, they'd both been so busy at work, and setting up the Monterey, that it hadn't seemed all that important after a while.

Emily had blossomed by his side, driven on by their shared vision. She was everything he could have wished for and he loved her deeply. She cared for and loved delivering babies as much as he did.

But today she looked exhausted. She must have been handling any last hiccups at the birth centre, working *and* having to deal with his accident and their families all by herself. No wonder she looked shattered. Had they put off the Grand Opening whilst they'd waited for him to recover?

For a brief moment he just lay there and stared at her, his heart swelling with love for the woman at his side, but after a minute or so he couldn't stand it any more and reached out to take her hand. Needing to touch her. To connect.

She blinked herself awake in seconds. 'Sam?'

He smiled and lifted her hand to his lips, pressed a kiss upon it. 'Sleeping Beauty.'

She glanced at her watch in confusion. 'I've been asleep for three hours!' She rubbed at her eyes and then glanced at him with concern. 'How are you? Are you in any pain?'

'Just a headache.'

'Should I call a nurse?'

'No, it's fine. It's understandable, considering my head got bashed. I'm sure there's some morphine being dripped in to me somewhere...' He looked up at the various drips and then smiled at her. 'I've missed you.' He squeezed her fingers, wishing he could be holding her in his arms. Wishing he could get her to come and lie beside him upon the bed. He needed to feel her next to him.

She looked a little apprehensive. 'You've been in a coma.'

'So you keep saying. But what about *you*? How are you doing? Any problems with Monterey I need to know about?'

Emily frowned and shook her head. 'No. It's all going very well.'

He let out a sigh. 'That's great news. How did Harry get on with the window treatments? Did he make the changes we asked him to?'

His fiancée looked at him, lines furrowing her brow. 'What?'

'The curtains and sashing in The Nightingale Suite. We decided to change them to that lighter gold colour. Has he done it yet? If he hasn't we need to get on that— the Grand Opening is only a few days away.'

She continued to look at him with puzzlement. 'What are you talking about?'

'The curtains were too dark. That suite is going to be our most prestigious—we want it right for the press tour. Think of the spread of pictures...'

'Press tour? We haven't had a press tour since...' Her voice drifted away and she suddenly looked at him, her eyes searching his face as she sucked in a breath. 'Sam, what day do you think it is?'

He closed his eyes and thought about it. He'd proposed on Friday, he'd been in a coma for ten days, so today had to be... 'Monday? Tuesday, maybe?'

She shook her head, her choppy blonde locks shimmering around her shoulders. 'No. I mean the month. The *year*.'

Month and year? What was she talking about? He'd been out for ten days, they'd said! He told her the date and watched as what little colour there was leeched from her face. She turned away from him, her curtain of honey-blonde hair hiding her face from his as she pulled her hands free of his grasp.

Her recoiling from him made him feel nervous. What didn't he know? 'Why are you asking? I'm not that much out of step, am I?'

He heard her sniff. Watched as she reached into her bag and pulled out a small hankie, dabbing at her eyes before she turned back to face him, bracing herself to prepare to say something she clearly thought he wouldn't be ready to hear.

'Sam... We've been married for *eighteen months*. The Monterey has been open and running for just over a year now.'

Sam stared at her hard. He swallowed painfully and his hands scrunched up the bedding as he made fists.

Eighteen months?

No! That's ridiculous...

'Why would you say that? Why would you even play a trick like that?'

A tear dripped onto her cheek and with clear-cut pain in her voice she said, 'I'm not lying to you.'

'Emily...'

'Sam, please, listen—'

But he wasn't listening. Not any more. Em was playing some cruel trick on him, and he didn't know why, but the doctors would have to tell him the truth! The nurses would. He'd make them show him a newspaper or something. This was completely ridiculous. There was *no way* that he'd lost all that time. He'd *know*. There'd be signs!

Sam stabbed at the button that would call a nurse to

his bedside and kept doing so, ignoring Emily's pleas, her cries. She was standing now, her hand covering her mouth, looking at him with those wide, tear-filled eyes…

The door opened and a nurse he hadn't seen before came in. She glanced at Emily in concern before turning to him. 'Mr Saint?'

'I need to see the doctor in charge of my care.'

The nurse kept on looking between the two of them, not sure exactly what had happened. 'Dr Waters has gone home for the evening. I can get—'

'Get *someone*! Someone who knows what they're talking about!' He glared at Emily, angry at her, and watched as she snatched up her handbag and ran from the room.

The nurse nodded and hurried out, and with both women gone he felt his anger deflate slightly.

Married eighteen months? Emily was crazy. Perhaps *she'd* had the bump on the head and not him!

He lay in the bed, fury surging through him, and waited for someone who knew what they were talking about to come and tell him the truth.

There was no way he had lost *that* amount of time.

CHAPTER TWO

EMILY RAN FROM Sam's room, throwing her bag to the
floor and sagging against the wall opposite. She slid
down it until she sat hunched on the floor, like a puppet
without her strings.

He couldn't remember! He had no idea of how much
time had passed! He thought…he thought that… She
heard his words once again, spoken with such certainty,
such concern. *'How did Harry get on with the window
treatments? Did he make the changes we asked him to?'*

Window treatments?

*I remember! It was a week before the Grand Opening.
He'd proposed just the night before…*

The nurse who had followed her out of Sam's room
came over to her, hunched down and draped her arm
softly around her shoulders. 'Are you okay, Mrs Saint?'

She could barely breathe…so, no, she wasn't okay.
But she managed to suck in a deep, steadying breath and
struggle back to her feet. Another breath and she nodded
that she was all right.

'The doctor told me… Dr Waters…she told me that
Sam had a little amnesia, but I thought that she meant
that…that he'd forgotten the *accident*. Not two whole
years of his *life*!'

It was so much for her to take in. And she couldn't

imagine how *he* felt! Well, she didn't have to, did she? He was furious at the idea. And she could understand why. Sam was a driven man, always pushing himself to fill every second of his life and enjoy it. The man didn't sit still for a minute.

And he'd forgotten it all. The opening of the birth centre. The massive celebrations...the parties. The first birth and all the births since. The amazing write-ups they'd received, the recommendations, the people who were attracted to the Monterey—celebrities, the rich... *Royalty* had even given birth there.

And not just everything that had happened at work. If it were true—if he really didn't remember—then he'd also forgotten their wedding. The preparations, the wedding night, the honeymoon in Paris...

The arguments... The fact that I told him I was going to leave him!

Emily bit down hard on her lip and accepted a plastic cup of water from the nurse, who had hurried to the small self-service station in the corridor. 'Thank you.'

'I'll page the on-call doctor.'

Emily nodded. 'Thank you.' She smiled weakly at the nurse, noting the relief on her face, her name badge—Melanie. 'And I think you'd better show him a webpage, or perhaps a newspaper. Prove the date to him. I'm not sure he believes me.'

Melanie looked uncertain. 'I think maybe the doctor ought to do that.'

'Maybe. Or perhaps I ought to do it? Do you have a copy of today's paper?'

Not that she *wanted* to go in there and do that to him. *Prove* to him that all that she'd said was true. That he was a man out of time with everyone else.

How did you get your head around something like that?

'I'd like whoever's on call to talk to both of us. I need to know what this means. Why it's happened. What we should be doing...' Her thoughts drifted off onto some nightmarish plane where Sam *never* regained those two years and she had to fill him in on *everything*. The long hours he'd put in, his absences from home, the arguments...

And somehow I need to tell him I'm pregnant too!

She felt sick. The weight of all this duty pressed down upon her. A thick ball of nausea sat low and curdled in her stomach and she could taste bile in the back of her throat, despite the drink of cool, refreshing water from the cup. Was there an easy way to tell a man that you were married, but that the two of you had been arguing constantly and that just under two weeks ago you'd told that same man you were going to leave him?

Because you refused to have a child with me and, oh, by the way, I'm actually pregnant! I found out after the accident. They did tests.

Yes, she really couldn't see that nugget of information going down very well with him.

It was all going wrong. Everything.

She tried to rack her brains for what she knew about amnesia, but apart from the general knowledge that it meant you couldn't remember things, she wasn't sure what else she knew about it. It wasn't something she'd specialised in. She was a certified nurse-midwife. She looked after labouring women.

She knew that there were different types of amnesia—some amnesia was permanent and some temporary. Dr Waters had said it might be so. If Sam's was temporary then he would regain his memories on his own and everything would be back to the way it was before...

But I was leaving him before.

She swallowed hard, seeing in her mind's eye that day she'd laid the suitcase upon the bed and stared at it. Then she'd lain a hand on her abdomen. This wasn't just about her and Sam any more. There was a baby to consider, and there was no way she was going to let her child be rejected by its father before it was even born. She knew what it felt like to be left behind and unwanted. It hurt. Left you bewildered. Made you question yourself. Your own value. She would not put her own child through that.

Emily swallowed the last of the water and crumpled the plastic cup. She put it into a trash can and walked back over to Sam's door, put her hand on it, waiting, taking a deep breath.

She was about to go back in when Melanie reappeared. 'I have a paper for you.'

She looked down. Saw the day's headlines. The date. 'Thank you.' Her mouth felt dry. There was a strange, tinny sort of taste in her mouth and she wondered if she were going to be sick.

'And the doctor will come down as soon as he's finished with a patient on the next floor. Ten minutes?'

Emily nodded, swallowing hard. 'Brilliant. Thanks.'

She watched as Melanie headed back to answer a ringing telephone and then with one final inhalation she pushed open Sam's door and stepped inside.

Their gazes met across the room.

If I'm going to get through this then I need to be strong.

'I've brought you something.'

'An apology?' He sounded bitter. Hurt.

'No. I don't need to give you one. But I will give you this.' She walked across the room and handed him the newspaper before stepping back. As if imagining that the second he confirmed the date for himself he would somehow explode. 'Look at the date.'

At first she didn't think he would look at it, but he finally lifted the paper and scanned the first page for the date.

She knew the exact second his gaze fell upon it. He seemed to stiffen, the muscle in his jaw flickering, the focus in his eyes intensifying before he flipped through, checking that all the other pages stated the same date, too. Then he went back to the beginning, scanned the headlines.

Sam dropped the paper as if it were contaminated, closing his eyes briefly as it all sank in.

'Two years? I've lost *two years*?'

He sounded so broken. So *hurt*. It made her heart ache. Made her feel like she needed to cross the room to him and take him in her arms and hug him better. She didn't want him to be hurting. She never had.

'I'm so sorry, Sam. But it's true. We've been married eighteen months now. We honeymooned in Paris. We were very happy.'

He instantly looked up, met her gaze, pinning her with his normally soft blue eyes. *'Were?'*

She tried not to cry. She seemed to be so emotional since finding out she was pregnant. She struggled to keep control of her voice. 'We're having one or two…problems.'

Sam bristled. 'What kind of problems?'

Emily shook her head. 'We can talk about those later. The doctor's coming to talk to you now. About the amnesia.'

'Are there problems at work? Is the Monterey *failing*?'

She could hear the fear in his voice. The concern. 'No. It's doing very well. The launch was amazing and we've had almost full capacity from day one. You haven't stopped working—working all hours to make it a success.'

At that moment the door opened and a new doctor came in, holding Sam's case notes in his hands.

Emily snapped to attention and crossed her arms, stepping back out of the doctor's way.

'Mr and Mrs Saint? I'm Dr Elijah Penn—how can I be of assistance?'

She managed a weak smile and went over to shake Dr Penn's hand. 'Hello, Doctor. My husband has just learned that he's lost two years of his memory after his head injury. We were in a car crash together ten days ago. We were wondering if you could tell us some more about what to expect, and what we can do to help him regain his memory.'

Dr Penn frowned. 'I've only had a brief read-through of your notes, Mr Saint, and without giving you a thorough examination and questioning you myself over what you remember I can't be precise here. There are many different types of amnesia caused by traumatic head injury and right now it would be hard to be specific.'

'Can you tell us what you *do* know?'

'I wouldn't like to guess, as I'm not your husband's physician and I wouldn't want to tell you anything erroneous. But if you'll give me a moment or two with your husband then I'll tell you what I can.'

Emily nodded. Okay. That sounded sensible. She left Sam's room once again and went and sat outside. From her purse she pulled out her cell phone and felt drawn to the photo album. Opening it, she began flicking through. Perhaps there was something here that might help Sam? Perhaps if he looked at their moments together that might provoke some kind of memory?

There were lots to go through. Many of the photographs were from work. Mothers-to-be whom she'd become great friends with, bouquets that she'd been sent as thanks. There were some pictures of the house after they'd had some work done on it. Other people's babies.

Why weren't there any pictures of her and Sam *together*? She had a few selfies. One or two of Sam in scrubs about to go into a Caesarean section, and then one of him relaxing at the house, reading a work journal. In neither of them was he smiling that beautiful smile she hadn't seen for such a long time. When had he last smiled at her? Apart from today? Because that didn't count any more, did it? He was of the mind-set that she'd just accepted his proposal. He thought they were *happy*.

If only...

She scrolled furiously through the rest of the photos. Nothing of them together except for one right at the beginning, when she'd first got the phone, of her and Sam, heads together, smiling at the camera.

When had that been? She checked the date stamp. It had been just after the Monterey had opened. Of course they'd been happy then. Work had been enthralling. They'd been busy. Passing like ships in the night, sometimes, but planning their wedding.

She felt the tears threaten once again and stood up abruptly, shaking them off. What on earth was she going to do? And how was Sam feeling? Thinking they were blissfully happy only to learn that he couldn't remember his own wedding and had no idea that over the last eighteen months he had slowly been distancing himself from her.

The doctor came to the door. 'Would you like to come in?'

Emily shoved the phone back in her jacket pocket and hurried through, glancing at Sam. He looked glum, but reached out his hand.

Puzzled, but hopeful, she went over to him and took

his hand in hers, her heart pounding in her chest because he'd reached out to her. Needed her. He hadn't done that for such a long time.

'Bad news?'

Dr Penn held his clipboard against his chest. 'I've had a chance to chat with your husband. Ask him a few questions. See what he understands of his situation. You've both been very lucky in that you escaped the car accident with a minimum amount of injuries. But from my understanding from this limited examination I would presume to say that Sam is suffering from a retrograde amnesia.'

Emily squeezed his fingers and looked at him. 'Which is...?'

'It can be caused by various conditions including head trauma, which Sam has gone through. Retrograde amnesia means that Sam's most recent memories are less likely to be recalled, but his long-term memories are easier for him to remember.'

'Right.'

'It's usually temporary, which is the good thing—though I have to warn you, of course, that not everyone will experience it that way. Sam may be unlucky. We have no way of knowing for sure into which camp Sam will fall.'

'But if it is temporary...is there anything we can do to try and help the memories come back?'

Dr Penn nodded. 'It can help to try and provoke those memories. Show Sam familiar things—photos, videos, possessions, favourite foods, smells, clothing. Anything and everything that might help the memories come back.'

'Places? Like if I took him to where we got married or our favourite restaurant?'

'Anywhere he can be immersed for as long as possible should help. Usually it's not just one item that makes memories return but a drowning in overall sensation—place, aroma, sounds, people. All of it at once. Like déjà-vu.'

Sam spoke up. 'So if I went home...that might do it?'

'It could, but I can't promise anything. Memories can take days or even weeks to return.' He swallowed. 'Maybe longer.'

'And would they all come back straight away?'

'It's different for everyone.'

Sam squeezed her hand. 'So can I go home?'

Dr Penn shook his head. 'Not straight away. I know you didn't suffer any broken bones or organ damage, but you did have a nasty hit to the head and you had a stent fitted to drain fluid. We need to monitor you for a while yet, and if you manage to stay stable, with no spikes of temperature or complications, and physio goes well, then maybe we'll look at letting you go.' He smiled. 'Now, if you'll excuse me, I have another patient to attend to.'

They watched the doctor disappear and Emily turned to Sam, aware that they were still holding hands. It was nice. It had been a long time since he had held her like that and she hated how much she needed his touch to re-assure her. She didn't want to let him go. She never had.

'How are you feeling, Sam? After all that?'

'It's a lot to take in. But I guess I ought to look on the bright side.'

She frowned. 'Bright side?'

He nodded. 'Yes. I know who I am. I know who you are. I still have all the knowledge that lets me be an OB/GYN. I can still work—eventually.' He waited until she looked him fully in the eyes. 'I know how much I love you.'

She swallowed and smiled, trying to still the beating of her heart. It was running away with joy at his words.

For how long had she yearned to hear those simple words from Sam?

But there's still so much you don't know!

Could she truly revel in those three simple words? He'd said he loved her, but he still didn't know the truth of their marriage.

He'd hurt her. She'd felt so rejected, so forgotten as Sam had stayed at work, or gone to fundraising galas without her, or disappeared to play tennis with his lawyer. All those arguments they'd had…all those harsh words they'd said to each other out of spite or desperation. How could she forget all they had gone through?

He had. Completely. Right now he was unaware of it all.

But she…? She remembered it all too well. Every argument was a scar upon her heart.

He was trying to be positive. She could see that. *Feel* that. Should she burst his bubble now? Tell him about the baby?

He needed to know. Needed to hear the truth so that he could be in full possession of the facts. The facts he needed, anyway.

'There's something more, Sam.'

'Oh?'

'You're not going to like it.'

He smiled. 'Let me be the judge of that.'

His smile twanged her heartstrings. It was so familiar! Held so much of that gorgeous cheeky charm that she'd fallen in love with!

But she knew. Knew Sam didn't want a baby. He wasn't ready for one after being married for *eighteen months*. Why would he feel ready for one when he'd thought they weren't even married?

'They…did some tests on me after the accident. Blood tests.'

He nodded, frowning. 'Go on.'

'They found something.'

His face filled with concern and she could imagine what he was thinking. Cancer. A mass. A shadow. Some disease…

'What did they find?'

She searched his face, knowing the response he would give, knowing how his face would crumple at hearing the news, not sure if she could bear the way he would drop all contact with her, let go of the hand that he was clutching so tight. Be angry with her again just as she'd started to enjoy the way he held her hand, the way he'd smiled at her before he started to learn the truth.

She'd missed *him.* So much!

But he'd made it clear he didn't want a baby with her, so telling him this was the hardest thing she would ever have to do. It might end them. But she had no choice.

'They found…' She paused, swallowing hard, 'I'm pregnant, Sam. I'm having our baby.'

He knew he was staring at her, but he couldn't stop. She was…*pregnant*?

Images of Serena instantly flooded his brain and he blinked them away. *No.* He would not think of her. That was all too raw, still. Because even though many years had passed he'd pushed away what had happened and stamped it down low.

Pregnant. *Pregnant!* Emily. His fiancée. No. That was wrong—Emily was now apparently his wife. For almost two years. And she was having a—

He swallowed hard.

He loved this woman. He loved her so much! He

should be pleased. But the way she was looking at him right now… Like she was *frightened* of his response? Like she was expecting him to start stamping around the room, or throwing things, or—

Sam knew what he ought to do. He should smile, say that it was *great news*, pretend that he was thrilled, but…

I'm going to be a father. I'm going to be…a father!

Surely she knew how he felt about this? What had happened to Serena had almost destroyed him. How had they been so careless?

Tentacles of fear wrapped themselves around him and tried to suck him down into that deep, dark well of pain he'd kept hidden for so long. Having that kind of responsibility, having to be the one to take care of a young baby every day, was just so…

His heart thudded in his chest so loudly he thought he could hear it in his ears. His skin grew hot, clammy, and he could feel the beginning of the shakes. *My body… it's surging with adrenaline…* The last time he'd felt this way had been after they'd found Serena…

Sam blinked slowly. Emily was still waiting for his reaction, and though the idea of becoming a father terrified him he loved her so much he just knew he couldn't let her see it. Couldn't let her see his inadequacies. Couldn't let her see his Achilles' heel. She would think him an absolute monster if he started on her about this, and both of them had been through too much just lately. His true reaction would have to wait. Maybe when he was out of hospital they could talk sensibly about this.

So he managed to let out a breath and grasped her fingers tightly. 'You're pregnant? Emily…that's so…' he forced the word, trying to make it sound authentic '…*amazing!*'

And he pulled her into his arms and clasped her

tightly, breathing in the delicious scent of her honey hair and closing his eyes with such intense pain in his heart, hoping that she could not sense his betrayal.

He felt her relax and sink into him, gasping with relief.

'You mean it? You're happy?' Emily pulled back to search his face, her own riddled with tears, unable to believe that this was true. But true it was. Because Sam was nodding and smiling and happy. And somehow *this* Sam— this version of Sam who had believed it was two years earlier and they were newly engaged—seemed *happy* at the idea of becoming a father!

And if he's happy then...maybe we can be happy too?

She kissed his face without thinking, clutching it with hands that were trembling. She'd been about to *leave* him! She'd almost packed her things. Had written him that letter. They'd crashed their car arguing over this. It was unbelievable.

His reaction, though welcome, was startling. Now the relief of telling him about the baby had passed without bad incident she began to feel pangs of doubt.

'Of course I mean it. How could I not?' He swallowed. 'How far along are you?' he asked, with real curiosity.

She smiled, almost shyly, amazed that she was getting to talk to him about this. Normally! Without him throwing a fit and storming out! 'About nine weeks, I think.'

'Nine weeks...' He looked up at her and smiled broadly once again. 'Still in the first trimester? I guess we really ought not to tell anyone yet.'

'You could tell your family if you want to.'

Sam shook his head. 'No, I...I think it's best we wait until you're in the fourth month.'

'Okay. Whatever you think is best. I'm so glad you're happy about this. I thought—'

'Thought what?'

She shook her head, as if her answer had been too silly to contemplate. 'It doesn't matter.'

This truly was an opportunity, Emily thought, for them to save their marriage. Sam loved her. He seemed happy to be a father. Was there any need to tell him what their relationship had really been like? This might be a chance for Emily to wipe their slates clean and start again.

Although it wouldn't be a totally fresh start. Because for her the upset of the last few weeks and months was still there. Just because Sam didn't know, it didn't mean that she'd forget too. But it might be a start. A way to save them, built on who they had been in the beginning of their relationship. In love. Supporting each other's hopes and dreams. There had been no need for her to get the suitcase out of the closet.

And what harm could it do? They'd nearly separated, but now...? Now things seemed to have changed. Sam seemed happy about the baby, despite everything, and that was what she'd wanted the most. She'd been granted her wish—only a fool would throw it all away now. She'd been desperate before, when she'd been on the verge of leaving him. But now she was being presented with a second chance.

And, yes, his memories might come back to him and cause them problems later, but what if they *didn't*? And if they did—well, Sam was happy to be a dad right now. If they both worked really hard on their relationship, then surely all that was in the past...could be washed under the bridge?

This was a second chance for them, and for the sake of their unborn baby Emily was prepared to risk it.

She'd always fought for their marriage. Had tried everything to save it. What was one last secret?

The second Emily left his hospital room to head home for the night Sam slumped back against his pillows, exhausted.

A baby...

It was such a huge responsibility. For years. A lifetime. And the weight of that responsibility was not something he thought he could bear.

What had he been thinking, getting Emily pregnant? Had they not been using protection? How had he allowed himself this colossal mistake?

He couldn't be a good father. Hadn't he proved himself incapable of looking after a baby? That was why being an OB/GYN was so beautiful. He could keep babies safe at work. Get them through their nine months of gestation as safely and healthily as possible and then make sure that the mother delivered her child without problems.

At the hospital he had a team. He was supported. He had the most recent advancements, tests and medications at his fingertips. Was able to experience joy with the family as he brought new life into the world. Holding a newborn baby...there was nothing in the world like it. It was a privilege. Magical. A brand-new person and he would be the first one to hold it, before he delivered it into the hands of its parents. The elation, the thrill in the room could not be surpassed. And then, once the umbilical cord was clamped and cut, Sam's job—Sam's *responsibility*—was over. He could relax. Let go.

Sam loved delivering babies. Hadn't he wanted to do that for so long? Hadn't he delighted in the miracle of birth so much he had made it his vocation? Deciding that because he hadn't been able to save Serena he could save others?

But after the birth?

No. That was when it could all go wrong. It was why he'd interviewed and hired the best, most elite team of neonatologists and paediatricians for aftercare at his Monterey centre.

He'd vowed *never* to put himself in that position again, and when he'd first met Emily he'd thought he'd found someone just like him. Someone who loved delivering babies but who didn't want one of their own.

Wasn't that what she'd said? Early on? He felt sure that she had. He had a blurry recollection of it.

They'd met in a delivery room. Their eyes meeting across a crowded stirrup. Em had been working as a private midwife and had brought in a couple whose home birth plan had gone awry. As the OB/GYN on call, he'd gone to the room to assist with a Ventouse delivery and had been physically struck by the sight of her beside her patient, clutching the mother's hand through each contraction, coaching her, intently focused on her.

He recalled a brief moment of wondering who this beautiful new midwife was before he'd got to work, and once the baby had arrived—safely, of course—he had left the room. Only for her to follow him outside and thank him.

I stared at her.

He smiled at the memory. He'd literally been struck dumb. Unable to speak. Her blonde hair had been messy, her cheeks rosy, and she'd been wearing these crazy dangly earrings with turquoise stones that almost matched her eyes. And she'd been wearing flats, so she'd seemed only as tall as his shoulders, and he could remember thinking that she was like an elf.

Eventually he'd managed to get his tongue and mouth to form simple words. 'You did a great job in there.'

'Me? No, it was nothing to do with me. You did all the work.'

'Well, it's my job.'

'Yes.' She'd stared back at him as if she'd been trying to work something out in her head. 'I love having babies.'

He'd frowned. 'You have children of your own?'

She'd shaken her head, as if realising she'd said something that she shouldn't. 'No! God, no! I don't want any yet.'

He'd smiled, intrigued. He'd wanted to know more about her. Wanted to see her.

His only focus had been to be with her. To soak her up. They'd had such fun together, shared so many likes and opinions.

It had been easy to get carried away in the whirlwind.

CHAPTER THREE

THE NEXT DAY a young man called Matt came to Sam's room to help him 'mobilise'. He was in the middle of trying not to feel too dizzy and light-headed after standing up for the first time when Emily came into his room.

His heart soared at seeing her, despite all his dark thoughts the previous night. She looked fresh and bright, a bohemian chic angel, as if she'd had a really good night's sleep, and she developed a huge smile on her face when she saw him standing up, holding onto a walker.

'You're up!'

'Not for long.' Sam collapsed down onto the bed and let out a heavy breath, clutching his head as if to steady it.

Matt cocked his head to one side. 'Dizzy?'

'Yeah, a little.'

'It'll pass if you take it easy. Try this: whilst you're sitting down, really push your feet into the floor and flex and release your calf muscles. It'll help pump the blood around your system and prevent a blood pressure drop next time you stand.'

Emily stood by his side and hesitantly laid a supportive hand upon his shoulder. She smelt minty fresh and was wearing a perfume he didn't recognise, but liked.

He looked up at her, expecting her to kiss him hello, but she didn't. Because of Matt's presence? It seemed unlikely. But now that she was here he wanted to show her what he could do. Show her that he was going to get stronger every day. He wanted to be back on his feet. He wanted to be up and about again. Working. Being Sam. He hated being stuck in a hospital bed.

Gripping the walker once again, Sam stood. Slower this time. He took a moment to make sure the dizziness wasn't about to make him collapse onto the floor and then pushed the walker to one side and took a step forward. Matt stood close, ready to steady him if needed.

Who knew lying on your back for ten days after a head injury would make you feel as weak as a baby bird? After just a few steps he was ready to sit down, but Sam was determined to push through. He kept going. Made it across the room, out of the door to the nurses' station and back again. By the time he got back to his bed he was exhausted, sweating as if he'd just done a full day's training in the gym, and he sank back onto the mattress with a broad grin on his face.

Matt smiled. 'So...you're one of *those* people.'

Sam raised an eyebrow in question.

'Type A. High achiever. It's good, but you also need to know when to stop.'

Emily sat beside him on the bed and passed him a towel to freshen up with. 'He's always pushed himself and strived for the best.'

'Yes, well, just keep an eye on that blood pressure. It won't always be as low as it was about five minutes ago.'

'I'm fine, Matt. Honestly. I won't stop pushing until I'm in my own home.'

Matt nodded. 'And probably not even then. I'll come back later, after your evening meal, and we'll do some more. In the meantime, rest. You're allowed to get up to use the bathroom only.' Matt saluted him and walked away.

Emily peered into his eyes. 'Do you remember home?'

Sam looked at her, tempted just to ignore the question and kiss her. Having her this close to him, smelling as good as she did, looking as beautiful as she did...

He reached up and tucked a strand of her choppy blonde hair behind her ear. 'Are we still in the apartment? The two-bedroom place with the sliding doors out onto the balcony? View across the city?'

He could picture that quite clearly. It wasn't a problem. He very much wanted to get back there.

But the slump in Emily's shoulders informed him that it wasn't the right answer. 'No. We don't live there any more.'

Sam tried to think hard. To force memories to the surface. But he couldn't. It was as if there was a thick wall in his head, blocking them, and no matter how hard he pounded against it, no matter how ferociously he yelled at it and fought to knock it down, it resolutely remained.

'Then where?'

'We have a house in Beverly Hills now. You found it for us. It's white. Very neo-classical—columns, balconies, topiaries, big doors...that sort of thing.'

He tried to imagine it, but was more concerned with the way she'd described it. 'You don't seem to like it.'

'I do. It's just...' She paused for a moment, looking down at the cover on his bed and straightening out a ripple on the surface. 'I guess we haven't made it *ours* yet.' She smiled weakly, but then stood up and tried to become more upbeat. 'But look at you! Only woke yesterday and already you're pounding the floors of the hospital!'

He could tell she wasn't telling him everything. Did

she not like their home? Was it a place that *he'd* liked and pushed her into buying? There was *something*...

But he dismissed it quickly as he thought of his triumph without the walker and stood up again, pulling her into his arms, searching her gorgeous blue-green eyes for that quirky happy girl he knew so well.

'I've missed you.'

She wrapped her arms around his waist hesitantly, as if it was something she hadn't done in a long time, as if she was trying not to make it seem like she was pulling away.

But why would that be? They'd only been married a short time—surely they were still very physical?

'Kiss me.'

'*Sam!* The physio said you should be resting. You need to get back into bed!'

'And I will! But only if my wife joins me.' Sam tilted her chin up and showed her a cheeky grin before he brought his lips to hers.

The last time he'd kissed her had been... Well, just after she'd accepted his proposal. In *his* mind, anyway. And he was still full of that celebratory need to show her how much he loved her, despite all that had happened— the car crash, the pregnancy, the head injury, the amnesia. As far as he knew he'd only just slipped that ring onto her finger and he was feeling full to the brim with happiness.

However...

They were *married*. And expecting a baby. So surely they had to be getting along. And, despite his trepidation, his fears and his doubts, there was one thing clear in his mind. His love for Emily. And right now he felt that he needed her. The last few hours had been a lot to take in. To believe he had lost two whole years of his life was...mind-blowing. His pet project—his dream—the

Monterey Birth Centre had opened and begun trading all without his knowledge.

Okay, so *technically* he'd been there. He'd orchestrated it, arranged it, even shown up to work there, apparently, but that was just what Emily had *told* him had happened. As far as he was concerned it still *hadn't* happened, and whilst he was stuck in this hospital life would continue to carry on without him. He needed to get home. Needed to see the Monterey in action. Needed to think about how he and Emily would tackle their new challenges.

He pulled back and looked into his wife's eyes. 'I can't wait to get home.'

She seemed breathless, her eyes glazed. 'Me too.'

It took two weeks before the hospital was even prepared to *consider* releasing Sam. In that time he received lots of welcome visitors—Emily, his parents, his siblings, some colleagues that, to him, were still relative strangers. *Those visits were weird.* He underwent a barrage of assessments—physiological, neurological, biological. He felt like every part of him had been poked and prodded or had blood drawn from it, and when that wasn't happening he had visits from occupational therapists, psychologists, neurologists and the surgical team, who'd given him the low-down on his small procedure.

Most importantly, throughout it all, he had remained *stable* and his observations had been normal. He was ready now. Anxious to leave the hospital walls and get home. Desperate to get back and see if being there would spark anything.

No memories had yet returned, despite Em's frequent visits with accompanying photos and videos of their wedding and the opening of the Monterey. She'd been so keen to show him what they had done. What they had enjoyed.

But it had been like looking at photos of a stranger, even though he was in them. It had left him feeling disconcerted. As if he was in a strange bubble.

The waiting to leave hospital was more than a little infuriating, and over the last few days he'd found himself snapping at various people. The psychology team had reassured him and Emily that this was normal, as he adjusted to his new self and situation, and offered to assess him every month, for as long as he felt the need to talk about it. Mood swings, apparently, were to be expected.

He wasn't sure he did want to talk about it. Not to them, anyway. They'd already cottoned on to the fact that he didn't seem delighted at the idea of becoming a father, and he'd grown to hate his sessions with them, knowing that they would return to the questions he dreaded. He'd even tried sharing his frustration with Emily, but it seemed as if she didn't know anything about Serena.

Was that possible? That they'd been married for eighteen months and he hadn't told her? That had kept him silent on all fronts and contributed to his anger.

So he was particularly pleased that *today* the doctors had finally decided that he could return home—with the understanding that he wasn't to work for a further three months.

'But I can go in and look around? Get familiar with what's going on?' he'd asked.

'Sure. But no working. You won't be covered insurance-wise.'

And with that dire warning they'd left his bedside.

And now Emily was at his side in the car, driving them home.

She seemed really nervous. Edgy. Fidgety. But he put that down to the fact that for the last few weeks the hospital staff had been around to look after him and make sure he was recovering properly. Now that safety barrier would be gone and it would just be down to the two of them.

Well...nearly three of them.

Sam swallowed and tried not to think of the baby. Emily was nearly eleven weeks now, and apparently she was booked in for a scan in a few days. He would have to go with her. Act the dutiful husband and hold her hand if she'd let him—he'd noticed a curious reluctance and hesitation on Emily's part to be physical with him—whilst they squeezed on that cold blue gel and then smile inanely at the images on screen.

He *so wanted* to be happy about this. And a part of him was. But whenever he thought about them having a baby he pictured his baby sister Serena and what had happened to her when he'd been left in charge...

A car horn sounded, pulling him back to reality, and he flinched, looking across at his wife driving the car.

'Aren't you scared?'

'Of what?'

He wanted to know if she was afraid of becoming a parent. It had to be a big deal for anyone, right? But something stopped him from asking that particular question.

'Driving. After the accident...'

She shook her head, her honey-blonde hair shifting around her shoulders like velvet. 'I was. Not now. But I'm being very careful. We can't just stop doing things because they make us afraid.'

Depends what worries you.

He smiled and glanced out at the streams of traffic. He knew this road. Knew this area. But he had no idea where they were headed except for the fact that Emily was taking them home.

Home. Would he recognise it? Would it spark a memory? Something—even if it was a little blurry? The doctors at the hospital had told them both that the memories *might* return, and that they might either come all at once or he'd experience the odd one or two at strange moments, in totally unexpected ways.

Brains were mysterious creatures.

Pulling off the freeway, Emily took a slip road and drove for a few more miles through beautiful streets lined with lush green trees and neat sidewalks. He saw a young woman walking a poodle that had been groomed to within an inch of its life, trotting along like a dressage horse. He saw beautiful properties, secure within their walls and at the end of long driveways, as they drove on beneath the heat of the sun in their dark saloon car, and then suddenly they were slowing and turning into a driveway.

He looked up.

A majestic house sat before him. Perfectly white, it glimmered in the midday heat against the glorious blue sky backdrop. It looked *palatial*. Like something fit for a film star or a minor member of royalty.

This is ours?

He tried to picture himself wanting to buy this and could see its perks. It was prestigious, and screamed quality, with tall oak front doors and what seemed like hundreds of windows flashing reflections of the sun into his eyes as they approached up the long, smooth driveway. It was very different from his childhood home.

As they neared, he saw grey clothed *staff* come near the car and open their car doors.

'Welcome back, Mr Saint! So good to see you up and about.'

He smiled at faces he didn't know and stepped out, looking around him. Emily appeared to be much more comfortable with her surroundings than he did, and she quickly indicated to the staff to take their bags from the trunk.

The bags were quickly hurried inside as Sam looked about him at the gardens, which were lush with green leafy trees and all-white flowers and blooms. 'It's beautiful.'

'You picked it. Don't you remember?'

He heard the trepidation in her voice. The hope that he would remember. He hated disappointing her. 'I'm sorry. I don't.'

He needed control of his life back. Something he hadn't had whilst he'd been stuck in a hospital bed as a passive observer.

'Let's go in. All your things are inside—there might be something...'

Something about the way her voice sounded made him look at her in question. Was it just the amnesia that was making him feel...? *I'm in the dark...*

It was a weird sensation, but the doctors had told him he would feel like this. That he was not to ponder on it, or worry about it, that it was normal. It was probably just him being over-sensitive right now.

Shrugging it off, he took her hand and clasped it tightly, kissing the back of it. Then he smiled at her and nodded. 'Let's do it.'

And they walked inside.

Sam had imagined that this would be *a moment*. A moment when a flood of memories would assail him. He would spot something—a chair, a table, a painting or piece of art, perhaps—that would ignite a memory that had lain dormant and hidden behind *the wall*.

But, looking around him, he felt—and remembered—nothing. He tried not to be too disappointed. But it was hard. He'd told himself in the hospital that when he got home he would remember. That walking through the door into familiar surroundings would give his brain the nudge it needed to start releasing the information he craved.

The fact that his brain was failing him—that his memories were refusing to leap to the surface of his mind—frustrated him. He was a man who had always been perfectly in control of everything, and the fact that he couldn't even force his own brain to do something made him feel angry inside.

Emily let go of his hand and stepped away from him to lay her bag and keys down on a table. 'Anything?'

Gritting his teeth, he shook his head, trying not to be angry with himself. 'No.'

She stared at him for a while. 'Don't worry. Something will trigger it. I'll show you around.'

And she took him from room to room. Sitting room, dining room, library, study, kitchen, utility, staff quarters, the guest bedrooms, the bathrooms, shower rooms, games room… Even all the storage rooms and up into the roof space, which had been converted into yet another guest room. They were all *beautiful*. Elegantly designed. Minimalist. Expensive and sumptuous.

Remembered?

Not at all.

All the belongings, all the possessions that Emily pointed out, convinced he would remember, meant nothing. He *felt* nothing.

A simmering rage bubbled away beneath the surface of his neutral face. And for some reason he felt anger towards Emily. As if it was somehow *her* fault that he couldn't remember. He knew it wasn't. It was just because she was the closest person to him and he so desperately wanted to remember for *her* delight. *Her* joy. Plus, it would also prove to him that he could somehow conquer the two years that had been taken from him. Two years of missed birthdays and celebrations. All of it. He could somehow claim it *back*.

There had to be *something*. Something that would bring back who he was. All that he had lost and then, hopefully, somehow he would have the strength to tackle the next great challenge that awaited them both.

Awaited *him*.

Because how could he be a father when he couldn't even remember creating their child?

'And this…'

Emily swept another door open. Another opportunity for his mind to let him down. He wasn't sure he wanted to look—wasn't sure he wanted to face that part of himself again—but he did, because Emily was being so supportive.

'…is the master bedroom. Our room.'

He stepped in, his gaze instantly drawn to the large king-sized bed in the centre, a mix of blindingly white bedding with gold-accented cushions. There were so many of them! Did they have to throw them all off the bed to get—?

Emily pinned to the bed, gazing up at him, smiling wickedly, her hair spread out in wild abandon across the gold cushions, the tassels weaving into her hair, making it seem as if she had strands of pure gold in it. His lips trailing down her neck, feather-light, her laughter, her—

The sudden onslaught of memory caused Sam to reach out a hand to steady himself.

'Sam—you okay?' She caught up to him and laid a hand upon his arm, her face full of concern.

'Yeah, I'm fine, I—'

A gold cushion being thrown at his chest from across

the room. Emily growling with irritation, stalking away from him, yanking the bedroom door open so hard it left a small dent in the wall. 'I hate you!'

Sam blinked and looked behind him. At the wall. There was a small dent.

'Sam? Have you remembered something?'

He met her gaze. 'You were angry with me.'

She blanched. 'What?'

'In this room—you threw a cushion at me...one of those off the bed. I was over here.' He stepped over to the part of the room that he'd seen in his memory. 'You threw it and you stormed out of the door and yelled from the corridor that you hated me.'

Emily looked awkwardly at the floor and he could see that she was biting her lip.

What had happened to make her say she *hated* him? She hadn't said he annoyed her, or irritated her, she hadn't said, *I really don't like you sometimes, Sam.* She'd said 'hate'.

What had they been arguing about? Had he done something wrong? Had she? 'What was that about?'

She grimaced. 'I'm not sure.'

He pictured the look on her face as she'd stormed away. 'You seemed pretty serious.'

Emily swallowed and sat down on the edge of the bed, fidgeting nervously. She patted the bedspread beside her and he sat down, waiting for her explanation.

'Things have been...tense sometimes.'

'Sometimes?'

'A lot.'

She seemed embarrassed to say it. As if she was letting him down by telling him this. But even though it was hurtful to hear he'd rather have the truth.

'What about?'

She sighed and her shoulders sagged. 'Family stuff. We had got to a point where we were hardly talking. When we did, we argued. Over and over again.'

'We were that bad?' He hated to ask, but Emily wasn't making it sound as if things had been good between them.

'We crashed the car arguing.'

He stared hard at the floor. 'God, Em, I'm really sorry.'

He felt the distance between them then. Even though they were next to each other on the bed she wasn't leaning into him for comfort—she wasn't seeking his support. She was stiff and straight beside him, eyes downcast.

How had things got so bad between them, so quickly? Was this why she looked startled each time he tried to hold her hand or kiss her?

'At least you remembered something...' she muttered.

He stared at the pristine white carpet on the floor. 'Yeah. I guess I did.'

Emily led Sam into his private office, hoping that *this room* above all others would mean something to her husband.

This was such a weird situation for them both. *She knew this man.* And yet because he couldn't remember the last two years it felt to her, in a way, that she was leading a stranger around their house. Seeing the way he looked at things in wonder and surprise, seeing things familiar to her but brand-new to him.

Hadn't he stood in this very doorway and kissed her? Hadn't he sat at this desk for many hours, talking on the phone, arranging galas and press nights for the Monterey? Hadn't they had one of their worst arguments in here? Leading to the first time Sam had stormed from the house, tearing down the driveway in the car so hard he'd left tyre marks?

He'd had a memory come back. A bad one. It was a scary sign. *Good* that he was remembering, but *bad* because of what it might mean for their relationship now.

It was clear that their problems weren't just going to disappear, the way his memories had. Whether he remembered their issues or not, Sam was still the same man and she needed to remember that. The issue here wasn't just the amnesia. They still had the problems of their marriage to solve, and if they were going to do that then they would have to start communicating and working together. Something they hadn't done for a long time.

She watched as he entered, noting the way his fingers trailed over the large glass-topped desk, the way he picked up the Murano glass paperweight that they'd bought in Paris, the way he stared hard at the picture of himself and Emily standing in front of the Monterey on the day of its Grand Opening. Their smiling faces, the green-garbed staff standing behind them, all with their hands in the air cheering.

She *wanted* him to remember it all. She really did. How else were they both going to recover? Right now Sam seemed happy about the pregnancy, and he was clearly wanting to be physical with her. Kissing her. Reaching out for her hand. Giving her the love that she'd craved. The *closeness* and *intimacy* that had been sadly lacking in their relationship since the arguments had started. But it was still difficult for her. Strange...

Because she *did* remember.

What would happen tonight? Would he sleep in their bed? Lately he'd been sleeping at work, and when he *had* made it home he'd either told her he'd sleep on the couch or go to a guest room. That had been embarrassing—the staff certainly knew—and also deeply hurtful.

Was it wrong to wish desperately that Sam wouldn't recall that part of their relationship? Was it wrong to be putting all her hope into this second chance they'd been given? Was it wrong to wish that Sam wouldn't regain his memories at all?

Of course it is! And I feel terrible for even giving those thoughts space in my head!

It was as if Sam were two different people right now, though she knew that it wasn't really true.

He's the same man and I need to remember that. The man who wouldn't talk to me is the same man standing next to me right now. And I'm not sure I know how we're going to sort this.

There was a baby that would need its father. Emily hadn't had one of those. Or a mother. Not really. She had been passed to an aunt by her mother so she could go rushing off after some ageing rock star and travel with him to gigs, and after that last time she'd just never come back. Even now Emily had no idea where or who she really was. Her mother had a name, but she didn't know more than that.

Staying with her Aunt Sylvia hadn't provided much insight either. Sylvia had not been a big fan of her sister, and had resented being left with a young toddler who made lots of noise and even more mess. Emily had soon stopped asking Sylvia and her Uncle Martin questions they never had answers to.

Who's my real mummy?

When is she coming back?

Does she love me?

The sound of drawers being opened and closed brought Emily back to the present. If Sam, now sitting behind his desk, was looking for something personal there he'd be disappointed. They only contained work-related paperwork and files. He looked lost in a world that should have been oh-so-familiar to him.

'It'll come back, Sam. Maybe not today. But it will.' She hated to see him hurting. It hurt her in return.

He smiled at her attempt to comfort him, but it was bitter. 'Well, a bit did come back today—only it wasn't what I expected.'

He shook his head, as if he couldn't quite believe all that she had told him. The bad memory had clearly rocked him to his core and he seemed to be thrown by that. He'd believed them to be happy. Why wouldn't they be? She wished she could explain it to him, but she didn't have any answers herself.

'We have to believe that things will get better.'

'Speaks the eternal optimist.'

Pulling deep within herself, she leaned over his desk and made him look her in the eyes. 'You're a fighter, Sam. We would never have got the Monterey started if it hadn't been for your vision. You've got to believe that all those memories in there...the ones that make you *you*... they're still in there. They're not lost. Not really. You just don't have access yet.'

'Like membership to an exclusive club?'

She nodded. 'Exactly.'

'I'm not sure I want membership to the bad marriage club.'

Emily stood up straight. 'Me neither. But we're in it, and we both have to work together if we want to make changes.'

He looked about the room one more time, before he stood and tucked his chair under his desk. 'You're right. We do.'

* * *

The telephone call came as they were heading downstairs. Emily's cell vibrated in her pocket and she knew immediately what the call was about the second she saw the name of the caller.

'Em? It's Marc—Sophie's husband. Her waters have broken and she's having strong contractions. We're coming in to the Monterey.'

Marc and Sophie were a couple who had come to the Monterey for fertility treatment and had conceived their much wanted first child through IVF. Sophie was terrified of both hospitals and needles—something she'd had to overcome to get through her hormone treatments and appointments. Emily had *promised* from the very beginning that she would be there to help them deliver their child, and Sophie had come to rely on Emily being there as her safe harbour, her port in a storm.

Emily's heart was torn between Sophie's labour and staying with Sam, whom she'd just brought home.

'Hi, Marc. I'm at home at the moment…hang on—' She held the phone to her chest so she could privately talk to Sam. 'It's clients. Sophie and Marc? The IVF couple? Sophie's in labour—I promised I would be there.'

Sam looked blank at the names, but he nodded anyway. He knew that work was important to them both. 'You should go.'

'You've only just come home. You need someone with you.'

He smiled. 'I have *staff*, remember? Go be with Sophie.'

She loved it that this part of Sam was still here. The need to be there for their patients, putting them first, staying true to the promises they made to care for their charges.

Em lifted the phone back to her ear. 'I'll come in. How far away are you?'

'I'm already driving, but traffic is heavy. Twenty minutes?'

'I'll meet you at the entrance. See you soon.' She ended the call and smiled at Sam. 'Thank you.'

'Hey, it's not a problem. It's what we do. Go on. You don't want to miss it.'

No. She didn't. She laid a hand on his arm, smiling, and then started running down the stairs, grabbing her purse and keys from the table and hurrying out of the front door.

She hated leaving him alone. But perhaps he needed some time in their home to wander about and look at things without feeling under pressure to remember.

She told herself it was a good thing she was heading in to the Monterey. She was about to see the outcome of a long, difficult journey for Sophie and Marc. This was what their work was all about. Welcoming new life into the world. Celebrating that.

And soon it would be her and Sam's turn.

One day. Maybe.

Sophie was labouring *hard*. Her normally calm and serene face was now red and creased, and her eyes were closed tight as she tried to breathe through a contraction.

Her husband Marc stood by her, one hand clutching hers, the other rubbing hard at the small of his wife's back.

Sophie had not wanted to get into bed. She'd said it had made her too uncomfortable. She wanted to get into the large birthing tub, which was currently filling with water.

'How much longer?' Sophie asked, blowing away the last of the contraction.

Emily checked the temperature of the water, which was perfect. 'Okay. You can get into the pool now.'

Marc helped his wife strip off the last of her garments and held her arm as she gingerly stepped over the side of the pool and lowered herself, settling into the warm embrace of the water.

'Oh, my God, this is bliss!'

Marc laughed. 'That's not what you said a moment ago.'

Emily smiled at them both. It was a surprise to a lot of husbands that their partners often felt so much better between contractions. Making a note in Sophie's file, she entered the time her patient had got into the pool and then got a Sonicaid device and listened to the baby's heartbeat by pressing the probe against Sophie's abdomen. There was a little sound of interference, and then a strong, steady heartbeat sounded out in the small room.

'Sounds perfect, Sophie. You're on track. Any urge to push?'

Her patient wiped her brow. 'I'm not sure. I think so…a little with that last one.'

'Okay, let's see how you are with the next few contractions and if that feeling increases we'll check to see if you're fully dilated.'

Sophie nodded, and then braced herself against the pool as another contraction hit.

Emily watched as Marc helped his wife through it, surreptitiously timing the contraction. It was good and strong. At least a minute in length, which was what they needed. Sophie had to be close, and Emily felt a ball of excitement in the pit of her stomach, as she always did when a birth was near.

This was what she lived for. Bringing new life into the world. It was something that had fascinated her ever since she'd seen a documentary on the television one evening as a child. Sylvia and Martin had gone out to an event at their local church and Emily had turned on the television out of boredom.

She'd hardly ever seen the television switched on. Sylvia and Martin had preferred to read, or listen to a play on the radio. But Emily had known it was a source of endless fascination for her schoolfriends and so she'd switched it on that night and found a documentary about a maternity unit. There, on screen, she had watched and learned about the way babies came into the world, and she'd been captured by its raw beauty, its power. She'd been surprised to discover tears trickling down her cheeks when she'd witnessed how overwhelmed the parents were by their new child.

I want to do that.

Seeing love, in all its raw glory, was something that she'd craved.

Did my mom act like that with me?

From that day forward she'd dreamt of finding a man who would look into her eyes like that, with so much love and pride. Of carrying her own baby and experiencing that rush of love and joy as she pushed her baby into the world. Never to be alone again...never to be forgotten. Never again to be that lonely little girl, sitting in her room, wondering where her mother was.

'Emily? I need to push.'

'Okay, just breathe through it this time. I need to check you first.'

Marc glanced nervously at her. 'Shouldn't she just push?'

'If she's not fully dilated yet it could cause swelling around the cervix and make her delivery difficult.'

Marc looked confused, but nodded, because he trusted her implicitly.

With the contraction over, Emily put on some gloves and checked Sophie. She smiled. 'You're ten centimetres! You're all set.'

Sophie started to cry. 'Oh, my God! It's happening—it's really happening! Marc?' She turned to her husband and clutched his hand as if she would never let go. 'We're going to have our baby soon.'

Marc kissed his wife. 'I know, honey. I'm so proud of you.'

Sophie laid her forehead against her husband's and then started grimacing as the next contraction hit. 'What do I do, Emily?'

'I want you to take a deep breath and then bear down into your bottom until I say stop, okay?'

Sophie bore down, the strain showing in the redness of her face.

'Seven, eight, nine, ten. Okay, another breath and push again!'

Emily counted the seconds away. Sophie and Marc were so close now to seeing their miracle baby. They'd tried so hard to get pregnant, and for a long time had thought that it wouldn't happen for them. Sophie and Marc hadn't met until they were in their early forties, and after a year of trying had come to the Monterey in desperation, afraid that time was running out for both of them.

Two cycles of IVF had failed, but on their third try they'd been successful. Sophie had been a model patient—eating right, exercising, looking after herself—and Emily knew this baby was going to be cherished.

'Oh, my God, Em, how much longer?' Sophie groaned.

'Not long! I can see a head of thick dark hair! Do you want to touch?'

'Really?' Sophie reached down and felt the top of her baby's head. 'Oh!'

Emily smiled and shone a light so Marc could see, too. 'What do you think, Dad? Takes after you?'

Marc blinked away tears. 'This is…' He couldn't speak any more. He just clutched his wife's hand and kissed the back of it. 'Come on, Soph, you can do it—you're nearly there.'

It took just four more pushes and the head crowned, emerged and restituted, so that the baby faced Sophie's inner right thigh.

'Head's out, Sophie! Just one more push and you'll be a mum!'

Sophie bore down as the next contraction came.

Emily supported the baby's head and body as it came out, and looked up at Sophie. 'Are you ready to take your baby?'

Sophie looked down, gasped aloud, and then reached for her newborn. 'Oh, my God!' She pulled the baby up-ward and rested it against her belly, and then burst into tears as her baby let out its first beautiful cry.

'You did it, Soph! You did it!' Marc laid his hand on his newborn child and began to cry.

The dads' crying always got to Emily. She had to bite her lip to stop *herself* from crying. She didn't know what it was, but she'd seen this so many times and it never got old. It was a privilege, and one that she cherished.

'Congratulations.' She clamped the cord and handed the scissors to Marc. "Cut between the clamps.'

He did so, and laughed, laying his head against his wife's.

'Did you see what flavour you got?'

Sophie and Marc had wanted it to be a surprise.

Sophie sniffed and wiped at her eyes, before she

looked down and lifted up one of her baby's legs. 'It's a girl! Marc, we have a daughter!'

Marc kissed her and put his arm around his wife.

Emily laid a towel over the baby. It soon got wet, but it helped to keep the baby warm. Sophie wanted a natural stage three, allowing the placenta to come out on its own, without the aid of drugs, and once that was done and had been checked, Emily helped Sophie get out of the bath and onto the bed.

She wrapped fresh towels around their daughter and checked Sophie for tears. All looked well. She'd done brilliantly.

'You haven't torn, Sophie. That's brilliant.'

She stared for a moment at the family picture of Sophie, Marc and their new daughter on the bed. A solid family unit.

She wanted that for her and Sam. That dream image that she'd built up in her imagination since she had first seen it on television. A mum. A dad. A baby. All wrapped together in the strong bonds of love. United.

There *had* to be a way for them to get there.

'Have you got a name for her yet?'

Marc looked up and smiled. 'Xanthe.'

Emily nodded. 'That's beautiful.'

She let the family have a few moments together, and then took Xanthe to check her over. All looked well, and she scored high on the APGAR, so she bundled Xanthe up again and handed her back to her parents. No doubt this little girl would be treasured and loved for her lifetime.

'I'll leave you guys alone for a moment. Give me a buzz if you need anything.'

Emily slipped from the room and went to write up her notes about the delivery. It was wonderful when deliveries went as smoothly as this one, and Sophie and Marc—who had been through the mill—deserved their happy-ever-after.

In her office, Emily was lost in thoughts about what would happen in the future for her and Sam. Would he regain his memories and know the whole truth about their marriage? Really, she *did* want him to, because then they could work through their issues. She just wanted them to have some time first. Time to reconnect, to fall back in love, time to strengthen their relationship.

Was that so bad? Wanting the best for them? Wanting their relationship to succeed? This time could give them what they'd never had before. The opportunity to open up to each other and work out whatever the real problem was. Because there had to be a reason Sam hadn't wanted to talk to her before.

Now, because of the accident, because of what had happened, Sam was still reeling, and he needed to anchor himself. Find himself. And if she could help him to do that then maybe, just maybe, he would see just how much she was fighting for their marriage. How much she wanted them to succeed. Surely he did, too, otherwise he wouldn't be so upset that it had gone wrong?

He'd loved her once—she just wanted to reinforce those feelings somehow. So that if everything went pear-shaped after his memories returned they would have a much better chance of staying together and having the perfect family that she wanted for them.

Her gaze fell upon the one picture she allowed herself in her office. It was of her and Sam, in front of the Eiffel Tower in Paris during their honeymoon. They'd had such a brilliant time there. It was an enchanting city, and the way she'd felt for Sam there had been overwhelming.

It was a pity they weren't there now.

But what if we could be?

The doctors had said that the best way to help Sam find his memories would be to immerse him in experience—the sights, sounds, smells of something familiar. What if they went back to Paris? Sam was signed off work for a few months. If they could get a Fit to Fly certificate from his consultant they could go back there and experience that magical place once again!

A spark of hope ignited in her chest and she stared at the photo once more. And if Sam's memories *did* come back by then it would be too late, because he would have fallen in love with her all over again!

They *needed* this.

In the past two years Sam had been working hard to get the Monterey up and running, working tirelessly behind the scenes. She'd barely seen him, and they'd argued when she had. This would be good for *her*—not just Sam.

Emily smiled and turned to her computer. Accessing the internet, she found a local travel agent and picked up the phone and dialled their number.

There was no harm in finding out.

CHAPTER FOUR

AIR FRANCE FLEW out of Los Angeles International, and after eleven hours and fifty minutes Emily and Sam touched down at Charles de Gaulle Airport, north-east of Paris.

Emily's excitement levels were high. Paris held such great memories for her and their relationship. When they'd come here before they'd been honeymooning, newly married, accomplished owners of a successful new birth centre business and blissfully happy. Everything had been going so well for them.

After making the decision to return to Paris, Emily had returned home from her successful delivery of Marc and Sophie's baby and blurted out her idea.

'Sam? We should go to Paris!'

'What?'

'We should go back to Paris. Where we honeymooned. Remember the doc said that we should immerse you in sights and sounds and aromas. Can you think of a better place than one where we were so happy?'

'I don't remember Paris.'

'Exactly! If your memory doesn't return there...well, we'll just make new memories. That both of us will remember this time.'

Sam had laughed at her enthusiasm, but then he'd seen

how determined she was. He'd called his consultant to check that it was okay for him to fly. His doctor had said that he didn't think it was a problem. Sam wasn't on oxygen, he didn't have any open wounds from surgery, and air travel was only usually restricted for seven to ten days post-neurosurgery. Sam had been recovering for a month now.

A Fit to Fly certificate had been arranged and before Sam had known what was happening they'd been booked onto a flight the next day.

Emily had meant it. The last time they'd visited she had truly fallen in love with the city, and had hated having to leave after their ten days there. As they'd risen into the sky on their way home Emily had looked out of the window at the city dropping away beneath her and whispered, *'I'll come back.'*

And here they were. Strolling through the airport, through the domed concourses, dragging their bags behind them, revelling in the hustle and bustle as hundreds of different voices and languages could be heard around them.

Despite looking in a shop window and gaping at a beautiful dress that she would normally have stopped to buy, she was so keen to get them to their hotel that she quickly hurried along.

Outside they found a *station de taxi* waiting to pick up passengers. They hailed one and got inside.

'Bonjour, monsieur...madame. Où?'

Emily smiled. 'Shangri-La Hotel, *s'il vous plaît.*' She turned to her husband and smiled.

'Shangri-La? Sounds...exotic.'

'It was where we had our honeymoon—*and* I managed to get us the exact same suite we stayed in the last time.'

Sam nodded in appreciation. 'You *have* been busy.'

'I'd do anything to get you back, Sam.' She felt her cheeks flush. 'I mean…to get your memory back.'

He smiled at her. He knew what she meant. Their relationship had clearly been faltering. From that one memory it looked as if it had become a war zone. It pained him to think how bad it had got for them and, like Em, he too wanted this trip to work.

And if you wanted to get the romance back, the love, where else to go but the most romantic city in the world?

'Thanks, Em. You've been great through all of this. The accident, looking after me… It can't have been easy.' She appreciated his acknowledgement of all her hard work. 'Well, morning sickness didn't help.'

She looked out of the window as her eye caught a glimpse of some hares or rabbits darting across the grass beside the road, so she didn't notice his gaze darken at her reminder of the pregnancy.

If she were honest, she'd admit that he'd been distant from her the last couple of days. They'd still not yet made love since his return from hospital, which didn't surprise her. Not after she'd told him how much they'd been arguing. Perhaps he had felt he couldn't approach her?

But she'd not pushed for it either. She hadn't slept with her husband for a couple of months, and it would have been strange for them to have tried, knowing how bad their marriage had become.

Sam had cited headaches, which she knew were to be expected, and she'd been grateful. She needed time herself to work up to the idea of becoming intimate with her husband once again.

It hadn't taken Sam long to return to his study in their house, determined to bring himself up to speed with what had happened in the last two years. Sometimes—just as before the accident—he'd fallen asleep there. It had removed the pressure and she'd been thankful for that.

Before, there'd always been a reason why he couldn't talk, or why he couldn't come home. It had made her uneasy, and she didn't want to return to the pattern they had fallen into. So arranging this trip together had been good. They were united in the idea of working to get each other back.

Emily *needed* to get Sam back. The good Sam. The Sam who loved her and adored her. The Sam who was happy about the baby and had beamed a smile whenever he'd seen her arrive at the hospital. The husband who wanted to hold her hand. Be near her. Touch her.

She missed his touch.

It wasn't just sex with Sam—it never had been. He had always made love to her, making her feel cherished and adored. As if he worshipped her. As if he couldn't get enough of her. The way she felt...the way she tasted. And afterwards, when they'd lain in each other's arms, sated and complete, warm and loved, she'd never wished for anything more.

To lose that—to lose that precious physical connection that they'd once shared—had almost torn her apart.

As she gazed out of the taxi window, her fingers fiddling with the pendant around her neck, she hoped fervently that back here, in this place, they would be able to reclaim that part of their marriage. Not just the sex, the making love, but the closeness she'd once had with him.

They'd had it good once. They could have it again.

The drive to the hotel took about forty-five minutes. Emily felt so happy to be in Paris and she clutched Sam's hand, squeezing his fingers every time she turned to look at him and smile. She gazed at the tree-lined roads, the relaxed unhurried pedestrians and the tourists ambling along the sidewalks, gasping when there was a break in the treeline or buildings and she caught a sweeping view of the city.

This feels like home to me.

She gazed at the varied architecture, from modern glass and steel to the more aged and authentic French buildings built during the reign of Louis XIV. There was such an eclectic mix here, and it never failed to astound her.

Sam, on the other hand, was looking at the city with new eyes. She watched him to see if anything seemed familiar—a sight, a sound. But he gazed at the city as if he had never seen it before and she felt her shoulders slump.

It's still early, though. We haven't got to our suite yet. Surely he must remember that?

It would be good if some of the memories, when they returned, were *good* ones! She hated to think that all he would remember would be the bad.

Arriving outside the hotel, they paid their driver and stepped out.

The Shangri-La was beautiful to look at. Positioned in the sixteenth *arrondissement*, it was a nineteenth-century decadent-looking structure, apparently originally the private mansion of Prince Roland Bonaparte, the nephew of Napoleon. Once named the Palais Iéna, it stood in a tasteful corner of Paris, resting within the shadow of the elegant Eiffel Tower.

Sam looked up at the hotel and felt a sense of awe. History, *seeped* from this place. The entranceway with its sturdy white columns, and above the mass of ornate curlicued iron balconies, made him feel a tiny bit insignificant against this backdrop of important French history.

A uniformed porter assisted them with their bags into

the hotel reception area and they stepped into a world of elegance. Even the floor was beautiful, and in the centre was a gold and glass table set with a generous, fragrant bouquet of lilies.

Sam stood back as Emily took care of all the arrangements and glanced around as he waited, studying the features, trying to see if anything would trigger a memory.

Nothing.

Maybe he needed a little more time? Perhaps if he relaxed a bit more then the memories might return? He'd had a couple. Back home. Fleeting ones, but still…it was better than nothing.

He was glad that he had agreed to this trip. Emily had seemed so sure that it was the right thing for them to do, and Sam had felt the same way after a moment or two of thought. It was what they needed—he wanted to get their marriage back on track as much as she did.

After learning that he'd lost two years of his life, and discovering that his business had become such a success, he'd felt keen to catch up on what was happening at the Monterey. But once he'd had that flashback…well, it hadn't taken him but a moment to agree to come here.

It was why he had closeted himself in his office, despite his physical need to reconnect with Em. Catching up on paperwork, accounts, reports, assessments, staff training was the only way he knew to allow her space. He understood her distance, her reticence to kiss him, to touch him.

The birth centre had been his dream and the fact that he'd missed its launch galled him. His wedding. His honeymoon. It was all gone—hidden behind *that wall*.

He'd noticed the little looks she'd given him when she had found him in his office yet again. The looks she'd tried to hide when he had not returned to their marital bed. Had they been looks of relief or upset?

He wanted to. Of course he did. He loved her. But... Sam was a driven man, and work was important to him. Now more than ever. Emily was carrying his child, and his sense of responsibility to take care of them both lay heavy upon his shoulders. But beneath that something didn't feel right. Knowing that they'd argued, that he'd upset her... The *timing* didn't feel right. It was awkward, and because he didn't do well with *awkward* he'd focused on the one part of his life where he did do well. Work.

His thoughts drifted back to the scan. He should be pleased it had gone so well. The baby had looked good, there had been no concerns over the measurement of the nuchal fold at the back of the baby's neck, growth looked consistent with dates. The pregnancy was going well.

He should have felt joy.

But all he had been able to feel was fear.

What if he couldn't protect their baby? What if he failed their child? What if the same thing happened as before? Serena had been in *his care* and she had died. How could he possibly get things right for this baby?

Had he been mad, thinking that coming to Paris was a good idea? Their relationship was not the joyful coupling he'd thought it was back when he'd proposed. They had been married for just over a year and already they were in trouble. But why?

Emily had mentioned his not wanting a baby, so she knew that much about his feelings. Obviously the married Sam had felt it easier to say than today's Sam. But it was becoming increasingly obvious that she knew nothing about *why* he didn't want a child. And that bothered him. He'd always assumed he would tell her at some point. Why hadn't he? Because of all their arguments?

Because you're afraid to admit what you did.

What would she think of him? An OB/GYN who delivered countless babies, head of a fabulous five-star birth centre, who had failed to realise that his baby sister had died?

The sound of the lift arriving brought Sam back to the present, and he and Emily followed the porter out of the lift and down the corridor to their suite.

'What do you think, Sam?' Emily asked as the porter swept open the door to their room.

It was tremendously beautiful. Painted in a soft cream, with original features and gold-draped windows, the room was littered with period furniture. Light from the sliding French doors that opened out onto a broad balcony welcomed them in, and just off to the right, almost within touching distance, was the tower that everyone recognised and thought of when they went to Paris.

'It's amazing.'

'It's our original suite. The one we honeymooned in.'

He turned to face her, hearing the nerves in her voice.

The honeymoon suite. A room built for seduction and intimacy. Was she nervous of being with him? Of beginning that side of their relationship again?

Sam tried to give her a reassuring smile. He couldn't blame her. She was doing so much to help him find his memories again. She was doing what she thought was right and he couldn't, *shouldn't* complain. But he was feeling the weight of her expectations and felt terrible at letting her down, because nothing about the room was sparking anything for him. And he was feeling terribly guilty about the state of their marriage. This trip *had* to work! He wanted her back. He wanted them *happy*.

Emily tipped the porter and he disappeared without

notice. Then she joined her husband out on the balcony as they gazed out over the city. 'Can you feel it, Sam?'

'Feel what?'

'The city, welcoming us back.'

He smiled and reached out to curl his fingers around her own. He just wanted to touch her for a moment. To acknowledge why they were here. But he wouldn't put any pressure on her until she was ready.

'Let's go out and explore. What should we do first, do you think?'

'Well, I don't know about you, but me and the baby are starving. Can we go get something to eat? Find a little café or restaurant?'

Her reminder about the baby pierced his conscience, but he pasted a smile over his face. He couldn't let her know how concerned he was. What would she think of him if he told her the truth? That he didn't feel able to protect the baby? At least whilst it still lay within her womb it was safe, and he had no concerns about her delivering. Both of them were trained for that. It was *afterwards* that worried him. He wouldn't be looking after the baby for one night, the way he'd had to babysit Serena. This baby—their baby—he'd be looking after for the *rest of his life*.

'Food sounds good. Let's go.'

They walked through the streets hand in hand, soaking up the sights, sounds and smells of Paris. Walking past a bakery made Emily salivate with anticipation, but walking past a *poissonnerie*—a fishmongers—made her feel a little queasy.

'Maybe you should stay away from seafood, Em,' Sam joked as he wrapped a reassuring arm around her shoulders and led her towards the River Seine.

They headed down to the Jardins du Trocadero, admiring the fountain and the views of the river, before heading deep into the city, wandering down small cobbled streets, looking for something small and chic and different. Eventually they found exactly what they were looking for.

Gino's Cottage was a rooftop restaurant. All the diners got to sit out on the terrace at long banqueting tables, with views towards the Palais de Chaillot in the distance.

They were soon seated, and they ordered themselves something to drink—wine for Sam and sparkling water for Emily—before they perused the menu.

'It feels so good to be back here.'

Sam looked at her over his menu. 'We came here before?'

'No, not this place. I meant Paris. I loved it here when we came for our honeymoon.'

'Can you tell me about it? Some of the things we did?'

She blushed a little. 'Well, not all of them. Certainly not in public!'

He smiled.

'I think I'm going to have the *bruschetta des tomates* to start. What do you fancy?'

'Hmm…' His eyes scanned the options. 'I think I'll join you with that. What about your main course?'

'Hmm…lasagne, I think, for me.'

'And I'll have the carbonara.'

She laughed. 'Can you believe we've come to France and ended up choosing Italian food?'

'We'll go full-on French tomorrow.'

They placed their order with the waiter and Sam took a sip of his wine. It was perfect. Fruity. Crisp. With just a tart enough kick on the back of his throat.

'So, tell me about our first visit.'

Emily's eyes became dreamy, which he had to smile at, and as he stared at his beautiful wife he couldn't help but think just how lucky he was.

'Well, we didn't come out of our room the first day we arrived. We took full advantage of Room Service after we'd...worked up an appetite.'

He noticed her blushes and smiled slightly as his own imagination supplied him with the possibilities of what that might have been like.

She straightened her serviette on her lap. 'We did lots of walking, exploring, trying to find the *real* Paris—you know, stuff off the beaten track. We didn't just want to do the traditional touristy stuff.'

He nodded. 'Tell me one of your favourite places.'

Emily sighed happily in recollection. 'We went to the Bois de Vincennes and rowed out across the lake to the temple on the island. There's a grotto underneath and we went there quite late, at sunset. It was the most beautiful thing I ever saw.'

'We should go again, then.'

'I'd like that.' She smiled at him, and then they said nothing for a while.

Sam gazed at her from across the table and it felt good to have his full attention.

'We have been happy, Sam. I know I said we'd argued, but...there were good times, too.'

'When did it all start to change?'

She shrugged, the shift in her demeanour clear. 'I don't know. It was gradual. I can remember sitting down to dinner with you one night, like we are now, across the table from one another, and I was excited because I was going to suggest we start a family. It meant so much to me, and I honestly believed that it would to you, too. Considering what we both do for a living, it seemed the next natural step. We were married, our business was getting off the ground, financially we were solid. I couldn't see why there would be any objection. I thought that when I suggested having a baby you'd think about it briefly. Mull it over as you sipped your wine and then we'd discuss when we'd start trying.'

'But it didn't go that way?'

Her gaze was downcast, her eyes darkening. 'No. You…you became a different man. The second I mentioned it a wall seemed to come down in front of you. You closed yourself off, told me it wasn't a good idea, and suddenly said you had work to do in your office. You got up and left. That's how it was with us. We never got to talk about the important stuff like that. Work—fine. Business? No problem. Personal stuff? You backed away.'

Sam looked down at the table.

'I left the subject alone for a bit. Things returned to normal. We worked hard. You were doing a lot of fundraising, a lot of galas, a lot of promotion. I started feeling lonely. As if I didn't have a husband any more. That the one I had was married to the Monterey. I tried to ask for a bit more of your time. I wanted to get you alone, so we could talk. But there was only one subject I wanted to talk about and you just kept getting angry so I stopped asking.' She sipped her water. 'We stopped talking to one another entirely—except about business.'

Sam let out a heavy sigh and rubbed at his forehead. 'It was bad, then?'

'It wasn't great.'

The waiter arrived with their starters.

The aroma of their food was delightful, the freshness and richness of the juicy tomatoes could not be questioned, and the bread had definitely been made by hand on site and flavoured with herbs and pepper.

Sam hadn't been sure he wanted to eat after hearing all that, but the sight of the food set his mouth watering.

They ate in silence, and it probably would have continued that way, but he reminded himself that they were here to *solve* their problems.

Sam sought for a brighter topic, so they could start talking again. 'Tell me about our wedding.'

Instantly she smiled warmly at the memories. 'It was a wonderful day. The weather was perfect. Everything went so well. Though I can remember standing outside, waiting to go in, and a honeybee flew under my veil. I panicked so much I think I might have screamed! But thankfully my bridesmaids were much braver than I was and they managed to brush it off me. It set my nerves jangling, but then…when the music started and I walked down the aisle towards you…all my nerves just disappeared. I knew that what I was doing was right, and that the man waiting for me—*you*—was going to make me the happiest woman in the world.'

He smiled and raised his glass to hers, clinking them together.

'We had a huge reception—hundreds came, mostly people *you* knew. We released a pair of doves from the balcony of the hotel, and we had all these cameras on the guests' tables and they each took pictures of what was special for them. I've got all the albums in the house somewhere. I can dig them out for you, if you like?'

He nodded. 'Tell me about the Monterey.'

'What can I say? It's doing better than either of us ever imagined. It helped, I think, that one of our first guests was a Saudi princess who gave birth to twins. She arrived with all these security guards, and she had so many staff, but we were able to accommodate them by allotting them the entire third floor. After that our success rates went through the roof. Everyone wanted to come to us. Everyone wanted to have their babies in the same place that princesses had been born.'

'And the fertility clinic?'

'I'm not sure of the exact numbers, but I believe so far we've helped over a hundred couples to conceive and successfully carry their children to term. Our manager, Edward, would be able to give you exact numbers. Didn't you call him before we left?'

'Yes, I wanted numbers and cost forecasting for the next year.'

Em nodded, aware that Sam had become work-focused yet again, despite all she'd said about the state of their marriage. It was something she was familiar with.

She finished her bruschetta, sliding her knife and fork together on her plate. 'How do you think it's all looking? I try my best to keep myself informed, but the money side of things is not my forte. I prefer the hands-on work.'

'It looks like we're exceeding expectations. I'm happy about that.'

'But...?' She looked at him with concern, knowing there was something else.

'But I'm not happy that our marriage has gone downhill.'

'We were both at fault. We allowed the Monterey to be our main focus, and sadly we forgot to put just as much work into us as we did that.'

'I should never have allowed it to happen.'

'Like I said, it was both of us.'

He appreciated her trying to let him off the hook, but he still felt that it was his fault. 'I still can't believe I don't remember it.'

'You were definitely there.' She gave a slight smile.

'But I don't remember, Em! I want to recall the experience of the rush of the Monterey's opening. The worry about whether we'd succeed and the watching and the observing as everything began to get better. The tweaking of the things that weren't quite right, answering our patients' needs and serving them, making their experience the best they could ever imagine. I don't feel I was part of any of that. I've just been handed dry forecasts and accounts of where we are now and apparently, according to you, work is just fine—but *we* aren't.'

She reached for her glass of water. Sipped it. 'We can be okay again, Sam. That's why we're here. And you *did* experience it. You worked so hard. The memory is in there—you've just got to be patient.'

'I know. It's just…'

'Frustrating?'

He nodded and sat back as their waiter arrived to clear their dishes. Once he'd disappeared, Sam sat forward again. 'I feel out of place, Em. I know the Monterey is ours, that we made it happen, but I don't *feel* like it's mine. I feel like it's something you've done. That it's been your project and you've just shown it to me. Does that make any sense?'

'A little, yes. But you have to know that it will all come back—you've already experienced one old memory. And when it does…'

He saw a shadow cross her face and knew why she looked so worried. 'Yes?'

'When it does, you'll know…everything.' She forced a smile.

'I hope so. I really do.'

'Me too.' She dabbed at her mouth with the serviette. 'I must just use the ladies' room. Excuse me.'

He watched her hurry away.

He knew why he was really so frustrated at not being there for the Monterey. It had always been *his* big project. *His* dream. He'd put so much work into it when really he should have been putting all the work into his marriage. He could vocalise his concerns about missing out on the Monterey. But he couldn't vocalise about what had gone wrong in his marriage—because Emily didn't yet know about Serena.

I've got to tell her. We won't survive otherwise.

Whilst he waited, he stared out across the darkening evening of Paris. The fairy lights had come on around the terrace, bathing them all in soft white light, but the brightest beacon of all was the lit Eiffel Tower, behind him in the distance.

It was a stunning sight—one they would no doubt be able to enjoy from their hotel window.

Sam hoped Paris would be everything they had planned it to be.

He needed his memories back.

He needed to be the man Emily had fallen in love with.

He needed to be strong.

Needed to know who he was and what he had gone through.

Why couldn't the accident have erased the memory of what happened to Serena?

Dinner was superb. The lasagne that Emily had ordered was deliciously sumptuous, and the chocolate mousse they shared for pudding was soft, rich and velvety.

As they sat drinking coffee Sam asked her an awkward question.

'Considering how things were between us, I take it the baby was a surprise?'

Hurrying to swallow her mouthful of coffee, she almost choked on it. 'Yes. It was a surprise. I didn't even know I was pregnant until after the crash, when they ran a few blood tests on me.'

'You were on the pill?'

'Yes, I was.'

He sipped his coffee carefully, not meeting her eyes. 'Did you get sick? Is that what happened?'

She shook her head. 'I don't think so. I certainly never missed any.'

'It's never been one hundred percent effective.'

'There was a lot going on, Sam. We were very busy. I was working long shifts because one of our midwives was off ill and I was covering for her. One night we'd both had a lot of wine and...'

'It happened?'

She nodded. 'Yeah. It happened.'

Emily remembered that night so clearly. She had been exhausted, tired and upset. She hadn't seen Sam for almost three days. He'd been in surgery, or in and out of meetings, and they'd barely spoken. He certainly hadn't touched her for weeks. Their arguments had grown so awful that they hadn't talked in what felt like ages.

Emily had gone back to their house and, knowing she didn't have a shift the next day, had poured herself a large glass of wine. She'd almost finished it by the time Sam had arrived home, and something about him had seemed strange. He'd been different.

He'd said he was fed up with their fighting and that he missed her. She'd not let him say another word, had gone straight into his arms, and it had been as if someone had lit a fire. Suddenly everything had been urgent. They'd craved each other's bodies intensely and they'd made love on the carpet.

Afterwards he'd scooped her up in his arms and carried her to bed, where she'd fallen asleep. But when she'd woken in the morning he'd been gone again. It had been a brief truce, a cessation in their arguments, but when she'd sought him out to talk to him about what had happened he'd been too busy, and had answered her sharply, and before she'd known it they'd been arguing again.

It had been a difficult time for her. She'd been devastated, and then hopeful as she'd lain in his arms that they might be able to work things out—only to be dropped like a hot stone afterwards. Cast aside, feeling used.

Emily didn't want to tell him any of that. How could she? Here? In this beautiful city? Sam didn't need to hear any of that. He'd hate to hear it. He'd feel so guilty, and she didn't want him feeling that. They were here to deepen their love. Not go over old, painful ground which neither of them needed to return to.

She wanted them to be happy! She wanted the fairytale that she saw being played out every day. A happy family, a *loving* family, with everyone eager and excited about their pregnancy, planning nurseries and buying tiny clothes, getting excited about the approaching labour and thinking of names and choosing godparents. All of it.

She wanted a husband who was thrilled to be a father! She wanted the love that she'd never had. To give her child the stable family home that she had never experienced. There was no way she wanted to go back to the way they'd been before.

When she'd married Sam she'd made a commitment, and Emily believed you should always honour a commitment. If you had a child, you stuck around to love it and raise it. If you got married—well, you worked with the other person to make the marriage the best it could be. You didn't just give up when things got rough. You didn't just walk out because life seemed easier chasing another dream.

She looked down at the table. Sam still didn't know just *how bad* their arguments had been. How close she had come to leaving him. If he knew what they'd really been like...the amount of times she had stood in the shower and cried...

'I just want this trip to work so badly. I can't imagine how you must feel, having lost two years of your life. To wake up to this...I've tried to imagine what it would be like if it had happened to me.'

What if she *had* been the one with amnesia? If she thought he had just proposed and she had forgotten the wedding, the Grand Opening of their business. Their arguments? She would still feel blissfully happy after the proposal, right? Would she want to hear that she had threatened to leave him? Would she want to hear that they *weren't* the blissfully happy couple she believed them to be? Would she want to hear about some of the things they'd said to each other in the heat of the moment?

No.

'I'm okay.'

'Are you? Without memories of the opening of the birth centre, our wedding, our honeymoon...?'

'I can get all of that back.' He reached for her hand. 'Isn't that what you keep telling me? Isn't that why we're here?'

She nodded. It was. But getting his memories back was a double-edged sword. On the one hand he would have the joy of recalling all the good times they'd shared, but on the other...they could slip apart.

'Then let's work towards that. If I have any questions I'll ask you and you can answer. At least until my memories come back on their own. Okay?'

It would have to do. 'Okay.'

He smiled at her, his eyes glinting beneath the fairy lights.

The restaurant was beginning to get busy now, but they finished their coffees, paid and headed back out onto the street.

'Let's walk for a bit,' Sam suggested, draping an arm around her shoulder.

Paris at twilight was even more beautiful than it was during the day. There were still just as many people bustling about, and the roads were filled with cars and bikes, but everything seemed just that little bit calmer. As if everyone was more relaxed. Cafés and bistros poured out their lights and their aromatic scents into the streets, and they could hear conversation and muted laughter and people *enjoying* themselves. They passed a busker or two, food and flower stalls packing up for the day.

Sam bought her a single rose and presented it to her. 'For *madame.*'

'Thank you, kind sir.' She lifted the bloom to her nose and inhaled its soft sweet scent.

These were the moments that she'd yearned for. The last time they'd been in Paris Emily had been soaking up the atmosphere as much as Sam, but this time she knew it all a little better and so could concentrate more on enjoying being with Sam. Holding his hand. Being in his arms. Being in Paris itself was an added bonus.

Sam and Emily headed back over to the Seine and began to walk along its banks, arm in arm. It was a truce of sorts. Both of them were keen to make this trip work. To become close again.

They could hear accordion music in the distance, against the soft lapping of the water against the banks.

A duck swam by, followed by a row of small ducklings, brown and yellow.

Emily sighed and looked about her. Couples sat on benches, hand in hand. Couples walked along the river, just like them. Couples sat on the stone steps, staring at the water. This really was a city meant for happiness. Not marital woes.

Sam kissed the side of her neck, inhaling the perfumed scent of her hair. He looked into her eyes. 'I'm sorry we've argued, and I'm sorry if I haven't been spending time with you. I guess you thought the same thing was happening again when I locked myself away in the office to catch up on things. Same old Sam, huh?'

She smiled. He was so unaware. So innocent of how bad things had actually become. She wanted to make him feel better.

'That's okay. I know you feel the need to catch up. I would do the same thing in your shoes.'

'I'm so lucky to have you, Em.'

She smiled back at him.

The music was getting closer now, and they could see an old man, sitting on top of the stone steps with a genuine accordion. It wasn't a recording, or a CD playing, but a real, actual musician. He had an ancient face, but it was filled with passion as he played an old-style Argentinian tango, his fingers moving over the buttons and shaping the accordion with ease. Around him couples were dancing against the backdrop of the river. All ages, all abilities. It didn't matter. People were just being in the moment.

Sam and Emily watched for a second or two, and then Sam took her hand and led her into the group of dancers.

'Sam! What are you doing?' She laughed.

'We're going to dance!'

She laughed out loud in disbelief! Did Sam not remember? He'd done this the last time! It didn't seem as if he knew that.

But who cared? Emily wanted to dance with him. Their honeymoon had been the only time he had danced with her. Apart from at their wedding, of course, and she loved to dance.

At least she loved to dance with *him*.

The beautiful music was at once sudden and jarring, and had Sam pulling her up tight against his body. At first she laughed, embarrassed, but then she could see Sam smiling, taking the tango seriously, staring deeply into her eyes.

The Argentine tango was a dance made for eye contact and a close embrace. They moved as one. Forward. Back. To the side. Their steps were in tune with the music, first fast, then slow. Their bodies pressed together.

Slowly Emily began to forget that there were other couples dancing with them in the same space. All she concentrated on was Sam's eyes locked with her own. *Feeling* the pace and emotion of the music.

Being close to him. Held by him.

He had such piercing blue eyes. Intense. Moving. And they bored into her own with love and adoration as he twisted her this way, then that. The music began to get a little faster. He twisted her out to the side and she swept her foot out wide, as if scraping the floor, her skirt billowing out around her, before he pulled her back in close once again.

He really was a masterful dancer.

Why don't we do this more often?

She stared once again into his eyes as he pulled her close, making her gasp. This dance represented their relationship so easily. Passionate...tempestuous. Intimate.

She slid her leg up and down his, aware of the way he was breathing with her now in the dance, enjoying their closeness to each other. Aware of the way his body felt against hers.

Oh, how I've missed this man.

As the music built to its climax Sam spun them round in tight little movements and then, at the big finish, he dipped her backwards, bending over with her. As everyone began clapping to thank the musician he brought his face towards hers and kissed her deeply.

She fell into the kiss, draping her hands around his neck, unaware that the music had begun once again and the other couples were continuing to dance.

Straightening, they simply stood in the middle of the 'dance floor' and kissed.

Emily sank into him, claiming her husband back, claiming his mouth, his tongue, his taste. She wanted him so badly. Did he want her just as much? She hoped so. It had been so long since she had felt his touch upon her like this, so long since he had stared into her eyes like this, and she craved him like a drug.

As the kiss ended they continued to stare into each other's eyes. For a moment neither of them said anything, and then she felt Sam slip his fingers into hers.

'Let's go back to the hotel.'

She nodded, understanding his intent, and together they left the dancing group.

CHAPTER FIVE

NEITHER OF THEM said anything on the way back to the hotel. They walked with purpose, through the evening light, and in their hotel room, surrounded once again by luxury, Emily suddenly realised just how much of a long day they'd had—the flight, the taxi ride, dinner, exploring Paris, and then telling Sam how bad things really were.

She felt she wanted to refresh herself. Wash away the travel. Take a few moments to prepare herself for this. They hadn't been intimate for such a long time and she wanted it to be perfect.

'I'm going to take a shower.'

Sam nodded.

Inside the shower room, Emily turned on the hot spray and removed her clothes. Stepping beneath the powerful refreshing water, she gasped at the feel of it on the back of her neck before turning around to face the water and look for soap.

That was when she became aware of the fact that Sam had joined her. She heard the glass shower door open and then sensed his presence.

Smiling to herself, she sighed in delight as she felt Sam's hands slide over the skin around her hips, before he slid them over her belly and pulled her back against him.

Emily closed her eyes with pure elation. She could feel him. Every familiar inch of him. His hands sliding over her breasts…his fingers splaying as they rubbed over her sensitive nipples. Leaning back into him, she allowed herself to enjoy the moment as his lips caressed her neck. She had not felt his touch for so long! *Too* long.

The last time Sam had joined her in the shower had been in this very shower, on their honeymoon. They'd just come back from visiting the top of the Eiffel Tower, watching the city from its viewing platforms and taking photographs. They'd hired bicycles and cycled around Paris in the midday heat, and by the end of the day they'd both been sweaty and tired. They'd fallen into the shower cubicle with giggles and laughter, holding onto each other as they kissed each other and covered each other in foam, their limbs sliding over each other.

Here they stood once again.

It gave Emily a strange sense of *déjà-vu*. Shivering, she closed her eyes as Sam's hands once again sought her peaked nipples. The heat and spray of the water, the feel of his fingers upon her, the way he kissed and nipped the skin on her neck and collarbone, his lips brushing like feathers…it was utterly delightful.

'Oh, Sam…'

He turned her to him and cupped her face, bringing her lips to his.

Oh, I've missed his touch…

A few weeks ago she could never have dreamed that they would be like this. She'd stood over a suitcase, planning to leave him! She'd felt angry at him, frustrated that he would never talk to her, or allow her to explain how she was feeling. He'd never listened—he'd ignored her, stayed away.

She'd never believed she would have *this* again.

Those days she'd spent worrying about what would happen when he woke from his coma had been swept away by the realisation that Sam couldn't remember the last two years. That, for him, their relationship was in a totally different place. And the baby! He'd not reacted badly to the news either—which she didn't want to think about. Didn't want to question.

All that mattered was the touch of his hands upon her, the feel of his arousal against her, the clear signs that he wanted *her*, wanted the baby, that he was happy despite his memory loss. And that they were reconnecting.

We can get through this. We can do it together.

A wave of tiredness swept over her, but she pushed it away. All these hours they'd spent awake—the travelling, the waiting in the airport, the long day. Her exhaustion was catching up with her, but she couldn't let it overwhelm her. She had waited for this moment with Sam. Had craved this intimacy between them. Something which had been sadly lacking for too long.

How many nights had she lain awake in bed, waiting for him to come home? Waiting for him to come to bed just so she could feel the security of him next to her on the mattress even if he did turn his back?

Too many times.

How many times had he stayed away? How many times had he left her wondering where he was actually sleeping? So she'd had to go tiptoeing through the house at night until she found the room that he was in?

Too many to count.

How did she know whether he would do it to her again? It had to be in him, didn't it? The rejection of her. The rejection of the baby. Even if it wasn't in him now it was *part of him*. He had already done it to her. He just couldn't remember. When would it start? Was it already brewing? Was he already having secret thoughts that he was holding back? What if he used her right now and then in the morning cast her aside?

Feeling afraid and confused, Emily turned her back to him. She needed a moment. To think. To *breathe*.

Sam ran his fingers through her long wet hair and reached past her for a shampoo bottle. Squirting some into his hands, he began to stroke it into her long locks, gently massaging her scalp, making sure he touched every strand, every length, trying to make the experience pleasurable for her.

She pressed her hands against the wall of the shower cubicle and gave in to the massage. It felt so good to be loved by Sam again. Cherished. But she wasn't sure what she should be thinking. Should she just enjoy what he was initiating? Or turn and tell him the full truth? Take the bull by its very sharp, pointed horns and tell him everything?

Emily pressed her hands against the tiled wall, feeling its reassuring, very solid presence.

I can't. I'd risk everything. It's best he doesn't know I was going to leave him.

The head massage was soothing. Too soothing. She felt as if she might almost drop off to sleep, it was so nice.

Emily held her head under the shower so that the shampoo would be washed away. The hot suds ran down her body, trailed by Sam's hands, his fingertips, a feather touch down her back, over the swell of her hips and bottom and the sides of her thighs.

Then he was reaching past her for conditioner, and as he smoothed on the cold creamy hair product, smoothing it down the hair that almost fell to her waist, she let out a long sigh of pleasure.

She dipped her head under the spray once more, then

turned to him. The heat within the shower was becoming too much. 'I need to get out. Cool down.'

He kissed her shoulder. 'I won't be a minute. Get into bed. I'll join you soon.'

Emily stepped out and grabbed a large fluffy bath towel, which she wrapped herself in, and then left the steamy shower room.

The hotel suite felt much cooler, and it was as if there was more air. Breathing more easily, she removed the towel and rubbed at her long hair, then padded across the suite in her bare feet towards the bed. She smiled as she slipped beneath the covers.

Tonight she would reclaim her husband.

Tonight she would get him back for good.

Sam turned off the shower and grabbed a towel to wrap around his waist and another to rub at his wet hair.

The shower had felt good. But it was even better to have shared it with Em. It was time for them to grow close—especially as he'd spent the last few days stuck in his office at the house, trying to catch up on all the paperwork that had accrued in his absence. Trying to look at business growth charts and financial losses, turnover and profit, stock ordering systems and staff training reports, and all the other reams of paper that had just seemed to grow out of nowhere and had almost brought on a headache.

Two years' worth of catching up had caused him to fall asleep there more than once! He felt sure that Em wasn't approving of that, but she hadn't complained. Not really. She'd given him a worried look or two, whenever she'd popped in with a coffee, or to say goodnight, but that was to be expected after his accident.

Now they were in Paris, and for him it felt like the first

time. Sitting across from Em in that restaurant and seeing the love in her eyes for him had warmed his heart. And then later, when they'd danced together, it had been clear they hadn't touched for an age, and it had been painfully exquisite to take her in his arms once more and see the hope and elation in her eyes.

He was eager for them to improve their relationship. To find the marriage they'd had at the beginning, before the arguments had started. They'd been good together once, but hearing how he'd been with her had rung too true. He could imagine himself trying to avoid the question about having babies—could picture himself staying away, thinking that if he did that at least then they wouldn't be arguing. That somehow he'd be trying to save her from pain.

Sam threw the towel he'd been drying his hair with to the floor and stepped out of the shower room. He'd only kept her waiting for a few minutes—he felt sure she wouldn't have minded.

Em lay in the bed, her naked back to him, her still drying hair spread out over the pillow.

Smiling, he lifted the covers, removed the towel from his waist and slid in next to her, his hand roving over her naked hip and around her thigh.

'Hello again, gorgeous…'

He waited for an answer, and when he didn't get one he propped himself up in bed and peered over at her face.

Was she *asleep*?

'Em?' he whispered. *'Em?'*

She breathed steadily, her eyes closed, her face in a truly relaxed state.

She's exhausted! Must be all those hormones…

His hand resting on her belly stilled. There was a

slight—ever so slight—roundness to it that hadn't been there before.

Our baby.

Sam laid his head down onto the pillow as he spooned his wife. How would he deal with what was to come? Could he do it? He'd have to, wouldn't he? The baby was already happening. Already growing within her.

He wasn't surprised that he'd not been able to find a way to tell her about Serena. He had always kept that part of him close. Tightly boxed away, never to be shown the light. But perhaps by doing that—by not telling Em— he had caused a different rift. One he could never fix. He hoped not. He hoped that there was still happiness ahead for them both. Perhaps he could find a way to tell her about his baby sister?

Sam swallowed hard. *I'm not sure I can.* He'd spoken about it to nobody. Even his own family didn't talk about it to each other. He'd learnt that from them. You take the hurt, you stamp it down and you bury it—bury it deep, where no one will ever see it. You don't mention the disturbed soil, you don't mention the empty crib, you don't say anything when you see someone crying. You stay away from all of that.

It had worked for him thus far, hadn't it?

No. Your wife was miserable!

He would have to hope this trip would give him time. Time to find a way through his concerns and fears about being a good, protective father.

Because it was real. The baby was in there, growing. He had seen it on the scan and it had taken his breath away.

Maybe a son. Maybe a daughter. Like Serena. If it was a girl, would he ever truly relax? Would he stand watch over her every night? Checking her breathing? Checking she was still okay?

Was that even possible? Not twenty-four hours a day. But how *could* he keep his baby safe? If something happened to their child Emily would be distraught! She might blame him.

And if it were a boy? Would he be any more relaxed? *No.* He supposed they could get a baby monitor that alerted you to your baby's breathing. He supposed he could get a camera for the baby's room, too. But would any of that make him feel better?

Sam wasn't sure. But what he *did* know was that they were against the clock. He had six months to get his head around this. Six months either to accept what was happening and get on with it, or…or what?

Sam cradled his wife's abdomen. The baby was safe for now.

He could only hope that it would stay that way. And they were making inroads in their marriage too. Coming here. Spending time together away from work. But there was work to do here too…on their marriage.

It took some time, but eventually he fell asleep, his eyes finally closing on the shadows crossing the room and the constant glow of light touching the ceiling, coming from the Eiffel Tower…

'Let's hire some bikes,' Sam suggested, a big smile on his face.

Indulgently, Emily smiled back, tearing a piece from her croissant as they breakfasted alfresco on their hotel suite balcony. It was a beautiful summer morning and she'd had an excellent night's sleep, waking to find herself snuggled into Sam's warm, inviting body.

'We did that the last time. And I don't want to get exhausted again.'

Em felt terrible for having fallen asleep last night. They'd both been expecting to *become more acquainted*, and yet the second she'd lain her head upon the pillow she'd gone off to the Land of Nod. Waking this morning to see the sunlight streaming through the windows, and having a distinctly empty memory of any recent love-making, had made her feel incredibly embarrassed and awkward. She'd slipped out of his arms and gone outside to the balcony.

'I meant those little moped things. I heard someone say yesterday that they rode around Montmartre and had an amazing time. Let's do that. No energy required.'

The buttery croissant was light and fluffy in her mouth and she swallowed it whilst smearing another piece with jam. 'Okay...sounds fun. What do you want to do in Montmartre?'

'Whatever takes our fancy. Let's just ride around and explore.'

'Okay.'

It sounded a great idea. They hadn't done *that* before, and she relished the idea of finding somewhere new to explore together. They needed to spend time like that. Who knew what might trigger his memory? Why not try something different?

'It's going to be another lovely summer's day.'

'It's always a lovely summer's day when I'm with you.'

She smiled. 'Ditto.'

'I'm going to get dressed. You enjoy breakfast. You need your strength. Don't want you flaking out on me.'

The croissant went dry in her mouth and guilt made the breakfast suddenly unpalatable. She hadn't meant to fall asleep last night, but the second she'd got into the bed she'd relaxed and closed her eyes for just a moment...

Sam must have felt so disappointed when he'd got out of the shower and found her fast asleep. Yet he was being so gentlemanly by not mentioning it.

But what could she do? It was done now, and he was obviously trying hard to not focus on it. She should do the same thing, too, and get ready for their day in Montmartre.

When she went into the bedroom she gasped to see a box upon the bed, tied with a bow. 'What's that?'

'Open it.' Sam grinned.

Puzzled, she sat on the bed and untied the bow, sliding off the ribbon before opening the box. Whatever was inside was wrapped in pale pink tissue paper, and when she opened that she gasped out loud. 'Oh, my goodness! When did you get this?'

Inside the box was the beautiful powder-blue dress that she'd spotted in the airport shop when they'd passed by at Charles de Gaulle. She'd pointed it out to him, had oohed and aahed at the dress in the window, but they'd hurried on, eager to get to their destination.

How had Sam arranged this?

'Sam...'

'I couldn't resist. I know it probably won't fit you in a few more weeks, but...I wanted you to have it.'

She stood up and draped it against her, checking herself in the mirror. 'I love it, Sam—thank you. I'm going to wear it today.'

'On a moped? Why not wear it tonight, when we get back? We could go out for a meal.'

She nodded. 'Perfect. Thank you.'

'You're worth it. I love you.'

She stroked his face, loving this side of Sam. 'I love you, too.'

He grinned. 'Okay. Get dressed and let's get ready to ride!'

At first Emily wasn't too good at riding the moped. But after a few false starts, where she kangarooed along the road, and a bit of extra tuition from a patient Sam, they finally got going and rode through the city, out towards Montmartre.

They stopped and parked on the Rue Jardieu, to get off and have a good look around the area, famed for its street painters and artists. They walked towards the Square Willette and gasped in awe at the sight of the Basilica de Sacré-Coeur—the beautiful, pure white Byzantine church that looked down the hill at them as if surveying all that it could see.

'That's just beautiful, isn't it, Sam?'

'It is. Should we go take a look around?'

She nodded.

They took their time—walking through the square, then up the terraced stairs, past a musician playing the harp, to whom they gave a few coins—and finally they stood in front of the wonderful, imposing building.

There were three arches, and above them bronze statues of a saint and a king, welcoming them in, After taking a photo or two, they stepped inside, into the cool interior.

The beautiful three-domed church was lit by dozens of stained glass windows, surrounding the building, and they walked around quietly, respecting their reverent surroundings.

Emily felt the need to slip her hand into Sam's, and she watched as Sam stopped to light a candle and stood back to stare at it, as if in contemplation.

She frowned, wondering who the candle was for. Sam still had both his parents and all five of his siblings. Was it for a grandparent? It seemed a strange thing for him to do, and she wondered about the Sam that she didn't know. There had to be something. Back in his past. And it was something he clearly hadn't forgotten about after his accident. An old memory? An old pain?

She knew Sam had secrets, and it had always pained her that he'd never chosen to share those with her. *Why* hadn't he? Was it because of the arguments, the distance between them? Why hadn't he told her about them when they *weren't* arguing? He'd had time. They talked to each other about most things back then. It hurt to think that he was keeping part of himself hidden, that he didn't trust her.

But she couldn't ask him here. Not with all these people around. She decided to wait until they were out of the church, maybe having lunch, and then she would ask him.

Watching Sam made her realise that she didn't have anyone to light a candle for. As far as she knew her mother was still alive. Her Aunt Sylvia and her Uncle Martin were too. No one had any idea who her father was. Grandparents? She had no recollection. So Emily had no need to make such a beautiful acknowledgement. It made her feel a little rootless, not knowing more about her mother and her family. As if a part of her was missing. That she was somehow incomplete. It was why she had fought so hard to save her marriage. She couldn't lose Sam, too. She would feel so lost.

They continued to look around, then eventually emerged outside, walking back around to the front steps and looking out over the city.

'It was so peaceful in there, wasn't it?' he asked.

Emily nodded. 'It was. Very.' She looked at his face

for a moment, wondering whether *now* would be a good time to ask about the candle, but she saw a shadow cross his face and decided against it. Not yet. There would be a time and place soon, though.

'Where do you think we should go next?'

'I'm not sure. Should we go back and grab the mopeds? Ride around?'

She nodded. The bikes would be good. Sam's mood had changed in the basilica, and she wanted to see the joyful Sam she had witnessed that morning. This was meant to be fun, and yet they had descended into a sombre mood.

They walked back through the square, enjoying the wide expanses of grass and the flowers, the singing of the birds in the trees, until they got back to their mopeds and donned their helmets.

Their engines roared into life and they set off into the small, winding streets, looking for treasures.

It came suddenly and without warning. Sam was riding his moped, following Emily. He'd been watching the traffic, enjoying the sight of his wife's hair billowing behind her, and the memory came from nowhere.

Emily striding away from him in a hospital corridor, anger pouring from every part of her body. Stiff shoulders. Purposeful.

He called her name in exasperation. 'Emily!'

She stopped walking. Turned and her face was full of tears. Her eyes red and streaming...

Sam blinked and a car sounded its horn at him as he wavered slightly. Straightening his bike, he raised his hand in apology to the driver.

What the hell had that been?

The hospital corridor had been at the Monterey.

He'd recognised it. It had been the corridor leading to Emily's office, because there'd been that picture on the wall. The watercolour of a pixie gazing at her reflection in a pool. Em had picked it out from an exhibition she'd seen.

In the memory his wife had been upset. Vastly upset. With him. *At him?*

What had happened next?

He cursed to himself, angry that the memory had been fleeting and brief. But then, strangely, his heart began to pound as he realised another memory had returned! Bad as it had been—*again*—a memory *had* returned!

Was this going to be it? Were they about to start coming back?

Should he mention it to Emily?

He pondered over that. If he told her he'd experienced another flash of memory she'd want to know what it was, and if he told her... Well, she might not want another bad memory being dragged up. Not here. Not on this holiday. She'd wanted them to enjoy this place. They were both hoping this trip to Paris would bring them closer again.

But hadn't she been the one to suggest that Paris would be the place for him to regain his memories?

This was what they were here for, after all. And, even though it was a bad memory, perhaps it seemed worse than it really was? Perhaps it was something that could be easily explained and Emily would laugh about it and tell him it was nothing?

Sam was desperate to get his memories back, and the fleeting one he'd just experienced enticed him to believe that others were there, waiting for him to claim them. If he explored this memory with Emily then it might cause others to come through.

He had to take that chance.

After they'd been driving around for a while Emily pointed over at what looked like a vast marketplace but was in fact a square, full of artists and portraitists, all sitting beneath large red umbrellas to protect themselves and their work from the sun or occasional inclement weather. The square was filled with laughter and French voices. Tourists and locals milled around, taking photographs or sitting for paintings beneath an avenue of leafy green trees.

Ahead of him, Emily removed her helmet, shaking out her hair, and slipped on her sunglasses. 'This looks great, Sam! Shall we get our picture painted?'

He loved her enthusiasm. Loved her smile. He didn't want to lose that. He decided to tell her about the memory later—perhaps when they were sitting for the picture.

'Okay.'

They locked up their mopeds, pocketing the keys, and headed into the bustling square.

There were some amazing artists there, using a vast array of techniques—acrylics, watercolour, pencil, paste, chalk. If there was a way of putting a picture onto paper or canvas, then it was here. And he knew Emily loved art.

They took their time looking about, trying to find someone they thought might capture the two of them perfectly, and stopped when they saw a caricaturist.

'Oh, this will be fun, Sam. Let's ask this one.'

Thankfully the artist spoke English, and they negotiated a price before they sat down together and smiled at the artist who soon set to work.

'You are here on holiday?' the artist asked.

Emily smiled at him. 'Sort of a second honeymoon. It's a long story,' she explained.

'Ah, *voyage de noces. La lune de miel.*'

'That sounds beautiful.'

The artist smiled. 'It is meant to be. *C'est romantique!*'

Emily and Sam shared an odd smile. The painter obviously saw them as a couple, very much in love, and only they knew the real truth.

As the artist worked, concentrating on his drawing whilst occasionally peering around his easel at the two of them, Sam decided to let Emily know what had happened.

'You know, Em…I think whilst we were riding here I remembered something.' He glanced at her to see her reaction and noticed with alarm that she seemed to freeze, pausing for a brief millisecond as if in fear, before she let out a breath and smiled.

'You did? What?'

He shook his head. 'It was brief. Barely anything, really. We were at the Monterey, heading for your office, but…'

She looked curious. 'But?'

'You were walking away from me, and when I called your name you turned around and you were crying.'

Emily looked away from him, frowning.

Was she trying to remember the incident? Had it been a common occurrence? He knew they'd been arguing.

'I see.'

'What was that about?'

Em shook her head. 'It's not important.'

'It is,' he pressed on. 'I need to understand what was going on if we're to make this work.'

She looked down at the ground. 'If it's the argument I remember, then I'd tried to track you down at work because you hadn't been home that night. I wanted to know where you'd been.'

He stared at her, afraid of her answer. 'And?'

'You'd been out wining and dining clients, and I was

annoyed because you were spending so much time woo-
ing other people that you never had time for me.'

'I see.'

'I wasn't being selfish, Sam. I hadn't seen you for what
felt like days! I'd been worried about you. Worried about
us. I'd spent hours huddled on the couch, afraid of what
might have happened, and then I learnt that you'd been
out having a good time.'

He looked away. 'Oh.'

'So I was hurt and angry and I stormed away from
you.'

Sam almost didn't want to believe it. But he could
imagine himself doing that. Avoiding the main argument
and throwing himself into something else instead, hoping
that if he just never talked about the thing that bothered
him then it wouldn't bother anyone else. It was what he
had been taught to do.

'So your memories are starting to come back?'

He gazed at her and he could see that she was sad.
But there was something else in her eyes that he couldn't
fathom. What was it? She was looking at him as if...as
if she was afraid.

No. That couldn't be true. Why would Emily be
afraid of his memories returning? She *wanted* them to.
It couldn't be fear. There was no need for it. She'd already
told him how bad it had become between them. For that
he was grateful. It would have been so easy for her to say
that they'd been getting on fine. He had to be wrong—it
couldn't have been fear that he'd seen.

Shaking his head, he decided to forget about it. The
artist obviously thought they were happy, because when
he showed them the picture—the two of them beneath a
backdrop of the Eiffel Tower—he had drawn red hearts
blossoming all around them.

Sam wondered briefly how the artist might have painted them if he'd known the truth? Would they have had blindfolds over their eyes? Hands clamped over their mouths?

He solemnly wished their lives were truly like the caricature.

They decided to walk through some of the streets, snapping pictures of things they found interesting. They found a very pretty vineyard—which seemed an odd thing to find amongst a bustling mass of streets—then a street of nineteenth-century villas and gardens which were in full bloom, and in another a windmill.

Montmartre was a place of contrasts, it seemed, and they could understand why it had once been *the* place to be seen if you were an artist or a painter.

'We ought to get something to eat,' Emily said, rubbing at her stomach. 'I'm getting very hungry with all this exploring.'

'What do you fancy?'

'Something quick.'

They found a small stall selling pitta pockets stuffed with a choice of chicken, beef or vegetables, served with plantains, avocado or black beans. They both chose a chicken pitta with plantain chips and two cold limeades.

'Oh, my goodness, that's delightful,' Emily said, savouring her sandwich and using her fingers to capture a piece of chicken.

'Something new for you?'

She nodded, smiling, her mouth full.

Sam smiled back. The food was indeed delicious, and he realised that he was loving today. Loving making these new memories with Em after the regret of knowing he had missed so much and that some of what he had missed had been awful. But he was determined to be positive and to look forward. He had a business that by all accounts was doing well, a gorgeous, wonderful wife whom he loved with his entire heart, and they were trying their best to tackle their problems the best they knew how.

And he was going to be a father.

That in itself was a scary thing to admit to himself, and he'd tried to put it in the 'positive' category but he couldn't. It was not something that he could escape from. He had to face it. Head-on. No matter if he had doubts.

Em took a thoughtful nibble of her pitta. 'This morning, Sam...back in the basilica...you lit a candle.'

He glanced at her, acknowledging her statement with a nod.

'Who was it for?'

So she definitely didn't know, then. He obviously hadn't told her about Serena. He supposed he knew why. He'd always kept that part of himself hidden. Had shared it with no one. And when Emily had brought up the idea of having a baby in the past he must have dug his heels in even more.

Was this the root of all their problems? His refusal to talk about his deepest, darkest secret? Had it been his fault all along? Hurting Emily by pushing her away? Causing her grief by refusing even to discuss something that was so important? It must have made her feel tiny. Belittled. She was his wife and he wouldn't even talk to her about what ailed him.

But did he want her to find out about it *here*? When they were trying to make new happy memories for themselves?

'It was for us. A candle to show the way.'

She smiled, relieved, and laid her head upon his shoulder. 'That's so sweet. For us? Thank you, Sam.'

Pressing down against the guilt he felt at lying to her, he kissed the side of her face, and he was just about to take another bite of his sandwich when something happened that seemed almost to occur in slow motion.

He looked out across the street and spotted an old man, looking for a place to cross. The road wasn't too busy, but there was a steady stream of traffic coming both ways. The side where the old man stood was clear, and he began to amble across. But halfway he spotted a motorbike, tried to hurry, then tripped—just before the motorbike collided with him.

Sam dropped his pitta pocket as the motorcyclist was thrown through the air and the old man crashed to the ground, spinning round from the impact.

His hands, frantically trying to control the steering wheel...

'Oh, my God, Sam!' Emily gripped his arm.

He was up. Dashing across the road, calling out, 'Call an ambulance! *Appelez une ambulance!*'

The rest of the traffic drew to a halt, drivers and passengers getting out to look at the crash.

The motorcyclist had been thrown clear and had rolled across the road. He was struggling to get up.

Sam ran to the old man first, who was lying motionless on the ground, with a wound on his head, bleeding profusely, his elbows and arms torn, his leg at a painful angle.

But he was breathing.

'Lie still! Don't move.' The man's eyes fluttered open as he came back to consciousness. 'Stop—*arretez*—don't move,' Sam ordered, holding the man's neck still to maintain his c-spine control. He glanced up and over at Emily. 'Check the other one!'

He watched as Emily hurried over to check the motorcyclist, who had now sat up and was trying to remove his helmet.

'No—*non*! Keep it on!' he heard her say.

The old man began to groan.

'What's your name? *Comment vous appelez-vous?*'

More groans, then, 'Alain...'

'Alain, do you speak English? *Parlez-vous Anglais?*'

Alain tried to nod, but Sam kept his head steady. 'Stay still, my friend. I'm a doctor. You must keep still—you've been hurt.'

Sam had never felt so useless in his life. He had no medical equipment with him here. He had nothing! How could he help this man and take care of him without the back-up of his team? And he wasn't an ER specialist. He dealt with labouring women. Not elderly men hurt in road traffic accidents.

Emily came running over. 'The motorcyclist is all right. His leathers and his helmet protected him, and he wasn't going fast.'

It was a pity the same could not be said for Alain. The old man was very thin and very frail. He'd probably broken a lot of bones.

'Hold his head for me. That's it. Alain? This is my wife, Emily. Lie still for her and I'm going to check you over.'

He grabbed at his own shirt and tore off a strip, folding it and pressing it tightly against Alain's bleeding head.

Sam started checking Alain for breaks. His collarbone seemed fractured, maybe a rib or two. His right arm probably. His pelvis? To be on the safe side Sam removed his leather belt and fed it under Alain's waist, looping it over and pulling it tight to secure the pelvic basin just in case. A bleed from a break there could be disastrous. His lower leg was certainly fractured.

'Alain? Where does it hurt?'

'*Partout...*'

Everywhere. He wasn't surprised. He'd been hit by a motorbike. How fast had it been travelling? Forty kilometres per hour? Maybe a little less? It was hard to tell.

In the distance he could hear sirens approaching. 'Help's coming, Alain. Do you have any health conditions I should know about? Any allergies?'

'*Non...*'

'Okay, *c'est bon.* Anyone we can call for you? Your wife? Family?'

'*Ma femme...* Celine...'

'Okay, what's her number?'

Sam listened and wrote down the telephone number Alain gave. He could hand all this information over to the ambulance crew.

'You're doing well, Alain. A few broken bones and a head wound, but I think you're going to be okay. The ambulance is coming.'

'*Merci...*'

Sam looked at the motorcyclist. He did indeed appear to be okay, which was good news, but he would still need to be checked over in hospital. He stood behind them, a stream of French words falling steadily from his mouth. Sam couldn't catch it all, but he thought the man was trying to say he had not seen Alain until the last minute.

Well, that was something for the police to sort out.

He felt a moment of fear. Had this happened at *their* accident site? Had people got out of their cars and stood watching as assistance was given? Had people gazed at *his* injured head, too?

Sam needed to keep Alain stable. The main thing was that he was conscious and breathing.

An ambulance fought its way through the traffic and

pulled to a halt a few yards from them. It didn't take too long for Sam to feed back to the crew what he'd seen happen and his assessment of Alain.

He stood back as they took over, fitting a proper brace to Alain's pelvis and returning Sam's belt, giving their patient oxygen, fitting a neck brace and loading him into the ambulance.

As they drove away Sam stood on the path looking after them, his arm around Emily. 'You okay, Em?'

'I'm fine. Are you? You look terrible…your poor shirt…'

'It's nothing. It's Alain I feel sorry for. Poor guy, lying on the road like that.' He turned to look at her. 'Made me think about what happened to us…'

She swallowed hard. 'We survived. So will Alain.'

'I hope so. I gave the crew my number. They promised they would ring with an update when they could.'

'You did all you could have done.'

He shook his head. 'It happened so fast…and yet I could see it about to happen, like it was in slow motion, like it triggered—' He stopped talking. Went silent.

Emily looked up at him. 'Triggered what? A memory?'

'I don't know. I need to think about it. But I think I saw…'

She looked scared. 'Saw what?'

'I think I saw *our* crash. I think I saw me spinning the wheel. I don't know…'

Emily laid a hand upon his arm. 'I think we need a strong coffee or two. Let's go find a café.'

He looked at her and nodded. That seemed sensible. He didn't want them to get onto the mopeds right after seeing that bike accident. He wouldn't feel right. And it had made him see how vulnerable Emily was, exposed like that on the bike. Anything could hit her. Could take her from him!

He couldn't have that.

'Good idea.' He resolved to get the mopeds returned as soon as possible.

CHAPTER SIX

THE COFFEE WENT some way to restoring their nerves. As did the slice of caramel *dacquoise* they shared. And once they'd returned the mopeds, and Sam had changed into a new shirt at the hotel, throwing his torn one into the wastepaper basket, they decided to head back out and reclaim the day for their own.

Em held his hand as they walked. 'So that's a couple of memories that have come back since we've been here. That's good.'

That day he'd followed her to her office at the hospital, after they'd argued about him partying, had been the day he'd accused her of being selfish, of only thinking of herself and what she wanted from their relationship.

'*Selfish? You think I'm selfish because I want to start a family with you?*'

'*It's all you ever talk about! "I want to get pregnant..." "I want a baby..." "I want us to start trying." Do you ever ask me what I want?*'

She'd shaken her head, confused.

'*What do you want, Sam?*'

He'd straightened, his face blanching.

'*I'm not ready to be a father yet.*'

'*Why? Please tell me.*'

'*I can't...*'

His voice had trailed away, and for a moment he'd looked helpless and lost. She'd feared, then, that he was unable to tell her something painful, so she'd broached the subject herself.

'Don't you love me, Sam?'

'Of course I do.'

'Then why don't you want us to have a child together? I don't understand. What's so wrong with starting a family? We help everyone else do it, day after day, why not us?'

He'd not answered her and so, frustrated, she'd stormed away from him, furious that she could never get a straight answer from him, furious with herself for allowing it to mean so much that it was tearing them apart.

She'd told him earlier today that she'd just been upset at him for staying out with those clients. Well, it had certainly been more than that. Sam hadn't come home that night but had worked straight through, and he'd only gone off shift when she'd clocked on in the morning.

It had been so humiliating! All the staff at the Monterey must have noticed. How could they not? They'd raised their voices in the hospital corridor and brought a personal matter into the workplace. Even Emily was appalled at herself for that. What must the patients have thought? A premier birthing centre set in the heart of a marital dispute!

Keen to put good memories back into Sam's head, Emily decided it was time for them to return to the Île de Reuily, otherwise known as the Temple of Love. They'd gone there on their first trip, and Emily was keen for them to go again. There was so much they needed to talk about and sort through, and now that his memories might be coming back she was keen to let him know and understand exactly where she had been coming from.

Before any more came back and completely blindsided him. Damaging them for ever.

They needed to talk about the family issue. About what had been keeping them separate. It had to be confronted—probably here more than anywhere, because they were now in a place where *both of them* were trying to save their marriage.

The distance between them had been scaring her. She'd known their marriage was failing, and yet every time she'd tried to get Sam back he'd just moved farther and farther away. She'd not known who he was any more, and it had made her fear that she'd never really known him at all.

This man had made her world shine brighter once and she wanted that back again. There had to be a way for them to get there.

Sam knew a little of her background, but she'd never gone into detail. Nor had he. Their relationship had blossomed quickly and ferociously. Both of them had been swept away on an intense new love, and if they hadn't been busy planning their wedding they'd been busy planning and running their business.

They needed this trip to get to know one another properly. Away from work. On neutral ground. They needed to understand each other—who they were and what had made them that way. Maybe then, and only then, would they begin to understand where it had all gone wrong.

So when Sam had returned to their room to change his shirt Emily had picked up the full picnic basket she'd asked the hotel to provide. The temple would be the perfect spot for them to talk, to clear the air and to watch the sun set.

'Where are we going?' Sam asked.

'On a magical mystery tour. Trust me.' She smiled,

making her way to the Line Eight Métro to get to their destination.

They people-watched for a while. Paris was filled with so many unique faces, both residents and visitors, but the city had a certain style, a *je ne sais quois* that oozed from every pore, every street, and the mix of cultures and voices helped provide that.

At the Michel Bizot stop they got off and began their walk up a long palm-tree-lined avenue. The weather was beautiful. Perfect for a picnic. Emily was looking forward to sitting down with him, enjoying his company with the good food that the hotel had provided.

They stopped briefly to look and take photos at the Musée National de l'Histoire de l'Immigration. It was a magnificent building that had figures and animals, trees and historic events carved into its exterior, like a stone Bayeux tapestry. Intrigued, they headed inside, and Sam asked if they could leave their picnic basket at Reception whilst they took a look around.

It was the perfect place to revive their sense of wellbeing after the accident they'd witnessed, and as they were looking around Sam received a call from the hospital to inform him that Alain was stable. Happy at the news, Sam draped his arm around Emily's shoulder and they walked around the numerous eclectic displays.

'I could spend all day here,' Emily said, knowing that they wouldn't. Knowing that she needed to talk to him. Confront him about the real issue. But for now she could pretend that all of that wasn't ahead of her. At least she could try to.

'Why don't we? There's a park nearby—we could eat the picnic there afterwards.'

She thought about it, but, no, she wanted them to go

to the temple on the island. 'I really want to show you the lake and island I was telling you about.'

She didn't want him to know why. Yes, it was the most beautiful place she'd ever been, but it was also isolated. The perfect place for them to talk. To share. To make up some of the ground between them, to forge new bonds and strengthen themselves once again. At least that was what she hoped would happen. But it was nerve-racking. What if it all went wrong? What if he refused to talk about his past? His issues?

He nodded, seeming happy to be guided by her. Paris had been her plan, after all, and so far it was working. He'd gained a few memories that he hadn't had before.

After an hour or two spent in the museum, they headed into the park of the Bois de Vincennes.

There was an exquisite flower garden, a kaleidoscope of colour, surrounded by neat swathes of pale green lawn and dark green trees, and with the heat of the summer sun it was the ideal place for them to be after their adventure that morning.

Emily smiled as Sam looked around, bowled over by the beauty of the place. 'I told you it was worth it.'

He turned to face her. '*You're* worth it.'

She smiled back and kissed him, revelling in the taste of his lips, the sun on their faces. In the warmth of not just being with the man she loved, but the joy of knowing that she was getting back the husband she adored. That he was trying as much as she was.

But nerves were bubbling under the surface. It was nearly time. Time to say everything. Explain everything. Dig deep and find out what had truly been keeping them apart.

Where would they both be by the end of this day? A

little closer? Understanding each other? Or would they be even further apart?

'Let's head for the lake. I hope you've got your arms ready to do some rowing?'

He nodded. 'I've carried this basket most of the afternoon. I'm sure my muscles are all warmed up for the oars.'

There was a long row of boats lined up by the lakeside.

'They've all got names on. I wonder if there's a rowing boat called *Emily*?'

'Or *Sam*. Not all boats are named after ladies, you know?'

The white boats were small, edged in red, with the inside of the boat painted in blue. Once they'd paid and Sam had helped Emily get in, making sure she was sitting down properly before he began, he took hold of the oars and gently pushed them out onto the lake.

It was very calm on the water. Poplars and tall grass bordered the lake, whilst weeping willows dipped their weary branches down into the water, creating little concealed areas where couples could take a boat and have a little privacy if they so wished.

But Emily knew exactly where she wanted to go.

There were hardly any other people out on the lake as she pointed across the still green water to the island in the centre. Upon the island stood a beautiful domed temple, supported by tall, slim columns of white stone. It sat on a grassy outcrop, and beneath it could be seen craggy rocks and what looked like, from a distance, numerous caves.

'Is that where we're headed?' asked Sam.

She nodded. 'It is. It's the place you first called me Mrs Saint.'

'Oh, yes? What else did I say to you there?'

She laughed. 'Lots of things! Some of them rather rude…'

'I'm intrigued!'

'Feels odd to think that we're back here and this time I'm carrying our baby.'

He glanced at her briefly, then looked behind him at the temple once more.

Sensing a shift in his mood, Emily tilted her head in question. 'Are you happy, Sam?'

He turned back to her. 'Me? Course I am. How could I not be? I'm here in Paris, with my beautiful wife, on a gorgeous day, and…' His voice trailed away.

'And…?'

'And I couldn't be any happier.'

'Really? You seem a little…sad.'

'Not sad, no. Pensive, maybe.'

'What about?'

He laughed and looked away. 'Oh, lots of little things. Nothing you need to worry about.'

But she did. This need for privacy, this *do not enter* that Sam had about him was what had caused a lot of their problems in the first place. He was *meant* to share his worries with her. *Meant* to share his concerns, his fears. She was his *wife*.

'Is it work?'

Sam shrugged. 'I am keen to get back. To me, even though logically I know the centre's open and I've worked there, I don't remember that. I want to walk the halls. I want to meet patients…'

'Of course. I have to keep reminding myself of that fact. That you don't remember. You don't know. That what's normal to me is still the unknown to you. I mean… I've *seen* you there at the Monterey. I've watched you work.'

For a while there was silence except for the sound of the boat moving through the water, the splash and the creak of the oars in their housing either side of the boat. The water had a pleasant aroma to it—of fresh and vibrant greenery, of summer, of *life*.

Emily laid a hand upon her belly, thinking of her child's future. 'Sometimes I can't quite believe the way things have turned out myself.'

She saw him glance at her belly, and then he turned to negotiate their arrival at the island beneath the temple. He got up and jumped out, using the chain from the boat to moor them to the wooden pier. Then he reached out his hand and helped her off the boat, before going back to retrieve the picnic basket.

They headed up the steps to the temple.

The round temple was beautiful in its simplicity, with a domed roof and gorgeous views out across the lake. The setting sun reflected light off the surface, glinting as if the water was filled with jewels, and they stood appreciating it for just a moment.

Sam gazed down at his wife and noticed that her hand was still laid across her gently swelling abdomen.

He loved her so much. Was he going to ruin everything with his doubts? Would she see him for the fraud that he was? But then maybe—perhaps—he wasn't the only one with doubts? Emily had never been a mother before. Perhaps she was scared, too?

'Does the future worry you, Em?'

She gazed over the beautiful lake. 'A bit. Becoming a parent is new territory for both of us.'

He nodded. 'It is.'

'Even though I wanted this baby, I know you didn't. But it happened anyway. I always thought it would be something we would want together. That we would make it happen together.'

'We did. Despite our arguments, it seems.'

'We were drunk.'

He let out a sigh. 'Lots of babies are conceived from a drunken night.'

'I worry about whether I'll be a good mother. It's not like I was given the best example of how to do it.'

Sam frowned. He couldn't remember much about her family situation. Had she told him before? He couldn't recall.

'Tell me.'

She looked back at Sam. *Yes*. These were the things they needed to talk about. But she couldn't imagine it would be a comfortable conversation, standing here like this. This was going to be a conversation that would take time.

'Let's see if there's a blanket in that picnic basket, because this stone step is uncomfortable.'

They opened it up and, sure enough, attached to the lid of the basket was a folded, padded blanket, which they laid upon the ground. Once they were settled, and Sam had poured each of them some sparkling water, Emily continued with her story.

'You remember I don't really have any close family?'

He nodded. 'Just your aunt and uncle.'

'That's right.'

'Have you told me much about them? In the last two years, I mean?'

'I've told you the bare bones, but never the full story.'

'So tell me now.' He laid his hand on hers.

She appreciated his support and comfort. Appreciated that he was ready to listen. Open to strengthening their bonds. It was why she'd wanted to bring him to this place. What they both needed to do if they were going to move forward together. And if she shared first then maybe Sam would do so afterwards.

'My mother had always been a rebellious woman, from what Aunt Sylvia told me. If there were conventions and rules and expectations to break, then my mother did that. She got pregnant with me, without being married—which, as my aunt was fond of telling me, caused a great scandal, as if it had happened in Victorian times. The fact that my mother never knew who my father was made it worse. Apparently there were many candidates.'

Sam rubbed her hand in sympathy.

'Anyway, my mother looked after me for about six months after I was born. I don't remember her, or that time. I was too young. I do have a photograph of me on her knee. My mother was into music, big-time, and she absolutely adored this one particular band. When they came into town to play she went to see them, was invited to an after-show party and that was that. She fell madly in love and simply *had* to be with this man, *had* to travel with him when they went on tour. Only a baby didn't fit into her plans, so she turned up at my Aunt Sylvia's house one day and asked if she would look after me for the night.'

'For one night?'

Emily nodded. 'Only she lied. She never came back and I got left behind. Forgotten about.'

'I'm sure she didn't forget you.'

'I never heard from her again. I can't have been a concern to her.'

'I'm sorry.'

'Sylvia and Martin were not best pleased—no one would be, to be honest. You agree to babysit, grudgingly, for the child of a sister you never really got on with and she never comes back… They were furious. My aunt and uncle did their best, but they weren't natural parents. I was a demanding baby, just starting to learn to sit up and grab things and squeal. They had nothing for me, apart from what my mother had left, and they suddenly had to find money to buy nappies, extra food, clothing, toys… Uncle Martin didn't have the best of health either. He suffered from a really bad back. And suddenly he had to work all these extra shifts, plus overtime, to help pay for me. I hardly saw him.'

'And your aunt?'

'She'd never wanted children. Not really. She'd grown up with my mother, who had apparently stolen all the attention of their parents. My mother was "the pretty one", the "clever one". Although Sylvia never said as much, I kind of got the feeling that she felt second-best. Never appreciated as much. Never loved as much. And now here she was, having to look after her sister's child.

'They tried to make me happy, but I could feel the resentment from them both. They never said anything outright, but…it wasn't right. So as a child I dreamt of happy, loving families, all sitting around a dinner table, laughing and joking and enjoying being with each other. I pictured what it would be like if we were happy. What our family portraits might look like. But we never did anything like that. There were photos, of course. Plenty of them. Just not the kind I wanted.'

'Your aunt and uncle sound like they struggled a bit.'

'They did their best. But my aunt never really got over her resentment of my mother, who seemed to have freedom and the world at her feet while they took care of her mistake.'

'Is that how you see yourself? As a mistake?'

'How could I not? I wanted to be loved so much. I

wanted them to put their arms around me and give me a proper cuddle. I wanted someone to tell me that they loved me and that I was their whole world.'

'*I* did.'

She smiled, feeling tears at the backs of her eyes. 'Yes, you did. Meeting you was the best thing in my life—after my work. The first time we met at the hospital there was something about you that made me feel as if I couldn't even breathe.'

'How did you become a midwife? What made you go down that path? Was it something Sylvia suggested?'

'No. I saw a documentary on television. Sylvia and Martin were out at a church dinner with friends, and there was a documentary on following the journey of an embryo from single cell to living baby. It was all so fascinating to me, and when they showed the birth... The miracle of the baby being born was one thing, but all I could see was the look in the eyes of the mom and dad. Such joy...such love. Pure elation. I wanted to experience that.'

'So you started training?'

She nodded. 'I worked hard at school and got to college. So I could experience that love again and again and again. I think a small part of me wanted to believe that was how my mother had felt when she had me. It's a privilege to be in the room when a mom gives birth. I didn't realise how special it would make me feel. How honoured. I loved it. I still do. But I've always craved experiencing it myself.'

Sam let out a big sigh. 'You had it tough. With your aunt and uncle, I mean.'

'Some people have it tougher.'

Sam sipped his drink.

'What about you, Sam?'

'What do you mean?'

'Tell me more about your family. I don't really know much about them, apart from their names and what they do for a living. We hardly see them. I think the most I ever saw them was at the wedding, and then they kept themselves to themselves.'

Sam let out a big sigh. 'Where do I start?'

'At the beginning.'

He gazed at her and nodded with some reluctance. 'There really isn't much to tell.'

'I think there is. Please, Sam. I feel apart from you. I feel like I'm stuck on this tiny island and you're far out to sea with a rescue boat but you won't come in to land. We need to talk...we need to share who we are so that we can start afresh. Unburdened. Nothing hidden.' She laid a hand on his. 'I know you have a secret, Sam. I don't know what it is, but I want you to feel you can share it with me. If you don't we'll always be apart. We won't get to fix *this*.' She brushed his wedding ring.

Sam's fingers enveloped hers and his thumb stroked the back of her hand. 'I don't want to lose you, Em.'

'I don't want to lose you either. Whatever it is, you can tell me. I won't judge. I won't say anything. I'll just listen.'

He exhaled. A big, heavy sigh. 'It's hard for me.'

'I know. These things usually are. But I know from experience that they always seem massive until you unburden yourself, and then you feel a little better. A little lighter. You know what they say. A problem shared...'

'Is a problem halved?'

She smiled. 'I love you, Sam. I'm your *wife*. You need to be able to tell me.'

'I've never shared it with anyone. None of us have.'

'None of you? Your family?'

Okay, this is a start.

He nodded.

'Then maybe it's time?'

She hoped he would tell her. Whatever it was, if he and his family had kept this burden under wraps for so long then it was time it was given some air. It was like carrying a weight. No matter how small the weight, the longer you had to carry it the heavier it got—until you collapsed from under it.

'You're sure I've never told you anything?'

'I'm sure. Come on—tell me. I want to know you properly, Sam Saint, and we've only ever skimmed the surface of who you are. I've spilled my family secrets. What are yours?'

She'd told him about everything. Her runaway mother. Feeling like she was a mistake. Being left behind. Abandoned. Emily didn't want their child to feel it was a mistake, too. Conceived on a drunken night, during a truce between its parents, and then abandoned by its father. Not loved enough. Worthless.

She wouldn't accept that. She wasn't just fighting for her marriage here, but for her child. *Their* child.

She saw the agony on his face. The internal wrangling going on inside his head. The anguish. She knew his instincts were to keep it hidden still. It was what he had always done. But her words had clearly had an effect on him and she could tell that he knew what she said was true. If they didn't tell each other everything then their relationship would be doomed to fail. Already so much of who he was, was hidden by the amnesia. He didn't need to hide even more.

'You know I have five siblings and Mom and Dad…?'

She smiled and squeezed his fingers in encourage-

ment, her heart beating faster. *He was going to share.*
'I do...'

'Well, the thing you may not know is that Dad and I don't really get on.'

'Really? You seemed okay at the wedding.'

It was true. Sam and his family had been nothing but delightful to one another. Sam had seemed incredibly warm to his mother and his younger siblings. To his dad he'd been... She saw the flash of memory. Sam standing stiff and formal, shaking his father's hand but keeping his distance. Not really talking, just a slight inclination of his head. An acknowledgement that his father had at least come to their wedding.

'Was there a free bar at the wedding? That would have kept my dad happy.'

Emily frowned. 'But he's not a drunk, is he?'

'He's a...social drinker. He has his friends that he sees every day down at the bar. I hated it that a lot of our money as a family got poured down Dad's throat when there were so many mouths to feed.'

'You're the oldest, right?'

'Yes. There's two years between me and Daniel, then a year later there was Clara then Warren, then Caleb.' He paused, looking out across the water. 'And then there was Serena.'

Emily blinked. *What?* But Sam was one of *five* siblings. Not six.

'Serena?'

Sam shook his head and got up to begin pacing, uncomfortable with this subject but knowing he had to tell her. They were married! And she was right—she had to hear this. Or they'd be torn apart because the guilt he felt over Serena's death was the one thing that was still tearing *him* apart, making him doubt his abilities to be a father.

'The only good thing my dad did was give me brothers and sisters—but all I saw growing up was my mother, heavily pregnant again, struggling to get things done. As the oldest, I had to help, and because Dad was never around, always at the bar, I sort of became a father as well as a big brother to them all.'

'That must have been hard for you.'

'Yeah, well…I don't like to focus on upsetting things.'

'I've noticed. You're a driven man. You've always wanted to be successful. Always busy.'

'It's how I was when I was a teen. There was always something to do—mow the lawn, fix a kitchen cabinet, a leaky faucet. You name it, I worked out how to do it. Because my dad couldn't.'

'Because he wasn't there?'

Sam nodded once. 'My dad was out drinking when my mom gave birth to Warren.'

'Home birth?'

'It was the same for all of us. I can remember being incredibly scared when Warren was born. Mom seemed in a lot of pain, but she was really cool about it in between contractions, you know? Like it was the most normal thing—which it was. But I was only eight. I didn't understand. The midwife asked Mom if she wanted me in the room for the birth and she said it was up to me.'

'And you said yes?'

'No. I was too scared. All the noise Mom was making was…incredible. I'd never heard anything like it. And that was *my mom*, you know? I can remember cowering in my bedroom, listening to her in the next room, wondering why my dad wasn't there to help her. It seemed to go on for hours—it probably actually did—and then there was this second of silence before I heard a new sound. A baby. Crying. And then there was laughter and joy and I could hear my mother crying again, but this time for another reason. I went back in and there she was, propped up in bed, smiling, tears of joy running down her face... It was the most amazing thing I ever saw.'

Emily smiled.

'I remember telling my schoolfriends all about it. They all thought it was weird!' He smiled at the memory. 'And then Mom told us all she was expecting again. I couldn't wait.'

'An OB/GYN in the making?'

He laughed ruefully. 'I guess. I was eleven when Caleb was born, and yet again I got to hear this miracle from the next room. I started telling anyone who would listen that I wanted to be a doctor when I grew up, so that I could deliver babies every day and witness the joy.'

She loved the enthusiasm in his voice at the memory of his happiness. She was elated that he still had all his past memories. They were important. He might have lost all sense of who he was and *that* would have been terrible.

'And Serena?' she asked with concern.

'I was sixteen years old when Serena was born. My mom swore this was her last baby, and once again I got to hear my baby sister come into the world. She was tiny. Only six pounds. But she was beautiful. She didn't cry. She seemed quite content and calm. That was how my mom named her. Because she was so serene. That was all she kept saying. *"She's so serene."* The midwife suggested it as a name.'

'It's beautiful.'

'Things were tough. Six mouths to feed, plus their own—my parents were struggling hard. Mom would clean other people's houses for extra money, taking the little ones with her in a playpen. I already had a paper round and gave my parents most of my wages to help out. But all our money seemed to go over the bar, and I hated my dad for doing that. My mom struggled to put food on the table every day, but she did it. She made sure we were happy. And then one day I thought to myself, *Who's making Mom happy?* Dad wasn't. She wasn't. She didn't have time. So I took on extra rounds. The second I finished school I'd be out on my bike, hauling papers across yards, all around the neighbourhood. I saved the money. Kept it. When Serena was about four months old I suggested to my dad that he ought to take Mom out for a meal. Nothing expensive. Just a burger or something. I felt Mom needed it, you know?'

Emily nodded.

'I said I'd babysit.' Sam gazed out across the water and watched as a swan glided across its surface, followed by another about a metre behind. 'My mom had never left us before. She didn't want to go. I made her do it. Said she deserved a night out.'

'You wanted her to have a break?'

'Yeah. I had some tests to revise for, so I fed the kids, made sure they had their baths, and after Serena had had her bottle of milk I changed her nappy and put her in her room for the night.'

Emily could tell the bad part was coming. Sam looked pained, with lines across his brow, and his narrowed eyes were stuck somewhere in the past. He kept rubbing at his forehead, as if the telling of the story was causing him physical pain.

'I checked on them all after an hour. They were asleep. They'd always been good sleepers. Never played up. They were all good kids.'

'What happened?'

'I thought they were okay. I made popcorn and sat down to watch a movie on the television. Mom and Dad came home and Mom, being anxious, went to check on them all.'

Emily laid a hand upon his arm to still him.

'Mom *screamed*. I can still hear it so clearly up here.' He tapped the side of his skull. 'Blood-curdling, it was. Like someone had wrenched her heart from her chest. Something *had*.'

'Serena.'

'They said it was Sudden Infant Death Syndrome. Nothing anyone could have done. Nothing anyone could have predicted. She just…died. The paramedics tried to revive her when they got to the house. I can remember sitting in the front room, hiding in the corner, hugging my legs and rocking, seeing the red-blue lights flickering through the windows and hearing footsteps above me. And all the time my mother crying. Wailing. Begging for it not to be so…'

'Sam, I'm so sorry.'

She pulled him into her arms and held him as tightly as she could. No wonder he had never told her this story. It was awful! Terrible! She couldn't imagine that happening. Not in her worst nightmares could she conceive how you would get through something like that. She knew that people *did*. They had clients at the Monterey who had lost children before, and she'd always been awed by their bravery and outlook on life.

Was this why Sam had never wanted children? Was this why they'd had so many arguments? He'd never told her before and now she could see why. And yet she'd pushed him, asking him over and over, until in the end she'd just given up and they'd stopped talking.

She felt so bad! Of course she'd wondered *why* he refused to talk to her about this, but now she knew. And she felt terrible for having pushed so hard.

'I should never have forced my parents to go out. I should have paid more attention to Serena. I should have checked on her more often. I failed her. I was meant to be looking after her and she died and—'

'Sam you were sixteen years old! You were still a child yourself. You can't shoulder that burden. They told you it was an accident. Sudden. It wasn't your fault.'

'It feels that way.'

'Is that why you never want to see your family? Why you never want them to visit?'

'I see it in their faces when they look at me. Like an unspoken accusation.'

She shook her head and grabbed his arms, making him look at her. 'They probably just miss you! Their big brother who always looked out for them suddenly doesn't want them around. They're probably hurt. They look up to you, Sam. Even I could see that. It's possible they're just wondering what they did wrong.'

He looked down at his wife's face. 'They did nothing wrong. It was me.'

'It was *not you*. You were babysitting. You did everything right. You bathed her, fed her, changed her nappy, put her to bed. That's what millions of parents do every night. They don't stand over their children's cots and count every breath. It's impossible.'

He still looked shame-faced. Still looked guilty. But he'd made a start in sharing his burden. She was glad that he had told her. And suddenly she realised. Suddenly she remembered.

'The candle was for Serena.'

He met her gaze. 'Yes.'

She let out a long, slow, steadying breath. 'Thank you

for telling me, Sam. Now I understand why you—' She stopped before she could blurt out any more. He didn't need to hear that. They were here to *heal*. Paris was healing their hearts as well as their minds.

'I'm afraid, Em. Afraid that I won't be able to protect *our* baby.' He laid a hand on her belly, gently stroking it, then knelt down in front of her, laying his head against her belly as if trying to hear a heartbeat. 'What if I fail our child?'

Her heart was almost torn in two as she heard the heartbreak in his voice. He'd agonised over this. 'You won't. It's okay to be afraid, Sam. It's okay to have fears. All parents do.'

He lifted his head to look at her. 'Do *you*?' He seemed to doubt her words.

Emily rushed to reassure him. 'Of course I do! What do I know about being a great mother? Did I have a fabulous role model? Did my aunt provide me with a loving example? No. Neither of them did. I worry that I'll get this wrong all the time. What if I'm awful at being a mom? At something that I've wanted for *so long*?'

'You'll be perfect.'

'And so will you. Believe me, Sam, I know you will. You care so much. But you know what? We can be afraid together and struggle together. We're strong that way. We're determined. Driven. Remember?'

Sam stood and looked down into her face. 'What would I do without you, Mrs Saint?'

'Let's hope you never have to find out.' She smiled. 'Look, we're here—in the Temple of Love. Let's make a promise to each other to always be open and share our fears. If there's a problem, we tell each other about it. Deal?'

'Deal.'

Sam pulled her towards him for a kiss. It felt like the start of something new. An opening. An honesty between them that had never been there before. Her lips on his sealed the promise that their hearts were making.

'Thank you for telling me, Sam. It means so much to me.'

'You're right. I do feel different for having said it out loud.'

'The pain won't go. Not totally. But it can be different now—just you see.'

'Thanks, Em.'

He pulled her close once more and they stood there, in the Temple of Love, enveloped in each other's arms, and just held each other.

Em knew they'd taken a huge step forward today. She'd been right to bring him here. To ask him to share this. It shed new light on all Sam's past behaviour. Perhaps she had enlightened him, too, on why having a baby had meant so much to her?

There was still so much for them to do, but right now things were moving in a positive direction.

She could only foresee it getting better.

CHAPTER SEVEN

THEY HAD A beautiful evening picnic. The hotel had packed some delightful food in the basket—a *salade niçoise* with mixed herbs, olives, anchovies and potatoes, a sausage and potato *galette,* a *haricots verts* salad with quail eggs and tiny shrimp, goat's cheese and tomatoes. There was also raspberry *clafoutis,* pound cake and *sables* biscuits, all served with a small bottle of white wine, sparkling and still water, and a tiny bottle of alcohol-free rhubarb wine.

They sat in the temple, overlooking the water, quietly eating their evening meal and enjoying the sounds of nature in the air: the occasional duck quacking, the lapping of the water below, the wind rustling the trees.

Eventually Sam packed everything back into the basket, and on their way down the rocky stairway to the boat they paused a moment to look inside the grotto. The stony caves were a mix of dark and light, jagged rocks and stalactites.

'This place is like us, really,' Sam observed.

Emily turned to him. 'How do you mean?'

'Well, there's the beautiful Temple of Love on show for everyone to see, and it all looks wonderful. But then you dig deeper, you come down here, and there's a dark place—forbidding and scary.'

Emily stepped out of the caves' darkness, through one of the openings, to move out towards the lessening light of the day.

'But, using your analogy, we've come through it together this time and we both know it's there.'

He nodded. 'True.'

Sam still wasn't sure that he should have told Emily everything. The uselessness of his own father... Serena's brief yet painful story. He wasn't used to sharing things like that. He'd never done it and it felt strange. It made him feel naked. Exposed when he'd always had a protective wall around him.

He knew the story was safe with Emily, but did she really grasp how much his past affected him?

He'd not had a great father figure. In his eyes his father had been good for two things—making babies and drinking beer. Sam had been a better father to those kids than his own dad had—but on the other hand he had also let them down. He'd devastated them. It had been *his* plan to send his parents out for the night. *His* plan to make his mother go out. When he'd checked on Serena that time and assumed she was sleeping because she was so still, so quiet, had she really been sleeping? Or had she already passed away?

It haunted him—the idea that he might have looked down upon his baby sister with love, not realising that she lay there dead.

I should have known.

The guilt still tore him apart, and the pain was still incredibly strong. And he still felt to blame. But Emily had welcomed the load. Had asked to take it on, no matter what it was. Had said that, as his wife, she was there to help him carry it. Make it easier.

But he doubted it would ever be that. Easier.

The plain fact of the matter now was, though, that Emily knew. Perhaps from here they could have a conversation about his fears about becoming a parent. About caring for this baby to come. His son or daughter.

They would need a strong marriage. Raising a child was not easy. He knew how difficult it could be. Okay, so he and Emily did not have the financial worries his own parents had had, but it was still hard. And they would need to be united. He knew from the flashes of memory he'd had, and the admissions Em had made, that their marriage had deteriorated—and quickly.

That concerned him greatly.

He loved this woman so much, and yet they had both allowed it to crumble so quickly because neither of them had been able to talk the way they had today.

Perhaps it took nearly losing your life, being in a terrible accident, having amnesia, to turn it around? To admit the problems and vow to work through them?

He reached out to place his hand in the small of her back and guided her safely down the steps towards the boat. She turned to look at him, flashed him a smile, and—

They were walking down the aisle. Newly married. Sun gleamed through the church windows and everyone was smiling. He looked up and saw his mother's face. She was crying with happiness, her hands clutched together before her chest as if in prayer, and she was mouthing something to him. He couldn't catch her words, and then as he passed her she reached out and took his hand.

'Live, Sam. Be happy now.'

He'd smiled back. Nodded. Promised that he would. And then he'd turned back to his wife and she'd looked at him and smiled and...

He helped Emily into the boat. Made sure she was

seated safely before he put the picnic basket inside and unchained the boat from the pier. With one of the wooden oars he pushed them away from the small island, and they drifted out across the water and he began to row.

His mother had wanted him to be happy. *Be happy now.* Had his own mother seen how unhappy he'd been at home after Serena died? He'd tried to make up for it. He'd tried his best to prove that he was still a good son afterwards. But nothing had made his mother smile after that.

But she smiled at the wedding. She was happy for me. She didn't resent my happiness.

Perhaps he ought to take the time actually to try and enjoy life. Was this why he was so driven? Filling his days with work and other distractions just so that he wasn't thinking about Serena? Was that why his marriage had begun to fail? Instead of looking at the faults they had created, the problems they shared, he'd done what he'd always done—pushed it to one side and filled up his time with work.

He'd thought that by ignoring the issues they would go away.

The revelation was startling.

He stopped rowing and the boat drifted quietly across the water.

Night had settled across Paris when they returned to their hotel. Emily donned the beautiful new powder-blue dress that Sam had secretly bought for her and stood in front of the mirror admiring it.

Sam came up behind her and slid his hands over her burgeoning abdomen. It was still only a slight swelling, but she smiled, looking at the reflection of his face in the mirror.

He looked content. And that was something she hadn't seen for such a long time.

'The dress is beautiful, Sam. Thank you.'

'You're more beautiful.'

Her cheeks bloomed in the mirror and she laid her hands upon his, their fingers entwining. She looked up at him, hesitant.

Was it too soon? Was it just right? If she pushed for them to make love now would it be wrong? Or just perfect?

She felt so much closer to Sam now. Before she'd described him as being on a rescue boat far out to sea, miles away from her, but since his confession—since he'd told her about his family and about Serena especially—she'd felt as if he was within arms' reach.

Should she test it and see?

She missed him. She missed the intimacy that they'd once shared. Surely now there was nothing that could keep them apart? Being together physically, emotionally, mentally, surely would just strengthen the bond that they were both trying to enforce?

She met his gaze in the reflection. 'Undo the zip.'

He looked into her eyes. 'You've just put it on.'

'Yes. And now I want you to take it off me.'

He looked hesitant. And for a brief moment she thought she'd pushed him too soon. Had asked, once again, for too much. But then—wonderfully—she watched in the mirror as his hands slid from hers, went to the zip at the nape of her neck and slowly, delicately, drew it down.

She could feel his heated breath on the back of her neck, and she closed her eyes as she felt him slip the dress from her shoulders, his hands following close after, trailing over her shoulders, arms, her hips.

The beautiful dress dropped to the floor and Emily turned to face him.

'I love you, Sam, and I want you to love me.'

'I do.' His voice was deep, emotional.

'Show me.'

Sam stared deeply into her eyes for a brief, yet agonising moment, before he finally took her in his arms and kissed her.

Emily sank into his embrace.

This was what she had craved! It had never been about the great sex, the making love. It had been about the deep intimacy they had shared when they had been together physically. The closeness, the connection. The unity.

Before, when they had been together, it had been great. Sam was a brilliant lover. But because she had never truly known her husband, never known all his secrets, there had never been that level of *trust* and *vulnerability* between them. Emily had always felt somehow, that she was being kept in the dark, and it had made her wonder if he had truly loved her.

But now she felt she *knew* him. Knew his fears. His pain. His hurt. She knew his vulnerabilities, as he did hers, and now they were equal.

She closed her eyes and gave herself up to Sam. *This* was what they needed to do. Be close like this. Intimate. They were working towards a greater good within their marriage and this was what both of them needed right now. To solidify that bond…to unite them in their vows.

As his hands and lips moved deftly over her body Emily found herself losing her train of thought. His lips upon her collarbone, her neck, were delightful. His hands had easily unclipped her bra and were now beautifully paying attention to her sensitive breasts, making her gasp and close her eyes…

Her hands were on his body...*too many clothes*...

He helped her remove them and once again she marvelled at his powerful, muscular body. The broad expanse of him, the wide shoulders, the narrow waist, the long, lean legs, his erection pressing against her stomach...

Sam scooped her up and placed her on the bed with a gentleness that belied his size. His thumbs hooked into her underwear and she lifted her bottom so that he could remove it, and then he covered her with his body as his lips began to explore even more.

Right now she just wanted to enjoy. Sam's lips. Sam's tongue. Sam's body. Moving over...*into* her.

Emily gasped, arching her body up against him as he drove in deep.

Afterwards, sated, they lay together in bed, Sam behind his wife.

It had felt good to be with her. It had felt *right*. This was where he was supposed to be. This was who he was supposed to be with. He knew it in his bones and he was feeling much better now about having shared.

It had brought them closer. Which was odd. That something so painful, so hurtful, had been the gateway for the two of them to connect.

Life was strange that way.

All this time he had kept it from her and in turn it had kept them apart. Obviously the old Sam hadn't been able to see that. Or maybe he had, but hadn't known what to do about it. How must it have felt to have seen his marriage crumbling?

He shuddered inside, glad his memories about that had not come back fully. He wasn't sure he wanted them—not now. Not now that things had changed. Now they were ready to face their future together. As one.

There was still fear about his ability as a father, but it seemed…less. How was that? All he'd done was voice it. Something he'd always believed would be the worst thing ever. He had feared that Emily would be appalled. How had he allowed himself to believe that?

But he guessed he had learned it from his parents. No one at home spoke about Serena ever. Mom was permanently depressed. Dad stayed away.

I stayed away! Was I being like my own father? A man I'd always hated for staying away and not being there?

Sam closed his eyes at the thought and pressed his lips to Emily's shoulder.

'You know, Sam, I've been thinking, and there are things that we can do.'

He frowned. 'What about?'

'When the baby arrives. Keeping it safe.'

She was so sweet. Thinking of his concerns. Knowing what he must be feeling.

'Oh?'

'We could get a monitor. Not just one of those walkie-talkie-type things, but one of those oxygen monitors—like a SATs device. We'd be able to keep an eye on it as the baby sleeps. We'd make sure it's in the *feet to foot* position in the cot, make sure no blankets cover it's head by getting a sleepsuit instead—things like that.'

He pressed the length of his body against hers. 'Thank you.'

'What for?'

'For trying to ease my worries.'

She half turned and reached for him. 'How could I not? You've already been through too much loss.'

'My whole family has.'

'I think you and your family ought to talk to someone. A counsellor, perhaps. Do you think they'd be open to that?'

'I don't know. All they've ever done is block it out.'

'And look what that did. I nearly lost you, Sam—we let it come between us. It was my fault, too. I kept pushing when I should have stopped to ask myself why.'

'You couldn't have known.'

'I could have if we'd been closer. If instead of just accepting what life had dealt us we'd fought against it. We both brought bad habits into our marriage and let them rule us, never pausing for a moment to think if it was right.'

'We worked it out in the end.'

'Yes, we did.' She smiled.

'Paris did the trick.'

'It always does.'

And as he moved to kiss her, and to make love to her once again, Emily pushed the thought of telling Sam the whole truth away.

Paris *had* helped—but not in the way they'd ever thought or hoped. They had found each other in another way, and it was better than anything she'd ever hoped for.

There was still time for Sam's memories to come back, too, and if they did she felt sure they'd be okay.

They were strong again.

They were close.

They were united.

CHAPTER EIGHT

THEY COULD NOT come to Paris without exploring the Eiffel Tower. They had deliberately left it till last, despite the way it overlooked them, like a guardian, whilst they slept in their hotel room.

'So, we have a choice. Do we want to climb the steps or use the lifts to reach each level?'

Em laughed. 'Considering my condition, I'm not sure I want to climb three hundred steps.'

'The lift it is.'

They stood at the base, craning their necks backwards to look up to the top.

It was an incredibly powerful sight. Only when you were close could you really understand its size and the work that had gone into its construction.

Emily took some photographs of them both, determined to get some pictures of them together into her phone. And then they were in the lift, travelling up with about eight others.

Opposite them was a woman, heavily pregnant, with her sprawling abdomen spilling over the top of her trousers. Emily smiled at her, imagining herself at that size in a few months. It wouldn't take long. And she couldn't wait to feel the baby kick and move around.

The woman was rubbing her hand over her abdomen.

'How many weeks are you?' asked Emily, hoping the woman spoke English.

She did. 'Thirty-five. This is our last trip before our world descends into chaos!' The woman laughed good-naturedly.

'You're British?'

'Yes. We came through the Channel Tunnel. I'm not allowed to fly now. You're American?'

Emily nodded. 'Second honeymoon.'

'Oh. Congratulations.'

'To you, too.'

The lift slowed to a stop and the doors opened. They got out on the first level of the tower.

Paris lay spread out beneath them and it looked so different. The rooftops, the buildings old and new, all basking in the afternoon sunshine.

'Look at that, Sam!'

'I see it.'

They both breathed in the view. There was something very calm and relaxing about looking at the city from here. Traffic bustled below, but up here there was a sense of peace. Of reflection.

Emily glanced around her and saw the woman from the lift. She was rubbing at the small of her back and looked uncomfortable. She nodded to Sam. 'Think she's okay?'

'I'm sure it's just backache. You'll get that big one day, and know exactly how she feels.'

Emily smiled. 'Remind me to enjoy it. I imagine I'll be quite nervous by the time I'm at thirty-five weeks.'

He draped his arm around her shoulders. 'I promise you I'll rub your feet.'

'Will you shave my legs for me?'

Sam smiled. 'I'll even paint your toenails.'

'Ooh. Can't wait, then!'

They took in the story window, showing the construction of the Eiffel Tower, and read about how the old hydraulic lifts had worked.

'Architects are amazing, when you think about it.'

'*You're* an architect, don't forget. You're building our baby. Think of all the work that goes into *that*!'

'Hmm, no wonder I get tired.' She ran her hand over her stomach. 'Should we go up to the second floor?'

Sam nodded, and back into the lift they got.

On the second floor they viewed the panoramic maps and a small red scale model of the original top of the Eiffel Tower from 1889. There was even a champagne bar.

'Hmm, not for me, though…' Emily mused.

'No. Got to look after the little one.'

She smiled at him and reached out to hold his hand. This was nice. Being able to talk about the baby easily to each other. Before it had always seemed a taboo subject. One that she shouldn't raise, knowing Sam's objections. But it was different now. And she could see them getting close to that ideal family picture she had of an excited couple preparing to welcome their new baby into the world. It was thrilling.

They got into the glass lift and ascended to the top. It was spectacular up there, but the wind riffled through her hair so much Emily had to keep tucking it behind her ears.

They were able to view Gustav Eiffel's office, which had been restored to its original layout, with wax models of the man himself and Thomas Edison, but they quickly headed back out to admire Paris.

It needed admiring. It was a truly magical place, and it had worked its magic on their relationship.

Emily felt grateful to it—so much so that her eyes

began to water and she thought she might cry. Surreptitiously she wiped her eyes and hoped Sam hadn't noticed.

Once they'd had a good look, and taken some more photographs, they decided to head back down to ground level. It felt a little sad to come back down to earth.

Emily had learnt so much this trip. Not just about Sam, but also about herself, and she'd set herself some new vows—never to let anyone push her away. And if they did to find out why. To see if there was something she could do to put things right.

People, relationships—they were important. Vital. What were any of them without those they loved? Alone. Lonely. Sad. That wasn't a life for anyone, and life was much too short to lose most of it in secrets or regret.

Sam had booked them into a restaurant for their evening meal.

It was a beautiful place. A large *conservatoire*, painted white and lit with lanterns. The wrought-iron furniture was softened by beautifully furnished cushions in bright colours, all complementing each other. Each table was adorned with a glass fishbowl, half filled with water, and in the water floated gerberas and daisies.

Emily took a seat and smiled at Sam. This was their last night in Paris. Soon they would be returning home. Back to reality. To work. The Monterey. Part of her didn't want to go back. She liked it here. She and Sam were in this nice little bubble and everything was right in their world. What if going back home changed everything?

As she pondered this she noticed the heavily pregnant woman from the Eiffel Tower entering the restaurant with her husband. They sat down at a table on the far left. Emily nodded and smiled when the woman looked up.

'I guess we've both got to return to reality when we go back,' she said.

Sam turned to see who she was looking at and nodded hello to the couple, too. 'We'll be okay.'

'I want us to be more than okay, Sam.'

'We will be.' He reached for her hand and squeezed it.

The waiter arrived and presented them with menus, and filled their glasses with water before disappearing.

Emily hid behind her menu for a moment, and then she looked over the top. 'What if we're not?' Her voice trembled on the last word and suddenly she was fighting back tears.

Claiming Sam had meant so much to her! It was her entire life. She loved him, worked with him, was married to him, was carrying his child. What if it all went wrong? She needed him to reassure her.

'Emily...' He put down his menu and leaned forward. 'I know it's scary, but we'll be all right. It's different this time. We won't return home the same people. We can't. We know the dangers now, and what to look out for. We're both fighting for this and I'm not going to let us lose what we have.'

'The Monterey takes up so much of your time, though, Sam. I'm worried it will suck you back in. You haven't seen it in operation yet—what if you're so eager to re-acquaint yourself with everything that's going on that I lose you to it? It was our dream to start it, but now—'

'But now it's already up and running. It's successful. And as the boss and CEO I can delegate, right?'

She nodded.

'Time for us, as a couple, will take priority.'

'Okay.' Slightly reassured, she looked back down at the menu.

Everything sounded delicious, and she felt hungry

enough to want to try it all. In the end she chose a French onion soup to start, a fennel and lavender lamb *noisette* for main and a *croquembouche* for dessert.

Sam ordered the same, not wanting to try the seafood, thinking it might make her feel ill.

Above them twinkling stars could be seen through the glass, and the French doors of the *conservatoire* opened up to a beautiful rose garden with a small fountain at its centre.

'It's beautiful here. I really don't think I'm ever going to forget Paris.'

'Nor me.' Sam smiled. 'Not this time.'

'Have you had any more flashbacks? Anything?'

'Not for a while.'

'It doesn't mean they've stopped.'

'I know. I'm not worried. They'll come back.' He took a sip of his water. 'You know what was great, though?'

'What?'

'For the first time today I actually pictured myself becoming a father. Wanting to be one. Holding our child in my arms. Looking down into its face.' He seemed wistful. 'I remember holding each of my siblings just after they were born, and how that felt, but to hold your *own child* must feel...incredible!'

'Oh, Sam, I'm so pleased.' She smiled back, knowing how much he'd feared becoming a father. To be thinking about it, imagining it in positive terms, was a huge leap forward for him. 'Is it scary still?'

'A bit. I was always so busy pushing the idea away, telling myself I could never be a father, that it never occurred to me to think about how much I might actually want to be one.'

'You do?'

'I do!' He laughed, incredulous. 'I'm sure you can imagine how surprised I am.'

Emily laughed with him, then sat back as their onion soup arrived, topped with herby croutons and a swirl of cream. The aroma of the onion and the richness of the soup tantalised her senses and she salivated in anticipation. 'Oh, that smells delicious!'

It was. The soup was perfect—not too thin, not too thick, rich with onion and vegetable stock. And the croutons were bite-sized crispy delights.

'It's strange. We came here to Paris to try and get my memories back, but instead I got a completely different gift.'

She smiled, pleased for him—for *them*. The last year of their marriage had been difficult, and she'd lost count of the amount of times she'd wanted Sam to want a child as much as she had. But now, since their talk on the island, they'd become closer, united, and Sam finally felt able to acknowledge that, despite his fears, he did actually want to become a father. It was more than music to her ears—it was a whole orchestra!

Everything was working out for them. And he was right. Paris had surprised them in such different ways from the ones they had expected.

Their lamb dish arrived, steaming and succulent, and the meat just melted in their mouths.

'You're going to make a great father, Sam.'

He smiled back at her with thanks. 'I hope so.'

'I know so. You care so much about getting it right. About being there for your child. How could you be anything else?'

'Well, I appreciate your vote of confidence. You're going to make the most amazing mom, too.'

She hoped so. Becoming pregnant had made her think

of so many things. Her own childhood, her marriage, what she wanted for her child... Above all she wanted her child to know without a shadow of a doubt that it was loved by both parents and that it would grow up in a stable family. Her feelings for her baby were already incredibly strong, and she couldn't imagine giving birth to a child and abandoning it six months later. Had her mother ever truly wanted her? Had there ever been that mother-baby bond?

It would be *so* different for their child. She would never make her mother's mistakes.

They were just about to start their *croquembouche*— Emily ready to tuck in with gusto, imagining those cream-filled choux pastry puffs—when there was a loud gasp from the other side of the *conservatoire* and a clanging sound as cutlery hit the floor.

The heavily pregnant woman from the Eiffel Tower had stood up, and was looking down at herself and breathing heavily. 'I think my waters just broke!'

At first Emily felt a surge of excitement for the woman. It might be a bit early, but she was about to meet her child and experience that rush of joy. But then concern filled her as the woman looked at her partner across the table and yelled, *'Something's wrong! I can feel it!'*

Waiters hurried to assist as the other diners all turned to see what was going on. The woman was gasping heavily and trying to feel through her dress.

'Oh, my God, there's something there!'

They could hear the panic in her voice—and rightly so.

Sam and Emily got up from their table and rushed over.

Sam stooped low to make eye contact. 'Remember us? From the tower? My name's Sam and I'm an OB/GYN. Do you want me to take a look?'

The woman looked terrified, and glanced to Emily for reassurance. 'And I'm a midwife. Let us help you.'

But they were in a busy restaurant, and it was almost full. There was no place for a private examination.

Emily looked at a waiter. 'Can you get some tablecloths so we can make a privacy screen?'

The waiter nodded and came back with an armful of cloths and some other members of staff. They all surrounded the frantic woman and raised the tablecloths so that she could be examined without the whole world seeing her so vulnerable.

Sam helped her lower herself to the floor and bundled up a jacket from the back of a chair to go under her head. 'I need to examine you. I won't touch, but I do need to look. Or would you prefer my wife to do it?'

The woman indicated she would prefer Emily, so they swapped places and Emily lifted the woman's skirt and adjusted her underwear. There was clearly something there that shouldn't be.

Emily turned to Sam. 'She has a prolapsed cord.'

A prolapsed cord was an emergency. The cord was what kept the baby alive, providing it with blood, nutrients and survival. If the baby's head or body compressed the prolapsed cord it might cut off all of that and the result would be foetal hypoxia, brain damage or even death.

If they'd been in a hospital they would have been able to deal with this immediately. They'd have had the equipment. They'd at least have had *gloves*. But here in the *conservatoire* they had nothing.

Sam immediately told the staff to call for an ambulance, and to bring them some hot water to clean their hands.

'What's your name?' he asked the panicking mother.

'C-C-Clare.'

'Okay, Clare, your baby's umbilical cord has prolapsed and we need to prevent compression. I want you to get onto your hands and knees and keep your butt in the air. You need to rest your chest and head against the floor. That's it. Now, my wife will have to press down against the baby, where we can see it. It's very important that she does this in order to ensure the baby is getting what it needs from the umbilical cord. Do you understand?'

Clare was crying. From fear, from embarrassment—he could only guess. But she had to do it if she wanted her baby to survive.

Sam looked at Em. 'Is the cord still pulsing?'

She nodded. It was, which was a good sign. It meant blood and nutrients were still getting to the baby. Now they just needed to keep it that way.

Normally this would never be done without gloves. With the amniotic fluid dispersed, the baby would be open to infection. But they didn't have gloves, so the hot water they'd been brought would have to do.

She found the presenting part of the baby's head pressing low. She provided pressure and felt the pulse in the cord strengthen. *Good.*

'Okay, it's working.'

Sam nodded. 'You're doing brilliantly, Clare. I know this isn't how you imagined it, but an ambulance is on its way, and before you know it you'll have this baby in your arms. Just keep thinking about that, okay? That's the important part.'

Clare nodded furiously.

They kept talking to her, trying to keep Clare's mind off what was happening to her. They even managed to make her laugh at one point. Just a small laugh. Nervous and timid. But she was looking braver.

Emily kept her eyes on Sam. He was being brilliant,

lying down low on the ground, face to face with Clare, keeping her calm, keeping her positive, telling her about all the babies he'd delivered and how he'd met his wife through one such delivery. How pregnancy and birth brought different surprises, and how at the end all that mattered was a safe and healthy baby.

By the time the paramedics arrived Clare was clutching Sam's hand and staring deeply into his eyes as if he was her own personal birthing coach. Clare's husband held his wife's other hand and she was very carefully manoeuvred into the ambulance.

'There is no room for all,' the paramedic said.

'They're all coming!' insisted Clare.

But with Emily still applying pressure, and Clare still clutching Sam's hand, her husband shouted that he'd take his car. His wife's safety was clearly a priority right now.

The journey to the hospital took minutes, and Clare was rushed into the *maternité* suite, given high-flow oxygen, as she had been in the ambulance, and rushed into Theatre for an emergency Caesarean section. Her husband had not yet arrived—obviously unable to keep up with the speeding ambulance in a city he did not know.

'I want George here!' Clare insisted.

Sam shook his head. 'There's no time, Clare. I'm sorry. They've got to operate.'

Emily tried to reassure her patient as they were whisked into Theatre, with Sam left behind to wait for Clare's husband.

Once they were in the operating theatre events moved at a frightening speed for the woman on the table.

Emily did her best, trying to reassure Clare, and within seconds her baby was being lifted out of Clare's womb. Instantly it began to cry.

Emily, who had been gowned by a theatre assistant,

had stepped back once the baby had been safely delivered, and she stood by the far wall as the baby was presented to the new mother. A little girl. As Clare took her new daughter in her arms the doors burst open and a frantic pair of eyes looked out over a mask, widening when they saw his wife and new baby.

Emily quietly slipped away from Theatre and found her husband. She reached for Sam's hand and they stood quietly, pondering the events of the last hour or so.

It didn't take long for their patient to come out of Theatre, and soon enough Clare and her husband George were in a postnatal room, enjoying their new daughter.

Emily and Sam wrote notes on what had happened in the restaurant to present to the hospital staff, and were about to leave when a nurse came to find them.

'Clare would like to see you.'

'Really?' Emily was delighted. She hadn't known whether they ought to say goodbye—whether they ought to intrude on Clare and George's first private moments with their baby. At the Monterey they liked to leave a family to get to know one another as quickly as possible when it was safe to do so. Those first moments together, alone as mum and dad and baby, were precious.

They knocked and went in.

Clare was sat up in bed, looking proud and happy with her baby in her arms, and beside her, his arm around his wife's shoulders, was George.

When Sam and Emily entered the room George stood up and came over to shake Sam's hand and give Emily a hug.

'Thank you so much! For all that you did.'

'It was our pleasure.'

'We were *so* lucky that you were there! If you hadn't been…' George shook his head as he tried to imagine such a terrible thing. 'We don't know what would have happened.'

'But we were and it all worked out—that's what's important. How are you feeling, Clare?'

Clare looked happy and content. Her face was a little pale, but there were two rosy spots on her cheeks from beaming at her new baby daughter. 'Fine. I'm absolutely fine!'

Emily and Sam looked down at the baby. Like all newborns she was squinting against the light in the room, snuffling, and trying to gnaw on one of her curled up hands.

'She looks hungry,' said Emily. 'And a good size for thirty-five weeks.'

'Six pounds one, they said.'

'Wow. She'd have been huge if she'd gone to term.'

They laughed.

'What are you going to call her?'

Clare looked at George and he nodded. 'We did think about calling her Emma, but we'd really like to call her Emily—if you wouldn't mind?'

Em gasped, clutching her hands together. 'Really?'

Clare nodded. 'Do you want to hold her?'

Emily took the baby carefully from her mother's arms and quickly glanced at Sam, who was smiling at her.

She'd delivered and held many babies, but this one seemed special. Perhaps because it had been such an emergency, happening away from a hospital, and they'd had to improvise with the hot water and the tablecloths and the *terror* that it could go so wrong, so quickly. She and Sam had met over a delivery and now, renewed, they had delivered another.

If that cord had become occluded, what would they have done? Performed a C-section in a restaurant without proper equipment? It would have been almost impossible, and Clare would have lost her baby.

They'd been lucky. All of them.

'She's beautiful, Clare.'

Emily passed the baby into Sam's arms. She felt her heart well up to see him standing there, holding the little girl. One day it would be their child. One day he'd be looking down at his own baby. Tears pricked her eyes and she sniffed and wiped them away as he handed the baby back to her mother.

'We'll leave you now. You need time alone.'

'Will you keep in touch? We'd love to send you a photo of baby Emily when she's older.'

They nodded, and wrote down their contact details.

It was hard to step away. But it was the right thing to do. They had merely assisted this baby to come into the world safely. It was like being back at work in a way. They'd done their part and now it was time to let the parents do theirs.

Sam sighed. 'I miss that rush.'

Emily looked at him and gave him a playful nudge. 'Well, technically you're still signed off from work for a while. You can't go back yet.'

'I know, and I'll stick to it. But it has made me wonder what I'll do when we get back. Presumably you'll be back at work?'

She sighed. 'Yes, I will. Don't forget you still don't have all your memories. You need to heal. Just because you don't have massive scars, or a plaster cast, or staples or stitches, it doesn't mean you're better. Your brain took a battering.'

'I know. But I *feel* good. Perhaps I could look to see which spare room we can make into a nursery? Start making plans?'

She turned to him, a smile on her face. 'Really?'

He nodded. 'Really. It'll be fun, I think.'

Emily laughed and reached for his hand once again. 'You make me so happy, Sam.'

'Good. Can I make you happy one more time in our hotel room? Before we have to start packing for our trip home?'

She looked at him, smiled wickedly and nodded.

They spent a rather pleasant few hours in each other's arms, leaving it until the last possible moment before they had to pack and get to the airport for their flight home.

It felt odd to Emily to be walking back through Charles de Gaulle airport. The last time she'd strode through here, through its concourses, she'd been nervous and excited. Wondering whether Paris would recover Sam's memories or not…whether it would make them or break them… whether they would rekindle their relationship and make it strong again.

Paris had exceeded her expectations. No. That wasn't right. *Sam* had exceeded her expectations. Paris had simply been a place. A setting. It was she and Sam who had done all the work. Both of them initially hiding from their feelings, being the people they had always been, but then slowly, after all their time spent together, they'd revealed their true selves.

They had eaten and danced and rowed a boat. They had biked through the artists' quarter and looked out from the Eiffel Tower. They had re-explored the city as much as they had re-explored themselves, finding places to go they had never been before and finding delight and joy and even peace in quiet, dark places.

They were returning to Beverly Hills with a united

front. With their marriage a hundred times stronger than it had ever been.

Her dream had come true.

And it didn't matter now if Sam's memories came back. He'd known they'd been arguing, he'd known it had been bad, and they'd both worked out *why*. Now they had a solution and they were strong again. Sam might feel a little sad if the memories came back. Being confronted with some of the things he'd said. Some of the things *she* had said, all in the heat of the moment. But they would get over them. They would be able to reassure each other that it was all in the past.

She knew him now. All of him. Secrets and all. And she loved him more than she ever had. She was so glad, deep in her heart, that she had stayed to fight for him. Stayed to give them both the chance they deserved.

Had she ever thought she'd be discussing how to decorate a nursery with him? Whether they should have an animal or a space theme? Whether to go for soft neutrals or rich primary colours? Had she ever thought that they would discuss names? Or what type of birth she wanted?

She was so looking forward to seeing Sam become a father. Watching him learn and grow, falling in love with their child and having that happy family that she had always dreamed of.

He'd admitted that he was still scared, but who wouldn't be? She'd be worried if he wasn't. *Everyone* was worried when they had a child. Worried that they'd not be able to look after it properly. Worried that they'd mess up. Worried that it might hurt itself one day.

But that was life. No one could be wrapped in a bubble, no matter how much you might want to protect someone.

They would do their best as parents. That was all they *could* do.

As they sat on the plane, and she read the book she'd brought along in her hand luggage, she laid her hand on her abdomen. Soon she would feel her baby move. Soon she would feel kicks and flips and all those little movements mothers-to-be talked about. She would walk the halls of the Monterey pregnant. She would deliver mothers whilst heavily pregnant herself, and they would ask her if she was frightened or scared?

And she knew that she would smile and rub her belly and feel that everything was right in her world.

Sam glanced at his wife, reading her book on the plane and absently rubbing her belly, and wondered if she was as scared of returning home as he was?

They'd got everything so *right* in Paris, and though he was keen to get back to work and restart their life together on a much better footing he still felt nervous.

He'd told Emily the truth when he'd admitted that he actually quite wanted to be a father. He'd come from a big family. He couldn't imagine it ever being just him and Em, even if he had rebelled at the idea of her getting pregnant. He'd loved having lots of siblings. Someone to play with outside, riding bikes and flying kites and making dens. And then, when it rained, playing indoors—hide and seek, cards, board games. Before Serena he remembered laughter. The way his younger siblings would look up to him for guidance.

He'd *loved* that.

To have his *own child* or even *children* do that would be the most marvellous thing he could think of.

But what if he became like his father again? It had been a revelation to him that he'd been doing the same thing. Staying away from home. Ignoring his wife. Okay, he'd not been out drinking their money away, but he'd been pretty much useless to her from all accounts.

Em must have felt so incredibly alone!

He was incredibly grateful to her, though. Because she had fought for him. Fought for their marriage. Fought for his memories. And she'd not mollycoddled him and lied about how they'd been. She'd told him the truth. Admitted they'd had problems. She'd even been scared to tell him she was pregnant!

That seemed such a long time ago. Stuck in hospital like that. Finding that out. He'd been so frightened.

He still was, really. What had happened to Serena would always haunt him, every single day, only now the pain wasn't as unbearable as it had used to be. He would worry about his own child every night. He knew he would. Perhaps he would have his fair share of sleepless nights. But he knew that every day he woke and found his child smiling up at him from its cot or bed he would feel joy and contentment on a scale he could never have imagined.

Work he would have to delegate, as he'd promised. Yes, he had a business to run. But what was more important? Work? Or his family?

He'd always put family first when he was little. He'd had to. Working to bring in money had taken up so much of his time it was probably why he'd found it so easy to let the Monterey consume him when he'd started having problems with Emily.

But he wouldn't let it do that any more. He wanted to be more hands-on with the births, not sitting in an office staring at a spreadsheet. That wasn't what he'd started the business for.

Sam laid his hand upon his wife's and leaned over to kiss her.

When they got back to America he would do everything in his power to make sure they had the life that both of them had dreamed of.

CHAPTER NINE

THEY ARRIVED HOME in good time, and the staff met them on the doorstep with huge smiles and welcomes before they hurried to the trunk of their vehicle to remove the suitcases.

Emily stepped through the door of her house and looked at it for the first time as a place she could call *home*. She'd always called it *the house*—never home. But perhaps now it could be? No longer would it be the shell that contained their failing marriage. Now it would be the *home* where she and Sam would be happy. Where they would raise their children and where they would grow old together.

Suddenly the white walls and prestigious art on the walls no longer seemed cold or ostentatious. The place looked inviting, filled with possibilities and hope.

She opened up the French doors out onto the beautiful garden and imagined children chasing each other on the manicured lawns. She could imagine a child marvelling as a butterfly perched on a bloom, or squealing loudly as it ran from a bee. They could have a swing set, a slide, a treehouse put in! They could even get a dog. As a child she'd always wanted one, but Sylvia and Martin had had cats. It was the idea of a dog that warmed her heart. Something large and fluffy with a big pink tongue, that was gentle and kind and would bounce around after her children.

'Doesn't it feel crazy to be back?' she said to Sam, who'd followed her out into the garden.

'A little.'

'We're the ones who have changed and yet it's this place that feels different.'

He looked out across the expanse of grass—at the herb garden, the large Pampas grass, the ornamental bridge. 'Or maybe just our feelings about being in it.'

She looked at him, squinting in the sun. 'What are you going to do now?'

'I'm going to get changed out of these clothes and maybe take a shower. Fancy joining me?'

She laughed and nodded. 'I'll be up in a minute. You get the water running, I just want to have a quick word with Rosie about dinner tonight.'

She wanted to continue their mood from Paris. She wanted to create a beautiful meal for them, to cook him some of his favourites, and she wanted to let the staff know they could have an evening off. Then they would be on their own, and she would arrange a nice romantic table for two, with flowers and candlelight and nice music in the background. There was no need for the romance to disappear just because they'd made it back to reality. She knew, more than anyone, the importance of making time for each other.

She watched Sam head back into the house and then went over to look at the flower garden. There were some pretty blooms there—roses, lilies, aliums. They would be perfect in a little arrangement for the table. She headed back inside to put her plan into action.

* * *

Sam trotted upstairs, keen to rid himself of his travel-worn clothes. Nearly twelve hours on a plane, and he'd spilt coffee on his trouser leg. And then, later, as he'd headed to use the bathroom, he'd had a young girl with a sticky lollipop walk into him.

He didn't mind. Accidents happened, and kids always got food on everything. Looking around at their pristine white walls, he smiled as he imagined the housekeepers shooing the children out into the garden so that they didn't get dirty handprints all over the paint.

They'd not had pristine white walls when he was a child. Their rooms had had cheap wood panelling, tough and resistant to handprints and smears. Not to mention the amount of soccer balls that had been accidentally bounced off them.

Soon this house will teem with happy life.

He was proud of himself. Of how far he'd come during their trip. When they'd left for Paris he'd never imagined he would open up the way he had. But he'd not been able to hold it back. All that wonderful time spent with Emily... He'd been so lucky that she had fought for them the way she had. All she'd gone through—the arguments, the accident, his injury, the induced coma, finding out she was pregnant and fearing his reaction—he couldn't imagine he would have been that strong!

Stepping into their bedroom, he began to unbutton his shirt, and as he undid the cuffs he stepped into the en-suite, turned on the shower and checked the water temperature. Perfect. Then he pulled off his shirt and went to put it in the hamper.

He had a small headache. It had been there since about halfway through the flight, and though he'd taken some painkillers he was due for some more. Where would they be?

He checked his bedside drawer, but there was nothing in there save for a book, a packet of gum and a phone charger. Perhaps Emily had some in her bedside drawer? He went over to her side of the bed and pulled it open. There, on top of everything, was a white envelope with his name on it—*Sam*—written in her beautiful familiar handwriting.

Intrigued, he turned it over. It was sealed. But it *was* addressed to him, so he stuck his thumb under the flap and ripped it open, and pulled out the folded piece of paper inside.

He opened it.

Sam,
I'm writing you this letter because I need to. There are things I have to say, to get off my chest, and you're not allowing me the time to sit down and talk to you properly.

You're killing me, Sam. It physically feels like you're ripping out my heart. I never, ever thought that the man who once professed to love me would be able to do this, and hurt me so effectively that I am barely able to function.

All I want is to start a family. Is that so hard? You could have said yes, and everything would have been fine. You could have said no and explained why, but you never do. You never have. Instead you just storm away. Stay away. And whenever you see me in the corridors at work you walk the other way.

Do you have any idea how that makes me feel? How small and how unimportant?

You are my husband, and I love you deeply, but I cannot stay in a relationship that is systematically destroying me.

Once you gave me hope. Now you only cause me pain. I can't live like this any more, and because you won't sit down and talk to me about it I've written this letter instead.

I'm leaving you, Sam. I'm getting out whilst I can, whilst there's still some of 'me' left. I'm not expecting you to come after me. I'm not expecting you to beg me to stay. I don't think you want that at all.

I'm doing this for both of us.

I'm sorry we didn't work out. I'm sorry we're so cut off from each other. I'm sorry to end it this way.

But you never gave me the choice.

Bye, Sam.

Emily

Sam blinked and stared at the words on the page. Was this *real*? It couldn't be! But this was Em's handwriting—he'd recognise it anywhere.

She was leaving me?

He went back to the first page and read it again. He'd not known what to expect when he'd started reading, but he'd never expected a *Dear John* letter.

She was going to leave me...

He frowned and read the words one more time, his heart thudding painfully in his chest.

And then it happened.

A flood of memories came crashing down around him, so fast and so hard he almost went dizzy.

The wedding music as he walked down the aisle with her, looking beautiful in that off-the-shoulder dress...

The honeymoon in Paris, tickling her in bed, hearing

her laughter as he turned her to face him and began to kiss her frantically...

Cutting the ribbon to mark the opening of the Monterey, the camera flashes, the cheers, standing in front of the microphone and delivering a speech...

Emily curled up on the couch, her face red with tears, her hand clutching a crumpled white tissue...

Arguing in the car. 'Stop the car! I want to get out!' she'd screamed at him. He'd turned to look at her, there'd been a blare of horns, he'd looked back at the road and...

Sam crumpled the letter in his hand, as his missing years returned with full, brutal force.

Emily had left instructions for the parts of the plan she'd need help with for Rosie to pass on to the rest of the staff.

'So Paris was wonderful, Mrs Saint?'

'It was the *best,* Rosie—you have no idea.'

'I'm so pleased for you. I know it's been difficult lately.'

Emily thanked her, blushing. She'd forgotten how much the staff must have seen. Heard. Though Rosie might be staff, she was also a good friend, and had often found Emily crying in one of the rooms in the house. She'd always done what she could. Brought her a hot drink. Something sweet and indulgent. Had tried to cheer her. Rosie had stayed late many a night, just to keep Emily company.

'It's all going to be much better from now on.'

'I'm glad.' Rosie shut the fridge. 'I'd already made rosewater pannacotta for your dessert tonight, because they needed to set. Do you still want to have those?'

Emily nodded. 'Sounds delightful. It'll save me some time. I never was any good at desserts—unless I was expected to eat them.'

Rosie laughed. 'That's fine. And I've got some lovely fillet steaks in the fridge—you could do them with a red peppercorn sauce?'

'Thanks, Rosie. Now, I'm going upstairs to wash twelve hours of aeroplane off me. Anything I should know about before I go?'

'No, I don't think so.'

'I'll pick up the correspondence from Sam's desk on my way up—he might want to take a look at that. I know how eager he is to get back to work.'

'Why don't you rest up there for a while? I can bring you up some coffee and cake about three? Would that suit?'

Emily thought that would be perfect. It would give her and Sam plenty of time to be on their own and christen the bedroom with these new versions of Sam and herself.

She left the kitchen quarters and headed up to Sam's office. There was a small pile of mail that had accrued on his desk during their few days away. And she had no doubt that their email accounts would have even more.

But all of that could wait.

She and Sam came first.

She didn't want to go into their bedroom and remind Sam that he had a pile of paperwork waiting for him, but she assumed he must be in the shower already. She could hear the water running.

I'll put it on the bureau.

Emily opened their bedroom door, and then jumped slightly when she saw a figure standing by the bed. 'Oh! Sam! I thought you were in the shower. What are you…?'

She saw his pale face, his stunned expression. Then she saw what he was holding.

A piece of crumpled paper. Her notepaper. And on the

bed behind him an envelope, torn along the top, with his name written on it.

The letter.

'Sam—'

'You were *leaving* me?'

She'd never heard him so shocked, so stunned, so hurt, so *appalled*.

Her heart began to hammer in her chest and her mouth went dry as she feverishly began to try to explain. 'Sam, I—'

'You told me countless times that we'd been arguing. I saw in my own head the memory of our arguing. But you said we were okay.'

'We were…'

'You were going to leave me. You said I was *killing you*…'

'Sam!' Emily couldn't think of what to say. His heartbreak was clear. His devastation was evident. Tears streamed from her eyes when she recalled what she'd put in that letter. She'd been *raw*, she'd been *hurting*, and she'd needed him to know that.

Why hadn't she destroyed that letter?

Because I thought I might have to use it.

She'd not known—could not have predicted—how well things were going to go. Not from the point they'd been at before his amnesia, before their trip to Paris and the strengthening of their love for one another. She hadn't meant for him even to *see* that letter. Not any more! She should have come up here the second they got home and got rid of it. Shredded it. Burnt it.

But she'd forgotten it.

And now he'd read it, and he was hurting and upset. There were even unshed tears in his eyes.

'You wrote this after the accident. You put the date.'

He showed her the letter, but she couldn't look at it. Couldn't face the evidence of her written words.

'You said that our marriage was over.'

'Sam, that was before I knew that you didn't remember. Before I knew that we would get each other back…'

'But you wrote it knowing you were pregnant? Knowing that you'd be walking out on us and leaving our child without its father?'

She heard the hurt, the accusation in his voice. 'Yes, I did. But—'

'You *know* how much I want to be a father, and how much it scares me, *terrifies* me, that I might lose a child—and yet you were willing to walk away from me with our baby?'

Emily hurried to his side, laid a hand upon his arm. 'I didn't know that *then*. All I knew was that you didn't want children! I thought that when I told you in the hospital you would go crazy! Maybe even ask me to get rid of it! I didn't know about Serena!'

'You were going to take my child from me…'

'Sam, that's not fair—'

But he wasn't listening. He dropped the letter and it fluttered to the floor as he stormed from their bedroom and began to run down the stairs.

Emily chased after him and stood at the balustrade, shouting after his disappearing form. 'Where are you going?'

'I'm getting out of here! I need to think!'

She heard the front door slam, the sound echoing through the house, and she stood there, her hands gripping the railings, knuckles gleaming white through her skin, and all she could hear was the sound of the shower running before a car roared into life and she heard the stones sizzle and spit as it roared away down the drive.

She sucked in a big breath and stared into nothing. *What have I done?*

Was Sam going to come back? Should he even be driving? He might have an accident. He might get hurt. He...

Emily sank to the floor and rested her head against the stair rail, feeling numb and broken. Her gaze was fixed on the open door.

He just needed some space. Some air to breathe—air that didn't have Emily in it, complicating matters.

Sam didn't even realise the direction he was travelling. He just drove. Blindly and furiously. His mind going over and over her letter. What it meant. How bad his relationship—his *marriage*—had been.

He never would have imagined he could let it get so bad that his wife would have felt that way. *She said I was killing her...* He swallowed, his throat tight and painful. He shook his head, disbelief filling him. He'd made her feel *that* bad? That was awful. He didn't deserve a woman like that. He didn't deserve all the effort she'd put into him. All the love. Her care. Her attention. That he'd done *that* to her! Made her feel as if she was the last person on earth he'd want to have a baby with...

The baby...

Furiously he wiped at his eyes, desperate to wipe away the stinging sensation burning them. He didn't deserve a child, either.

And suddenly he was at his mom's place. On her driveway. He couldn't remember the journey at all, and as he sat there, blinking, staring at the familiar building where he had spent his childhood, he tried to recall the drive, hoping he hadn't gone through any red lights.

He'd made it here safely, anyway. That was one thing.

But it was strange to be here. He hadn't come back

home for over a year. More, he figured, since he'd been married for eighteen months. He'd spoken to his parents on the phone, of course—they'd not been complete strangers—but it had been infrequent and rare. And now he could feel the weight of that guilt upon his shoulders.

Was his mom even in?

His question was answered when she opened the door and peered out to see who had arrived.

She looked the same. A little greyer, maybe, but not much. She still had on those slippers he remembered so well, with the sheepskin inlay. Still seemed to favour those 'mom jeans', with the high elasticated waist, and tucked into them was one of the simple, stripy tee shirts that had always seemed a staple item of her wardrobe.

He stepped out of the vehicle. 'Hi, Mom.'

'Samuel!'

She walked over to him, her arms outstretched, and pulled him into a hug that was as familiar, as comforting, and as painfully heart-warming as he'd remembered them to be.

'Let me look at you! Oh, you look so handsome.'

She smiled as she looked him over, but then, as she gazed carefully at his face, she must have seen, must have sensed something that concerned her.

'What's wrong?'

'Why does something have to be wrong?'

'Because you're home, Samuel, and you swore you would never come back here. Something made you come back. Don't get me wrong—I'm glad. But what is it?'

He hated it that she was so astute. He hated it that he had come here. To this place. To the house that had once held his most painful memory and the people who populated it.

It didn't hold his most painful memory now. Not any more. He had a new pain.

'I just needed to see you, that's all.'

She looked at him sideways, not quite believing him but willing to put it aside for a moment. 'Well, come on in. I'll get you a drink.'

He followed her into the house, sucking in a deep breath before he went through the front door.

It was like stepping back in time. The place looked exactly the same. The same furniture, the same paper on the walls, the same lamps, the same throw rug over the back of the couch. There was even that same old aroma of just-made coffee and freshly baked cookies.

She settled him into a seat and bustled away into the kitchen, making them both coffee and then sitting down with him in the living room.

'How are you feeling after the accident?'

He nodded. 'I'm good.'

'I did visit you. Can you remember?'

'Yeah.'

Of course he remembered. He remembered everything now. All of it. Every hurtful moment.

I can't believe I cut Emily off like that! I walked away from her when all she needed was an answer from me! I was so angry! So afraid.

He swallowed hard. 'Do you ever talk about her?'

'Emily?' His mom looked confused.

'Serena.' He hated having to ask, but he needed to. They'd never mentioned it in this house after she'd died. It was like the elephant in the room.

His mother reached for the necklace at her throat and looked back at him. 'Why do you ask?'

'I wonder about it. We never spoke about her. Not after.'

'Not in the house, no. We chose not to discuss it. You children got so upset.'

'Not in the house? So you *did* speak about her?'

'Of course! She was my baby. For a brief time there I thought I might die too, but my pastor helped to get me through.'

'I didn't know you were religious.'

'I'm not. But he met me one day in the supermarket. After the funeral. We began to talk about her and…well, we met every week after that.'

He stared at his mother. 'Every week?'

She nodded. 'I had to. If I'd kept it inside me, then who knows how I might have ended up.'

He was dumbstruck. All this time! All this time he'd thought it was a forbidden conversation, that no one dared speak her name. And yet all this time his mother had been talking her way through her grief. He was glad. Glad she'd had an outlet. But there was still a question on his mind that haunted him. A question he needed the answer to.

'Did you ever blame me?'

'*You?* Samuel, *no!* Of course not! Why would we? You were a child…you were still in school. It wasn't your fault. It was…' She leaned forward and reached out to lay her hand on his. 'What's going on?'

'I've ruined my marriage.'

She didn't gasp, didn't look shocked—just sat there calmly. 'How?'

'Because of what happened I was afraid to… Emily wanted a baby… No. That's wrong. She wanted to *talk* to me about having a baby and I wouldn't let her.'

'Oh, Samuel…'

'It never occurred to me that as I denied her a family I was hurting her. I just thought I was protecting myself.

I was selfish. The way I treated her…it made her feel as if she were nothing. We kept arguing and I stayed away from home. Stayed away from Em. She was getting ready to leave me when the accident happened.'

His mother sucked in a deep breath. 'I knew she was tense when I saw her in the hospital. I thought she was just worried about you. I never knew any of that was going on.'

'She found out after the accident that she was pregnant. Of course I was in shock. I'd just learnt I'd lost nearly two years of my life and now I was going to be a father? I tried to act pleased. Tried to hide it. The fear, the guilt, eating me away inside.'

He paused.

'We went to Paris to get my memories back. Instead we got close. Closer than we'd ever been before. It was amazing. We shared things. I told her about Serena. She understood where I was coming from. And I finally, *finally* felt like everything was right between us. And then I discovered today, when we got back, that she was going to leave me. Knowing she was pregnant. She was going to walk away. Because of me. Because of how I was with her. I hurt her, Mom. Emotionally. I don't deserve to be with her. With our child…'

She gave him a sympathetic smile. 'I'm going to be a grandmother?'

He nodded. 'Congratulations.'

But he wasn't smiling.

'I don't know what to do. I got my memories back. All of them. I saw what I did. What I *said*. Quite frankly, I'm amazed she stuck around at all.'

'Oh, Samuel, it sounds like she was trying to protect you.'

'Trying to protect herself, more like.'

'I think you're being harsh.'

'I'm not. What if we've always been doomed? We couldn't tell each other basic facts about each other— even after we were married! I had to wait eighteen months before she told me about her childhood, and then I found out that she'd withheld a basic truth from me after we'd promised not to keep anything from each other ever again. We weren't just having the odd argument—we'd been drifting apart for months! We were on the verge of separating.'

He shook his head, still unable to believe how bad things had been.

'I let Paris and our hopes for the trip carry me away. The place wove some sort of magic spell because it had been our honeymoon destination, the city of romance... all of that.'

'Does she still want to leave you now?'

'Probably. After how Dad was I vowed to myself that I would be the best husband there ever could be. I would work hard, but I would be *around*. I'd be home. I'd support my wife, we'd have this great love, this mutual respect—and it turns out I was a huge disappointment. Some of the things I did...said...I was cruel.'

The more he thought about his actions, the more he hated himself. He'd become everything his dad was. Apart from the drinking part. He'd been useless! Distant. Unsupportive. Argumentative. And had he shared with her? No.

He'd let them all down—Emily, Serena, his mom. Himself.

Nobody could be more angry than he felt right now.

His marriage was in tatters.

His mom let out a heavy sigh and reached forward to take both his hands in his. 'Samuel? You deserve to be with Emily. She has *fought* for you! You can't let her down. Not now. Not now you're going to be a father. This isn't just about you any more.'

'Yeah, but—'

'Do you love her?'

He stared at her, saw the intensity in her eyes. 'Of course!'

'Then why are you still here with me?'

Rosie came up the stairs carrying coffee and fresh slices of cake and found Emily sitting on the stairwell.

'Mrs Saint?'

Emily looked up at her with tear-filled eyes.

'Are you okay?' Rosie put down the small tray and hurried over to her employer.

'I think it's all over, Rosie.'

'How? You were just saying earlier how good everything was.'

'He found this.' She pulled the letter from her pocket and passed it over, cringing inwardly as she imagined Rosie's thoughts as she read it. Would Rosie judge her, too?

'Oh…'

'I screwed up. I should have thrown it away. But I forgot it was there. I was just so excited. Sam seemed happy about the baby, we were going on a trip, and I…' She let out a heavy sigh. 'Just as everything was working out right between us. After all those difficulties…you know what I mean. You must have seen. Heard.'

'It was hard not to hear sometimes,' Rosie replied with sadness.

'I'm sorry. You shouldn't have had to hear it at all. We should have sorted it. Been open with each other right from the beginning. We could have avoided this.'

'Mrs Saint, I don't understand everything that's happened, but there is one thing I do know. You and Mr Saint may have had your difficulties, but I have always said that you two were meant for each other. It's not my place to suggest anything, but please don't give up on him. He's a kind man. A good man. This is bound to have shocked him. It would have shocked anyone. Give him time to reflect. Sort things out.'

Emily took back the letter. 'You're very kind, Rosie, but this is what happens to me. People walk away and leave.'

'You think he's going to walk away?'

'I'm used to it, after my mother…I should have expected it.'

'I'm sure he'll come back.'

Emily looked at her sharply and Rosie quickly stood. 'I've spoken out of turn. I'm sorry. I'll leave you on your own. Call me if you need anything—I'll just be downstairs.'

Rosie hurried away and Emily instantly regretted the sharpness of her gaze. But she hadn't been able to help it. Her first thoughts had run to the fact that he was abandoning her a second time. Her mother had done it once, her husband twice. Was she going to let him do it a third time? A fourth?

It was time to draw a line in the sand.

This wasn't just about her any more. A baby was involved. She'd always vowed that when she had a child of her own it would know love from both its parents. It would grow up in a warm, loving home and would never feel the sting of rejection—certainly not before it was even born!

She was failing her child already.

CHAPTER TEN

'OKAY, SAM. I'M very happy with your progress. You may officially return to work.'

His doctor had given him the good news, expecting Sam to smile.

He hadn't.

He wasn't in a smiling mood.

Sam had spent the last few nights sleeping in his old bedroom at his mother's house, squeezing himself onto a bed that was too small and staring at the ceiling for half of the night. As each morning approached he would re-sign himself to the fact that he wouldn't get any sleep and then somehow he would, falling into a deep sleep literally an hour or so before he was due to wake up. Then his alarm would blare into his brain and he would jerk awake, bleary-eyed and instantly sad.

He'd not spoken to Emily. He didn't know what to say. How could he go back there? Could he ever say he was sorry enough times? He didn't deserve to be happy with her any more. Surely he'd given up all his chances?

His mother had tried to argue for Emily's side, saying that she must have done what she had to protect him.

Was that true? He tried to imagine himself in her place. Her situation. If it had been Emily in the coma with a brain injury, not him, would he have done the same thing?

Perhaps.

But there was a new equation in all this. The baby. All his life he'd pushed the idea of being a father away. It had been too scary a concept, too terrible even to imagine how that would feel. And because he'd been so busy pushing the idea away, refusing to accept it, he'd never taken a moment to think about whether he really wanted to be a dad.

Hadn't he sworn that he would never be like his own father? So he must have thought about it a little, right? Perhaps it hadn't all been about his guilt over what had happened to Serena? Perhaps his fear had come more from being given the opportunity to have what he wanted most in the world, but then failing miserably? Had it had been easier to lose his temper with Emily and refuse even to talk about having a child than to face up to the possibility that he might fail?

As he drove along the freeway, heading to work, he pondered this. Had it ever really been about Emily? About Serena? Or had it always been about *him*? He was a driven man. He'd provided for his siblings, looked after them, had sent himself to medical school, specialised, set up a thriving business... He'd been successful at everything he'd put his mind to except for what had happened to Serena. He'd failed his sister, and the weight and pain of that failure *haunted* him. Was it that same fear of failure that was driving him now? Having a baby with his wife meant an uncertain future. He couldn't possibly know if he would get it right. Was that why he'd fought against it for so long?

His memories had proved to him that he'd got his mar-

.riage wrong once already—did that mean he would continue to get things wrong?

The painful ache in his heart was almost unbearable.

He indicated and pulled over, breathing deeply, his brain trying to sort through all the memories, putting them in order. He saw them all. The bad. The good. And he remembered their arguments—saw how he had behaved. The words that he'd said. The numerous ways that he had tried to protect himself. He'd not been thinking about Emily! He'd known he was hurting her, had seen how much she wanted a child, but he'd been so concerned about his own vulnerability that he had pushed it back on to her.

He felt sick. Nauseated. He saw over and over again how Emily had kept trying. Trying to talk to him. Trying to find a time that was good for him. Trying to understand why he kept saying no without getting a decent answer from him. He saw how she had begun to retreat from him, hurting and in pain, but how she had still tried. The times he'd come home late and found a table set for two with candles and flowers. The times he'd found her asleep on the couch because she'd been trying to wait up for him.

She fought for us. Despite what I did, she fought for us.

It must have hurt her terribly to consider walking away. To have written that letter.

Sam felt ashamed.

He'd been in the wrong and he'd allowed his fear to keep them apart.

Emily had fought for him. Always. Should he really be giving up on her? Or seeing whether she would give him one last chance? A chance to show her how much he loved *her* and how much he wanted to fight for *her*.

No one had ever fought to stay in her life.

But I'm determined to be the one who does. No matter what.

Desperate to put things right, he picked up his mobile and with trembling fingers called the Monterey.

'It's Sam. Is Emily there today?' He didn't care if the staff were wondering about why he was asking. Surely he should *know* if his wife was working?

'She's at home today, Mr Saint.'

'Thank you.'

He took a deep breath, indicated again, and pulled back out into the traffic. He knew now. He knew what he had to do to put things right.

He was not going to fail at his marriage.

Emily sucked in a deep breath and closed her eyes as she stood in the garden, the sun shining down upon her face, hoping to find the peace and calm that mindfulness— a technique she sometimes used with her labouring patients—should bring.

It had been an upsetting time since Sam had left, and she'd worried about where he'd gone until she'd received a whispered phone call from his mother to let her know he was safe and well and at her house.

She'd been grateful to his mother for letting her know. It had put her mind at rest.

The garden provided solace. Their private garden, at the back of the house, was in full bloom, populated by some of the flowers that she'd carried in her wedding bouquet—Calla lilies, baby's breath, white roses. They reminded her of that special day they'd had. The day she'd thought all her dreams were coming true.

But the worst had happened. He'd found that awful letter and reacted badly to it. But they could put it right, couldn't they? It didn't have to mean it was the end of everything. No, she hadn't told Sam the whole truth, but she'd been doing it honourably, protecting him from all the harmful things that had been said. Surely he'd be able to see that when he calmed down?

Her cell phone rang in her pocket, disturbing her thoughts.

'Em? It's Sam. I'm coming over.'

She slipped the phone back into her pocket and felt a nervousness start deep down low in her belly. She hadn't expected him to call. He'd said nothing to her for days. Why was he coming? To say goodbye?

Feeling sick, she absently rubbed at her belly.

If he was coming here to say goodbye then she would make sure she told him, one last time, that she had always fought for him, always protected him, always loved him. She would make sure that his last memory of her was one that proved she had never given up on him—even if he was going to try to give up on her.

So she quickly returned to the house, put on the powder-blue dress from Paris. When he arrived she would remind him about their wedding day and remind him of the vows they'd taken. Vows that, to her, had meant everything. She would not be meek and accept him walking away.

She returned to the garden, seeking that earlier sense of peace she was so desperate to feel again, and waited for him to arrive.

She didn't have to wait long.

She became aware that someone was looking at her, and as she turned back to the house there was Sam, standing on the stone steps leading down to the garden. He had a strange look on his face. He certainly didn't look as angry or as upset as he had the other day, when he had walked away.

Tell him now.

She stepped towards him, but he raised his hand. 'Can I speak first?'

Emily closed her mouth and nodded. She would listen to what he had to say.

'How have you been?'

It wasn't what she'd been expecting. She'd thought he'd come straight out with it. Keep it short. *I'm leaving you for good.*

She refused to cry, but already she could feel tears pressing against her eyes. 'How do you *think* I've been?'

He nodded, his gaze dropping to her belly and then moving up again, to her face. 'I should have told you where I was.'

'You were at your mother's house. She told me.'

'She did?' He seemed surprised, but then he nodded, smiling. 'I should have known.'

'You should have done it yourself.'

He looked right at her, then. 'You're right. I'm sorry.'

Seeing him like this was painful. This man was someone she'd thought she would get to love for ever. Now he was standing across from her like a stranger, and all she could think about was how it felt to be in his loving arms!

'You don't deserve someone like me, Em. Someone who's hurt you like I did. I'm sorry I made you feel that way.'

She sucked in some air. He was building up to it, wasn't he? Why didn't he just say it? Get it out in the open so that she could weep and wail and cry when he was gone?

'Well...'

'Can you give me another chance?'

She stopped breathing. What? What had he just said? She looked up into his face. 'I'm sorry?'

Sam walked up to her. 'I remember.'

Emily frowned. What? He remembered? 'Have you had another memory come back?'

He nodded. 'I've had them *all* come back. I remember it all. The good, the bad. The ugly.'

A small divot formed between her eyebrows.

'I've come here to say I'm sorry. I should never have walked away from you the other day. It was…an old habit. You see, I've learned one or two things since I left. I've realised that most of this—our problems, our disagreements—they were all my fault.'

Really? He was actually saying all these words? Words that meant so much—words that were on the way to healing them. Mending them. Bringing them back together. Was it possible?

Her heart began to pound. But she couldn't let him shoulder all the responsibility.

'No, Sam. It was me. I kept pushing you. Pushing you to commit to a family because I thought if I didn't push you would drift away from me—like everyone else. And you weren't ready.'

'I *was* ready, though. I was just terrified of failing at it.'

She shook her head, not understanding.

'I've always succeeded at everything, but when I lost my baby sister I experienced feelings I didn't know how to deal with. I was sixteen, and no one at home talked about it, so I had to process it myself. Something in me must have decided that I was *never* going to feel that way again. Like I was losing myself. Like I'd lost control. When you asked for a baby that wasn't unreasonable, but I saw it as something I could fail at. I had no certainties, no assurances that everything would be fine and so I pushed it away. Pushed you away. And then I began to fail at my marriage. And though I saw that it was crumbling I tried to pretend that it wasn't happening. I'm sorry.'

'Oh, Sam! I should never have pushed you so hard. There were so many things I'd never been given answers to, and there you were doing it too! I couldn't stand that, when I loved you so much. I still don't know why I was so easy for my mother to leave me behind, but when *you* left me too? I feared there might be something wrong with me. That there was something inherently unloveable about me that made people leave.'

He reached for her hand.

'Or perhaps I pushed them away? I pushed you.'

'No Em. You were never in the wrong. You were—are—incredibly loving and loveable. You didn't push your mother—or me. To me, you said what needed to be said. And I'm glad you did, because it forced me to confront myself. I needed to do that, to see why I behaved like I did, and I'm sorry if I hurt you with anything I have said. I never meant it. I just lashed out verbally because it was easier than dealing with my own issues. I'm sorry, Em. I truly am.'

Emily sank into his arms, her head against his chest. 'Don't be. I trust you, Sam. With my whole heart. I would give it up to you right now.'

They held each other for a moment—a beautiful moment in which the birds sang in the trees around them and the gentle breeze played with the hem of her dress.

'I love you, Sam.'

'I love you, Em.'

They looked at each other, seeing the love they needed, thrived on, lived on. Emily pulled him to her so that her lips could meet his.

The kiss was gentle, solemn, heartfelt. Emily was

thrilled that his memories had returned at last, and that he appeared to have worked through his issues. Obviously his time away had helped heal him. If he and his mother had talked about Serena, then hopefully she was healing, too.

When the kiss ended Emily looked up into his eyes and smiled. 'I'd marry you again right now if I could. To prove to you how I feel.'

Sam looked at her and laughed. 'Me too. But, you know, I remember the first lot of vows, and they were pretty damn good.'

'They certainly were.'

He stooped and scooped her up into his arms, and she laughed, surprised.

'Allow me, though, to carry you over the threshold.'

He started heading back towards the house and Emily laid her head against his chest.

This was the dashing Sam she remembered. The man who'd used to be full of romantic overtures. The gentleman.

The man she loved.

She knew they would be okay now. There was nothing left to break them. No secrets that Sam didn't know. No memories left unremembered.

He knew everything. The good, the bad and the ugly.

Now they could focus on creating more of the good and more of the amazing. She and Sam were united. Husband and wife. Soon to be a family.

The baby would start kicking soon.

And then they would both enjoy their new adventure as parents.

Together.

EPILOGUE

SAM HAD SEEN many babies come into the world, and each of those births had put a smile upon his face. But nothing could have prepared him for the way he felt when his own daughter made it into the world.

Emily had been great. She'd not written a birth plan. She'd just told everyone that she would do what her body told her to do. And when the contractions had got stronger and longer she had chosen to get into the tub.

Her labour had been very relaxed and soothing. Even during the most intense of contractions she had breathed carefully through it, her eyes closed, intent on what was happening within her.

He'd held her hands as she'd got onto her knees in the water. He'd coached her.

'One…two…three…four… And breathe…'

When she'd begun to push the strain on her face had been incredible, but she had borne the pains well and worked with them, using them to help deliver the baby slowly and safely.

As Mia Saint had slithered into the water Emily had gasped and reached down between her legs and brought their daughter to the surface for her first breath.

I'm a father!

She was so beautiful! So perfect!

He hadn't known he could cry so much. He wasn't even aware that tears were pouring down his face until Emily looked up at him with so much love and reached up to wipe them away. He pressed her hand to his face and then kissed her palm, before he laid his hand upon his daughter's head.

No matter what was to come he would protect them both. He would love them to the end of his days. And if there were challenges or difficulties then he knew they would face them together.

These last few months he and Emily had just got stronger and stronger.

He'd delegated, as promised. He'd never worked more than sixty hours a week. And when he was home, he was *present*. Sometimes things didn't get done, but that was okay—because the most important thing was his family.

And now, as he held Mia in his arms, he realised that he was still scared of the responsibility, but he knew in his heart that every father felt the same way. It was natural. Normal.

And, as a father, he knew his daughter would rule his heart.

He would grant her every wish.

If he failed at something, then he would learn from it, and if he needed to lean on Emily then he knew she would be there for him.

He didn't have to do anything alone any more.

He kissed Mia's squashed little nose, then leaned forward and kissed Emily. 'I love you. I'm so proud of you.'

She smiled back and stroked his face. 'And I love you. Don't forget—we're a great team, you and me.'

He kissed her. Slowly. Softly. 'I never forget.'

* * * * *

LET'S TALK

Romance

For exclusive extracts, competitions
and special offers, find us online:

MILLS & BOON
A ROMANCE FOR EVERY READER

- **FREE** delivery direct to your door

- **EXCLUSIVE** offers every month

- **SAVE** up to 25% on pre-paid subscriptions

SUBSCRIBE AND SAVE

millsandboon.co.uk/Subscribe

JOIN US ON SOCIAL MEDIA!

Stay up to date with our latest releases, author news and gossip, special offers and discounts, and all the behind-the-scenes action from Mills & Boon...

 millsandboon

 millsandboonuk

 millsandboon

might just be true love...

MILLS & BOON

MODERN

Power and Passion

Prepare to be swept off your feet by sophisticated, sexy and seductive heroes, in some of the world's most glamourous and romantic locations, where power and passion collide.

MILLS & BOON
True Love
Romance from the Heart

Celebrate true love with tender stories of heartfelt romance, from the rush of falling in love to the joy a new baby can bring, and a focus on the emotional heart of a relationship.

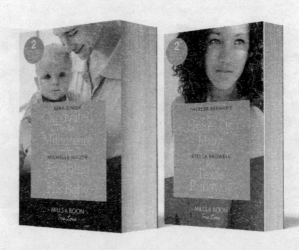

Four True Love stories published every month, find them all at:

millsandboon.co.uk/TrueLove